BOYS OF
LIFE

Published in the United States by Cleis Press, an imprint of Start Midnight, LLC, 101 Hudson Street, Thirty-Seventh Floor, Suite 3705, Jersey City, NJ 07302.

Printed in the United States.
Cover design: Scott Idleman/Blink
Cover photograph: iStockphoto
Text design: Frank Wiedemann

First Edition.
10 9 8 7 6 5 4 3 2 1

Trade paper ISBN: 978-1-62778-172-5
E-book ISBN: 978-1-62778-173-2

BOYS OF
LIFE

PAUL RUSSELL

CLEiS
PRESS

To the memory of
Karl Keller
Robert Mapplethorpe
Pier Paolo Pasolini

ACKNOWLEDGMENTS

My thanks to Harvey Klinger, my agent; Arnold Dolin, my editor; and Matthew Camicelli, assistant editor. To Ann Imbrie, James Lewton-Brain, Catherine Murphy, Steve Otto, Bob Richard, Harry Roseman, and Michael Somoya, early and encouraging readers of this manuscript. To Matthew Aquilone, Christopher Canatsey, and Karen Robertson. To the late James Day, mentor, master-reader, friend. Especially to Tom Heacox. And finally to my lively and constant companions of Barhamsville, Abby, Darrell, and Sugar Baby.

Even if their adventures were sometimes so cruel as to be revolting by our standards, if they were obscene in such a grand and total way as to become innocent again, yet beyond their ferocity, their eroticism, they embody the eternal myth; man standing alone before the fascinating mystery of life, all its terror, its beauty and its passion.

—FEDERICO FELLINI

T HE FIRST TIME I MET CARLOS REICHART I WAS standing in the Nu-Way Laundromat folding up a bed sheet, which is probably a strange way to meet the one person who's going to ruin your life.

It was September, and there was this light drizzle coming down past the windows of the laundromat. The fluorescent lights made everything look even more depressing than usual—concrete block walls painted yellow, these blue and green palm trees painted over the yellow. The concrete floor and the stale heat smell that comes from dryers.

The Nu-Way was the only laundromat in Owen, Kentucky, and doing laundry there was one of the things I hated most. The clothes in the washers went round and round, and in the dryers too. In two weeks there you'd be back again, washing the same clothes over and over. That was exactly what your life was.

I remember hearing on the radio, years later, about some tropical depression out in the Atlantic that was being upgraded into a storm. We were making a movie on this estate in the Hudson River Valley, and Seth Rosenheim, Carlos's cameraman, made the joke, "That's what happened to Carlos—a tropical depression upgraded into a storm." What it suddenly made me remember, though—those words *tropical depression*—was the Nu-Way Laundromat: maybe the clothes spinning in the dryers, and those green and blue painted palm trees that were supposed to cheer the place up but only made it more depressing. Or maybe because I met Carlos on a day when it was raining and some-where, some ocean, it really was the season for tropical depressions and storms.

I was tugging bed sheets out of the dryer, stuffing them back in the plastic garbage bags I'd brought. When I looked up, this man was staring at me. He was sitting on the wooden bench that ran along the windows in the front of the place, and he had a little spiral notebook in his lap, the kind you buy for school. He must've been writing something down, only he'd stopped and was looking around. I guess he'd seen me because he was staring, and when I glanced up we were looking right at each other.

I expected him to look away, but he didn't, and for some reason I didn't either. But then I did, I went on folding those sheets. I had this feeling he was staring at me the whole time, and when I looked back at him it was true, he hadn't moved. It was this questioning look, like you give somebody when you think you might've seen them before, or you might know them but can't remember from where. Only he looked like he knew exactly who I was. That's what I felt—here was somebody saying, Oh, I know exactly who you are even though I've never seen you before. Like he'd been waiting to meet me for a long time and he'd known he would—he just didn't know when or where it would happen and now here it was.

Maybe I'm making all that up, but I don't think so.

There wasn't anybody but us in the laundromat. I hadn't noticed him till I noticed him staring at me. He was maybe forty years old, not gone to flab anywhere but tight like the head of a drum. With his high cheekbones he looked like he might have Cherokee blood in him. His black hair was combed back from his forehead, and he was wearing this black long-sleeve shirt buttoned all the way up to the collar. His eyes were black too, crazy glittery eyes like country people sometimes have, and that thin hard hollowed-out face. Only he wasn't any country person. He was definitely somebody from somewhere else.

I kept on folding sheets, but he was starting to bother me. I felt like he was studying me, but when I looked up again he'd gone back to writing in his little spiral notebook. Just then, he looked up right when I was looking at him—it was like I was the one who'd been looking and not the other way around, and he'd caught me.

There was something about those eyes, more like some animal's eyes than a person's—some really smart animal that's always on the lookout, the way you see hunting dogs go on the alert. Like even here in this laundromat some keen sense of smell in him was sniffing out things other people wouldn't pick up on.

I pretended I was trying to see past his head to something passing by on the street. All of a sudden he came bolting up at me from where he was sitting. I must've looked surprised—he sort of raised his eyebrows in a friendly way and sailed right past me to the washing machines, where he started pulling out clothes and tossing them into the dryers. He probably opened up fifteen washing machines, nearly every one in the place, and threw his stuff across into that many dryers. I had to laugh—each time I thought that must be all of it, there was still another washer for him to open and pull clothes from. He stopped loading the dryer and looked at me. What's so funny? was what that look said.

Before I knew I was going to say anything, I said, "You got a pretty big family."

"You might say that," he said. "You got a pretty big family yourself." He was looking at the stack of laundry I'd piled up—with my mom and my brother, Ted, and my two little sisters, there were five of us. "You married?" he asked me.

"Do I look old enough to be married?" I said. I was sixteen.

"Around these parts," he told me, "sure. Don't you people marry when you're about twelve years old?"

He had this sharp accent, and I knew then he had to be this total stranger to Owen. Nobody in Owen ever talked that way. It sounded sort of snide. I couldn't know at the time that was just the way he was with strangers; you'd never guess it, but he was this shy person really.

"Hey, just kidding," he said. "Don't you hate doing this stuff?" He took in the whole room. "I mean, isn't it the worst?"

"It's pretty bad," I told him. "But you really do have a lot of clothes. Using up all the washers in the place."

"See," he explained, "I'm doing laundry for a bunch of people." "That's nice. How'd you get suckered into that?" I wanted to pay him back for that line about my being married.

He looked at me with a kind of odd look.

"Suckered?" he said.

"You know, doing everybody else's laundry for them."

"Just think," he said, like it had any kind of connection with anything, "we'd never've had this stimulating conversation if I hadn't brought all their laundry in here."

"Yeah, right," I told him.

I'd finished putting my laundry into garbage bags, but since it was still raining outside I hopped up on a washing machine to sit and wait for it to stop. I wished it wasn't raining because I sort of wanted to be out of there. I was afraid this guy might talk to me some more, and I didn't really have anything else to say to him.

And I guess he didn't have anything else to say to me either—he finished shoving everything in the dryer and then went back to his bench and started writing in his notebook again. From where I was sitting on the washer I couldn't really see him. Not that I wanted to, but something kept getting the best of me and I'd look over my shoulder to where he was. But he was never looking up at me, which I was glad for. He just kept writing in that notebook.

I couldn't figure out what he could be writing, and I sort of wanted to ask him, but I didn't want to start us talking again—so I sat there trying to be as blank as I could and watched the rain, listening to it drum the roof and wondering if it'd take long to get a hitch back to the house, or whether I'd have to walk it in the dark. The more I thought about all that, the more depressed I got. Like everything else, it was something I seemed to be doing all the time with no stop to it.

I wondered where he could be from, what reason he was stopped in the Nu-Way Laundromat with more dirty clothes than practically the rest of the town put together. There was something I liked about him, the way he sat there writing in that notebook and never looking up at me even though I knew he knew I was still there—some kind of lonely feeling I got looking at him, some queasy kind of loneliness I knew from when sometimes I'd lie on my back on the ground and look into the sky wondering if it ever had an end to it and knowing it didn't. It nagged at me, this feeling, which was why I kept glancing over at him the way I did. Like maybe I could surprise something and then I'd know what it was I was looking for and not being able to find.

Part of it was, to be honest, I was just bored sitting there waiting for the rain to be over and watching the whole row of dryers with their loads spinning behind glass and the rain just kept on and finally the dryers came to a stop.

They'd been stopped a minute or two and he hadn't made a move. "Your stuff's all ready," I told him.

"Thanks," he said. "You can go now." He started tucking stuff away into garbage bags.

"It's raining," I told him. "I don't want to get wet."

"Smart kid. And I see you're into the garbage bag fashion statement too."

"It's just that I have to walk. It's easier to carry that way."

"Yeah sure," he laughed. "I know a garbage bag buff when I see one. Where do you have to walk?"

"A ways," I said. I thought maybe he'd offer me a ride, but he didn't, he just concentrated on stuffing his bags full of clothes. Okay, I thought. I'm out of here. If he sees me walking in the rain he can get the point, or if he doesn't, then fuck it. But I didn't go. It was still raining, and I just sat there watching him stuff piles and piles of clothes into his garbage bags, probably fifteen in all, till finally he was done. He looked over at me and grinned this tight grin, like something was paining him. "So," he said with that sharp accent of his, "you want to help me stow these in the van? Since obviously you plan to sit there all night."

"I've done worse," I told him.

"Yeah? I want to hear about it."

I shrugged.

"No really, I do."

"How about giving me a ride home instead?"

We were lugging the bags out to his beat-up orange VW van in the parking lot. He opened up the back. "Careful," he said, "don't just go slinging things around. You'll break something."

"What's all that stuff?" I had to ask. The back of the van was totally full of junk—worse than some handyman's station wagon. "Equipment," he said. "Cameras and whatnot."

"You take pictures?"

He made some sound like "anngh."

"It's this movie project," he said. "All these clothes, they're for my crew. They go through them like diapers. I was the only one not hung over today, so here I am."

"A movie project," I said. "Like what kind of movie project?"

"Like a movie movie. Like we're making a movie," he said as he piled the last bag on. It made a pretty impressive heap. "I'm Carlos Reichart," he told me all of a sudden. "I'm not famous, so don't pretend you've ever heard of me, because you haven't. Now hop in and let's go."

The front seat was as filled up with junk as everywhere else in that van—pieces of paper torn out of a spiral notebook and tools and empty beer cans and Barbie dolls missing an arm or a leg.

"Excuse the mess," Carlos said. "I didn't exactly expect to go ferrying local youth around town."

"You never know," I told him. It got to me, the edgy way he had of talking—but at the same time I felt pretty easy with him. It was strange. I wasn't sure if he was pulling my leg about making some movie—but that was okay, he was still the most interesting person right at that moment that I knew in Owen.

"But let's talk about you," he said. "What I'm always curious about is other people. People who live in little towns and carry their laundry around in garbage bags. I don't know anything else about you except that. I'd like to, though. Maybe I'll write a movie about you."

"Some movie that'd be," I told him.

"Well, you never know," he said. "But right now—where're we going? Where's home? Or we could go somewhere and talk. Surely you don't have to go home and cook dinner too? But are you hungry? What time is it? I have no idea of what time it is, but I haven't eaten all day—I'm starving. That pizza place serves takeout, doesn't it? What's the drinking age in this part of Kentucky? Ten? Eleven? We could get a six-pack and takeout pizza and live it up in the back of the van."

It almost made me laugh—he sounded like he was afraid if he stopped talking I might say something, and then everything'd be ruined. Like I might bolt in between sentences. I never heard anybody like that before, and I guess it interested me.

"Sounds okay," I said, not knowing exactly what I was okaying out of all those things he said, but definitely excited by the prospect of some beer. I knew my mom wasn't coming in till late—it was a Friday, and lots of Fridays she was out all night. And my little brother, Ted, could take care of my sisters fine. He definitely had sense enough to heat up something or other from a can.

We picked up a pizza and two six-packs and then drove a ways out of town to where the road turned off to Tatum's Landing. You could put boats in the river there if you wanted to—there was this concrete apron that sloped down into the water. With night coming on, and the rain, nobody was out there.

When we'd climbed over all those garbage bags full of laundry, his and mine both, into the back of the van, Carlos said, "Pretty cozy, huh?"

"Well, at least it's different," I told him, which it was definitely that.

I downed those first couple of beers like no tomorrow, which he did too, and then once we were both on our way to relaxing, he started asking me questions again. Did I go to school, what was it like at home, did I have a lot of friends? He kept watching my face the whole time he was talking, the way nobody ever watches you. He kept asking me questions. I guess I was sort of flattered.

"Yeah, I go to school," I told him. "It's pretty feeble. I live out on Route 27—back the other way out of town." Like Carlos could care less or anything.

"A farm?" he asked, like that was what he wanted it to be.

"Nah," I had to tell him. "It's just this trailer. It's me and my mom, and I got a brother and some sisters. It's okay, it's better than this house we used to live in that was falling down at the time."

"And where's your dad?"

I sort of had to laugh—I guess I never knew what else to do. "My dad," I said.

I hadn't talked to anybody about my dad in a long time—it wasn't something any of us ever talked about.

"I'm just this stranger," Carlos told me. "Don't say anything you don't want to."

"No, I got no secrets," I told him. "I don't care."

"Good—if you don't, I won't," he told me, again looking at me like he did all the time. I remember wondering at the way he kept looking.

"There's these two theories about my dad," I told him.

"Theories?" Carlos asked.

"Depending on who you talk to," I told him. "One theory says he's laying out in the Wahrani swamp."

"What?" Carlos seemed really alarmed.

"Yeah. Where he got knocked off by some of Mr. Hodge's men for getting himself involved in this liquor running scheme over in

Christian County. See, it was a dry county back then—six years ago. So that's one theory. But then this other theory goes, my dad just up and left one day. My mother thinks he's in Louisville living it up right now."

"And what do you think?" Carlos asked.

"I don't think anything. I was just this little kid back then. All I know is, my dad used to beat up on my mom a lot. Or he'd go lighting into one of us."

"What do you mean, lighting into you?"

"Well, if she wasn't around. You know, at night. He'd go asking us where she was, and it didn't matter what we said, he'd still light into us. So we just always made stuff up."

I had to laugh—suddenly I was remembering something.

"What's so funny?" Carlos asked. He was taking all this in, like it was serious stuff—which I guess it was.

I told him, "I was just thinking." I had to laugh again before I could go on. "This one time, my brother, Ted, heard my dad stomping back to the bedroom where we were sleeping, and I guess Ted just couldn't take it one more time. So he went diving under the bed. Which when my dad saw that, it gave him this total fit. He completely forgot about my mom and went tearing after Ted, and the whole time Ted's yelling, Leave me alone, and my dad's yelling how Ted better not be hiding from his own dad. He's cussing and screaming, and Ted's screaming, and my dad finally manages to grab hold of Ted's underwear, which is all Ted's wearing, being asleep and everything. So here's Ted screaming and my dad tugging at his underwear to try to pull him out and Ted hanging onto the bedpost for dear life. Then pow! The elastic band just pops and my dad goes flying across the room."

Carlos was still studying me.

"I guess you had to be there," I told him. The way he watched me made me sweat.

"It's a pretty funny story," he said. "It's a hoot." He said it in this way that you couldn't tell whether he thought it was a hoot or not.

"It wasn't too bad for me," I told him. "Live and let live—that's my motto."

"It's a good motto," said Carlos. "It's my motto too." He handed me another beer, my fourth or fifth I guess. I remember thinking how great it felt to be talking like I was. I didn't have too many friends, none really since everybody I knew at high school was so feeble-minded and boring. So most of the time I didn't say anything much to anybody. But Carlos really did seem to want to know about me. It's funny I never thought that was weird, it was just something I accepted about Carlos from the very first. Plus I never minded telling him anything he wanted to know, which I wouldn't normally do with somebody.

He just let me talk, and he listened, and he never told me much about himself in return. So you could say that even ten years later I still don't know major facts about him.

Not that major facts tell you anything. The Carlos I knew was never the major facts that everybody else knows—his movies and his awards and what all the magazines said about him. What I knew was the Carlos who'd sit there and listen to you ramble on about anything and study you like you were the most interesting person he'd ever met.

It's stupid little things I remember—the way he never ate a slice of pizza till it was cold. I chalked it up to his being so interested in listening to me talk—but later I learned he always did that. He was scared of burning his tongue; I mean, the way other people are scared of drowning, or snakes. Maybe that's bizarre, but it's why Carlos never drank a hot cup of coffee or ate a bite of hot food straight from the oven.

It's a stupid little thing, but it's Carlos. It's just as much Carlos as all those movies he made and everything the newspapers said about him after he got famous, or maybe I should call it notorious.

"So what I want to know, Tony," Carlos asked me, "is what did you think about all that stuff with your mom and dad? I mean, when you sat down and thought about it. That's pretty rough stuff."

I had to shrug. "I guess I never really sat down and thought about it," I told him.

"But don't you ever try to put it all together? How one thing leads to another, what it all means?"

All I could do was make a face.

"I'm dead serious," he said. "You really should think about these things." He leaned forward, like he had some secret to tell me, and I remembered thinking how he was looking right through me like some maniac, all bright black eyes I couldn't look away from. "Otherwise," he said, "if you don't think, then who're you going to be? How're you going to know anything? Look—try this: every night before you go to sleep, choose one thing you remember and then think about it. Try to think what came before it, and then what came before that, and try thinking back as far as you can."

"Okay," I said. "Sure."

"See where it gets you," he told me. "I guarantee—you'll find out all sorts of things. Useful things. You'll be amazed." He pointed to his head. "It's all in there. You discover you're a totally different person from the one you think you are."

I'd stuffed myself on pizza and he hadn't had a bite. But his eyes were fired up with a kind of excitement. I was pretty skeptical.

"The kind of nightmares I have," I told him flat out, "I can just see the trouble I'd go getting myself into if I was to lie there thinking about things before I went to sleep."

"Exactly," he said. "Exactly. That's why you have those nightmares. You're not thinking about those things you need to think about. And they have to get out somehow."

Maybe if Carlos had left me just with that—gotten up and walked away right there—then that would've been enough. That would've done it. Who knows? Here I am ten years and a few thousand miles down the road, and there's not much else to do except lie around and think. And think and think. Who knows? It hasn't helped the nightmares any—Carlos was wrong about that. But sometimes I get the feeling, if I think about things long enough, if I try and remember the way things happened and not the way I might wish they'd happened, then—who knows? Maybe I might really be able to think my way to something that's on the other side of all this mess. I don't know.

Carlos finally took his first bite of pizza, which by that time was bone cold. He folded the wedge in two before eating it, and I noticed how his fingernails were cut smooth down to the quick. While he ate, I told him about the part-time job I'd had for a while loading flats at the lumberyard till it closed down and I hadn't found anything else since then, and how I was going to drop out of school and as soon as I was eighteen I wanted to apply for a job as a penitentiary guard since they made good money.

All of a sudden, in between bites, he looked up at me, right in the eye, and said, "I bet you're a big hit with the girls around here. I bet you've got fifteen girlfriends."

It kind of took me by surprise. "Don't I wish," I told him. "It's emptier than the moon around here, girlwise."

"Tell me about it," he said. He wasn't eating anymore, just looking at me.

I tried to think of something interesting to tell. "Well, I used to go out with this girl," I said. "It's sort of amusing, I guess. There was this guy Wallace, he worked at the lumberyard too—in fact, he was how I got the job there. He was older than me by I guess about five years. Anyway, we used to go out with these two girls. What happened was, they were sisters, and Wallace wanted to go out with the younger one, only her mother wouldn't let her go out unless her older sister was chaperoning. So the way Wallace got around that was, he set me up with the sister, who was about three years older than me, and Wallace went out with the one who was my age. We'd go out on these sort of double dates."

"Yeah?" Carlos said.

"Yeah. There wasn't much to it. Those girls weren't really into much."

It felt good and drowsy to be lounging around in the back of that van, with the rain still coming down steady and it getting dark outside. It was our last beer.

"Like what?" Carlos asked.

"Nothing much."

"Surely they were into something?"

"Oh, kissing," I said.

"Yeah?"

I had to laugh. "A little hand action," I said.

Carlos just kept studying me. He had thin dry parched-looking lips. "Tell me more," he told me.

"There's not really anything to tell," I said.

"Oh, there's always something to tell," he said.

He made me laugh, he was so curious. He had this way of sucking in his cheeks that made him look even thinner than he was.

"Well," I told him, "if you have to know."

"I don't have to know," he said. "But I'd like to—I'm new around here."

"Yeah, well. We'd park somewhere and Wallace and his girl were in the front seat and me and the sister in the back, and we'd all be necking around. You know—the windows getting all steamed up and it was almost like those two girls'd gone and rehearsed everything in advance."

"What do you mean?" Carlos wasn't going to let me out of this story once I was into it.

"Well," I said, "they'd both say almost at the exact same time, like they clocked it—okay, that's enough, you got to take us home now."

"That's a drag," Carlos said. "So did you take them home like they wanted?"

I'd totally forgotten those girls, but now I was hating them all over again. "So what else were we supposed to do?" I said. "It was so frustrating. Jeez was it frustrating."

Carlos stopped chewing on his pizza. "Did you ever come when you were with them?" he asked me, looking at me with this look that made something turn over inside me.

I laughed—nobody had ever asked me anything like that before.

"Well, did you?" Carlos asked me again. I got the feeling he thought this was funny—which I guess it was, me and Wallace trying all the time and never getting to home base with those girls.

"Nah," I told him. "They'd always cut out way before that."

Hearing that must've relaxed him. He took another bite of pizza and chewed it up. "That must have been pretty rough," he said.

"Well." I didn't know why I was telling him all this. Like I said, I never talked to anybody like this. "See," I told him, "usually after we dropped them off, Wallace would ask me if I wanted a beer, which I usually did, and then he'd just go crazy about what cockteasing cunts those two girls were, and how if they didn't watch out they were going to be in for a surprise one night. Stupid pig cunts, he'd call them."

"That's funny," Carlos said. "Stupid pig cunts." He said it like he was trying it on for size.

"So then what would happen?" he asked.

"We'd sit on the floor in his living room. We'd drink beer."

"Yeah?" He daubed at the corner of his mouth where a string of cheese was.

"We'd watch each other jerk off," I admitted.

It felt strange to say that to somebody I'd just met, especially somebody who was more than twice as old as I was. Especially somebody who was making me sweat under my armpits the way he did—nervousness, I guess. But it also felt, well—exciting, like here was this secret thing I was suddenly talking about.

"Sounds kind of depressing," Carlos said. "Did you do anything else?"

I shook my head. "The yard closed and Wallace moved away. I didn't see those girls again after that."

"Did you want to?"

I shook my head. I'd never really thought about it. "I guess not really," I said.

We'd finished the beers. I wished I hadn't told Carlos that story— suddenly I felt more depressed than I'd been all day. But all at once he reached out and put his hands on my shoulders so that we were face to face looking right in each other's eyes. I felt full inside, like something in my chest had expanded a couple of sizes and was pressing against my heart and lungs. I was a little drunk. I dared myself to keep looking into his eyes.

He held me there at arm's length, not saying anything, the two of us studying each other. There was this fine stubble on his chin, and I noticed how his eyebrows met above his nose. I could smell my sweat there in the van, and maybe his too, this sweet-sour smell.

I was very aware the whole time of beer building up in my bladder, and how I really needed to piss something awful. But that didn't stop me from returning Carlos's stare right back into his eyes and locking him there, not moving, just letting it go on between us to see when it would have to break.

After what seemed like forever he said in this quiet voice, "I think you're very special. Do you know that?"

"What I know," I told him, reaching up and putting my arms on his shoulders the way his were on mine, "is that I really, really have to piss."

He laughed out loud, a really loud laugh, and leaned his head forward onto my shoulder. "You're funny," he said. "You're crazy. Go piss. I have to piss too." I relaxed a little and managed to haul myself over all those garbage bags and open the side doors of the van. Carlos followed me. It wasn't raining so hard as before, but it was still raining. We stood in the rain next to each other and pissed these long streams of piss, mine clear and Carlos's dark yellow. Carlos aimed his so that it intersected with mine, and they hit the ground together in one single stream.

I could tell Carlos was staring at my dick the whole time I was pissing. Well, I thought, it wasn't like I hadn't glanced over at his.

When he finished he didn't stuff himself back in his pants. He just stood there with it hanging out, waiting I guess for me to finish. Which I did, and zipped up.

He reached over and put his hand on my belt buckle. I didn't move. I didn't brush his hand away. I didn't do anything.

He crouched down in front of me, looking up at me the whole time with our eyes locked. Then he undid my jeans and slipped them down. I kept saying to myself, Tony, do something, but I couldn't do a thing. It was that animal thing in him, which I picked up on from the first. I felt his hands on me and I couldn't move. My dick was starting to crank up under his touch, and I realized it'd been half-hard back there in the van when we were talking, only I hadn't wanted to admit it.

Before I knew it he was touching my dick with the tip of his tongue. He ran his tongue up and down the sides of it, and then he slid it in his mouth.

I'd never felt anything like that—before I knew what'd hit me, whoosh! I gave out this huge groan, and there I was shooting off in his mouth. But he didn't seem to mind, he just kept going at it harder than ever until finally he came up for air.

"Oh man," I said to him. It was like somebody'd gone and knocked the breath out of me. I was sorry I'd come in his mouth without telling him I was going to—I thought he'd be upset. "I didn't mean to do that, really I didn't," I said.

He wiped his mouth but kept on crouching in front of me. Then he started to laugh. He couldn't stop laughing—and I had to laugh too, so hard it was almost like crying. Laughing at how crazy it was, what'd just happened with us.

"You know," Carlos said when he finally stopped laughing enough to get his words out, "I've got you now. I've got you."

"What do you mean?" I had to ask. Suddenly I thought—maybe he's crazy. Maybe he's some kind of lunatic.

"Here's a scientific fact for you," he said. "A person's semen contains every piece of information about that person. It's all coded in there, genetically. And you know what? I think that's miraculous, Tony, I really do." Then he started laughing all over again. All I could think of was to grab both his ears and ease that laughing mouth of his back down onto my dick, which hadn't stopped being hard even after I came.

That shut him up, and it felt great to be inside there again. I started pumping into him, pushing my hips against his face till I came again.

This time he jumped up and sort of scooped me into his arms, and before I knew it he'd kissed me. It was pretty surprising—his tongue just pushed on in, and it was like he had a mouth all gooey with snot. Only it wasn't snot, I figured out in a flash.

"Yecch!" I pulled away from him. I didn't want a mouthful of come, even if it was my own. It tasted slimy and disgusting. And I didn't exactly like a guy trying to kiss me, either. "Why'd you go and do that?" I said.

"Oh, I don't know." Carlos was still clinging onto my shoulders and talking right in my face. "Passion of the moment. That's what I love about you crazy kids." He let go of me and did this little dance. "All that energy," he said. "I bet I could make you come three times in a row if I wanted."

I was getting back into my pants and it was my turn to laugh.

"Any more and it'll fall off," I told him.

I wasn't feeling bad or anything. In fact, I was feeling pretty great, even if he had tried to kiss me.

Back in the van, driving back to town, he didn't have much to say— but every once in a while Carlos would start laughing to himself, like he was remembering something—or like some little kid who's so pleased with himself he just doesn't know what to do.

"Well," he said. "All in a day's work. Anything else I can do for you?" We were driving down Main Street, and I was looking at everything thinking, It all looks the same, it's like nothing happened to change anything. And I guess I felt glad about that.

"You could buy me," I said to Carlos, "a bottle of Canadian Club whisky."

I knew it was straight out of the blue, but what the hell?

"A what?" he said.

"Yeah," I told him. "A bottle of whisky." I pointed out the Main Street liquor store, which was the only thing in downtown Owen that stayed open in the evenings.

"Never a dull moment with you kids," Carlos said. He swung the van over to the curb and hopped out. The van was still running, the keys were in the ignition. "Now don't try to drive off or anything," he told me. I don't know where he thought I was going to go.

When he came back out, he handed me the bottle in its paper bag. "Notice," he said, "how I'm not asking any questions."

I just smiled at him. I was feeling pretty content. "It's time for me to go home," I said.

My mom's car was in the drive. We stopped by the steps that led up to the trailer, and I pulled the laundry bags from the back of the van and hefted them onto the steps so they wouldn't get in the mud. "Thanks for the ride," I told Carlos. It didn't seem like the right thing to say, but I couldn't think of anything else. I couldn't believe everything that'd happened.

"So—see you around," he said, like the whole thing had been kind of amusing to him.

I stood there watching the taillights of his van down the road. Then they were gone and it was just me. I felt incredible and scared at the same time, and completely empty too. I took a swig from the whisky bottle and then stashed it down under the trailer, behind one of the concrete block foundations. Then for about half an hour I just sat on the steps beside the black plastic garbage bags that were tied up to keep the laundry dry inside them. It was chilly out there, the clothes I was wearing got soaked though with the rain, my hair was all stringy and falling down in my face. But that was okay, that was what I wanted.

I WROTE ALL THAT DOWN YESTERDAY IN ONE SINGLE
breath—at least that's what it felt like. It came whooshing out. I don't
want you to think I'm just writing a bunch of porn, though if it gets you
off, fine. Why shouldn't it get you off?

I keep talking to "you," but I don't even know who you are. All I
know is, there're a lot of folks out there clamoring to hear about Carlos
Reichart, I guess because most folks are basically buzzards when it
comes to famous people. And you know what? There's nobody in a
better position to tell you about Carlos than me. Because I was there. I
know.

I also know you're probably not that much interested in me. But if
you're going to get the dirt about Carlos, then you're going to have to
hear about me too. I say that because I want to be honest and tell the
truth. There's a lot I could be tempted to make up, but I'm not going to.
I'm going to try to remember the way things happened, connect them
all together—the way Carlos told me I should do that first day I ever
met him.

It's funny—when you're a kid, you think you've got forever to figure
things out. Then one day you're not a kid anymore. One day, before you
ever thought it'd happen—time's up, the movie's over.

Here at the Eddy—which is what they call this place—the movie's
definitely over. I have to face up to that.

Though nobody here seems to care one way or the other about what
I did, unlike the newspapers. I guess I sort of respect the Eddy for that—
I've always had to respect people who felt they could be indifferent
about things. Not that I see anybody much—this protective custody

stuff gets pretty exclusive. There's this one guard, Earl, who comes to see me, and we've gotten so we talk. I'm not a suspicious sort of person, so I don't really care what he's up to with his visits. Maybe they pay him to talk to me on the off-chance I might say something, but I don't think so. I think he's just curious about me. I think, of all the people here, he's the one who thinks he's got something in common with me. Or maybe I should say he's worried he does.

I'm not sure what I mean by saying that. Earl's a regular family man and everything. But four different times now, he's brought me this picture of his two kids. He never says anything, he just shows it to me, like it's always the first time he's showed it to me. Maybe he doesn't remember he's showed it to me before, though that's a little hard to believe.

They're about seven or eight, his kids—twins but not identical twins. It's odd—whenever he shows me that picture and I look at it, I can tell he's watching me. Like he's trying to figure something out. Like that picture's going to have some kind of effect on me and Earl's going to be able to tell by looking at me what the effect it's having is. But I don't think he ever gets the effect he wants, and the reason he keeps showing me the picture is, he knows there's something there and he's desperate to find it. At least I think that's what it is. Maybe he's just weird—he's a prison guard after all.

I said those kids were twins, though you wouldn't really guess it unless Earl told you. They've got sandy hair, but that's all you can really tell about them because the picture's sort of blurred. And anyway, it's winter so they're all bundled up.

It's not such a great picture, it's just a snapshot. But I guess the one thing about pictures I learned from Carlos is—how they always say a lot more about the person who took them than about the people who're in them.

"Don't be naive," Carlos would say. About everything, even about some snapshot a dad takes of his kids. So since Earl took the picture, you might say I don't know anything about Earl's little boys, but I know a lot about him.

And I think I can definitely say this—Earl's scared for his kids. That's what that picture says to me loud and clear. They're at a sliding board, it's in some park and it's winter, and one of them's standing on the ground beside the sliding board with his head crooked to one side.

He's holding up his left hand to shield his eyes from the bright sun, while the other kid's perched up at the top of the sliding board just ready to go down the chute on his stomach. They don't seem aware of each other, those two kids—like each one thinks he's the only one in the picture.

I never know what to say. I say stupid stuff like "cute kids," and then Earl tells me they favor their mother, or that he's sending them to Olive Branch Christian Academy because the public schools're no good anymore. He says to me, like it's a secret only him and me are supposed to know, "Tony, the problem's not drugs or blacks or Hispanics per se, the problem's people who come here not understanding fundamental American values." He always leans close to me when he talks like that, and lowers his voice even though of course there's nobody to hear. He says, "This country's letting itself go to ruin because it's just opened its borders wide to anything that wants to come through. A country that can't control its own borders, now where's that country going to be?"

I never have much to say to all that. I guess my life's pretty much been one big open border. And anyway, it's what you'd expect from Earl. It's what I grew up with in Owen and if things hadn't been different, it's probably what I'd be like now. There're even times when I wish I was still like that—everything would be a lot easier and clearer. Anyway, who's a murderer to go saying to Earl's face how it's bad attitudes like his that start to break a country down, not people coming in across its borders because they don't have any other place to go?

But back to that photo. I think it's odd for some prison guard to be showing a murderer pictures of his kids. I think Earl looks at that picture and he knows there's something there he's not getting. Then he looks at me, and I think somehow he's pleading with me to tell him what it is. That's why he's so interested in me—he thinks if you kill somebody then you know things other people go through life never knowing. Terrible things that a man who's got kids needs to know if he's going to keep those kids safe.

Maybe that's why, last week, instead of showing me that photo again, he went and pulled out a newspaper article he had all folded up in his wallet.

"So what's that?" I asked.

"Something I thought you might want to see," he said.

I wasn't too surprised—it wasn't the first time in my life I ever saw my name in print. "Tony Blair's long nightmare is over," it started off, "and another one begins." I read a little ways into it, and it made me pretty sick to my stomach what they said about me. Not that it was a bunch of lies, but just that they didn't have a clue. So I told Earl that. I told him what really snared me was how whoever wrote that article thought they could figure something out about me—like they had some kind of inside information.

"I got a drawer full of clippings if you ever want to see them," he told me. "Newspapers, magazines."

"I've got no interest," I said.

"I'm keeping them if you ever want them. I made a sort of album—you know, to keep things straight for you."

It struck me as sort of creepy, him pasting away at that scrapbook in his spare time. I could just see him sitting around the kitchen table at night, sipping coffee—I'm sure Earl doesn't drink. I'm sure his wife won't let him. I guess it's a free country, though—if that's what he wants to do.

I asked him, Did he read those articles?

"I read them all the time," he told me. "There're some things you just can't get out of your head."

"Tell me about it," I said.

"I still can't figure you," he said. "Nobody can."

Which made me laugh. "There's nothing to figure," I said. "I mean, once you know. It's just that nobody ever asked me my opinion about any of it."

Earl didn't say anything to that. He just shuffled off in that Earl way of his, and I didn't think any more about it till about a week later he brought me this spiral notebook and a blue ballpoint pen. He said he'd been thinking about it, and he thought if everybody else was going to have a say, then maybe I should write my own side of it too. He said he was sure it would be fascinating, and he thought I could sell it to some magazine for lots of money.

"What's a person like me going to do with lots of money?" I asked him.

"Well then," he said, "write it to tell the truth."

So here goes, Earl. Though there's just one other thing I want to say before I get on with it.

The summer when I was fourteen I got this completely strange idea. I thought a wood tick, one of those little brown things about the size of a pinhead, had managed to crawl up into my dick and get lodged in there. It made this itch I couldn't get at; kept me squirming all summer long. All I could think about was that tick getting fatter and fatter. I could feel it getting fatter, its little, brown body bloating up like you see ticks on dogs, till it was a big gray pellet all mushy with blood. Every time I pissed I kept expecting to somehow be able to piss it out—but I couldn't because of course nothing was up there.

Which is how I feel these days, only the tick isn't stuck in the slit of my dick anymore—it's crawled all the way to my heart. I can feel it hanging there, attached to that blood pump, feeding off it and itching me like hell. But no matter what I do I can't get at it.

I'M TRYING TO REMEMBER EVERYTHING I CAN AND BE completely honest, so if I think about something and find I haven't exactly remembered it right, or told the truth about it, I'm going to go back and change what I said, or add to it. Which is what I have to do right now—meaning, I wasn't completely honest when I told Carlos about me and Wallace, watching each other jerk off. So I should tell you the whole story now, for the record.

By the time I was sixteen or so, I guess I was probably an alcoholic. Maybe you already guessed that from what I said earlier. It wasn't my fault, exactly. What happened was this: ever since I was a little kid, I had these terrible nightmares. The kind you wake up screaming from in the middle of the night. And something new every night. I'd be standing in front of a mirror picking at my nose, and my nose would come off like raw hamburger. I'd go on scratching at my face, and it would just peel off under my fingers. Or I'd be in this dark room and something would be in the room with me, and I knew if I yelled out it'd go away—but I'd keep trying to yell and nothing happened. Then I guess I really would yell out loud and wake myself up in a sweat. You get the idea.

I remember my dad would come into the bedroom and take me up in his arms and walk me around, singing this song to calm me down. "Red River Valley" was the song, and I always used to think Red River Valley was the place where we lived. When he sang, "From this valley they say you are going," I always felt sad and empty—and then when he up and left us, a couple of years later when I was eleven or so, I knew why I'd felt that way.

With no more Red River Valley, I was pretty much on my own—

but when I was fourteen, I made this great discovery. I remember that afternoon: I was in the trailer watching after my two little sisters, who at the time were about four and five, and because I was feeling restless I decided to have a shot of Mom's whisky to maybe relax me. I knew she kept it in the cupboard and did shots of it at night before she went to sleep—but somehow it just never occurred to me to try some myself. It was bitter-tasting, but nice to feel go down warm in my throat, and then spread out in my stomach. I decided to have another swallow, and then after a few minutes I was feeling so good I had another, and before I knew it I was drunk.

I remember walking outside—it was a cloudy day in the middle of summer and the green of the trees about knocked me over, it seemed so close and heavy and I couldn't get enough of looking at those trees and taking it all in. Then I came inside and fell asleep on the sofa, which was the first good sleep I'd had in, it seemed like, years.

Pretty soon I was taking so many shots of Mom's whisky that I had to figure out how to get some on my own. There was only so much doctoring it up with water that I could get away with. Which leads to Wallace.

I can't really remember how I met him—it seems like he was always around, and we always sort of knew each other even though he was four or five years older than me. I never really thought about it at the time, but now I think probably he and my mom had something going for a while. But then it must've stopped, and they stayed friendly afterward. That was more or less the way my mom was with her men—after my dad left, she didn't get too emotionally involved. I think she was out for a good time and that was all.

I liked Wallace because he was funny and smart, unlike most of the people I knew. We went hunting a few times, and I remember he took me to a turkey shoot once where he won a turkey that he gave to my mom on the condition she invite him over to Thanksgiving, which she did. After the meal Wallace and I went on a little walk in the woods behind the trailer, and he brought out this pint of bourbon and we sat on a log and drank it and talked about girls and what a dead place Owen was, and how he had these big plans about moving to Detroit, where he had a cousin. With the bourbon and all, we got to talking about various things about ourselves—I don't know what got into me, but I up and told him about the dreams I was having, and how I needed to get whisky so I could sleep.

He sort of laughed and said, "Yeah, sure; we all know how it is." But then he went on to say, if I could pay him he could get stuff for me, no problem.

The only problem was, I didn't have any money because I wasn't working, and they wouldn't hire at the lumberyard till you were sixteen. So Wallace said he'd think about some way I could pay him, and in the meantime he'd get me stuff from the liquor store.

About a month went by, and he'd brought me about four bottles of Canadian Club and hadn't asked for a dime, and I thought, This is great, I've got it made. But I also sort of wondered what was up—though of course I didn't say anything. Then one night he came over. It was late Saturday night, and he stood there banging on the trailer door. He was pretty drunk. In fact he was blasted—you could tell just by smelling his breath and how bright his eyes were. He leaned against the door like he was bracing himself and looked in at the living room. "Your mom here?" he said.

I told him, no, she was out with this guy Bruce she'd met. "Figures," he said. "Then let's you and me go somewhere too."

"I can't go anywhere," I told him. "I'm watching the kids." Which in fact I was.

"So are they asleep or what?"

"They're asleep," I admitted.

He grabbed my arm. "Come get in the truck. We won't be all night. They'll be just fine."

"Sure, okay," I told him, because after all it was Saturday night and the kids'd be fine just lying there asleep. Plus, I thought, if he's so drunk there's probably more where that came from. I was running a little low on my current bottle, so I thought it might be a good idea to be drinking his liquor tonight instead of mine. And who knew? Maybe he'd give me another bottle or something.

The truck ride was pretty severe. Wallace was having a little trouble holding it to just one lane, and we kept swerving onto the shoulder—but fortunately his apartment was only about five minutes from our trailer. Even though he was already completely drunk, as soon as we were in the apartment he poured both of us two big glasses of bourbon, which

was just fine with me. Then he put the Allman Brothers on the stereo
and started sort of dancing around the room. I'd never seen Wallace so
stoked before, but that was okay. Sometimes I thought the guy was a
little too serious, but now he was being pretty silly. Definitely he was
somewhere else, though I was drinking fast to try to catch up. This is
great, I thought. I'll pass out when I get home and won't have to worry.

"So it's time for you to pay," Wallace told me. He was still dancing
around, not looking at me at all.

"What do you mean, pay?" I said. He knew I didn't have any cash.

"Like I said, pay. We agreed, right? I was going to think about how
I was going to get paid."

"Yeah, you were going to think about it."

"Well, I've done thought about it." He was still dancing, and as he
was dancing he slipped his T-shirt off over his head.

"I don't get it," I said.

"Come on over here," he told me. Then, when I didn't immediately
move, he danced over to where I was and put his hands on my shoulders.

"You're a great pal," he told me.

"You're a great pal too," I said back, still thinking he was just being
drunk.

But he wasn't—and, well, one thing led to another and pretty soon
it was clear how I was going to pay.

"Go on," he said, "it's not going to kill you. Lots of people done it
before this."

I wasn't too thrilled, but I wasn't freaked out either. I guess I was
pretty drunk. I did some quick calculating and figured out it was probably either do this or no more whisky. What the hell, I thought—he's
right, it won't kill me. We were in his bedroom by then. He was lying
with his hands behind his head and his half-hard dick flopping across his
belly. Well, I remember thinking, here goes nothing. So I went down
on it.

"No teeth," he said.

I tried again, and I must've done better because he started moaning
and moving his hips around. I didn't get any thrills from it—basically it
just made my jaw ache. I don't even remember now if I had a hard-on
or anything. I went up and down on it for a while, and then when
I got bored with that I started experimenting with how deep in my

throat I could make it go. I couldn't get all that far down on it without gagging—so I went back to doing what I could handle. Pretty soon he said, "I'm going to come," so I pulled off because at the time the last thing in the world I wanted to do was go swallowing a bunch of come. Taking his dick between my two palms I jerked him off the rest of the way. He came in a big white puddle right on his belly. I'd never seen another guy's come before, and it was sort of interesting. I remember I rubbed it around his belly with my fingers and then lifted my fingers to my nose and smelled. More out of curiosity than anything else.

When I looked up at him he was completely passed out. I poured myself another big glass of bourbon and sat in the living room and watched a little bit of *White Christmas* with Bing Crosby, which was the late movie on TV that night. When I looked in the bedroom again, he was still passed out, only now he was snoring. I left him like that on top of the covers, sort of half on and half off the bed, and I walked back home feeling pretty drunk but okay.

He never mentioned what happened, and I sure wasn't going to, but he kept the whisky coming, and I guess probably four more times we did the same thing, always more or less exactly the same, with him being drunk and me sucking him till he was about to come and then jerking him off the rest of the way. We neither of us ever said anything about what we did, and after about six months Wallace up and moved to Detroit. I never saw him again after that.

Now that I've told the truth about Wallace, something else comes back to me. I'd totally forgotten about it till just now, but about a year before the stuff with Wallace, my mom and I were driving back from Paducah, and I had to piss. We stopped at a rest stop on the interstate, and I went into the toilet. At the next urinal, there was this older man. I thought it was odd he wasn't pissing—he was just standing there holding his dick—but I didn't really think anything about it. So I went on and pissed and when I was through, before I could stick myself back in my pants, he reached over and put his hand around my dick.

I was shocked as hell, but also hard in no time. I just stood there, I couldn't move a muscle. He jerked me off and himself at the same time, and I came almost instantly. I was back in my pants and scooted out of there before the guy had time to come or anything.

The strange thing was, the instant I was out of there it was something behind me, it was just something that had happened to me and that was that. I didn't think about it on the car ride home or anything.

I never thought about it again till just now, when thinking about all that other stuff must've dredged it up. Carlos would like that.

I N THE DREAM, WHICH IS ALSO A MOVIE THAT'S BEING
filmed, they're wearing gas masks that make them look like people
from some other planet—big round empty eyes and elephant trunks that
hang down, plus heavy clothes and gloves. When I first see them, they're
coming over a rise, about five people trudging toward the camera. It
looks like some World War I battlefield with craters and mud and no
trees or anything except some blasted trunks and branches.

No matter what's happening in the dream, I never forget it's all
being filmed, even though I never actually see the camera crew. But I
know they're outside the frame, and somehow that's comforting because
I know if they're filming it then it's all just acting. But it's also scary
because somehow I realize—but they don't, and this is what makes
dreaming it so bad—that they think it's all being acted but it's really
not. It's the real thing.

The people in the gas masks stop in a grove of dead trees where
the bark's been peeled away and is hanging down in big strips—like
it's been burned off by acid. Somehow in the movie the bark hanging
in strips is connected with the melting sickness. Because there's some
kind of melting sickness in the air that the suits and masks are supposed
to protect against. One of the people in the group—a kid—has gotten
exposed. His skin's melting off like some snake shedding its skin: only
not clean and dry like that, but wet and horrible. He's not wearing the
same protective suit as everybody else, instead he's wearing this army
flak vest that leaves his arms and chest exposed.

They come to a stop in the grove of trees. Everything's happening
with no sound, like in some silent movie. The leader of the group holds

up his hand to tell the others they should halt here. The kid lies down because he can't go any farther, and his father, who's the leader, kneels down beside him and takes out a handkerchief. He dips it in this can of gasoline that's there beside him. He cradles the kid in his arms, and I can see now how his skin is melting off in these horrible pools of flesh. The father very gently takes the handkerchief with the gasoline on it and smothers the kid, and that's the end of the movie—only the people who're filming it don't know yet that it's not a movie, that there really is this terrible disease in the air that's making people's skin melt off.

I DIDN'T GUESS I'D SEE CARLOS AGAIN. THE NEXT DAY
I moved the bottle of Canadian Club he'd bought me down to this
hollow tree stump in the woods where I'd stash stuff when I had it. If it
wasn't for that bottle, I probably would've thought I was crazy and made
the whole thing up. But the bottle was there, and I remember resolving
how I was going to make it last as long as I could. Every time I took a
hit from it, I thought, Carlos bought me this bottle—and that made me
feel empty and charged up at the same time. Carlos who I'd never seen
again, who I couldn't even really remember what he looked like once a
couple of days had gone by. But there were things I didn't forget—his
mouth on my dick, all slick and warm and me feeling like I belonged
in there. I could jerk off to that, and I did—and thinking about him
kissing me too, which didn't feel so bad to think about. Especially since
it wasn't something that was ever going to happen again.

Then one day I was riding this beat-up old bicycle I used to get
around town on, and here comes a car horn beeping practically in my
ear—it's the kind of thing that annoys me like crazy, when cars do that
to me and I'm on my bicycle. I turned around ready to give the finger
when I saw it was Carlos in the orange van.

"So I guess you think that's funny," I told him. He was grinning at
me, this mean ugly grin that made me hate to see him again. I felt all
sick to see that face and remember everything it'd done to me.

"Not really," he said, "but I had to get your attention somehow. I'm
so happy to see you."

"Yeah, well," I told him. "I could say the same. So you're still in
town," I said.

It was weird to see him again. He was still wearing that black shirt of his buttoned to the collar.

"We're making a movie," he said. "I told you that."

"Yeah, you're making a movie where?" I said. I hadn't seen any evidence of anybody making a movie. I figured it was just this thing he'd told me to try and make himself interesting. But he sounded disappointed.

"I thought for sure you were going to come out and see us."

It was honestly something I hadn't even thought about. I'd figured— whoever he was, he was long gone from Owen.

"So where is this movie?" I asked him.

It turned out it was about a mile past Tatum's Landing, where we'd gone that night.

"Throw your bike in the back of the van and come on out—I'm going there right this instant."

It was the last thing I wanted to do right then. "I can't," I lied. "I got to run some errands."

"Well tomorrow, then. Tomorrow afternoon. I'll be looking for you.

"We'll see," I told him.

"Gotta go," he said, and honked his horn again, and then he was off.

I stood there breathing his fumes, straddling my bike. I remember saying to myself out loud, "Jeesh," like that was going to solve anything. I never talk out loud to myself.

But my heart was beating fast and I had this prickly sweat. I was really happy, I wanted to shout something right there, I wanted to clap my hands and high-five it. It also made me feel queasy right down to the bottom of my gut.

Without another thought I started peddling fast as I could in the direction Carlos took off in.

I thought—if I just peddle and don't think, everything'll be okay. It made my legs ache, I peddled so fast without letting up—but I liked that. I liked concentrating on the way my muscles started to burn.

I was past the turnoff for Tatum's Landing in no time. There was a little rise, and then the road dipped down, and suddenly what I saw was this: an old dilapidated shack sitting in the middle of a field, and in front of that shack there were about twenty black plastic buckets with tall weeds growing out of them. Somebody'd lighted those weeds on fire, and they were flaming away. This huge black woman in an apron and a bright purple kerchief was hanging out of the cab of an old pickup truck, driving it around and around those burning weeds in a circle. She was whooping it up, shaking her fist at those weeds. Then all of a sudden she fell right out of the truck on her face and the truck kept going on without her, sort of in a circle but sort of not. Some old man who'd been standing on the sidelines, where the cameras were, scrambled up to make sure she was okay, while another guy took off running after the truck to jump in the cab and put the brake on.

I hadn't known what to expect, exactly, but it definitely wasn't this. Carlos seemed happy to see me. He turned his back on everything that was happening in front of the shack and walked over to where I'd gotten off my bicycle. He put his arms around me; then he stuck his tongue in my mouth. I was panting like crazy from the ride. It made me squeamish, him hugging me in broad daylight like that, and kissing me, but I could tell nobody was watching because they were all still running around trying to put out the fires in the buckets.

"I knew you'd come," Carlos said. "You're a godsend. See that shovel? Take those buckets out in the field, dump out the burned-up weeds, then dig and pot me about twenty more. And bring them back over here, okay? Netta'll help you."

He pointed to this wild-looking woman who came up to where we were standing. She had a bug-eyed look, and frizzy black hair she kept running her fingers through. She was wearing this tight black dress that followed the shape of her body.

"Well finally," she said. "Let's get this thing done right." She went over and started pulling the burnt weed-stalks out of the buckets. I didn't say anything—I was too surprised, and Carlos was suddenly involved in a very intense conversation with this big bearded guy with a movie camera. I followed Netta down to the field where we dug up the tall brown weeds that were growing there and potted them in the buckets.

"You wait," she kept muttering under her breath. "You'll find out." I couldn't tell if she was talking to me, but I sort of thought she wasn't. I sort of thought she must be talking to the weeds she was pulling up with her bare hands. She kept wiping her face with those hands, and her hair, and she left dirt smudges across her cheeks and her forehead, and little bits of weed in her hair.

"Slash and burn," she said. "When in doubt." And she pulled up another stalk of weed and plugged it down in a bucket.

We brought the buckets back from the field and set them in front of the shack the way they'd been last time.

Carlos was talking to the black woman, whom he called Verbena. She was breathing hard. "Hoo," she told him, "I ain't that young no more." Up close, she had the worst teeth in the universe—four or five scraggly stumps in the front of her mouth and that was it. But she kept smiling this big smile, even when Carlos put his arm around her and told her the bad news: she had to do that stunt with the pickup truck one more time. "And you're not supposed to fall out of the truck," he told her.

"I know I'm not supposed to fall out of the truck," she said.

"Then don't do it."

"I got carried away," she told Carlos. "Maybe I'll get carried away again."

"I'll kill you," he said, "if you get carried away again. I'll drive the truck right over your body."

Carlos had forgotten all about me—there was nothing to do except watch. Somebody was splashing gasoline on those buckets of weeds we'd brought up from the field, and somebody else moved in with a movie camera while Verbena tugged at her dress that'd gotten twisted on her body, the way some little girl might go squirming and tugging, and then what happened next was the most amazing thing. I couldn't believe it.

Verbena walked over to those buckets. She hiked up her skirt and squatted down. She took out a cigarette lighter, and held it around behind her, where her butt was sticking out, and she flicked it. Whoosh! Out came this humungous fart like a cannon. It ripped right through that lighter spark like a flamethrower, this long tongue of fire that went licking out over all those weeds in the pots till they blazed right up. Verbena let out this yelp and ran over and jumped in the truck, and away she went, driving around those burning weeds, hanging on for dear life even while she kept slinging her big body as far out of the cab as she could, steering with one hand and yelling and shouting and shaking her fist while the truck went round and round and the fire climbed up the stalks of those weeds till you couldn't see the weeds anymore, just the fire.

The camera was getting it all down, from start to finish. And my heart, I have to tell you, was beating like no tomorrow.

Nobody knew it at the time, naturally, especially not me, but that movie they were making was the one that'd make Carlos famous—*Ur,* which when they showed it in New York at this film festival got a lot of attention from everybody, and I still have the photo from *Time* magazine of Verbena hanging out of that truck with all those weeds on fire.

But that was all a couple of years down the toad, and if you ask, Did any of us know we were doing something that would be famous one day? I'd have to honestly say, No, we didn't. Except maybe for Carlos, and I know even Carlos was kind of surprised when he got to be famous—I mean, famous in the way he did. He worked such a long time with nobody paying any attention to him, he figured it was always going to be that way. And he didn't care—he'd already made his peace with that a long time before I ever knew him.

The take Carlos finally ended up using, by the way, was the one where Verbena fell out of the truck. Somehow, once you saw it on film, it looked totally inspired.

After the last shot, nobody seemed to know what to do. Verbena'd drifted down to the weed field, and now she was walking around in circles, sort of dazed and farting these big watery farts I don't think she thought anybody could hear, but they were really loud, like explosions.

The big burly guy who'd been operating one of the cameras handed me a beer.

"I'm Seth," he said.

"Tony," I said.

"Get drunk," he told me and walked off. Which was a little strange, but at least I had a beer. Nobody else seemed curious about me or anything, and that was fine. I just leaned against a tree trunk and drank my beer.

After a while Carlos showed up, totally involved in leafing through that spiral notebook he'd had in the Nu-Way.

"Oh Tony," he said. "Stay for supper. You can do that, can't you?"

"Yeah," I told him, "I can do that."

"Then go help Sammy," he said. He never looked up from his notebook, he just nodded over to where this little old man was cooking something on one of those kerosene stoves like hunters use. He was wearing this funny-looking cap, and this T-shirt with KILL THE BASTARDS stenciled on it. He had tiny little thin arms. I thought it was pretty funny, what his T-shirt said.

"Kill what bastards?" I asked him.

"Kill the bastards," he said, like he meant it.

"Okay," I said. "I was just trying to make conversation."

"Make dinner instead," he told me. "Slice those potatoes over there. Here's a knife."

"Are you French?" I asked him. I'd never met a foreigner before, and he had this accent like you never heard. Plus he was wearing that funny little hat.

"And you, you are perhaps a schlemiel?"

"A what?"

"Never mind. Peel the potatoes and don't talk to me. I got things to do."

I pointed to his hat.

"A Hungarian Jew invented the beret in the eleventh century, long before you were born," he told me in that high-pitched little voice of his. "Now I'm busy," he said, and he turned his back on me like I'd gone and offended him.

I sat down and started to peel. There're worse things than peeling potatoes, I guess, especially if you don't know what else to do with yourself.

Before I knew it he was standing over me—he was about as tall standing up as I was sitting down—and he was screaming. "No, no, no, no, no," he screamed, and each time he said no he raised both his fists up to the level of his ears, and then dropped them again. He looked like a little wind-up doll that'd run down if it went on very long.

"What's up?" I asked.

"Slice. Not peel, slice." He made slicing motions with his hand against the palm of his other.

"I was peeling them first."

"This youth thinks peels are not healthy?" he said. "Vitamins," he yelled at me. "Roughage. Better people than you have made whole lives off the peels of potatoes."

This one's a crazy one, I said to myself. His weird little accent made me want to laugh. Plus he really was upset, the way crazy people can get themselves totally upset over little things like that.

"Okay," I said, "sure. Vitamins."

"Vitamins," he said. We eyed each other for a minute—then all of a sudden there was this twinkle in his eye, he was winking at me, there was some little joke between us. It lasted for about a second, and then he went back to whatever he was cooking in that big pot of his.

When I finished with the potatoes, I decided it might be best just to rest out of harm's way. I went back to my tree and sat down with my back up against it.

I wasn't there but a few minutes when Seth came over. He squatted down beside me and took a long swig from his beer. "So, you're Tony," he said. Which I'd already told him was my name earlier.

"Tony," I said. "That's right."

He was this big ape of a guy, greasy black hair all tucked up in a red kerchief and this huge black beard. He studied me like I was something the cat dragged in. I could tell he was sizing me up, which is a thing that always makes me bristle when people do that to me.

"Hmm," he said. "So how tall are you?"

It was sort of an odd way to start up a conversation. I didn't like him much.

"Why?" I said.

"Tell me how tall you are. Five nine, five ten?"

I shrugged. "I don't go around measuring myself all the time," I told him.

"You're still growing," he said—not like it was a question, but something he just knew about me.

How was I supposed to know if I was still growing? I didn't say anything, and he rubbed his beard with the palm of his hand. These big flakes of dandruff fell out of it. I could see them raining down, they were so thick. He took another big swig of beer.

"You know what causes that?" he said.

"Causes what?"

"Dandruff." He rubbed his beard again, and again it started to snow.

I had to shrug one more time. I never liked tests, I was never very good at them.

"Deficiency of zinc and selenium," he said. He swigged from his beer again. With his sleeveless denim jacket and army boots, it was like he'd taken me prisoner in some kind of jungle battle, the way he was crouching in front of me and me with my back up against that tree. I practically expected him to come out with the bamboo torture instruments any minute now.

"Do you know," he said, "what causes a deficiency of zinc and selenium in the human body?" He looked at me like this was something any idiot's supposed to know.

I just looked back at him.

"You jerk *off* too much," he said; "You lose zinc and selenium through your semen. Now isn't that interesting? I bet you didn't know that." All the time he kept peering at me, pinning me to that tree trunk.

"There's lots I don't know," I told him. Anyway, he was the one with the dandruff, not me. "Are you trying to tell me not to jerk off too much?"

He laughed his bear laugh. "Consider it a friendly warning," he said. "Take me as an example."

"Yeah," I told him. "You and my gym teacher."

"Fair enough," he said. "We all got vices. You smoke?"

I shrugged again—sometimes I did, sometimes I didn't. I used to smoke when I was around Wallace, because he did. Kools, which I always thought tasted pretty grim.

"Well—either it's yes or no," he told me. Suddenly it was like he was angry with me for no reason. "I guess that means the hell no," he said.

I couldn't figure out what I was supposed to be saying to him. But just then he took out this joint from his pocket and stuck it in his mouth.

I never smoked dope. I knew my way around booze like a pro, but I'd never touched any dope. I knew what a joint looked like, but that was basically from TV. Believe it or not, even though it was 1979 there weren't a whole lot of drugs in Owen, Kentucky—even the home-grown kind.

He went ahead and lit up right there in my face. Then he blew smoke at me. It smelled smoky and sweet.

"That bother you?" he asked.

"No," I told him. This treatment of his was sort of freaking me out. Suddenly he jabbed with one hand to the left of my head, then to the right, these two split-second moves so fast I hardly had time to react.

"Hey," I warned him. It seemed crazy this guy might be trying to pick a fight.

But he only smiled. "You're just fine," he said. He stood up and looked down past his big belly at me. Then he walked away without saying another word.

Okay, I remember telling myself. Fine. You're just hanging out, you can get up and walk away from this any time you want. Because I was pretty rattled. It was sort of the same way I'd felt with Carlos in the laundromat—how somehow this guy I'd never even met before knew all these things about me. Things I didn't even know. I wondered if he could tell just by looking at me how I jerked off too much.

It never occurred to me Carlos might've been talking about me to these people. It never occurred to me one bit.

In the field on this side of the shack were some tents set up and people milling around. There was Carlos's orange VW van, and a pickup truck with an old homemade camper on back and this ancient church bus painted sky blue with the words RISING ZION HARDSHELL BAPTIST on the side. Hardshell is right, I remember thinking.

It was getting dark. That whole scene started to look like some kind of strange movie I was making in my head. Sammy in that KILL THE BASTARDS T-shirt of his over there stirring something in a big pot, and Verbena still down in the field walking around in circles and farting. Nobody there knew they were in my movie right then, but for a minute they were. Which was weird—I'd never looked at anything like it was a movie before. But it sort of worked.

Everybody was gathering over where Sammy'd started dishing out food. I looked around for Carlos, but I couldn't see him anywhere. I remember thinking—of course he was going to go off like this, and all these strange people around. But I couldn't leave—and I guess I didn't want to. I stuck my hands down in my pockets and wandered over to where everybody was sitting around in a circle on the ground. There were bottles of wine, which cheered me up, and everybody was talking and laughing.

"Come on, shy girl," Verbena said. "Sit yourself down. We don't bite round here."

I sort of had to laugh. But I sat down anyway. Verbena poured me some wine into a paper cup, and I took a big swallow.

"Watch you don't lose your head on that stuff," she told me.

"I'm okay with it," I told her, and with another swallow I finished off the cup. I was pretty nervous, and I needed some calming down. "Fill her up again," I told Verbena. I held out my cup to her.

"This boy," Verbena told Seth, "he's a regular gas guzzler."

"He's okay," Seth said. "He's just frisky."

I didn't like Seth. There was something about him that bullied me. And I kept watching all that dandruff flake down his chest. I tried not to imagine him jerking off—it was too gross.

Finally Carlos showed up. He sat himself down next to me but he didn't say anything—he just patted me on my thigh to show me he was there. Carlos, I wanted to say—but then I didn't know what'd come next. So I didn't say a word but just dug into that stew Sammy'd made, which actually wasn't bad if you liked that kind of thing.

Carlos wasn't eating anything. I noticed that in a minute—my spoon was scraping the bottom of the bowl and he was just sitting there studying everybody, watching all of us eat like it was the most fascinating thing. He could've been taking notes in that spiral notebook of his and it wouldn't've looked any stranger.

All of a sudden, like it was something he'd just remembered, he said in this loud voice that interrupted everybody else, "This is Tony. I haven't introduced him the way I should, but he's a very good friend of mine and I want everybody to like him, okay?"

Not the greatest way to introduce somebody, I thought—telling everybody else they have to like him.

Everybody in the circle sort of nodded at me, except Sammy, who I felt really disapproved of me for not knowing to leave the peels on his stupid potatoes. They all seemed a little stressed by having me there, which I could understand, since I was a little stressed by being there.

Carlos didn't exactly make it better. "You're new to all this. It'll take time." He laced the fingers of both his hands together. "We're strong, like this. We hold together. Utopia is what we are. And now you come in from the outside. It's hard."

While he said that, Sammy was handing around blackberries he'd dished into bowls. When everybody had a bowl, Carlos held his up in front of him. "It's been good," he said. "A good day, and they can't take it away from us. Whatever happens tomorrow, we've had this." Nobody said anything—they all just lifted their bowls up. Like a salute—not to Carlos, just a salute to everything. It impressed the hell out of me, it sent chills down my spine, and I thought about the way Carlos had laced his fingers together, and said that word *Utopia*.

Everything that'd been going on for the last several days just focused right then for me, because I remember looking around at those people and thinking, I've got to remember this. And that's what I realized Carlos had been doing earlier, when he first sat down. Looking around and trying to remember it all. I thought about him lacing his fingers together, and I thought to myself, so clear it was like saying it out loud—These people trust each other totally, like people never do. It was stunning for me to suddenly think that, because I'd never before had any cause to think about trust except in ordinary ways, and now suddenly I was saying to myself, looking around at Carlos and Verbena and those bowls of blackberries—These are people who totally trust each other. I thought about Verbena sending out that spout of fire right in front of everybody, which should have been gross and disgusting but somehow wasn't. It was just something that could happen if you wanted it to, and it was okay, it was one more thing. You might think it's strange to say, but I was glad I'd seen that. It was something I wanted to remember. It was stuff like that that held them together, and I wanted that stuff.

It'd gotten completely dark. Even though I was feeling totally at ease, I also thought I should be getting back home. It's like the way you wander into deep water. You're surprised you've gotten that far, and you know you could probably go farther, but you don't want to trust your luck anymore. You want to turn back with just what you have.

I touched Carlos on the arm to say I had to go. He looked at me like he was surprised I was still there. He'd let me see these things I'd seen, but I didn't know what he was trying to tell me with them. "I'll walk you a ways," he said.

I was scared. Some funny bone had gotten struck deep inside me, and I was ringing from the inside out. It just didn't seem likely, after this afternoon, we could go back to being the way we were. That Carlos could just scoop me up out there in the dark and go down on me like he did before. Every step, as we walked out into the dark where my bike was—anything could happen. But Carlos seemed relaxed. He put his hands in his pockets and sort of whistled a tune. We didn't have that much to say but that was okay.

It made me feel better, somehow, to know he was in some kind of control. And it made me feel better to know he was connected to those people back there around the fire that Seth had managed to make roar up in a big flame with some leftover gasoline from the shoot. It made me feel better to know Carlos hadn't dropped in out of nowhere, which is the way it'd felt at first.

When we got to where my bike was, he stopped and said, "Well." But he didn't say anything else.

"Maybe I'll stop by tomorrow and see how things are going," I told him. "That was all pretty interesting today." I wanted to make it sound like I was in control too. Like I wasn't quivering.

He still didn't say anything, and I remember thinking it was like he was calculating something in his head. Finally he said, "We won't be here tomorrow, Tony. We're leaving."

"For good?" I said. "You didn't say anything about going tomorrow." I think it probably sounded like a whine.

"We finished up early," he said, the way you might just shrug some body off. But then he grabbed my arm so hard it hurt. "Look, this is crazy," he told me. "I haven't slept in three days. I've been up all night. Writing, see? I've got this great idea, it's a magnificent idea for a movie... And you should be in it. It's for you, Tony. I wrote it for you, a script and everything. To star in."

It took me a second to get it.

"A movie for me to star in?" When I said it, it didn't sound right at all. But he suddenly seemed to believe in it.

"We'll start shooting in, I don't know, about two months. We can get some money, I know where we can get some money I'm pretty sure, and we can start shooting it and go from there. Two months. Start to finish. It'll be over before you know it."

He made it sound like an ordeal, but I sort of liked the idea of starring in a movie—even though I have to say it freaked me out a little too.

"That's what I have to offer," he said. Then he sounded sad, and it kind of swept me off my feet. "That's all I have to offer," he told me.

"But I don't get it. How are we going to make this movie when you're leaving?" I pointed out.

"You're leaving too. You're coming with us. The instant I saw you, I knew you were perfect. I've been looking a long time for the one perfect person for this movie, and you're it, Tony. You're that person."

"What kind of movie?" I was suddenly suspicious. "I'm not going to be in any porn film."

"No, of course not," he said. And kind of laughed. I have to admit I wasn't exactly thrilled either with the idea of my movie career being to drive a pickup truck around in circles till I fell out on my face, or to go farting fire out my butt or some stupid stunt like that. Not that I'd ever spent too much time thinking about my movie career up to that point.

"I can't just up and leave," I told him.

"No, I guess not," he said.

"Wow," I said. "I have to think. I mean, there's school and things. I have to take care of my brother and little sisters."

"I guess so." He sounded disappointed, but not as disappointed as I guess I wanted him to sound. I was going up and down on his movie idea like a seesaw.

"There's no mercy," Carlos said. He had this edge to his voice that took me off guard. To tell you the truth, it sort of scared me. "You stay in one place," he said, "you fall behind. You fall behind, you don't count anymore, you're not worth shit."

He sounded angry. Not at me: just angry. But I didn't know anything about what he was talking about. I said, "I don't know anything about any of this, and you're dropping it all on top of me pretty fast."

"You've got it," he said. "But then we just met, right? And I'm leaving tomorrow, right? So where does that leave us?"

"What kind of movie?" I asked again, because he hadn't quite answered that the first time I asked him.

He laughed. "Not like any movie you've ever seen before. Not by a long shot."

Which after this afternoon, I could pretty much believe was true.

"It's not just movies," he said. "Think about it. It's other things too."

"Look," I told him, "I'm not a fag or anything, if that's what you're thinking."

I think he must've been smiling. But it was dark, so I couldn't see.

"I don't think you're a fag," he told me. "I never said you were a fag."

He was right. Though I also had a hard-on from standing there talking with him. I expected him, any minute, to move in on me. But he just stood there with his hands in his pockets, not making any move at all, and I suddenly realized he wasn't going to. If this was my last chance, then I was losing it even while I was standing there waiting for it.

"We're pulling out about six," Carlos said. "Think about it. I want you to come, but I'm not going to say anything else."

If only he'd touch me, I thought—somehow all the rest would happen. But he just started to walk away.

"I'll think about it," I told him, though as soon as I said that, it felt like something that comes too late. Like he'd completely lost interest. I could see the fire going, and shapes moving around the fire, and hear their voices, and it made me feel empty inside, like here was this door that had opened and I'd gotten a peek inside and now it was closing. I'd never get a chance at anything like it again.

But at the same time it was just too much to think about, and I sort of shut down. "See you around, Carlos," I said, feeling all hurt and angry inside. But I don't think he heard me. Or if he did, he pretended he didn't—which is probably what really happened, now that I think about it.

I must've stood there for a minute wondering what to do, thinking maybe Carlos would come back and give me a second chance. But he didn't. I could see him settle down around the fire with everybody else, and it was pretty clear he'd totally forgotten I was even alive.

So fuck you, I thought, and hopped on my bike and rode home in the dark—something I always liked to do, sliding along with only the whirr of the bicycle tires in my ears, this cool clean sound that's like nothing else. The country roads around Owen get pretty dark at night, but I knew them by heart. I'd spent a lot of time pedaling them up and down trying to burn off all the things in me I didn't know what else to do with.

When I got home, I didn't go up to the trailer. I went down into the woods and found my stash of whisky Carlos had got for me, and I took the bottle that was still about half full and walked way down in the woods, completely out of sight of the lights from the trailer. I sat down—it was pitch black because there wasn't any moon or anything, there weren't even any stars. I took a long swig and felt how it spread out in my stomach. Home at last, I thought, settling down to welcome the only feeling I was ever really comfortable with, that warm feeling of whisky in my gut.

I remember sitting there absolutely quiet, hardly able to see even the trunks of the trees around me, just able to sense they were there, and the woods were quiet except for that cicada drone that once you get used to it, you just don't hear anymore. After a few minutes my hearing tuned itself way up—I could pick up traffic I knew was miles away, conversations black people were having on their front porches over in what we called Niggertown, even the sounds little tiny insects were making while they burrowed down inside tree trunks.

It wasn't the first time I'd sat in the woods like that, just listening to everything till it roared in my head. But this time I had the strongest feeling something out there—or maybe it was inside me—was about to burst. I could feel the whole woods tense up. Some bomb was ready to drop, and I was waiting for that thing to happen, which didn't happen yet but it was going to. Every second that went by it was more likely to happen. Now, or now, or now. I don't know what I thought it was going to be, or what it was supposed to mean if it did—I just thought now would be the perfect time.

But nothing happened. I just sat there and strained to hear the farthest-away sounds I could, and nothing happened. I took another swig of Carlos's whisky, and another, and I waited, and nothing.

Instead my brain was burning up with things I remembered from the day. That pickup truck going round in circles, and the field where Netta and I dug up weeds, and Sammy's blackberries in a bowl, and of course that long shooting flame coming out of Verbena's big behind like a flamethrower. I looked down and realized I had the fingers of my two hands laced together.

I'd finished off the bottle, though it wasn't the whisky I was drunk on. It was all those pictures coming one after another in my brain, like in one of those action comics I'd always be reading in back of the classroom instead of paying attention. *Pow! Crash! Zam!* Piling up one after another in each new frame till you couldn't tell who was beating up on who anymore. I'd hide the comic book down under my desk and take peeks at it all through class, and get a hard-on that I'd rub my arm against so nobody could tell what I was doing.

I stood up and tossed that empty whisky bottle as far as I could. It didn't shatter like I wanted it to, it just fell with a thud. If anything was happening in those woods, it was me.

Back at the trailer, my mom's car was gone. No surprise for a Saturday night. Inside, everything was quiet. I guessed the two girls were asleep, but Ted should still be up. It was always good to be with Ted—just to talk to him, because even though he was only fourteen he was sharp for a kid that age. He could put his finger on things. Not that I'd ever in a million years tell him about Carlos.

I started back toward the bedroom but then stopped. I guess my ears were still tuned to all that quiet outside, because with the bedroom door closed the sound was so faint I'd probably just have barged in on it otherwise.

From the sound of it, Ted was dry humping the mattress. He must've been lying on his stomach rubbing his dick against the sheets, because he was really plowing away. The more I listened, the more I could hear. It made me want to laugh, but it also depressed the hell out of me. I stood there in the kitchen and listened to the noise my little brother was making, and now that I was paying attention I could feel the trailer shaking ever so little on its rickety foundations.

My little brother getting his rocks off. It was an odd thing. The bed just creaked away, a regular motion that sounded like plain hard work, and then I heard him groan, this really loud groan like he was totally cutting loose when he came, and that was it. I couldn't stand it anymore, couldn't stand the thought of all those days jerking off in Owen, days stretching out as far as I could see, one after the other and each one jerking off and jerking off. I bolted without letting Ted even know I was ever in that trailer.

I was totally calm, like I was watching everything from a distance— which is maybe a dumb thing to say but it's true. I remember thinking— it was very clear in my head—I'm not going to see any of this again: my mom's ashtray piled high with ashes, Ted's sneakers on the floor by the door, those stupid little colored-glass elephants my mom kept on a shelf and that were always getting knocked off and broken so most of them were missing a leg or a trunk. A door opening, and I walked through it and then it closed shut behind me.

T HERE'RE THESE TWO WASPS FLOATING AROUND
the ceiling in big lazy loops, back and forth, trying to find their
way out. I lie on my back and watch. It's amazing. They steer clear of
the fluorescent light, which is probably some kind of death to them.
They drift down the walls a ways, then boost themselves back up to
the ceiling. Drowsy is what they are, which means that outside there's
been a frost and that's stunned them—they don't have much time left.
Something in their bodies tells them they should come in here where
it's warm, maybe try and stay alive a little longer than they're meant to.
I wonder if it works, if they really do stay alive longer this way, or if
they die just the same? Probably just the same—but I like the way they
try to keep on living.

I don't have any idea how those wasps got in here, since I'm in what
you call an inside wet cell, which means no windows. At least I've got
my own toilet head. This so-called protective isolation is getting to be a
real drag, though. Not having anybody to talk to except Earl, who goes
a long way in little doses.

It's why I like those wasps up there on the ceiling—they're some kind
of message from the outside world. There was this one day last week
when Earl and another guard were taking me down to the infirmary for
a checkup, and we passed by a window. Not one of the windows that
looks out on the workout yard, but one where you could see hills and
trees and the river in the distance. The trees had turned these dull reds
and golds, and suddenly I realized it was fall out there in the real world.
I hadn't known that before—I could be in some spaceship or an underground cavern for all I know about what goes on outside.

About a month ago there was a thunderstorm. I could hear the thunder, but of course I couldn't see any lightning. It must've been a pretty violent episode, because the thunder was sharp and exploding right out of nowhere, not those low rolls from a distance but breaking out right on top of you. Then afterward everything got quiet and the place filled up with that clean, clear smell you get after lightning. Ozone, they say it is. It was just barely there, but it was definite—I couldn't get enough of it. And then a little later the smell of rain, again faint and hardly there—but after a while you live off little changes like that. I think I lived off that storm for days.

Seeing those trees was even better, though. It wasn't just the trees I was seeing, it was a whole memory opening up, and I'm still thinking about it even now: how when I was six years old and first went to school, I hated it. I hated the ugly green walls, and the green-and-white tile floor, and the ammonia smell—sort of the way I came to hate the Nu-Way Laundromat when I was a little older.

Every morning at recess I wouldn't play games with the other kids— I'd hightail it straight for the swingsets. They were these big sturdy playground kind with long heavy chains and plastic seat bottoms that curved around your butt—all except for the middle swing, which still had a wooden seat from the old days. That was the one I always took. I'd concentrate on making that swing go as high as it'd go, till if I got high enough, almost level with the top bar, I could just barely see Barton's Ridge, a few miles away. It made my heart feel sick to think how far the distance was between me and it. I'd swing higher and higher, trying to imagine I was over there on the other side of that ridge—till one of the teachers would call for me to stop and get off and let somebody else have a turn.

But I never would. I'd keep swinging higher and think if I concentrated hard enough I could wish myself out of that playground and over the ridge into the distance where I'd be safe, where nobody could find me. By that time I'd be swinging so fast and furious none of the teachers could stop me, and they'd just have to let me go on for the half hour of recess. I'd catch hell when I got down, but even though they'd tell me when I came down I couldn't swing on the swings anymore, that didn't stop me. The only thing that was important to me during the whole day at school was seeing Barton's Ridge in the distance. I liked to think nobody else even knew it was there. Next day I'd be back on that swing, and let them try to stop me if they could. Which they finally gave up trying to do.

The last time I ever saw that playground with those swingsets and the sooty brick school building I'd always hated so much was from the window of Carlos's VW bus the morning we left. I'd gotten out to where they were camped as early as I could—I didn't want to miss them. The sun wasn't even up, and there was this cold mist. They weren't exactly raring to go, it turned out—they'd all gone and gotten drunk after I left, and it was the kind of hangover you could just see in their faces. Carlos especially. He was looking about ten years older than usual, and in addition he was wearing this black headband.

"What's that?" I touched his forehead. "Playing Indian chief?"

But he pulled back. "Don't touch," he said in this sharp voice.

"Oh, excuse me," I said, chalking it up to his hangover.

"Just don't ever touch the headband, okay?"

"Does it keep your head from falling apart?" I asked him.

"Something like that," he sort of mumbled.

It was one of those things that, after you've made up your mind to do something, sort of gives you a warning signal like maybe you shouldn't do it after all. But I decided Carlos and I were both just jumpy that morning, for obvious reasons, so I let it go.

Like I said, we drove past the school, and then out along the road where I lived, and pretty soon we were driving past the trailer. I could see my mom's car parked in front, and I wondered what they were all doing in there. Probably still sleeping—but even if they weren't, it was too early for anybody to miss me.

Carlos didn't say anything when we drove by the trailer, though he must've noticed me staring at it out the window as we passed. Maybe he didn't remember it from being there just once, but I think he probably did. Carlos didn't forget things.

I think what it was: Carlos was scared to death. Of course, he never let on to that, not even years later when I'd ask him. He'd shrug and say he wasn't particularly worried that morning, because the first instant he ever saw me in that laundromat, he knew it was fate. And if it brought him down, if it got him in trouble—well, that was part of the fate too. He wasn't going to turn aside from any of it.

Which strangely enough I always took to be some kind of compliment to me, though I don't really know why.

"So where're we going?" I asked, because it occurred to me that that was one big question I'd totally forgotten to ask the night before.

But now that we were passing Barton's Ridge, it seemed like maybe the time to find out.

"Ever been to New York City?"

He must have known I hadn't.

"Do you live in a skyscraper?" I asked. You'll laugh, but I really did think everybody in New York lived in skyscrapers because there wasn't anything else.

"I live in a slum," he said. He let that sink in, and then he said, "Which you'll love, I guarantee."

"A slum," I said. "Is it dangerous?"

"No more dangerous than you are," he told me.

"So—pretty dangerous," I joked.

"Pretty fucking dangerous," he agreed.

There's really only one other thing I need to tell about that first day. After we finally stopped for the night—we'd driven about two hundred miles away from Owen to somewhere in Pennsylvania—Carlos and I took a blanket and a bottle of scotch and walked about a mile from camp, up along a ridge to where some high voltage power lines cut across. There was this mowed space underneath, and there on that mowed space under the power lines was where I had the first real sex of my life.

It came as a total shock to me, because I really had no idea. Carlos spread out the blanket and we drank down about half that bottle of scotch in no time, me because I was dying for a drink and also excited as hell at the blow job I knew Carlos was going to give me, and Carlos because that blow job wasn't all he wanted to do to me and he must've been nervous to see what would happen if he tried everything he wanted to.

Those power lines were humming, this eerie sound that sort of came and went the way cicadas do in summer.

I got drunk in no time. Carlos lay there on that blanket, propped up on one arm looking at me. For some reason I jumped up and started singing this Bruce Springsteen song from off the radio, "Thunder

Road," I guess to let off nervous energy from being cooped up in the van all day. I pretended I was playing guitar, and I stomped around some and then pretended I had a mike in my hand and I was pumping out the words to the song. "Oh, oh, oh, oh Thunder Road," I sang. Carlos lay there watching me with this faraway dreamy look. I took another deep swig of scotch, and then I was really into it.

All of a sudden, Carlos must've decided something: he stood up and put his arms around me and held me so tight I thought he was going to crush me. He kissed me and kept holding me with his arms around me so the kiss went on and on—I couldn't get my breath even if I'd wanted to. But after a while even Carlos had to breathe, so he pulled back and looked me straight in the eye and started to unbutton my shirt one button at a time.

It made me dizzy to look at him like that, though it was also probably the scotch. Even if I'd wanted to, I couldn't have moved because of the way his hand was reaching inside my shirt and rubbing my skin just barely with his fingertips and touching my nipples—which was something nobody'd ever done to me before. It got me excited like crazy. My dick was so hard in my pants it hurt.

I thought for sure once he had my shirt off me he was going to open up my jeans and go down on me. But he didn't. He kissed me again, this time really slow and romantic the way you see guys kiss girls, and all the time he kept running his hands over my bare back and slipping them down my pants along my butt.

Then finally he did go down on me, but only after crouching in front of me and rubbing his face against the front of my jeans where my dick was pressing up hard against them; unzipping my jeans really slow, teasing me with it so I was going totally wild; then when he had my dick out in the open just barely touching it with his tongue. Which made me even wilder. When he went down on me completely it was almost a relief from all that excitement.

I remember reaching my hands down to feel his lips and the base of my dick where it disappeared into his mouth. I was suddenly feeling totally peaceful. I had the weirdest feeling I was traveling somewhere, even though I knew I was standing completely still there in that stretch of field. But I felt like I was going somewhere, all this was taking me someplace I didn't know—I'd never seen it before, but that was okay, that was just fine. And the hum of those power lines up above our heads with all that electricity zinging along for miles and miles to who knew where, and here we were right in the middle of it.

In the meantime Carlos was untying my sneakers, then he was sliding my jeans off me, and there I was butt-naked—which is a pretty amazing thing, to be butt-naked like that outdoors. Even for somebody like me, who used to traipse deep in the woods sometimes and strip down totally except for my sneakers—then I'd run around for a while like some wild Indian until I got so excited being like that I'd jerk off.

Carlos pulled me down on my back on the blanket. He bent over me on his hands and knees and kept his mouth going on my dick, but also on my balls and my belly button and my nipples and meantime his hands were everywhere, light as feathers that just as soon as I'd feel them somewhere they'd be gone and cropping up somewhere else to give me goosebumps. Then before I knew what was happening he grabbed both my ankles and pushed my legs up in the air over my head and went right to my asshole with his tongue.

If you'd hooked one of those power lines to me right then, it wouldn't have been any more of a shock. I'd never dreamed in a million years of one person doing something like that to somebody else, but the feeling was so incredible I came right there, groaning like some wild animal and shooting all over my chest. But Carlos just kept going, pushing farther up with his tongue, then sliding a finger up me, at first just a little ways till I tensed up around it, but then all the way in.

It hurt like fire and I grabbed his wrist to make him stop, but the way he was moving it around in there was like electricity. I started to get hard all over again, even though it still hurt, and I could feel my asshole clenching and unclenching like a fist. Somehow he'd gotten his pants down around his knees, because the next thing I knew he was pushing his dick up me. It hurt ten times more than his finger, and I remember thinking, No way, he can't be going to do this to me—but there it was. I thought I was going to pass out it hurt so much, but he just kept pushing it in farther and farther even though I didn't think it could go any farther in and I thought I was going to explode there was so much up there inside me already—like when you have to shit really bad and you don't think you can hold it in another second, but then all of a sudden something just gave way and I remember letting out this huge yell and banging my head back against the ground five or six times and bellowing like I was a million miles away from everything and he was all the way inside me. He kept it there for a minute with my asshole spasming around his dick, and he bent over and kissed me, which must have been the best kiss of my life because I kept concentrating on that kiss so I wouldn't have to think about that thing stuck up my butt and how scared I was that what with everything it took for him to get it up me, he'd kill me if he tried to pull it out again. It'd be like pulling out a plug and my guts would just go whooshing out.

When he must've figured I was ready, he pulled out a little way and then pushed back in. I just kind of melted. It was like that warm feeling when a swallow of whisky spreads through your stomach, only now it was my whole body and not just my stomach that warm feeling was spreading through, and when he moved inside me again it was another warm wave and then another and they just kept on coming the way water comes bursting up from a spring in the ground and spills over on top of itself with no end in sight.

We never spoke through the whole thing, which from start to finish must've lasted more than an hour.

I WROTE THAT LAST PART YESTERDAY BEFORE LIGHTS out. I have to admit, writing it gave me a hard-on. I stripped into my shorts, and crawled into my bunk, and I jerked off. I jerked off to remember Carlos way up inside me, somewhere near my heart and filling me up like I never knew anybody could be filled up. It was great to remember that—it sent these shivers starting in my balls and running all through me, even now when ten years've gone by—and then suddenly I was so upset about everything, I couldn't stand it. I started crying, sobbing like some crazy drunk to think how that's all gone, nothing like that's ever going to happen again and the only thing I can do is try and remember it.

Lying in that bed with my hand jerking my dick raw, I see how I am. I'm this guy kneeling in the bushes, looking in through the window—and it's me I'm seeing, it's me I'm jerking off to. Me when I was sixteen years old and nobody'd ever fucked me in my life before. Suddenly I've got to get it all exactly right, every little detail that's coming back to me, and I'm jerking harder and harder, till my hand cramps and my dick aches, and I've got the middle finger of my other hand stuck as far up my asshole as I can get it—but everything just gets worse and worse, the harder I go at it, and when finally I get myself to come I'm feeling so miserable it's agony I'm groaning with.

Afterward I fell asleep in a second, which I never do. I guess I was so depressed my whole body just sank right down into sleep, like all it wanted to do for a while was not know it was alive anymore.

Now this morning I'm remembering other things, better things. I still feel sad, but it's clearing—and just a minute ago I was thinking about this one time when, I don't know why, I was looking through Carlos's wallet and I found his driver's license. On the back was this place to sign so you could donate your organs if you got killed in some car crash, what they called an "anatomical gift." There were these two boxes you could check; one said you'd donate all your organs but the other box said "only the following body parts." Carlos had checked that one, and then in the space where you were supposed to list what body parts he wrote, "penis, gizzard and testicles," and signed it. Then he got two people whose names I never heard of to sign as witnesses. When I asked him about it, he didn't know what I was talking about, so I made him take out his driver's license from his wallet and I showed him on the back where it was written. He just looked at it and shook his head, and all he said was, "I must've been really really drunk for that one."

Maybe things like that aren't interesting to you, but they're what I carry around with me, and I think somehow they have to matter. If they don't matter, then nothing does. And if I'm going to talk about any of this, then I have to talk about all of it.

For example, this dream I had last night that I'm just remembering now. It's something I don't understand—how writing all this down must be setting off these depth charges in me somewhere, and so all this stuff floats up to the top. It's some other secret story that goes along with the story I think I'm telling.

They always take place in Owen, my dreams. I never dream about New York, or Sammy or Verbena or Seth or Netta. I never dream about Carlos. In last night's dream I'm walking down in the woods behind the trailer, and it's wintertime. I notice somebody's set a brushfire, though it's burned itself out and all that's left is a charred circle about twenty feet wide. In the circle there's a big old stump, some tree somebody cut down years ago. When I look closer I see the brushfire has burned away the side of the stump, and it's hollow inside. The hollow of the stump's filled with skulls and other bones—people's skulls, which at first I think are old Indian skulls, but then I know they're not. Where the hole in the side of the stump is, skulls are spilling onto the ground, and beside one of the skulls that's spilled out there's a charred piece of paper, a driver's license. When I pick it up and read it, it says "Mattie Parr" on it—not a name I ever heard of in real life, but in the dream I know who Mattie

Parr is, and I look down at the skull and I somehow recognize that it's Mattie Parr's skull.

In the dream I know people have been looking for her—she's somebody who's disappeared, and in fact lots of people have been disappearing and nobody knows where they went to. But now suddenly I know who it is who's been making all these people disappear—it's these three farmers who live down the road. In the dream I know them, I know what they look like. They're these three old black men who wear overalls and they all three live in this farmhouse together. They're killing people and hiding their skulls in the hollow stump.

I know I should call the police and tell them about this, but I'm afraid to because the farmers'll know it's me that found the stump—though I think maybe in the dream I do call the police, or maybe I stick the driver's license in an envelope and mail it to the police telling them where they can find Mattie Parr. It gets sort of hazy—but I think in the dream somebody says the police have found eighty-five bodies in that tree stump, though by that time I'm living somewhere else, on a sea coast. I'm eating ice cream with Ted—he's wearing sunglasses so nobody'll know him. We're way up on a cliff, sitting in lawn chairs on a kind of terrace with pots of red flowers and the ocean way down below us.

How the story of that dream connects with the other story I'm trying to tell, I still don't know.

I T TURNED OUT CARLOS WAS RIGHT WHEN HE TOLD
me he lived in a slum. That apartment on Avenue C was about the
seediest place you can imagine—not even really an apartment, just this
one huge cold empty room on the third floor of an old brick building.
There wasn't any bathroom—only this toilet head in one corner of the
room, and curtains somebody'd hung around it to give a little privacy.
The same person—I never knew who it was—had hung some around
another mattress in another part of the room, and that was the bedroom
where Netta and Sammy stayed, and that was it for rooms. There was
also this filthy old stove and a refrigerator that couldn't even make ice it
was so broken down.

There were windows along the front of the apartment, facing the
avenue, but somebody'd tacked heavy sheets of plastic over them, I guess
to keep the cold out—but it also meant you couldn't see out. Every day
looked the same in that apartment—this cold, cloudy light that didn't
have anything to do with whatever real weather was happening outside.

Carlos wasn't around most of the time. He'd go over to Brooklyn
during the day to edit *Ur* with Seth and Verbena, who were both living
over there. The first couple weeks I stayed around the apartment a lot
in the day, reading X-Man comic books and then when afternoon came
hitting the Canadian Club Carlos kept me supplied with and trying not
to jerk off while waiting for him to get back at night.

As for Netta and Sammy, who stayed in the apartment's other
room—if you can call curtains around a mattress any kind of room—
they were always there too, especially Netta, who never left the apartment a single time, as far as I could tell, till she moved out for good

sometime in the middle of that winter. They'd yammer away at each other in that foreign language they always spoke with each other. It always sounded like they were arguing, but I guess they weren't because they spent hours in there together. Sometimes Netta would get in these moods and play tapes of opera singers on a little cassette player she had—she'd play each song over and over like she was trying to figure out something about it before passing on to the next one.

When that'd happen, Sammy would always move out into the other room where I was. At first it made me nervous. We hadn't exactly hit it off with each other that first day back in Kentucky. But for some reason, maybe because he was as bored around that apartment as I was, he seemed to take some kind of liking to me. At least he'd talk to me, which was more than Netta usually did. Ever since we'd dug weeds together in that field, she'd pretty much acted like she couldn't be bothered with me.

Sammy's real name was Szlama Finkelsztajn, and he was born in the year 1900, which in Jewish years was the year 5661, something I thought made sense: the world was older for them than it was for us. He told me about how he used to live in Poland, and what happened in 1939, or 5700, depending on how you wanted to call it.

"Everywhere," Sammy said, "there were the signs." He never looked at me when he talked. He was going over this stuff again and again in his head, and I could've been anybody there to listen. We were both sitting at this rickety kitchen table, and I had a tea cup with some Canadian Club in the bottom of it. "But we would not believe the signs," he said. "No one would believe. How could you go on living and believe those signs? But this one day there is no longer any doubt. I am walking and it is hot, it is summer. Because I have not eaten I am very weak. And I pass a church, a Christian church. The Church of the Virgin Mary it is called, and from the very first that they closed the ghetto this church was closed up also. No one is allowed in it. But today I see it is open. The doors are open, and there are women, Jewish women walking in and out of the open doors of the Church of the Virgin Mary. What is this, I ask, that you are going in and out of the Christian church? And a woman tells me, it is the Institute of Feather Cleaning. And she points to a sign beside the door and it is true, it says Institute of Feather Cleaning. So I go inside, and what I see is, everywhere white feathers piled up on the floor and floating in the air. When I take a step white feathers float up into the air of the church. Every breeze that comes through the door, white feathers float up and sink back down. All over the carved altar and the great organ and the statues of saints white feathers are floating. And everywhere Jewish women are at work."

"I don't get it," I told him. Lots of times I got the feeling Sammy thought I knew things I didn't really know. It always made me want to dive into the Canadian Club a little deeper than I already was.

"There in the Church of the Virgin Mary," he went on, "Jewish women were ripping open the pillows and featherbeds of the Jews who had been murdered, and cleaning the feathers, and sorting them, and shipping them to Germany, to German merchants who sold them. And from that day on I knew. I knew what was happening without any doubt, and I said to myself God have mercy on us."

"I'd have gotten a gun," I told him. "I'd have fought back. I'd hide in the woods and eat roots and they wouldn't take me alive. I wouldn't just let something like that happen to me."

Sammy picked up my tea cup and sniffed at the Canadian Club, and then put it back down on the table.

"Every day people were jumping out of buildings," he said. "Or they would walk to the barbed wire where the sentries were, right up to the wire without any fear, and the Germans would shoot them. And all this time there were concerts, and even with no food the cafes were open, and people got married and there was crime, like in any city."

"Sounds like New York," I said. At night I could hear gunshots out in the streets, and sirens, and in the day it wasn't too much better. I wanted to get out and around, but the neighborhood scared me a little. I'd never been anywhere in my life like Avenue C before.

"There was a bread we used to make," Sammy went on like he hadn't heard me. "From potato peels and brick dust. That was what we ate when we were hungry."

"Potato peels," I said. "And so you kept yourself alive, and now you're here, now you're making these crazy movies with Carlos. I don't get it."

Sammy looked at me for a long time. "I will tell you this," he said. "When you are old, maybe you will remember. There was this one man, a photographer, a young man, very shy. He worked, I think, for the bureau of statistics that gathered information. How much the food ration was today. What was the weather. How many people died or were born, and for what causes. And this photographer, Mendel was his name, before the war he had wanted to be an artist, he had wanted people to admire the beautiful pictures he took of flowers and girls."

This is hopeless, I thought. But what was I going to do? I was raised to have respect for older people.

"But now," Sammy went on, "he was not interested in beauty anymore, this Mendel. Now he was taking pictures of everything. Everything that was happening, he took pictures. And it was forbidden in the ghetto to take pictures. He would be shot if they caught him taking those forbidden pictures. But every day he was walking the streets, or climbing on rooftops or hiding behind a window to take pictures."

"Fine," I said. You can only have so much patience. "What does this have to do with anything?"

The whole time we were talking, Netta's tape recorder was blaring out opera music in the next room, those big busty voices heaving away at the top of their lungs. As soon as the song was over, she'd rewind and play it through again.

"He was not in good health," Sammy said. I was thinking maybe he couldn't hear me for the opera music. I was thinking maybe this whole conversation was pretty pointless, and I should just leave, only I didn't want to leave. I wanted Sammy to leave. "His heart," Sammy said. "So many times I would go with him, I would carry his satchel for him. And we would go around. His camera he kept under his coat, because it was forbidden. And his hands he kept in his pockets. You see, he had cut his pockets open on the inside so he could work the camera through his coat. And when he would see something, he would turn his body to aim the camera, and he would open his coat just a little—it was very dangerous—and *click,* there would be the picture. Everywhere we would go, and he would take those pictures. And all those pictures, do you know where they are now?"

I wanted to take a sip of Canadian Club—a good swig is more like it—but the way he was looking at me, I couldn't do it. It was the first time in the whole conversation he looked at me.

"Vanished," he said. "Gone into thin air."

I was never sure how much to believe. I mean, I knew a little from school and TV, but I never really thought about it.

"Not every single photograph," Sammy said, not looking at me anymore. "But most." All of a sudden I felt squirmy inside, like I didn't want to hear any more of this. But I couldn't leave, because where was there to go? Sammy smiled. Not at me. Not even a happy smile, not even a smile I realized, though for a minute it'd looked like one.

I saw he needed a shave in an old man kind of way.

"One day," he said, "we were in the street. Mendel and I were in the street and a whole family passed us by. They were hauling shit. It was good money in the ghetto, to haul shit away from people's houses. It gave you money for food. But nobody lasted long because of the disease, so only the most desperate people would haul shit for money. And here was this family. Mother and father, son and daughter. The parents in front of the cart pulling. The children on the sides pushing. And Mendel was about to take a picture of this, the way he took a picture of everything that was happening, but then he stopped. And I knew what he was thinking. How can I do this? he was thinking. How can I take a picture of these people in such shameful degradation? And he was not going to take the picture. But the father saw him, and he knew Mendel, everybody in the ghetto knew Mendel and knew he was taking pictures because he would give people pictures to keep. He thought if he gave enough pictures to people some would have to survive the ghetto. And the father who knew Mendel asked him please to go ahead and take the picture. Let them know, he told Mendel. Let others know how we were humiliated here."

"Kill the bastards," I told him. But he only looked at me. I felt ashamed for saying that, like it was completely the wrong thing to say. But I didn't know what was the right thing to say. I was sure Sammy didn't think I could ever understand any of this, and he wasn't even telling it to me—he was just speaking it out loud where I could hear it if I wanted to.

A couple days after that he took me to the public library. I went because Carlos never took me anywhere, and I thought, What the hell? Plus Netta was in her opera mood, which I think was driving Sammy as crazy as it was me. The afternoon was one of those cold New York afternoons when the wind blows right through you and trash is everywhere in the air. He took me through this room where people were busy reading and back into the shelves of books till he found exactly the shelf he wanted. It was like he'd memorized where it was. He reached up on his tiptoes and pulled down a book, and standing there in the aisle between the shelves where the light was dim he opened it up and showed me. It was a book of pictures, mostly out of focus like somebody snapped them in a hurry. But there they were, about fifty of them by Mendel the photographer whose satchel Sammy used to carry. I flipped through those pages, picture after picture, a little freaked out to actually see them, since I only sort of half believed what Sammy'd been telling me. But now he didn't say a word. He just stood there and looked at me looking at the pictures.

I never knew exactly how to behave around Sammy. I always felt a little bit off-guard, so mostly I just didn't behave at all. Which is what I did that day. I looked at the pictures and handed the book back to him, and I guess I said something like, "That's pretty amazing." He didn't say anything. He didn't seem pleased or disappointed or anything—he just took the book and reached up on tiptoe again and slid it back in the space on the shelf where it'd been. And that was that.

Except what I never told Sammy was—I used to go back to that library from time to time to look at that book. I didn't think I could find it again but I did—I went right to it. At the time it seemed like a good sign of something, but of course you never know. I'd take it to a table where other people were reading, and turn the pages looking at those pictures. There was this one picture that completely got to me— a kid about my age feeding a little girl some soup from a sort of canteen. I used to study that picture for a long time. I'd find myself wondering how he died, because he must've died. Did he have to become one of the shit carriers Sammy told me about? Did they take him out in the woods and make him dig a grave for himself, and then shoot him? I couldn't get enough of looking at him, and wondering—till one day I did know. It came to me like it was something I'd known all along, how one morning he just walked up to the barbed wire and let the guards shoot him. He scooped his little sister up in his arms and they both walked right into the bullets.

I'd sit there and look at him and wonder what it must have felt like when he finally decided to do it—how he must've been incredibly scared, so scared I couldn't even imagine being that scared. But I also wanted him to be completely calm. I wanted him to be watching all this from some distance that didn't have anything to do with him. I wanted him to be indifferent to it.

I knew it wasn't like that.

I'd slam the book shut and shove it back up on the shelf and I was out of there—I was wandering the alphabet avenues where it pretty much looked like a ghetto already and all they'd have to do was put up the barbed wire and there we'd be.

T HAT FIRST TRIP SAMMY AND I MADE TO THE PUBLIC
library did a lot of things to me—and one of the things it did was
release me from that apartment. I started going out more in the day to
avoid having to listen to Sammy drone on, even though in little doses
he was fine, and also to get away from Netta's opera music, which could
drive you crazy. But most of all, once I'd taken the subway uptown,
and came back in one piece, I felt free to be totally out on the streets.
And once I was there, I just kept going. I went all over the city. I loved
just wandering around, walking everywhere, or jumping the stile like
I saw other kids do to ride the subway if I was tired of walking and just
wanted to get home. Or to see where I'd end up, which you may think
is crazy but it never occurred to me back then. I guess I thought I was
immune. I'd pop up everywhere, take a look around, then be back on
that train rattling along underground till I popped up somewhere else.
The only trouble was, I never knew how things connected up with each
other that way, and what I finally ended up doing was giving up on the
subway for a while, and walking everywhere—just to get the hang of
things.

At least by day that's what I did. I never went out at night at all—I
was always back at the apartment by the time it was dark. I was waiting
for Carlos to show up, because I didn't want to miss a minute of Carlos,
but also the nighttime in New York made me nervous. It took on
this air for me. I didn't know what was going on out there. I could
hear sirens, and people yelling down in the street—just yelling for no
reason—and sometimes gunshots. At least that's what I always thought
they were: gunshots. And probably they were. I think I told you how

the windows had plastic over them, so I never knew what was going on out there once it got dark. I could only try and imagine it. I'd picture Carlos making his way back from Brooklyn, slinking from cover to cover, hiding behind garbage cans, dashing across empty streets. All these narrow escapes—from what, I didn't know. I'd lie in bed in that apartment and follow him like it was different frames in some comic book, and then I'd get to the end but he wouldn't be home yet; so I'd have to start all over, slow it down some, add a few more scrapes. And then finally he was home. I'd hear him tramping up the stairs. He never knew how happy I was to see him come in that door. How I wanted to throw my arms around him just for making it back—because even if he didn't know how close a call it'd been, I did. I knew he'd barely made it back.

All that was just at night; the day never bothered me. The scary stuff went away, and I was free as a river. I could go anywhere.

Partly it was what Carlos wanted me to do—be out on my own having adventures, learning about things. "You got the universe at your feet," he'd tell me. "The stars, the sewer, the semen—it's all yours, kid. Now go out and take it." At night he always seemed really happy to listen to me tell him where I'd gone, what I'd done, so I started saving up stuff to tell him. When I'd get home I'd lie there and figure out ways to put it together so it'd be interesting to him. The more outrageous, the better he liked it.

I remember—there was this one man with a golf club, this grizzled old fellow. I don't know who he was or where he was from, but he walked around with a golf club all the time and would just start yelling for no reason, and banging with his golf club on garbage cans and stair railings or whatever he could find—making a racket, and not caring who heard. I'd see him all over the city, carrying that golf club over his shoulder and yelling—not at anybody, but just to hear himself yell, I guess.

One time I came out of the apartment, and he was standing across the street like he was waiting there for me. There was this little tree somebody'd planted, or maybe it was just growing up from a crack in the sidewalk—it was the only green thing around. I'd watched it lose its leaves that fall, and now it was all spindly and naked. I liked that tree. The old man stood there beside it; then all of a sudden he hauled off with his golf club and started whacking it. "Only God can make a tree," he was yelling. "Only fucking God can do that. Listen, all you queers and niggers, listen to this you Jew, only God can make a fucking tree. Just you try." All the time he was yelling, he kept swinging the hell out of that club till he broke the little tree trunk right in half.

I couldn't move—I stood there watching him do that, and then when he was through, he shut up and moved on down the street. I went over to the tree, but it was a goner. And a second ago it was as alive as you or me.

I don't know why, but we were always showing up in the same place. It got to be so that old man would recognize me. He'd watch me—I could tell he was watching me. I saw him in Central Park, by the lake, and over on the piers by the Hudson River, and where the tram goes across to Roosevelt Island.

One day I took the ferry to Staten Island. I was down at the tip of Manhattan where the boat was leaving from, and all these people were crowding into the building there. I wandered in, curious what was up, and since it only cost a quarter to go, which was all I had, I thought why the hell not? Staten Island was someplace I'd never been before.

The boat was terrific—it kept thumping along in this high wind, and spray pumping up, all the time the city with its tall buildings back there behind us getting smaller and smaller and we're staying exactly the same. Suddenly I heard this yelling in my ear. I turned around and there he was, standing practically behind me on the deck at the back of the boat to watch the view from.

"All the fucking saints of this goddamned city go walking around on craw-asses and nails," he was yelling, "every fucking one of them. And out of nowhere too. Did you ever see the stinking lightbulb that could crank out all the saints that're walking on their craw-asses and nails in this fucking city, did you ever see that?" Then suddenly he started swinging that golf club of his. It nearly hit me, but I was about an inch too far away, and then it did hit this man who was standing next to me right in the shoulder, and it hit an old lady on the leg. People were yelling and screaming and pushing. About five guys jumped the old man and started punching him down and tugging at his golf club—but he wouldn't give it up. He kept yelling, only now everybody was yelling. I didn't do a thing—I stood there watching, looking over my shoulder at the city getting smaller and smaller behind us, and then back at the heap of people on the floor with that old man and his golf club at the bottom of it. Finally these two security guards came down with billy clubs and worked their way into the crowd and took the old man off. I think he never let go of that golf club.

"He'll show up again," Carlos said that night, in bed, when I told him about it. "He's bound to—when you least expect it. But I guarantee, you'll see him again."

It'd sort of freaked me, there on that boat—it was such a close call. Every once in a while the city'd give me some close call like that, and then part of me wouldn't want to go out for a few days. But I made myself. Back in Owen, at the city pool, if I had a bad turn off the high diving board I'd always climb right back up there and jump again. Otherwise I knew I'd get spooked. It was something Ted and I'd call each other on—we'd make sure the one of us who flubbed scrambled right back up there and did the dive again.

There was an even closer call than that day on the ferry. It'd been lousy out all morning—rain and sleet and stuff—so I stayed put there in the apartment. Sammy talked to me for a while, and I was doing shots of Canadian Club and cups of tea to keep me from getting too bored. Somehow what Sammy was telling me got me all impatient—talking to him could make me want to walk till my legs ached. I'd shoot out of that apartment and do this quick clip for maybe ten blocks till I was breathing hard and the air cleared my head. Which is what I did now.

I was pretty drunk so I sailed right along. It was days like this when I longed for my bike back in Owen, to cover the whole town in no time. I'd see bike messengers zooming in and out of traffic like maniacs, and I'd wish that was me. I guess I could probably have picked up some bike somewhere, if I really wanted it—but I just never did. Though I did pick up a few bike messengers, I guess to make up for it, when I started doing that sort of thing a few years down the line.

I should tell you one thing before I go any further. In those days it wasn't bike messengers I was into, or any of the guys I saw when I was out walking. I didn't look at other guys. But I did look at girls a lot—I guess because if you'd asked me, Was I a queer? I'd have said of course not, no way. I mean, looking back on it, I don't know what I thought I was doing with Carlos—I guess I didn't put any kind of name to it as long as I could get away with that. One thing's for sure—I never said to myself I was queer or gay or anything like that, and like I say, when I was out on the street I kept seeing these women I thought were so gorgeous, they made my heart ache. Maybe it was knowing somewhere inside me I really was a queer that made me look at those women the way I did; maybe I was saying goodbye to something, even though I didn't know that's what I was doing. All I know is, every once in a while I'd find myself following some girl I thought was really great-looking, and feeling this kind of homesickness. That might sound strange, but it's the only thing I know to call it. I'd follow her for blocks, till she went into some building or store and I lost her. I'd follow her down into the subway, and ride the same car with her, which is the way I got around to a lot of those neighborhoods I'd never have thought of going to otherwise. I didn't want anything from those women I followed, I never made any move to walk up and try to start a conversation or anything. I just wanted to be near them for a while before I lost them.

Sometimes one of them would notice me, and I'm sure she thought I was this total goon hanging around like I was—and I'd have thought the same thing if I was her. But I wasn't doing it to be creepy. I was doing it out of some kind of sadness that was inside me.

But back to my other close call. I'd gone to the public library, to find that picture from the ghetto I had to touch base with every once in a while. I'd been sitting in the big reading room, where there're these long tables with lamps, and probably a hundred people in there all being quiet and reading to themselves. I'd take that picture book and spread it open and study it for maybe half an hour, always feeling like somebody was going to come tell me I shouldn't be there, though nobody ever did. And I guess I came to feel at home there, in some weird way, because I kept coming back. Which is hard to believe—me, Tony, in a library—but there I was.

I put the book back on the shelf, feeling sad but also happy from studying that picture. When I went outside the sun had come out—it was one of those blustery winter days when you think maybe spring's going to come sometime. There on the front steps of the library, standing by one of those stone lions, was this girl talking to two black guys. She was just leaving them, they were saying "Catch you later" to her, and she held up her red sequined pocketbook and pointed to it. She was about my age, blonde hair so white-blonde she must've dyed it, and black boots and a black skirt and a black leather jacket. At first I thought she was some kind of boy in drag—but then I made up my mind, no, it had to be a girl. Actually, I have to say I knew right off she was a hooker, just by the way she was walking and sort of keeping her eye out for stuff. I followed her down Forty-second toward the Square, being careful the whole time to keep her from noticing me. I didn't want her to talk to me or anything—I wouldn't've known what to say. I was just interested in her, I just wanted to see where she went.

I haven't thought about that girl in ages. She's probably dead now, which is a weird thing to say, but I'd be fooling myself about everything if I didn't think it was true. Just like that boy and his sister in the ghetto. What I remember is how interested I was in her—about everything in her life, and also how far away she felt, like I was never going to know anything about her. She had these slim hips to die for, and a way of walking down the street that totally melted me.

She wandered all over Times Square, stopping to look in the windows of camera stores, and talking to people here and there—mostly other hookers, I could tell. Then around Thirty-ninth Street she went into a movie theater, one of those XXX places showing *Barbed Wire Dolls* or some other movie like that. Actually, I think it was something called *Chained Heat*. I waited for a minute on the other side of the street, thinking, Okay, that's it. I've lost her. These things always ended somewhere, just like that. But then for some reason, instead of walking on like I usually did, I crossed over the street and went inside the movie theater after her.

I'd never been in a place like that before—Carlos hadn't yet started taking me out to the Adonis on what was his idea of a date—so I didn't know what to expect. There was this dull red lobby with nobody around except a guy in a greasy silver jacket.

"Looking for something, kid?" he asked me.

I sort of felt like bolting right there, but that was back in my totally fearless days, and I thought, What the hell? I'd wade on in. If the water got too high, I knew how to swim.

I told him about the girl with the white-blonde hair, how I thought I knew her—I'd seen her from across the street, and if she was who I thought she was, she was somebody I needed to talk to about something important.

I have no idea what he thought about that. All he said, in this Spanishy accent, was, "You not here to see no movie, I take."

"I'm just here," I told him.

"Well, then you follow me," he said. He took me downstairs and we went along this hallway with dim red lightbulbs hanging every ten feet or so. It smelled like vomit. There were some doors, but they were all closed. At the end of the hall was another door, and then we went down another flight of stairs into another room, which I guess was supposed to be a bar. There were some chairs and tables, and a couple of fat men sitting at them drinking, and in the back of the room was a stage.

On the stage this short little white man was fucking a black woman in her behind. She was bent over on her hands and knees, and she had these great big breasts like cow's tits flopping back and forth while he fucked her.

I'd never seen two people fucking before, only dogs and such like, and it made me feel queasy. Every time he pushed in, she made this grunting sound, and they were both covered in sweat that was all shiny under the red lights. He had this black curly hair, bushy like an Afro, and a sort of hook nose. He was really ugly. I just stood there and watched, and in about a minute he groaned and screwed up his face and you could tell he was coming.

She let out this howl, and he held himself inside her for a second; then he went and pulled out. He had this enormous dick, especially for such a little guy. He was almost a midget, he was so short, but his dick looked about as thick around as a wrist. Somebody handed the woman a towel and a drink, and she sat there crosslegged on the floor, toweling herself off and drinking that drink, like nothing ever happened. The man climbed down off the stage and went over to one of the tables where two men were sitting. His big dick was still half hard and flopping around while he walked. He stood there talking to the guys at the table, these two fat men in suits, and smoking a cigarette. The white-blonde girl was nowhere down there—the only woman in that room was the black woman sitting on the stage.

She started gesturing in my direction.

"Hey, white boy," she said. I looked around, but there wasn't any other white boy. "Come here, white boy. You like what you see here?" She took one of her breasts and sort of shook it at me—it had to be at me, because there wasn't anybody else in the part of the room where I was. Everybody was looking at me, though—the two fat guys, and the guy with the big dick, and these three other men in dark suits who, I suddenly noticed, were standing by the bar. They were all looking like they were really interested in me—in what I was going to do.

I felt like I had to get out of there. I shook my head at the woman, who was calling to me, "Hey kid, whyn't you come up here and get some of that pussy you been needin'? I know you been needin' it bad. I can see it in your face. You got a pimple on your cheek there, I can see—it's from not gettin' enough pussy juice. I know. Come on up here, let Mama give you some. Whip out that white boy dick and come on up here. Let Sugar Mama give it to you."

The two fat men were turned around in their chairs, craning their necks to see me. I remember the little man with the big dick standing there with his hands on his hips.

When she saw I was making to leave, she started saying, "Buy Mama a drink, won't you, honey? Won't you at least do that? One drink for Mama?"

I started to go up the stairs, but the three men in the dark suits were standing in my way.

"Don't you hear the lady?" one of them told me. He reached out and held my arm. The other two sort of clustered around me, so there was nowhere to go. "She wants you to buy her a drink."

"I got to go," I told them, trying to shake free my arm. "It's important. I got to be somewhere."

"Let's see your ticket stub," said the guy who was holding my arm.

"What ticket stub?"

"You got to have a ticket. You got to pay admission," he said. "You think this is a free show? Yolanda here's an artist. Joseph's an artist. You got to pay to see artists. You can't just wander in and take a peek and then go trot along your merry way. You got to pay for this."

"I don't have any money," I said, which was pretty true. "I didn't mean to come here. I was looking for somebody."

"Well, I think you found them." He was rubbing his fingers together to show he wanted cash. The other two guys were sort of jostling me, just enough to make me nervous. I took out my wallet.

"See," I told them, "no money." I had two dollars in there, which the guy took out. He looked at the bills like he didn't believe them; then he held one of them up, like it was dirty or something, and he spit on it, and then he spit on the other one. Then before I knew what was happening he punched me in the stomach.

The other two guys were holding my elbows, so even though I doubled up there wasn't much I could do. "Don't," I croaked, but he punched me again, and again—probably about five times. I couldn't breathe.

"I think that about pays the price of admission," said the guy who'd worked me over. "Now, kid, you want to buy the lady a drink?"

I could hardly see, I had tears in my eyes, and I couldn't breathe to say either yes or no.

"I think he wants to buy her a drink," said one of the other guys. "I think he wants to buy her a two-dollar drink."

The guy who'd hit me gave me back the wallet, minus the two bucks. Then the other two guys gave me a shove up the stairs. I stumbled and slammed my palm against one of the steps, but I kept on going like a pack of dogs was barking at my heels.

I could hear the black woman calling at me from the stage. "Bye," she said. "You have a nice day now, you hear?"

I went scrambling up those stairs and down that long dim hallway and up the next set of stairs and through the lobby. Nobody followed me, and the lobby was empty—that man in the silver jacket had totally disappeared on me.

Out on the street the sun was shining, there was traffic, people walking by, billboards advertising XXX movies. I was shaking all over and sweating this cold sweat—though I was at least beginning to catch my breath. I had to start laughing. I went swaying along Broadway, bumping into people, reeling around like I was half drunk, laughing up a storm. And sobbing like a baby too, if you want to know the truth. It was blocks till I calmed down.

I never told Carlos about that afternoon. It wasn't that I was afraid to—just that I didn't have any idea how. I couldn't get it straight in my head. I just kept seeing these pictures: that little guy with the big dick standing there with his hands on his hips, like everything was totally normal, and the black woman saying the things she did, and then wanting that drink from me. It all made me squeamish to even think about—it was shameful somehow, like some disgusting dream you have and then would be embarrassed to let other people know about. Now that I've finally told about it, there doesn't seem that much to it. It's been ten years, and worse things have happened—but at the time, it bothered me so much that, if my belly hadn't hurt where I'd gotten punched, I might've talked myself into thinking I'd made the whole thing up.

The only other thing I never told Carlos about, at least not for a while, was going to the library with Sammy, and that book with the pictures in it—but that's another story.

SOMETIMES IT'D HIT ME, HOW EVERYTHING HAD gone by so fast. I'd been in New York about a month, and it was like a series of pictures that had no connection. There I was living at home in Owen, this so-called normal kid with his mom and his brother and sisters, and then all of a sudden here I was in New York living with this man who was probably crazy. I mean, how many sane people go driving around the country picking up kids in laundromats and giving them blow jobs the first time they meet them? I thought, maybe I've just gone off the deep end for a while. This thing came along that was so different from anything I was used to, and I fell for it—but pretty soon I'd wake up.

Sometimes I tried to imagine sitting down and explaining to Ted what I was doing. I told myself, if you can explain it to Ted, then it must be okay. But I couldn't imagine it. All I could imagine was Ted looking at me with those blue eyes of his, skeptical like always, and then sort of narrowing those eyes and shaking his head at me. I couldn't figure any way to talk to him that wasn't going to make me ashamed, that wasn't going to creep him out. And that upset me.

You have to understand how I was totally crazy about Carlos all during that time. Here I'd spent years of my life in Owen thinking about certain things—things I'd never have told anybody about even *thinking* about—and then Carlos came along and turned them into reality for me.

What I'm talking about are the things we did in that bed of his.

Things I spent a lot of hours in Owen dreaming about and jerking off to, but never expecting them really to happen to me. Never thinking there was somebody else who wanted them the way I did. Somebody who wanted *me*.

Carlos totally loved my body—every bit of it. Which shocked me at first, that anybody could love everything about somebody else's body the way he did, but it also completely excited me. With Wallace it was always how this was getting his rocks off, but where girls were concerned I was definitely second best. And with Cindy in the back seat of the car, well, we'd just fumbled around—if you asked me what did she look like, I couldn't even tell you anymore. But Carlos treated my body like it was some amazing discovery of his he just couldn't get enough of—sniffing my armpits, my asshole, licking my nipples and between my toes and behind my calves, all those places I never even thought about. He'd graze the top of his tongue along my skin— exploring my whole body that way, pulling all the different parts of me together into this one complete shining body.

You could say he took this comic book kid, all jerky freeze-frames, and threaded him all together into a moving picture. It's what nobody else in my life ever did with me, before or since. Just trailing his dry tongue around on the surface of me, he could cause me to explode on him.

Then he'd go inside me.

One of the things about Carlos was how he looked at me. It was rude, and scary, and I never got used to it. He'd pin me there on the bed with those glittery black eyes of his, and then ease his dick into me, all the way up inside me. I'd take a deep breath, and he'd be balanced up above me, locking my wrists down with his hands, his dick in me and his eyes boring a lot deeper into me even than that—and me forcing myself not to look away, to keep staring back at him no matter how scary it was to lock eyes with him like that.

He'd flex his dick in me, just once, and I'd practically faint.

The only thing about all that stuff we did was, Carlos never wanted me to do any of it back to him. He wasn't interested in that, like his body was something he already knew all about and so he was on to other things. I'd try, sometimes, to give him back what he was giving me—try to go after that wiry, fighter's body of his. He had stomach muscles I could die for, and I loved the big veins in his arms. After he'd been inside me, I'd want to go down on him and get a taste of where he'd been. But he'd just say no, and push me aside to where he could get at me again. I guess you could say he was greedy with me, but I didn't care one bit once he started in on me. In some weird way, it made him even more exciting to me—the way he wouldn't let me really go at him the way he went at me. Like it was different for him in some way. Like he'd already been to all the places he was taking me too many times to want to go back anymore.

I don't really know about all that. Sometimes here at the Eddy I'll be lying on the mattress dreaming about the things Carlos and I used to do—or I guess I should mostly say, what he'd do to me—and I just have to wonder. When I think about it now, I realize there were lots of things I never knew about him, and I guess, being just a kid back then, I never felt like I wanted to know. I can't believe all the things I never asked him, but they just never occurred to me. But now I wonder sometimes. I wonder where he'd been, all those years before he met me, that made him so crazy for this sixteen-year-old kid the way he was. Crazy to the point where he didn't want anything from me except me, and nothing else.

After Carlos died, there were lots of newspaper articles—junk, mostly, which was pretty easy to shrug off. But one of them that Earl showed me from his scrapbook got under my skin like some wood splinter and stayed there. It was this famous movie critic writing in *The New York Times*, and I'm putting what he said in here just so you can see how totally different the Carlos I knew was from the one everybody else thought they knew.

> *The single time I was in the presence of Carlos Reichart, at a film festival here in New York, he was so closely sheltered by members of his famous troupe, The Company, that there seemed to be a conspiracy afoot to keep him in some kind of protective custody from the world at large. He radiated what I can only describe as a remarkable aura of depravity, as if having come straight from unspeakable debauches. He seemed curiously disoriented—a master actor who suddenly and inexplicably finds himself onstage in the wrong play. And I suddenly began to realize something terrible about this man, or rather about my sense of him: that there are great directors whose films make one long, intensely, to know the man behind the film.*

But with Carlos Reichart, one must finally say that, however much one might admire his films, one had no desire ever to know the man himself.

I guess I feel sorry for the guy who wrote that. I picture him going home from that day, and being really happy to see his wife, and the dog, and washing his hands with soap for a long time, and suddenly realizing that's what he's doing. I picture him telling his wife how much he loves her, which is something he hasn't done in a long time, but seeing me and Carlos that afternoon scared him in some ways he doesn't want to think about. Because he's not dumb—he's seen Carlos's movies, he knows they're better than anything anybody else is doing these days. And he also knows if he's going to go on watching them, if he's going to understand what they're really about, then he can't go on living the way he does. Which is too much for anybody to ask. He looks at his face in the mirror. What's wrong with me? he wonders, and so he washes his hands again. He can't get Carlos and me out of his head, that picture he has of Carlos walking into that room.

It's Earl all over again—getting nervous about something he sees and he's not sure what to do with it. Maybe I'm being defensive.

O NCE A WEEK THE WHOLE COMPANY WENT TO THIS little Italian place about five blocks from the apartment—long tables, benches, candles stuck in big fat wine bottles. The guy who owned the place owed Carlos some favor—at least that's what Seth told me—and it must've been a pretty big favor too, for him to feed all those people so many times. But it seemed like he was happy to be doing it, and lots of times he'd come sit with us and get drunk along with everybody else. I remember his name was Gianni, and he had these sad eyes and big nervous hands he never knew what to do with.

Carlos loved those meals more than anything. Some glasses of wine and some bread and a little spaghetti and a bunch of other people talking and laughing—that made him completely happy. He never ate or drank that much himself—he just liked watching everybody else, he liked to listen in and feel like he was part of something. He told me once that he thought that was what life was all about—people eating and drinking together. "People and food," he'd say. "There's nothing else that matters. Everything else that happens is just an imitation of that."

There was this Cuban grocery down the street from the apartment, where we used to stop in to buy a six-pack from time to time. There were always about seven or eight out-of-work guys hanging around, all jabbering away at each other in Spanish, so when you stepped inside, past all the jungle plants blooming in the steamed-up front windows, and the cans of black beans and guava juice with rust spots on them on the shelves, it felt like maybe you were in Cuba. At least it's how I always imagine Cuba: this cheesy music on the radio, everybody smoking cigarettes and drinking beer. They drank these extra tall cans of Budweiser, even the women.

Whenever Carlos walked in, the three little kids who were always in the store, usually sitting on the floor playing some game with bottle-caps I could never figure out, would jump up and just start shrieking, they were so happy to see Carlos. I don't know what for, exactly, since he never gave them anything that I saw—but there was just something about him that made those kids go wild. Like it was a holiday. And the women and old men would talk to him—he knew some Spanish, I don't know where from—and they'd babble away, gesturing with their hands and laughing these big laughs that were like gunshots going off.

Carlos was in some ways a really shy person, and he always seemed embarrassed a little by all their attention. But he also loved it. He knew they thought he was special, even though he'd never have told you that. But it brought him out of himself—the way certain things, some pretty kid walking down the street, or rain coming down in the morning, or just anything somebody might say that was odd to him, could bring him out.

I remember one time we were in that grocery, and they were all whooping it up—Carlos was grinning that nervous grin of his and the little kids were clamped onto his leg and he was patting the tops of their heads. Then this man started talking to me. They never talked to me, and at first I couldn't even understand what he was saying, his English was so terrible. But he was saying, "I give you job."

It sort of freaked me a little.

"You want," he said, "I give you one. Like that. You very fine boy for job."

"What's he talking about?" I asked Carlos. I felt like just some other kid clamped around his leg for protection.

"You want a job? He's offering you a job. They like you here."

"They don't know me."

"I'm sure that's why they like you so much. You could work here and live a regular life."

Carlos had never talked to me about getting a job. It always seemed like it was okay with him if I just hung around the apartment.

I hated the idea of getting a job. How was I going to drink if I had a job? Though it was true, all those Cubans seemed to be drinking beer all the time. But they made me nervous—I didn't want to work for a bunch of Cubans.

The man who'd asked me did I want a job just kept smiling. He was missing one of his front teeth, and he was wearing this T-shirt that said STAYING ALIVE across the front, and also what looked like a blood stain or maybe it was grape juice.

I had this sudden fright—Carlos was trying to unload me on these people.

"A job," I said. "Do I have to?"

"Gracias, no," Carlos told the man with the STAYING ALIVE T-shirt. "Tony's got better things to do. He's a genius. He sits around all day and thinks."

I couldn't tell whether Carlos was criticizing me, and I guess he knew that.

"I'm serious," he told me. "You *should* just sit around all day and think. A boy your age."

Even if he was being straight with me I could never tell if he was also spoofing. I think he was probably doing both at the same time, all the time, and that's maybe one of the five hundred secrets about Carlos that made him tick.

He shook hands with all the men in the store, and pried the little kids loose from his waist, and this big fat woman kissed him on each cheek. He took the six-pack from them like it was made out of gold, and handed over the three dollars, which they took like it was three dollars they were going to frame instead of ever spending. Then we were out of there, the street was full of trash, it was starting to spit snow and this wasn't Cuba anymore, it was New York.

I guess it was Carlos's idea of a compliment, but we never stole from the Cubans. I don't know why—we stole from just about every other grocery in the East Village. In fact, we'd go all over Manhattan. The way we'd work it was this. Usually it was me and Carlos and Sammy and Verbena—we'd make a regular Saturday afternoon outing of it. We'd go into some store, Sammy would grab a basket, and the four of us would wander up and down the aisles.

I remember the first time we did that—I didn't know what was happening. Carlos walked me around the store, asking, Did I like to eat this? Or this? Picking up fruits and vegetables and cans of things.

But whether I said yes or no, or I don't know, he just put it back on the shelf. Meanwhile Sammy was loading a few things in the basket—a loaf of white bread, a can of pork and beans. Okay, Carlos said after a little, we're through. "You go with Sammy," he told me, "and we'll wait for you outside."

So I stood in the checkout line with Sammy, while Carlos and Verbena stood out on the sidewalk and made faces in at us through the window. Verbena in this faded maroon winter coat she always wore, with about six pieces of costume jewelry pinned to it. And Carlos with his headband on, since we'd had a little too much to drink the night before, and this funky black leather jacket that had just appeared on him one day, I don't know from where.

Sammy handed the things in his basket out onto the counter and then started to fumble around in his trousers pocket like he'd lost his money. Finally he pulled out this little change purse, the kind old grandmothers carry, but then he couldn't get it open because his hands shook so much.

Because I didn't know what was up that first time, I was incredibly embarrassed standing there with Sammy while he took forever. I tried to catch the eye of the cashier, this Asian girl, to say I really didn't have anything to do with this old man. But she was bored with him and me and everything else too—all she did the whole time was inspect one of her fingernails.

Finally, after about five minutes, Sammy managed to pull out a folded-up ten-dollar bill, which he took forever to unfold. The whole time there was this line of other people formed behind us, but he didn't seem to notice.

Then while the cashier was getting him change, he managed to drop the change purse on the floor right where she was standing, so in the middle of giving him change she had to bend over and help him pick up the pennies and quarters that were rolling off in all directions. After about ten more foul-ups like that, Sammy managed to get the right change, and in a minute we were out on the street with Carlos and Verbena.

"You carry the bag," Sammy told me. "It's a great honor."

"This isn't very much," I told them, hefting the bag and thinking how it was maybe one meal and that was it.

"Not to worry, shy girl," Verbena said. And right there in the middle of the street she opened her maroon coat—inside, the pockets she'd sewn in were stuffed with tomatoes and packages of Oreo cookies and cheeses and a Danish ham, all from the grocery.

"Miss tricky fingers," Carlos said. And at the same time Sammy was brandishing his folded-up ten-dollar bill, which I could see in an instant was the exact same one there'd been all the to-do about back in the store.

I practically fell down laughing right there. It was the first of at least a thousand trips I must've made with them over the next few years—food zaps, Carlos called them. Finally I think that ten-dollar bill just came apart, it'd been used so many times.

T HE ONE PERSON WHO COULD OUT-TALK SAMMY was Netta Abramowitz. He'd sit down with me and talk and talk, but with Netta he'd sit down and more often than not he was the one who got talked to. I'd hear her back in that so-called room they shared, which was just curtains around a bed, talking and talking to him in these fierce whispers, and not a word out of Sammy. Then after a while Sammy'd come trudging out into the front to find me, so he could get his turn to talk.

At first I thought maybe Netta was his daughter, or even his grand-daughter—she looked to be about Carlos's age. But she wasn't either of those things. She wasn't any relation to Sammy at all. They were just two people who'd had a lot to say to each other over the years.

Netta never really noticed I was around, I think; and anyway, the beginning of my stay with The Company was the tail end of hers. One of the only times she ever talked to me, because she wasn't ever very talkative with anybody except Sammy, I was giving myself a little sponge bath at the kitchen sink. There wasn't a shower or anything so fancy as that in the apartment. I had my shirt off and was washing my chest and under my arms, and Netta came in eating some kind of fish out of a little can. I say "some kind of fish," but I know exactly what it was—cuttlefish, it's called, which is like octopus and it comes in its own ink. There were cans and caps of it on a shelf in the kitchen. Stolen, I'm sure, like everything else around the place. I used to be fascinated by the thought of anybody eating something like that. I even sneaked a can of it one day, just to see what it was like—but I couldn't stand it. It was like eating little pieces of tire. But it's about all Netta ever ate.

When she came into the kitchen that day I was washing, she just stood there watching me, in between bites. Like seeing me standing there at the sink with my shirt off made her remember something.

"Carlos has no business," she said.

I had no idea what she was talking about.

"Just look at all this," she said. "What does Carlos tell you?"

"What do you mean, what does he tell me?"

"About anything. About any of this."

"He doesn't tell me much of anything," I had to admit, "but then, nobody does."

"Of course he doesn't," she said, like she was suddenly putting her finger on something. "He doesn't tell anybody. Nobody knows what's going on. Ever." She said it like she was furious. "He doesn't even know what's going on. It's just like him—hoping if he doesn't talk about it nobody'll notice. But everybody notices anyway. All the time, everybody notices everything. Even you probably notice things."

I wanted to ask, What things? But I didn't want to sound more in the dark than I was.

"He thinks you can go back and salvage, and you can—but my God, not the way all this stuff has to be salvaged. There're just too many pieces."

I couldn't tell exactly what she was talking about. But it scared me a little—the way when you meet somebody and you think they're just great, but then you hear somebody else saying these terrible things about them, and you get worried that maybe you're wrong. You get this little knot in the pit of your stomach.

"What do you expect?" she went on. "The man doesn't know how to use a movie camera. He can't even do a zoom without Seth. And if you're expecting him to direct you—ask anybody who's acted for him. You have to just completely ignore every single thing he says. If you're crazy enough to wake up one day and find yourself in one of Carlos's movies, all I can say is—you're completely on your own. Not a clue. And besides, what's this stuff about revolutionary movie-making? He watches other people's movies and steals their ideas, and then he does the same thing. Only he does it so crudely everybody thinks he must've meant it to look like it does. I could've had a career without Carlos. I can tell you that right now."

I didn't know. It could all be true, what with me not knowing anything about movies at all. I had to admit—what I'd seen that day when he was filming back in Owen didn't look much like any movie I'd ever seen. It scared me to think maybe he was crazy after all, and I was just some dumb kid falling for a gimmick anybody else could see right through. Because I have to tell you—even though I went right on thinking Carlos was the greatest thing in the world, there were lots of times when I was pretty miserable that winter. Times when I'd wake up and not know where I was, or what I was up to. I'd lie there in bed in this total panic, not remembering. And then I'd remember and that'd almost be worse. To think how I couldn't go back from wherever it was I'd got to now.

But back to Netta—it was like this anti-Carlos talk was some speech she had to give me, and once she gave it to me, then, whatever happened, she'd given me some kind of fair warning. And that's fine—that's the way she was, the way she related to people. I remember that first time, after she'd gone on destroying Carlos for a while longer, she looked at me and said, "Do you really know what you're getting into?"

"I think so," I told her. I felt like I had to stand up to her or she was going to take Carlos away from me with her talking, so I said, "I think I'm getting into what everybody else gets into."

"You make me want to weep," she told me.

"Save it," I said. "I can take care of myself."

She studied her tin can of cuttlefish. "We all say that, don't we?" I was feeling a little put out with her.

"Do you say that?" I asked. She smiled at me, but I could tell she didn't mean it.

"No," she said. "I don't say that anymore."

She looked straight at me.

"You're so young," she said. All of a sudden she sounded incredibly sad, and she just kept looking at me. She reached out with her free hand and touched my hair—only for a second. Then she looked away toward the floor. "I was just thinking," she said. But she stopped and didn't say anything more.

One more thing about those cuttlefish. I'd been out shoplifting enough with The Company to know what food was brought home, and I knew we never brought home any cuttlefish. And as far as I could tell,

Netta never left the apartment to go out shopping on her own. But the shelf was always full of cans. Then one day I figured it out—how it was Carlos who brought them for her. I heard him one night, restocking the shelf. I was sure that was what the sound was, and when he came to bed, I asked him. He looked at me like I'd surprised him, but then he just nodded, Yes, this harsh abrupt nod that said he didn't want to talk about it.

I knew that nod from Carlos, but I wasn't letting go. "That's so strange," I told him. "We had this cat back home—it used to bring little dead mice around when you were asleep, and put them in your shoe, or under the covers with you. Like they were little presents."

I don't know why that popped in my head, but it did, and I said it.

"You're so smart," Carlos told me—and he started to lick my ear. If you want to drive me completely crazy that's the one thing to do—get your tongue down in my ear.

"Stop it," I told him. "I'll laugh. I'll get a stomachache." But he kept it up. "I'll piss on the bed," I told him.

"Promise?"

"You're gross," I said. "Tell me about Netta."

"Why? You hit the nail on the head."

"What do you mean? What nail?"

"About your cat. That's exactly what it is."

"I don't get it."

Carlos laughed. "It's a peace offering," he said. Then he just lay back in the bed and laughed and laughed like somebody invisible was tickling him. It almost made me worry.

"It's been a long, long war," he told me.

"She doesn't like you," I said.

"Personally speaking, she's not so crazy about me, no."

"Then why's she living in your apartment and everything?" Which was something I still hadn't gotten quite used to—all these people camped out here like they owned the place.

"It's not my apartment," Carlos said. "It's The Company's apartment. You know, share and share alike."

Carlos had this way of putting me in my place. At the moment, though, I was more interested in Netta than I was in the apartment. "Why doesn't she like you?"

"She's seen through me," Carlos said. "She's used me up. I've used her up. It happens to people, you know."

Which I guess I had known, but still it came as a surprise. I wasn't old enough to have thought about things like that yet.

"She's going to leave us," Carlos went on. "She'll be the next one to leave."

"There've been others?" It seemed to me like The Company must've been the way they were forever.

"Lots," Carlos said. "We're the leftovers." He smiled. "The ones who didn't have any other place to go."

"But how do you know she's leaving too?" I asked him—though from what she'd told me, it wasn't too hard to guess.

"I can tell these things," he said. "It'll take another month or two. But she knows she's used us up, and she feels sad about that—but it's the way it is. She's been with us a very long time, since the beginning. We did some wonderful things with her."

That was what I remembered later—how Carlos said that, like she was some very accurate tool you could use where nothing else worked. But then he went on to say, and this just sort of stunned me, "You know, everybody's been in love with her around here, in their time. Everybody." And he left it like that.

I'd think about it from time to time, even though we never talked about it again. I think Carlos wanted me to piece it together, and I think that's finally what I did. Who knows? Maybe I'm all wrong about it—but what I think is, once upon a time, way back in the beginning of everything, when The Company was just getting started and a long time before Carlos ever took up with his first boy, Carlos and Netta were lovers. Maybe from when they were teenagers—I don't know. But they understood all about each other. Then over the years lots of things happened, things I'd never know anything about, and they hadn't been lovers for a long time. They'd gone their different directions, but here they still were. They were still working together because it was something they both believed in, even though they knew each other so well that a long time ago they'd lost faith in each other but not in what they were doing.

Maybe I'm saying that not because it has anything to do with Netta and Carlos, but because it's what I wish I'd been able to say about me and Carlos at some point in our lives together.

Maybe none of what I've said here is fair to Netta. Carlos was right that she was the first to leave—by the middle of that winter she was gone, moved to an apartment in Jersey City, and she never came back the rest of the time I was with The Company. Sammy would take the train out to see her every once in a while, but he never talked about her, and since I never had more than that one conversation with her, I never asked. There was something about her, though, that made an impression on me—like she was standing in for all the things I never could know: about lots of things, but especially about Carlos. She'd starred in four or five of his most important movies, but by the time he was making *Ur* Carlos had lost interest in her, or used her up, or they were just making each other crazy over stupid little things. I don't know. All I know is that about all she got to do in *Ur* was dig up some weeds off camera and put them in buckets, and you didn't need to be a genius to do that. Even I could do that.

Ur was Netta's last movie with The Company, and I don't know what ever happened to her after she left, whether she went on to be a star somewhere else or not, because I never heard anything more about her—which at least is something nobody'll ever be able to say about me.

Y OU KNOW THE WAY LOGS AND TRASH'LL CLOG UP
under a bridge pier, and one day for no reason it's too much, and
the whole thing gives way?

Carlos had come home late from Brooklyn that night. I was lying in
bed, feeling all agitated—it was the way I got sometimes, for no reason
I could figure out. Those were the nights I'd take to doing nightcaps
from the Canadian Club, waiting desperately for Carlos and trying not
to get too drunk and pass out, but also bored to death and fighting off
the urge to jerk off I was so bored, and lonesome, and I'd read every
comic book in the apartment ten times.

Carlos always said he could tell if I jerked off during the day, because
when I did, then there wasn't as much come when I came at night, and
Carlos liked lots of come. So I was always trying to save myself.

We were sitting crosslegged facing each other on the mattress in our
so-called bedroom, and I remember wondering whether he ever got to
craving me during the day till he couldn't stand it. Even though he said
so, somehow, deep down, I was afraid he didn't.

"So was it a good day?" he asked. It was what he always wanted
to know when he got home—it was important to him that the days
be good days. That's when I'd usually tell him where I'd gone, what
I'd done. But that day, I hadn't gone out. It was too cold, and I told
him so.

"I stayed home," I told him. "Sammy talked to me. I ate a can of
mushroom soup."

He looked in my eyes and grinned. "Are you all drunk again?" I
couldn't ever tell when he was kidding me.

"Nope," I told him. "I only had two or three drinks. I had a nightcap waiting for you," I said. "I had two or three."

"Nightcaps—that's fine. It's heavy drinking I'm worried about."

"No heavy drinking," I told him. "Heavy sex."

"Heavy sex," he said. "You working-class boys are all the same."

"At least I'm not the one on welfare," I said. Because Carlos had figured out some way so he'd been getting welfare checks for years and that was what we were living on, at least sort of.

"Yeah," he said, "and I'm not the one who sat on my butt doing caps all day."

"It's work," I told him. "My elbow's sore. Actually, I did go out."

He pretended like he was all surprised. "Oh you did?" he said. "So what's his name? How much did you charge him?"

I didn't like it much when he talked that way. It made me wonder whether he secretly meant what he was saying. Sometimes I wanted him to want me to stay around the apartment waiting for him, and not to be out there running all over the place.

He grabbed both my wrists and pushed me back on the bed.

"I went to the library," I told him. I don't know why I said it. I hadn't really been to the library that day, though, like I've told you. I'd been there a lot before. But for some reason I'd never told Carlos about the library, and how it was the library that'd started me going everywhere else. The library was my secret.

He was straddling me, pinning me down, but he let me go and put both his hands to his head. "The library?" he said. "The library?" He thought it was hilarious, which I didn't see any reason he should.

"You never told me you had this other life," he said. He was still sitting on top of me so I couldn't get up. "But it's good," he said. "A boy should go to the library. Read books."

"Cut it out," I told him. "It's not what you think. There's this book, this picture book with pictures of the town where Sammy grew up, and people like you and me, and the things that happened to them there, the church full of pillow feathers and the shit carriers, some of them just little children, and the kid who keeps looking out from the page at me, the kid with his little sister and them both begging in the streets for some food, maybe some bread baked out of brick dust and potato peels." All that stuff came pouring out of me in one long breath. Pent-up stuff from deep down inside me, which I hadn't realized I'd been thinking about as much as I must've. "There they were living their lives and thinking nothing could happen to them, and then all of a sudden it did happen. And here we are thinking we're safe from all that and everything, but who are we to be safe? I mean, who do we think we are to be safe?"

That outburst pretty much took Carlos off-guard, like when somebody starts telling what you think's going to be a joke and then it turns dead serious. I don't think he knew just then whether to laugh or be worried about me.

"You've been talking to Sammy," he said.

"Who else am I supposed to talk to?" I said. "You're never here. And yeah, I've been talking to Sammy. No—change that—Sammy's been talking to me. He's been driving me crazy with his talk, and then those pictures in the book—it could be you or me or anybody they did that to."

He rubbed my shoulders. "Tony," he said, "you're a really exceptional guy and I mean that, but I have no idea what you're talking about."

"I'm talking about the Jews," I told him. "I'm talking about Sammy and all that. If we woke up and they decided to do that to us, what would we be able to do? They'd just do it."

"Who's us?" Carlos asked. I looked up at him where he was still straddling my chest—it was an odd position to have a conversation in.

"Anybody," I said.

"Not to worry. You'd get your heinie back to Kentucky." Carlos said it like he was really impatient with all this stuff. "You'd fit right back in like you never went away. You're not a Jew or a nigger or queer or anything you have to worry about. So relax, enjoy. Somebody like you, in America—you're not going to have to worry."

It made me think. He was right, I could just go back to Kentucky and keep on living the way I used to think I'd be living my whole life.

"I wouldn't leave," I told him. It surprised me to hear myself say that, but once I said it I knew it was completely true. It was like one more door closing behind me. And I didn't even like Sammy—he was the most self-centered old man I'd ever met, thinking I was always just sitting around waiting to hear another story about Jews in the ghetto.

Besides, he had this way of sucking the saliva in at the edges of his mouth when he talked that was completely disgusting.

"I'd become a Jew," I said. Carlos laughed really loud.

"Yeah right," he said. "Wear a little beanie cap. Tony the yeshiva boy."

"What's a yeshiva boy?"

"Never mind," he said.

"It's something I've been thinking about a lot," I insisted. Actually it wasn't till that minute, but I knew if I had thought about it I'd have come to the exact same conclusions. And Carlos was making me angry, the way he wasn't listening to what I was saying. Like he thought it was something I needed to get out of my system and that was that.

"But why?" Carlos asked. "If they told you you didn't have to. That you could just go back to being normal and you'd escape." He looked at me with his serious look and sort of massaged my arms. I could tell he was trying to figure out if I might be having a nervous breakdown or something classy like that.

I didn't have any kind of answer to his question "Why?" I didn't know why I'd do what I said, but I knew I would. I could see that guy in the picture in the book really clearly.

Carlos sort of ruffled up my hair. "Anyway," he said, "There's nothing safe anywhere. Look at you."

"Look at me what?"

"You're doing your laundry and look what happens."

"Oh that," I told him. "Was that a bad thing?"

"Was it?" He was making me uncomfortable again. "Do you want to go back to Owen?"

The trouble was, I did sort of. I wasn't being very happy in New York, doing nothing all day except roam around on my own—The Company sure wasn't much company to me—or like today, sit around and read comic books and drink by myself, and then feel hung over so drink some more.

I asked him, "Are you trying to get rid of me or something? Trying to send me back home?"

Carlos laughed, but this time it was a quiet laugh. He started unbuttoning the buttons to my shirt. One at a time and slowly, and looking the whole time right in my eyes. I looked at his face, his eyes that were very serious-looking right at that instant, and I just lay back there and let him unbutton my shirt because what could I do? It was always like that when he started to touch me, especially that winter in that apartment where I was always cold and my skin felt cold and my hands and somehow Carlos's hands weren't cold like mine, they were warm and rough. When he'd start to touch me, laying his palm on my bare chest and stroking my nipples with his thumbs—something went all over me. I couldn't do anything except let him do whatever he wanted to with me. It was like I was dead and in the grave and here were his hands warming me up and back to life.

"I'm not trying to send you anywhere," Carlos said. He pulled my shirt off me and rubbed his hands along my belly, right where the waist of my jeans was. "You're right here," he said, slipping his fingers down under the waistline to where, even though I didn't really want it to, my dick was starting to get hard. "You're in for good," he said, "and you're right—there isn't any going back."

"Then I'm not going anywhere," I told him. He ran a hand along the front of my jeans, and my body arched up to meet him like it had a life all its own. I sort of moaned. He unzipped me and pulled out my dick, and rolled it around in his hand, looking at it even though he'd seen it a hundred times before. But he was always interested in what it looked like. Then he bent forward and took it in his mouth. He'd done that to me also about a hundred times and still it made the floor drop out from under me. I loved touching my fingers to the base of it where his lips were wrapped around.

Now that we were like this, it seemed even more upsetting to think about that kid caught in the picture. Stopped there forever, and us going on, moving around like we were. Alive. Not that I didn't like us like this, but I just kept seeing that kid in front of my eyes, and that one expression on his face that was going to be caught like that forever.

Carlos raised up and started pulling my jeans off me, lifting one ankle and then the other to free me up completely. "Look, don't go getting goofy on me, okay? Sammy's just a paranoid Jew, so forget it. I mean, if anybody's earned the right to be paranoid it's Sammy, but don't let that fuck you up. Okay? It doesn't have to have anything to do with you."

"Sure," I said. "Why should I listen to some paranoid old Jew?"

"Right," Carlos told me. "How do you know he's not making all that stuff up just to impress you?" Which was something I never thought of before.

"Besides," he went on, "I need you." He was taking off his shirt, sliding his pants down so we were both completely naked with him straddled on top of me, which is something I really loved when we got down to that point. "I'm counting on you," he said, "for that movie."

"Yeah?" I said. "Tell me more." I wanted to hear him talk about that movie. It was the reason he'd gotten me here, and now two months had gone by, and nothing. I thought maybe if I gave him a blow job he might keep on talking, so I guided his dick toward my mouth.

"That's nice," he said. "That's great."

It wasn't something I'd ever done with him before. Usually Carlos was the one who wanted to do things, and I just lay back and enjoyed them. But this time felt different. I wanted to ask him more about the movie, but my mouth was full, and then I got to thinking about other things. I got the idea—strange to say, I'd never gotten it before—that since it was something he did to me that I liked, maybe I should do it to him too. So I reached my hand around his butt and squirmed a finger down his crack till I found his hole, and I started to press my finger up it.

He grabbed my wrist. "Sorry," he said, "off limits."

I pulled off him. "And mine's not?" I said.

He sat up and kind of rocked back—then he spread my legs and started rubbing his finger into my asshole. It sent hot chills right up me.

"Do you want it to be off limits?"

He could have me groaning in no time. "No way," I told him as he pressed his middle finger all the way up. "No way."

It was hard to tell who was winning, but after that it was pretty much whatever he wanted to do with me was fine, he could do it.

Still, all I could think while he was doing it was: the Jew kid in the picture, didn't he die hungry, of bullets, when he lived past the picture they'd got him in? It was what I couldn't get out of my head.

Later, after we both fell asleep, I could only sleep about half an hour before I was wide awake and staring at the ceiling. Next to me Carlos wasn't moving, or even breathing as far as I could tell. But then that was the way Carlos always slept—on his back and completely still. If you went to sleep with him like that and woke up eight hours later, you might've been in fifty different positions but he hadn't moved an inch. I think some of the time he wasn't even sleeping, he was just lying there thinking. He'd lie completely still, and if he couldn't get to sleep it was still a way of resting—his arms folded across his chest and his eyes closed like some kind of Egyptian mummy.

I propped myself up on my elbow to watch him. In the orange glow that came in through the plastic over the windows, I could see his face—thin lips, and smooth tight skin, and those high cheekbones that could make him look like a Cherokee Indian. It never occurred to me at the time that Carlos might be a Jew.

I thought about some of the pictures in that book, people the Nazis killed in some riot. After they took the bodies to a warehouse before carting them off somewhere else—Sammy told me this—Mendel went in there in secret and took pictures of the faces, so people could look at those pictures and know for sure whether their son or wife or whoever was one of the ones that got killed.

Lying there in that orange light, Carlos looked like he could be dead too. His skin could've been ice cold to the touch. I thought about the faces of those dead people in the pictures, how their eyes were open with a kind of shocked look like they'd just been going along alive one instant and suddenly the next they were dead. It was sort of the look you might have if death was some invisible wall that you were walking along and just ran smack into without any warning.

Which is the sort of thinking you can only do so long. I crawled out of bed, careful not to wake Carlos up. I put on some clothes—it was way too cold in that apartment to be wandering around butt-naked—and went into the kitchen, where I sat down in the dark with my bottle of Canadian Club.

I thought about getting really drunk, as a way of putting all that stuff out of my head. But I didn't drink. I took a sip or two and realized a drink wasn't what I wanted. That was probably the first time in my life I ever realized something like that, which shows how far gone I was that night. Somehow I guess I'd thought Carlos was going to be able to say the one simple thing that'd get rid of everything that'd been going around in my head, and that's why I blurted everything out. I hadn't meant to do it. But now it was worse instead of better—with the worst part being that I could see nobody was going to help me. It was something I was going to have to work out by myself.

I grew up on Carlos right then—not that I ever thought he was going to get me through stuff, but I do think I hooked up with him back in Owen because I could see I needed some kind of help. And now that fell apart.

I still don't quite know why I did it, but I got up and walked over to the door and unlatched it, and stood there for about fifteen minutes. I felt the way a skydiver probably does before a jump, leaning way out into space and knowing once he lets go, that's it, free-fall and a long way down. Then I left.

I closed the door behind me and told myself I knew exactly what I was doing. Of course I didn't know, and when I think back about that whole night it's like I was totally drunk even though I was completely sober. But there I was out on Avenue C at what must've been three in the morning—and I've already said how the nighttime in New York had a way of freaking me. I started walking west.

I didn't get too far, as it turned out—just to Tompkins Square Park between Avenues B and A. Even though it was freezing December and the middle of the night too, it was still full of people—guys standing around these trash cans they'd lit fires in to keep warm, and other guys sitting on benches all wrapped up in army blankets, or just wandering around with dazed looks on their faces like they had no idea where they were. In the middle of the park where all the sidewalks came together, this black guy was standing there just saying, Smoke, smoke, smoke, over and over in this dead voice even though nobody was buying. But it was like once he got going, he couldn't stop.

There were also men who kept watching me with these hungry eyes. They'd walk up close to me and then veer away at the last minute, like I was somebody they thought they recognized but then didn't. Or maybe it was the other way around—they were the ones who wanted me to recognize them. I knew what they wanted—I'd seen queers in New York, I knew all the ways they'd look at me when I passed. Now here they were, roaming around in the middle of the night still looking, and here I was too.

I guess whatever carried me out of the apartment just all of a sudden gave out and I was standing there without a clue when these two Puerto Rican kids came up on bikes. They must've been about eight and ten, just little kids, and when they said, "Yo man, what's up?" I asked, "What're you guys doing out here? Why aren't you home?" Which may sound dumb, but it was the first thing that came into my head—I guess with the park so full of guys cruising for a chance with little kids like that.

"Don't look like you're home neither," the older one said. He was missing one of his front teeth.

"Don't worry about me, man," I told him. "It's late. You guys should really go home." I think I was suddenly thinking about Ted and how I wouldn't want him out in a place like this.

"Yeah, fuck you too," the little one told me. They'd moved up so their bikes were on either side of me.

"You a faggot?" one of them asked.

"Do I look like a faggot?"

"Everybody looks like a faggot to me," the older kid said. "Just don't try nothing."

"Am I trying anything?" They'd sort of locked me in between their bikes and all of a sudden I wasn't sure what they were up to.

"He's no fag," the little one said.

"Naw, he's no faggot," said the older one.

"So what're you two up to?" I asked, since obviously they'd decided to let up on me a little.

"Eh," the older kid spit on the ground and wiped his mouth on his sleeve. "Whatever."

I remember thinking how strange it was, those two kids on their bikes in that park in the middle of the night—totally out of bounds, and at the same time acting like they owned the place.

"We're just hanging," the little kid said. "Want to hang with us?"

"I don't know," I told them. "Maybe for a while."

"Yeah, hang with us for a while," the older kid said. "Should we ditch the square or what?"

"Should ditch it," said the other one. The square being Tompkins Square, where we were. We went east along some streets back toward where the apartment was, then past it over to Avenue D, and I knew we were looking for something but I didn't know what it was supposed to be. The older kid was whistling this tune but I didn't recognize it. Nobody was talking or anything, so I didn't try to talk either or ask what we were doing. I was just hanging with them for a while—it was strange to be with kids instead of an old man like Sammy for a change. I remember I was liking the cold air. I kept taking it down deep in my lungs and living off the flat hard taste of it. It was clearing me up like no drink ever did—plus I wasn't thinking about Carlos or Sammy or anything, which was the first time in a long time.

In front of us on the sidewalk was this old man lying up against a building with his face to the wall—asleep, I guess, and he had this old coat with newspapers stuck to it. You know how leaves and dirt'll stick to some piece of candy you drop on the ground? That was the way this old man looked, like somebody'd rolled him in a bunch of old newspapers and they'd stuck to him. The two kids got off their bikes and leaned them against the wall. Then, like it was something hilarious, they snuck up on that old guy—he was either asleep or completely passed out, you couldn't tell which. The older kid mouthed one two three, and suddenly they were both kicking the shit out of him. I mean, kicking so hard you heard the sound of their shoes hitting him in the ribs, these thumps that were incredibly loud and made you sick to hear.

He yelled and swatted at them, but not much, because mostly he just lay still like he'd passed out again. They kept kicking at him; then they rolled him a few feet to sort of unwind him out of those newspapers he was wrapped up in. Their hands were all over him—in his pockets and feeling up his coat—and I could tell the little kid had found a couple of dollar bills and some change in one of the pockets.

I stood there next to where their bikes were leaned up against the wall. I never saw anything like it, and it took me a minute or two to figure it out—and by then they were already through doing what they were going to do. I think when they saw I wasn't going to help but just stand there like an idiot they didn't pay any more attention—they just dropped me like that. When they were through, the older one sort of slapped the top of my head with his hand.

"Faggot!" he said, and they both laughed and jumped on their bikes and rode off. Which left me standing there with this old man on the pavement—I didn't know if he was alive or what, because he wasn't moving even though there wasn't any blood I could see. Like I said, I couldn't do a thing—I just stood there like he was an old bag of trash somebody'd dumped. I probably should've seen if he was okay, but everything was feeling more and more like some kind of bad dream.

I remember thinking, if I just turned and walked away it wouldn't've happened—it just wouldn't be there anymore.

I couldn't do it. I went over to where he was lying on the ground, face down, and I turned him over to see if he was still breathing. I didn't know what I was going to do next, but that seemed the place to start.

When I rolled him onto his back, his face was staring right up at me, and it was then I recognized he was the old man with the golf club, who Carlos had said I'd see again.

I left him right there. I wasn't going to touch him—it spooked me too much. I turned around and walked off quick as I could, and I was probably even whistling while I was walking just so I wouldn't completely freak out.

Then suddenly it came to me right on the street there between Avenues C and D, like I was actually saying it out loud it was so clear and upsetting: those queers in the park are just like Carlos. The only thing is, Carlos found me in a laundromat and not in a park. It made me break into a run when I thought that, and I ran all the way back to the apartment. Carlos was still asleep, and I went right to him and shook him really hard.

"You're wearing your clothes," he said. He was really groggy. "You're cold." He was like somebody swimming upstream to try to break out of his sleep.

"Look." I was shaking him pretty hard. "Are you just fucking with me or what?"

"I don't know what you're talking about." He was sort of giggling, like he thought this was some kind of joke. I could tell he was pretty confused. I think he liked me shaking him awake like that in the middle of the night; he thought it was different and fun.

But I was really upset, so I asked him again, "Are you just fucking with me?"

It must've gotten to him finally that something was really wrong, because he sat up in bed and grabbed both my arms.

"You find this kid," I told him, "and you start fucking with him and you tell him anything so he won't know what's what and it's all so you can have everything right where you want it, right?"

I was yelling at him with the words coming out and me not even thinking about them. "Who said you could act like that?" I remember saying it over and over, and I didn't care if Sammy or Netta heard. Of course they must've heard, but from the first I'd always sort of pretended they didn't, even though they must've heard us fucking around every night of the week. I guess I just didn't care, like when I was a kid and had to piss in a restroom. If somebody was standing next to me, I'd get nervous and couldn't—but if it was some black guy next to me I'd say to myself, He's just a nigger, and then I could piss fine because it didn't matter. "You're just a fucking New York queer out hitting on any kid you can get your pervert hands on," I yelled, and I think I was punching at him, because he grabbed my wrists and before I knew it he was holding me in a power lock.

"Listen to me, Tony," he said. "Listen to what I'm saying." Because he'd been talking and I wasn't even listening, I was just yelling at him these words I wasn't even paying attention to.

"Are you going to listen?" He was squeezing my wrists together really tight and it hurt, so I nodded.

I could barely see him with the orange streetlight glow coming in through the heavy plastic over the windows. It was like a fire burning somewhere that was lighting up the room.

"I could tell you I love you," Carlos said. It was a terrible thing for him to say. I remember I started shaking my head and trying to break away from him but he held me and I couldn't get away. "Does that make it any better," he said, "if I tell you that? Is that what you need?"

"That's bullshit," I said, "that's what it is. It's got nothing to do with anything." Which at the moment I really did believe, and the last thing I wanted Carlos to do was start telling me he loved me.

"Then what're you doing here?" Carlos asked me straight out, and when I didn't say anything—which I couldn't, I was just too surprised— he said, "There's got to be an answer to that question, Tony. What is it you want? Somewhere there's got to be an answer to that."

He knew I didn't have an answer, which was why he asked. He knew I didn't know what I wanted, even though I was walking around thinking I did, and if you'd asked me before that instant, Did I know what I wanted, I'd have said, Of course. But now when he said it, it was like everything I ever wanted fell into some hole, and all that was left was the hole and nothing to fill it up with. Suddenly that part of me that'd always been jabbering away about everything suddenly forgot what it was talking about and didn't have anything more to say and I was speechless.

I started crying like a lunatic—the first time in about five years I'd cried like that. I mean howling, just completely letting go and not caring who heard me. And Carlos did the one perfect thing he could do. I'm sure he knew it was the one perfect thing, even though I'd never have thought of it. He put his arms around me and hugged me and wouldn't let me go—which is a very simple thing and maybe obvious but it was the perfect thing to do anyway, and what counts is that he did it. He eased me down into bed with him, not saying anything, and just held me. He didn't kiss me or fuck with me or anything, he just held me there like I'd die if he ever stopped holding me, and he let me cry my heart out about everything I hadn't cried about: Ted, and my mom, and being this fucked-up kid who was taking it up the ass from a queer—which was bad enough, but wanting to take it up the ass, which meant I was having to say, for the first time, I was a queer like Carlos was a queer, and I wasn't going to be anybody else than exactly who I was. Which can be a pretty terrible thing to suddenly realize.

I KNOW PEOPLE TALK ABOUT CARLOS CORRUPTING kids that couldn't know any better. But speaking only for me, all I can say is: whatever was there for him to corrupt would've gotten corrupted anyway, and everything I did, I did because I wanted to do it. Maybe I'd have done it in different ways—but I'd still have done it. So you can only pin it on me. People say, Well, he put those ideas in your head. All I say is, if he hadn't put them there somebody else would have, or they'd've put some other ideas there to take their place. Either it's somebody like Carlos who puts ideas in your head that other people don't want to be there and so if you want those things it's bad, or the other people put their ideas in your head and so if you want those things it's good because that's what they wanted you to want.

The only trouble with Carlos I can see is, he wanted things other people didn't want him to want, and those other people were the ones who were able to say what people are supposed to want and not want—especially what kids like me are supposed to want, whether we really do want it or not. And as far as I can see it, that's what Carlos's life was all about. Pointing out the way all that stuff worked.

So you could say Carlos corrupted me into seeing things the way he did. But then I never knew any adult who wasn't trying to corrupt you every time they talked to you, even if it was just to say do this because it's right or don't do this because it's wrong.

Which is all something I've been thinking about, and I just had to say it for the record.

C ARLOS MUST'VE HAD EVERYTHING WORKED OUT from the start. Either that, or he knew how to make things look like he'd wanted them to be exactly the way they were. It might've been his biggest talent—taking things the way they came, and then fitting everything else around that.

A couple days after that night I just told you about, he came bursting into the apartment.

"So, can you read?" he said.

I was sitting at the kitchen table with an X-Man comic and my Canadian Club and hot tea, and I was really surprised to see him in the middle of the day.

"What do you mean, can I read?"

"Well, these days you can never be sure."

"Of course I can read," I told him. Not that I ever did in those days, except for comic books and stuff like that. But I could if I had to.

"Good," he said, and he handed me a bunch of papers in a folder.

"So what's this?"

"Read," he said.

I'd never seen a movie script before, but even if I had I might not have recognized what Carlos handed me—it wasn't really a script, it was just this set of suggestions. Later I'd learn that was the only kind of script he ever used—he wanted people to be free to make things up on the spot. It could drive you crazy—the movie was always changing directions out from under you, depending on what other people did. But then nothing about Carlos's movies ever had much to do with normal movies. He didn't care if his movies didn't look like the stuff that came out of Hollywood—in fact he wanted them to look completely different. What his movies always looked like was, somebody went and invented movies from scratch without ever seeing a Hollywood movie.

Like sync sound. He could do sync sound if he wanted but he never wanted to. We'd do a scene or takes for a scene and usually we'd be just saying anything. Sometimes it was good and we could use it and sometimes it was bad, but it didn't really matter, because Carlos went back and wrote the dialogue after he'd filmed everything and then dubbed the voices in. Sometimes he'd have the person do their own voice, but sometimes not: sometimes he'd get somebody else to do the voice—strange, because here was this one person and then this other person's voice. But it grew on me, and after a while I sort of started to see how Carlos was looking at things when he made his movies.

Not at first, though. "So this is the movie I'm supposed to be the star of?" I asked Carlos. Because I couldn't make a thing out of what I was looking at.

"You bet."

"But I don't get it. What'm I supposed to do?"

Because in the so-called script there would just be a number and then something like: *57; Sammy becomes a seagull on the rooftop,* or *81: Tony as a principle of unconscious motion.* There were about two hundred of these, no lines for us to learn or anything, just Tony this or Sammy that and we didn't even have names except our own names.

My heart sort of sank when I realized it was basically just me this and Sammy that through the whole movie. Like what I needed just now was more of Sammy.

Also, I was afraid there was something in this script I wasn't getting.

"Nope, no secret," Carlos said. "The secret is, you make up the secret as you go along."

And that's exactly what we did. I never would've believed it, but we made a whole movie that way—which I guess just proves that Carlos was crazy and a genius like people said he was.

Making that movie turned out to be both harder and easier than I thought. Most of it was just standing around waiting to do something, and then you'd do it, and then maybe do it again a couple more times. Then you'd stand around waiting for the next thing to do. It was pretty boring. And also freezing, since it was February and snowing, and when it wasn't snowing it was even colder than when it was.

Since Sammy and I were supposed to be these sort of street people, basically the whole thing was outdoors shots. Being so old and frail, Sammy really suffered. He'd stamp his feet and rub his hands together to try to keep warm, but you could tell it didn't help. In between feeling my ears and nose to see how I couldn't feel anything in them anymore, I was always trying to find places in the neighborhood where we could go get a cup of coffee and warm up—which on the farther alphabets there weren't a whole lot of back in 1980.

Sammy never really complained much about the cold, just about everything else—mainly me, and how I wasn't doing things right. As far as I could tell, there wasn't much of a right or a wrong, there was just whatever we happened to be doing at the moment. All bundled up, Sammy was like some rag doll you could pick up and toss around if you wanted, and sometimes I almost did—except then I'd look at him and think about all that stuff he'd told me about Poland and the war. If you thought about it, nothing made any sense—him going through all that and how could he have ever known back then he'd still be alive in 1980 and making this crazy movie in New York City in America with some kid from Kentucky?

Sometimes he was really enjoying himself with it, though—doing things that if I did them he'd be all over me for ruining the movie, but Carlos thought anything Sammy did was great so sometimes Sammy just cut loose. I remember one morning he showed up with this amp meter, the kind you test circuits with. I don't know where he got it, but he explained with a straight face how it was his invention to measure animal magnetism.

"What's animal magnetism?" I asked him.

Carlos and Seth were getting it all down on camera. Lots of times it was like that—we'd be making the movie before I even had time to realize we were making it, which completely threw me till I got used to it.

"For years I have worked on this machine," Sammy told me. "It is my crowning achievement." We were walking along Avenue C and it was so cold steam was rising from the manhole covers and when we'd walk through the steam it was warm like stepping into a bathroom where somebody just took a shower. Sammy took the two wires of the amp meter and touched them to a metal stair railing that went up to a brownstone. He shook his head. "No animal magnetism," he said, like it was the most tragic thing. "Stair railings do not have animal magnetism."

He moved along and I followed after him, since what else was I supposed to do? Seth was walking backward ahead of us with the camera, and Carlos was making sure he didn't back into anything by accident. He tilted a garbage can out of Seth's way, and when Sammy came to the garbage can he stopped and touched the meter to it.

"No animal magnetism," he said. "Garbage cans exhibit no animal magnetism."

I was desperately trying to think of something to say to all that, because usually Sammy was the one to think things up and I couldn't think of a thing, and after a while Carlos would hold up his fingers, which meant I was supposed to say whatever numbers came into my head and he'd figure out something to dub in there later.

"Four thirteen seventy-two thirty-three," I said in my most convincing voice.

"I have raised a brilliant son," said Sammy.

Just up ahead there was this guy lying asleep on the sidewalk, with about five wine bottles sitting around him and a cardboard sign propped up against the wall beside him that said NEEDED 1 MILLION $ FOR VINO-LOGICAL RESEARCH. Before you knew it, there was Sammy bending over him and touching the wires to the wino's shoulder where he was rolled over on his side.

"Animal magnetism," he said, nodding his head and looking very proud of himself. "I have proved animal magnetism."

But then a few days later Sammy got sick, being out in the cold every single day like that, and he started this hacking cough that once it started would go on for five minutes till you thought he was going to choke. Carlos didn't even seem to notice, or if he did it was like he didn't care—it was just one more thing that was getting in the way of everything else.

I collared him with it one afternoon when Sammy was shivering and these violent coughs kept racking him. "So how're you planning on finishing your movie when Sammy up and dies?" I asked him. Partly it was because I was freezing to death too, but also I was worried Sammy really was going to do something like die if we kept this up.

Carlos made a face, like that was something he really didn't want to hear right then. "Well, I guess we could always do a death scene," he said.

"Fuck you," I told him.

"It's not up to me to do anything," he said. Then he did what he never did—he turned his back on me and walked away to where Seth and a guy that helped Seth were setting up some lights for the next shot we were supposed to do. I couldn't believe it. I didn't even *like* Sammy all that much. He was supposed to be Carlos's friend, and Seth's and Netta's, but none of them seemed even worried he might be dying of pneumonia.

During my little argument with Carlos, Sammy'd gone over and sat down on this pile of bricks in an empty lot next to where we were filming. He hunched over in another of his coughing fits, this old man alone out there in all that rubble, and suddenly I thought—it's the way animals in the forest go off in a corner somewhere to die. The wind was really sharp that day, these stinging gusts that cut right through you. Suddenly I had this idea. Over in the corner of that lot, chucked next to the side of a building, was one of those big cardboard packing boxes, the kind refrigerators come in. I dragged the box over to where Sammy was, and without saying anything to anybody I took out my pocketknife and cut a sort of door in it, and a window in the door so he could see out. Ted and I used to make these forts out of sawhorses and old packing boxes when we were kids, and putting this shelter together for Sammy made me remember Ted, and when I was a kid, and I guess I was really getting into fixing that shelter up because I didn't even realize Seth was getting the whole thing on film. Carlos was loving it. When I'd finished that box and helped Sammy into it and out of the wind, he threw his arms around me in this great bear hug and whispered in my ear, "I always had faith, Tony—always." And maybe it was just a gust of wind blowing something in my eye, but I teared up right when he said that to me.

So that's the story of that scene in the movies where I build a cardboard shelter for Sammy to die in. Like I said before, that was the way Carlos always worked; you could hate him for it, but somehow it always worked.

Another thing I remember is how one day these two guys about my age, maybe a little older, were standing on the corner watching us and every once in a while calling out, "Yo, faggots," trying to get our attention or show off or whatever. People were always stopping to watch what we were doing. I guess, even though it was New York, it wasn't every day you saw somebody out on the streets making movies. Anyway, after about ten minutes of those two guys yelling, Carlos walked right over to them and I thought he was going to tell them to fuck off, but instead he asked did they want to be in a movie? They looked at each other like that was the last thing they expected—you could see they were sort of daring each other to say yes. Finally one of them said, Sure, they'd be in the movie—but that didn't mean they were any kind of faggot actors or anything. They didn't have to worry, Carlos told them. Nobody would think they were a bunch of faggot actors just for being in one film like that.

So that's how Rafe and Nicky got in the movie. And again, up to that point I wasn't supposed to have these two friends in the movie—it was just basically me and Sammy—but then Carlos wrote them in right on the spot and by the time it came time to dub the movie he'd already lost track of them so he got two other guys to do the voices. The line about "I'm a walking death warrant"—my favorite thing in the whole movie—Nicky never said that in real life at all; Carlos only added that later when he was dubbing the voice. But you'd never be able to tell it just watching the movie.

I really sort of liked Rafe and Nicky, only they had so many tattoos they made me a little nervous. Especially Rafe, who had about five running down the length of both his arms—eagles and roses and a skull wearing a top hat and this big green dragon all coiled up in itself. He was always wearing a black sleeveless T-shirt under this beat-up old leather jacket, and anytime you got him indoors he'd take off his jacket so he could show off his arms. I used to sit in this bar where we'd go after shoots (the bartender didn't care what age you were) and I'd just look at his skinny arms with those tattoos up and down them. It made me shiver. What those tattoos said was, he was completely lost and he was going to die pretty soon. I don't know why they made me think that, but they did, and I liked him for that reason. Plus he had a motorbike he'd let me ride sometimes at night, up and down Avenue C where there's not much traffic.

Some of the other people Carlos picked up for the movie weren't as great as Rafe and Nicky, and I told him that. We'd just done a shot over in Tompkins Square Park, where I was supposed to be warming my hands over a trash-barrel fire with a couple of bums. One of them starts handling me while I'm standing there. I mean, he reaches down and grabs my ass and smiles this gross smile with no teeth in it.

"What'd you want?" Carlos asked. "Hire a stuntman?"

"Sometimes I get this feeling you're just joking with me," I told him. "I mean, all the time. Getting your kicks that way."

He looked at me and asked, "Aren't we all?" like nothing else ever occurred to him.

Sammy was sitting in his stupid little cardboard tollbooth, watching us out the window.

"What do you mean, aren't we all?"

I remember thinking, I bet Carlos is feeling sorry right now he can't get this on film too, like everything else—but he wasn't supposed to be in the movie and Seth couldn't shoot me without shooting Carlos so for once we were safe. I wasn't changing the plot for the hundredth time by opening my mouth or doing something I never planned to do. Anyway, Carlos was terrified of anybody ever taking a picture of him, let alone with a movie camera—which I always thought was strange from somebody who spent their life making movies.

"Aren't we all just getting our kicks?" Carlos asked. He seemed really surprised by it all.

"Getting felt up by some wino's not my idea of kicks," I said, with the wino standing right there where he could hear everything since we'd raised our voices and with this completely sad look on his face. I felt sorry for him, since it was Carlos who asked him to feel me up in the first place, and if he got his kicks out of it, it wasn't *his* fault.

"Maybe feeling you up's his kind of kicks. Maybe being in a movie's your kind of kicks. How about that?"

Of course it was a point, the way Carlos always made points.

"Anyway," Carlos went on, "anything for art. Right?"

"I thought it was anything for a drink," I told him.

"I always forget," he said. "You're the future and I'm just the past." Which meant things sort of ended there, with us doing a retake and that wino's hand on my butt one more time and Carlos getting his way completely. That was how things always ended up and I guess you could say how *Next Year in Gomorrah* got made. That being the name of the movie starring Tony Blair and Sammy Finkelsztajn, him as the old Jew from the ghetto in Poland, like he was in real life, and me his son and a Jew too, which of course I'm not in real life but like I told Carlos, I'd become a Jew on purpose if they ever started doing the concentration camp thing again.

I guess it was only a long time after we finished making that movie and it was all history that I started to see how much Carlos was fooling around with me. I'm not sure how to explain it. How he was fiddling with my brain in all sorts of ways I didn't have any hope of understanding at the time—just to see what he could get out of me for the movie. And by the time I started to realize all that, it was too far in the past to worry about. It was just the way things were—and by then I pretty much knew how things were anyway.

IT'S BEEN FIVE YEARS SINCE THE LAST TIME I SAW Sammy, and three years since he died, which is something I'll tell you about later. But now that I'm thinking about him again, I remember all these things I thought I'd forgotten. Stupid stuff—these beat card games he used to try to teach me, which I never could get the hang of, or this one song they used to sing in the ghetto in that yammering Yiddish of his. He used to sing it to me all the time: about the young girls in spring, he used to say, and for some reason he wanted me to remember it.

But I can't remember it. Right now I just sang some of it out loud, but it wasn't right—wrong tune, and I forget the words. But other things I remember—Sammy's tomatoes: how he'd go over to the markets on Second Avenue and come back with a paper bag and three tomatoes, which he paid for I'm sure with that same ten-dollar bill he always used. He'd hum his song about the young girls in spring and sit at the kitchen table and dump those tomatoes out of the bag. With his salt shaker, he'd sprinkle a little salt on the tomato, and then bite in, this big juicy bite like it was some sloppy apple he was eating—and then another shake of salt and another bite, juice running all down his chin and his fingers and him with his eyes closed, slurping away. The first time I heard that sound, it was so scrumptious and noisy I thought somebody in the apartment was having sex, the juiciest blow job of their life.

Of course, I found out it was just Sammy eating his tomatoes. But every time after that, when I heard that sound, I still liked it, and I wondered if Sammy lay in bed at night listening to Carlos and me and if it sounded just the same. I was sure, even if his ears were just an old man's ears, he still could hear us through those curtains that were the only walls in the apartment. I wondered if somehow the sound of us slurping away at each other was as comforting to him as the sound of him eating his tomatoes was to me.

It never seemed to bother Sammy too much, what me and Carlos were doing. I remember sometimes our room could get to looking pretty rough after we'd been at it for a night. Carlos would always be gone by the time I woke up, and I'd lie around in bed till noon or so—I never knew what time it was in those days. I liked the sweaty body smell of the sheets. We used to go for weeks without changing the sheets, maybe because the laundromat was ten blocks away and as you probably already know I hated laundromats, I'd do anything to stay away from them, but maybe because we both liked lying in there with our smell all over the place. Just to remind us.

Anyway, some mornings I'd be lying in bed and I don't know what would get into Sammy, but he'd bring me a cup of tea on a tray and sit on the edge of the bed while I sipped at it. It was like some kind of joke to me, but I went along with it. I used to imagine we were in some movie where I was this Russian prince and Sammy was my faithful servant, and I could almost make it work too, especially on cloudy days when the light was this pale light coming in through those white curtains that were the walls of the bedroom, and Netta's opera music was playing on her cassette player in the so-called other room.

While I'd drink my tea Sammy would flip through the porn magazines that were always lying around, because Carlos loved porn magazines. I don't know where he got them, but he was always bringing them home. I think Sammy just thought they were really peculiar things, not good or bad but just interesting. He'd flip through them and just shake his head. "So adventurous, these boys," he'd say. "See what they do here?" He'd show me some picture of a kid with a dildo stuck in his ass. "Why do they want to be doing that, I wonder?"

Why did they? Sammy'd lived through that ghetto. I guess nothing surprised him anymore, which was why he was with The Company— but nothing other people who hadn't been in the ghetto did made much sense to him. I think he always felt sad about the way people were living their lives. I think he was always thinking about those people he knew who never got a chance to be living their lives one way or the other.

"I guess it makes them feel good," I told him. But it occurred to me—I really didn't know why somebody'd want to do stuff like that when there was this camera watching them. Somehow I'd never thought about there having to be other people around—guys working the cameras, and lights, and everything like that. Suddenly it made whatever those two boys were doing on a bed seem different. It was a job, like they were actors, and they could be good or bad but it was still a job. It was something they were out there doing for the rest of us—so we could watch, whatever the reasons were that we wanted to watch them. And I thought—why not? Why not do it in front of a camera if that was what you needed to go and do. Because I guess I was happy they did. Not that I spent much time jerking off to those magazines, I was never much for looking at porn, though like I said before Carlos could never get enough of it.

"It just breaks my heart," Carlos told me once. He was holding up some magazine called, I don't know, *Hotter Than Hot,* or something like that—they all had stupid titles. What he was showing me wasn't any different from any of the other pictures, but he said, in that excited voice he sometimes got, "Look at it, look at it—the expression on that kid's face." He thumped the pages. "Right when the blond guy's putting it in him. See how they caught it just like that, that instant when the kid thinks, I'm gonna die. It's too big. I'm not gonna live through this. But he loves it. He loves that feeling of I'm gonna die. See—his eyes're kind of crossed, his mouth's hanging open, you can just hear that *ouff!* he's moaning when it sinks into him. And they've got it there, just some guy with a camera and he's catching this kind of death that's happening for this kid—this one single instant that turns him clear as some pane of glass. You're looking all the way down into him, to where he's giving away something he didn't even know he had."

Carlos could get inspired—he'd talk himself into these excited states. It was true, the kid did look kind of shocked, not bored like they usually did in Carlos's magazines. But still, it was just some guy getting fucked. Carlos was always seeing things I never could, even in some stupid porn magazine.

"My God," Carlos went on, like it was something he was trying out for the first time, like it'd been lying there under his nose all along and he never noticed it. "Do you realize what we could learn from all that? I mean, for really getting the truth about somebody. That instant when some cock's going into them and they just give everything away.

A single look. That's what's real—not all this posing around, but that one real second when you think you're going to die. That's a true self, that second there. It's too scary even to look at. You could go to jail for the right kind of picture like that, and everybody knows it. It's why everybody's so scared and no good."

I lay there on the bed and just looked at him. He knew I thought he was peculiar.

"It's an idea," he said, shrugging his shoulders.

"You have all these ideas," I told him. It was why he sometimes wore that black headband, I thought—to keep all those ideas from exploding.

"Yeah, I do," he said. "And for what? Who cares about any of this?" He let go of the magazine that just a minute ago he'd been holding like it was the greatest thing, and it fell on the floor. "Why make movies," he said, "or porn magazines, or anything?" He sounded sad. I just sat there, my eyes locked on his. I knew he didn't want me to answer his question. With his hand he reached down under the covers and closed around my dick that was hard for him.

"It's because this won't last," he said. He pushed the covers aside and leaned forward and put my dick into his mouth. Then there he was, slurping away, like the noise Sammy made with his tomatoes.

If his question was going to have any kind of answer, I guess that was it. I guess there's some reason why I started out talking about Sammy and ended up talking about Carlos. Sammy would sit there on the side of the bed while I sipped the tea he'd brought me. He'd turn those porn magazines this way and that way, like he was trying to figure out something, and every once in a while he'd say something like, "Tony, I count three boys on this bed, and three heads and three impolite things and six legs and seven arms. Now can you tell me why is that, Tony? Does that ever happen to you?"

W E SHOT *NEXT YEAR IN GOMORRAH* DURING THE
whole month of February, and Carlos and Seth spent most of the
spring editing it down. I'd sometimes go out to Brooklyn to the film
collective where they did the editing—not that there was anything I could
do to help. Besides, Carlos didn't want my help. Like Sammy and Nicky
and Rafe, I'd already done whatever it was I was supposed to do—Seth
was the only person Carlos wanted now. Which I guess made sense, seeing
how the instant he turned that camera of his on, Seth was Carlos's eyes.

The collective was this run-down building that a bunch of movie
people used, though that spring there was only one other person in
there regularly, this woman named Jean who'd made a documentary
movie about some banker who turned into a drug addict and then got
better, and now he was teaching deaf children how to sing in some
school in Harlem. It was a pretty okay movie—she let me watch parts
of it—only the kids couldn't sing worth shit, being deaf and everything.
She got a little huffy on that score and said it was beside the point what
they sounded like. It was doing it that counted. Still, I thought that was
pretty neat. Carlos said she'd been making that movie for ten years, and
he didn't think she was ever going to finish it. I think Carlos liked her
a lot—he was always very nice to her at the collective and all—but he
thought she was pretty hopeless. All Seth ever said about her was, she'd
picked the perfect subject.

I sort of liked watching the little bits of film Carlos had finished
editing. They'd be hanging in long strips from a clothesline. I'd take
them down and spool them through the viewfinder for ten or twenty
seconds of movie action till it ran out.

It was something to see myself there—me and Sammy carrying on, riffing with each other out on the streets and so cold the breath coming out of our mouths was like talk-bubbles in a comic strip. What it made me remember was something I hadn't thought about in years. When I was a kid—I think I might've mentioned this—we didn't have a TV set. So what I'd do instead was, I'd go through the funny papers on Sunday, the color ones, and cut out the ones I liked—Dick Tracy, Snuffy Smith, Li'l Abner. I'd paste them onto a long strip of paper so you could watch them like a movie. I even made a little box, with two wooden sewing spools you could thread the strip of paper onto, and a window cut in the box that was like a screen. When you rolled the spools, each frame of the comic strip moved by the window. You could stop at each one and look at it, and then go on to the next.

I must've been ten when I made that, and I was pretty proud of it. I made a show of watching my movies, and how interesting it was, but I never could get anybody else to pay attention. I'd set up special show-ings, march around the house announcing to everybody, come see Dick Tracy at the movies, three o'clock. And I'd set everything up on the kitchen table ready to go, but when three o'clock came, nobody was there. Not even Ted. Maybe my mom and dad weren't crazy about me pointing out how we didn't have a TV. But Ted should've liked it. It was for him as much as for me.

It was odd to think back on all that, and now here I was making real movies. I'd sit on a stool and watch Seth and Carlos putting the different clips together—which, to tell the truth, was about as inter-esting as watching somebody sew. Carlos knew that. "Go on," he'd say. "Get outta here. You're driving me crazy."

"I'm just watching," I told him.

"You are radiating boredom so intensely, if there were plants in here they'd fall over and wilt," he said. "Now scram. Go bother Verbena."

Verbena lived in this apartment about five blocks from the collective.

"What'm I supposed to do with Verbena?" I asked.

"I don't care," Carlos told me. "Anything. Just don't let her sit on top of you."

"You're disgusting," I said. And with that, and a laugh, he swatted me out the door. Actually I was glad to go. I loved being in that room with Carlos, watching him do his work, seeing how careful he was when so much of the time it could seem like he was the most careless person you ever met. It was one more of those things that filled in the blanks for me. At the same time, I could only sit there and watch him edit for so long—after that, I was happy to know there was work going on, and one day there'd be a movie out of it.

Verbena's apartment was this dingy place filled with pot plants—some scheme she had going with Seth to grow plants indoors and sell them. She had the windows blacked out, and tin foil and mirrors all over the walls, and bright lights set up to shine on the plants. Carlos said she'd figured out some way to steal electricity from Con Ed—they had no idea her apartment was even hooked up to them. There must've been twenty-five plants in there, so many they filled up almost the whole room. Actually it was sort of great-looking, like being in some jungle. And very warm and humid.

Verbena was sitting at a table listening to the radio, some preacher raving on about the rapture—how when it came, those that were saved would just disappear. A man driving a bus, or a pilot flying a plane. The preacher was laughing this big belly laugh to think of all the plane crashes and bus crashes the rapture was going to cause.

"How can you listen to shit like that?" I asked her.

"I like the melody," she said. She held this painted fan and was fanning herself and sweating all over. She had on these huge gray sweatpants and a bra—her breasts looked the size of New Jersey at least.

I hadn't been to visit her in about a month. Whenever I saw her, she always pretended not to remember my name. At least I thought it was pretend.

"Tony," I told her.

"Shy girl," she said, "I seen so many white boys in my time—they all look alike. But I'm happy to see you. I was itching to get out of here."

"Where're we going?" I asked her. The idea of being seen around Brooklyn with Verbena wasn't totally my thing.

"To the roof," she said. "If we can make it that far. The elevator's broke. But we can rest on the landings."

"What's on the roof?"

She smiled, that big gap-toothed smile of hers that was the ugliest thing, you had to love it. She wrapped herself in this flowery robe and we were ready to go.

It took forever, what with stopping every flight up: but in that building of hers, even that could be interesting. On one floor, this little black kid came tearing toward us down the hall. Then all of a sudden he just fell down. He didn't make a noise, he just fell down, and when I looked I saw why he fell down—he was wearing two left shoes, both of them about five sizes too big.

Verbena leaned with her weight against the metal door at the top of the stairs—it gave way into bright sunlight, and there we were on the roof. Somebody else was already up there.

"T.J." Verbena called to this tall black guy—really tall, like seven feet. He was standing in front of a tar-papered shed. On the roof of the shed were about a hundred pigeons, all standing there crowded together.

T.J. was cooing at them and they were cooing back, all of them cocking their heads in his direction while he talked pigeon talk to them.

"Hey," he said to us. "Ya'll just in time to see us slap off."

"What?" I said.

He picked up this bamboo pole with a red flag on the end of it and waved it through the air. It was like this explosion—a hundred pigeons all flying up in the air at the same time.

It was a slap off all right.

T.J. jumped up on the roof of the shed where the pigeons had been and started making these sharp cries, not the soft ones he was doing before—and waving his flag around in these 8 shapes. The birds went up and up—it was great—and then they started hooking around in 8s just like T.J. was making with his flag. I never saw anything like it. They went up as far as you could see, almost till they were out of sight. There was a helicopter flying over, and they were up even farther than it. T.J. stopped waving his flag and jumped down off the shed.

It must've been some kind of signal. All those birds came spiraling back down, like water funneling down a drain, like that shed was the drain and they were funneling right to it. In half a minute it was like they'd never been up there in the sky at all—they came in through a trap door and were sitting there peacefully in the shed, cooing away.

My heart was beating like no tomorrow.

"That was a fine spay," T.J. said. "Don't you think so?"

"It was a fine one," Verbena told him.

"That was great," I said. "That was the most amazing thing."

"That was nothing. You just wait. King Kong's up today."

"King Kong?"

"This guy who lofts birds about five blocks over. He's got such a huge flock, I call him King Kong. But I'm ripping away at him. I got six rippers this past month."

"I'm totally in the dark," I said.

I thought to myself, what am I doing standing here on this roof in the middle of New York with two black people and a hundred pigeons? What would Ted say to that, or anybody back in Owen? Not that I was ashamed to be hanging around with black people—I just couldn't get used to the thought of it. I told myself these black people weren't like the ones in Owen. Though maybe they were. I'd never hung around with any of the blacks in Owen.

Just then T.J. gave a shout, and Verbena did too—I looked to see what it was, but couldn't see a thing.

"Over there," Verbena pointed.

"What?" I shouted. The two of them were so excited, I didn't want to miss whatever it was I was supposed to be seeing. With a big whoosh, all T.J.'s pigeons lifted off the roof into the sky. The instant they did that, I saw what it was Verbena was pointing to. From a roof way off in the distance, this other flock of pigeons had taken off. They went rising up in a black cloud, changing shape all the time like a soap bubble does when it floats, sometimes drawing way out and other times shrinking close back into itself.

"King Kong," T.J. said. The two flocks of pigeons moved closer together in the air, till they were on top of one another and then they were all swirling together like one big flock. T.J. was busy throwing corn down on the roof. The two pigeon flocks swung in and out of each other, sometimes two flocks, sometimes only one. We watched them like that for a while, making patterns in the sky, changing direction quick as a finger-snap, whipping back and forth—the way you see sheets of rain whip across a lake in a windstorm. Then T.J. started swinging the corn bucket over his head and making pigeon noises like I'd seen him doing earlier.

The flock that'd been one flock for several minutes all of a sudden was two again, with one of the flocks funneling back down to the roof where we were. They hit the roof of the shed like thunder and then immediately jumped down onto the roof where we were and started pecking away at that corn. All except one bird that stayed on the roof.

"Shh," T.J. said when I was opening my mouth to say something. "Just watch."

We all moved away, behind a roof divider. They were watching the one single bird that was on the roof of the shed. "It's King Kong's all right," T.J. was telling Verbena.

"How can you tell?" I whispered.

"Got a red band on his foot there. See my birds? They got yellow bands. Oh, he's a beauty, isn't he? What I call a blue splash—see all that blue color in his neck." As far as I could see, it was just a pigeon.

"There're kinds of pigeons?" I asked.

"Lots," he said. "You can tell by the colors. There's blue splashes, dun nuns, beardeds, lots of kinds."

The pigeons on the ground had filled up on corn, and now they were going one by one through the trap door into their cage. Once T.J.'d said that about the colors, I could see how each one was different. Their necks were all shimmering in the sun—if they hadn't been pigeons they'd have been gorgeous.

I'd never thought to look at pigeons before.

All the birds were inside but the one on the roof. It was looking around but it wouldn't come down.

"Shy bird," Verbena said. "Maybe it's thirsty."

T.J. went over and got the water pan and stuck it right inside the trap door. All the time he was talking pigeon talk to that bird, trying to coax it, but the bird wouldn't talk back. It just kept eyeing him, like it was the smart one and T.J. the odd bird here.

For ten minutes T.J. kept up his bird talk. Finally the bird hopped down. Looking around all the time, he waddled over to where the water was. He looked around, one last time, and stuck his head in to get the water—the instant he did that, *wham,* T.J. had the trap door shut and the new bird was inside.

"You got him," I said.

Meanwhile T.J. had let himself into the coop and was looking around at his birds. "King Kong's done ripped three of mine," he said. "Damn, that nigger's too good."

I understood that the game had been to steal each other's birds away.

"Oh well," T.J. was saying. "This time last year I couldn't rip a single one of his birds."

"You'll be T.J. Ripper," Verbena told him, "before you know it."

T.J. mucked around with his birds some more, separating them out into cages that were inside the coop. When he was done, we went back downstairs to Verbena's apartment.

"How do you stand it in here, girl?" he asked. The instant we walked in he took off his shirt, and I did the same. After the cold air of the roof, it was stifling.

She opened a bottle of Colt .45 for each of us—those big bottles we used to call nigger bottles back in Owen.

"I was raised in Alabama," Verbena said. "I'm used to heat. Got it in my bones. It's these winters that kill me. Shy girl, you want to roll some of that weed, you go on ahead."

"I don't smoke," I told her, "but thanks."

"That's good," T.J. said. "Smoking that stuff'll kill you. There's so much shit you can put inside your body." He shook his head.

"Don't listen to him," Verbena told me. "He's a old dope hog talking."

"Used to be," T.J. said. "Used to be. But I quit. I quit putting any of that stuff inside me."

"Quit shooting dope and took up flying pigeons," Verbena said. She was walking around the room with her bottle of Colt .45 in one hand and a plant mister in the other. She was giving those pot plants a good dousing.

"Tony here," she said to T.J., "has gone and made a movie with Carlos."

"That so?" T.J. studied me. "Carlos ain't too much in my book."

"Well, he is in mine," I said.

T.J. kept studying me. He nodded his head. "Yeah," he said, "I bet he is. Keep your eyes open is all I can say." And he squinted at me, like he had trouble seeing who I was.

"I could tell you something about Carlos," I said, "that'd totally change your mind."

"So go on ahead, mystery man," said Verbena. "Tell us something about Carlos that'll change our mind." I could see she thought it was going to be amusing to hear something about Carlos she'd never heard before. She took a swig and went on misting the plants.

For a second I was blank—it'd seemed so totally clear, what I had to say about Carlos. How it had to do with everything—the pigeons on the roof, and T.J. and Verbena. Everything that'd gone on in the last hour. It was like I'd seen it out of the corner of my eye for a second, and now it was gone.

But then I saw it again, and I launched in. "I had this friend Wallace," I said, "back in Kentucky. He'd come round, we'd spend time together. Down the road from where I lived there was this old black man. He lived in a total shack. Heaps of garbage out in front of it—he used to pay people to dump their trash in his yard and then he'd go through it, find what he could use or sell. It always pissed Wallace off when we drove by, to see all that trash out there."

T.J. was still studying me, and Verbena'd stopped misting the plants and was just standing there. But all the water drops on the leaves were catching the light—they were glistening.

"I have to tell this story," I said. "If I don't tell it, then I can't be here. I mean, right here in this room. Up on your roof. Whatever. So let me tell it, okay?"

They were both looking very serious.

"That old black man had this mangy hunting dog he used to keep tied up in the yard. Thin—you could see its ribs sticking out. Well, one day Wallace and me were doing some serious drinking—we'd gone out hunting, but we didn't bag anything. It was drizzling all morning, and we'd been drinking to keep warm out in the woods.

"Wallace was this kind of crazy guy, but I liked him. We were driving by that old man's shack, and the dog was out front where he usually was. I don't know why, but Wallace stopped the pickup there in the front yard, and the dog started barking like it always did when anybody came around. The dog started barking and Wallace started yelling Shut up! at the dog. It was very funny. The two of them going at it, Wallace yelling Shut up! over and over, and the dog keeping up with its bark. I don't know why—it made Wallace madder and madder, the more he yelled and the more the dog barked. I was laughing, I thought it was so funny. Then Wallace said, I'm gonna get that damn dog. He took one of the rifles off the rack, yelling Nigger dog, nigger dog, while he was aiming out the truck cab. I thought it was this great joke, and I was laughing and laughing till all at once he pulled the trigger.

"That dog was in the middle of a bark—it was like you just sliced through its bark with a knife. But it wasn't dead. It was lying on the ground making this whine that was terrible to hear. Nigger dog, Wallace kept yelling, but now he was the one who was laughing, this crazy scared laugh that was like hiccups. I think he was totally freaked at what he'd gone and done.

"He threw the truck in gear and we drove forward, right over that dog. You could feel the truck go over its body, like hitting a speed bump."

T.J. and Verbena were looking at me. They didn't say anything.

"I had to tell you that story," I told them. Sweat was pouring off me, these cold drops on my ribs. It was seeing those birds on the roof—how they broke loose into the air like they did. How they came funneling back home to T.J.

"You were going to tell us some story about Carlos," Verbena reminded me.

"I know," I said. "I just did. Carlos lifted me out of all that."

I WANT TO TALK MORE ABOUT SETH, HOW HE AND
Carlos would sit up for hours arguing about movies and other direc-
tors and politics and the best way to shoot a particular scene. They never
seemed to agree about anything, which was maybe why they worked
so well together. At the collective where they edited the movies, they'd
both be hard at work, concentrating on their little bits of film and
talking nonstop at each other, arguing with Seth yelling all the time
at whatever Carlos would have to say—and neither one of them ever
looking up from their work. They'd just yell at each other and keep on
concentrating on sewing their little pieces of film together.

I think Seth's secret was that he was angry all the time—this scary
powerful anger that kept him going, and that would've ripped him apart,
if it hadn't been for the dope that kept it just barely under control. For
anger to rise to the surface over all the dope he smoked to keep it down—
that was some anger that had to come from deep down and be incredibly
powerful. I always thought of Seth as having this grizzly bear locked
inside his body. Sometimes I'd think how that big angry bear was trying
to bust out of Seth's human skin to get at the world with its teeth and
claws. And if you looked at him the right way when he was angry about
something, you could swear you saw that bear coming right on through.

Lots of things made him angry—more things than I even knew were
going on out there. Things in foreign countries like El Salvador and
Nicaragua I'd never thought about before, fundamentalist preachers,
the mayor of New York, fishermen from Japan and Iceland who were
killing whales, a bunch of people called the Kurds who lived in Turkey
and were getting ripped to shreds by the army.

When he got going, Seth could be as talkative about what was going on in the world in 1980 as Sammy was about the ghetto in Lodz and everything that happened back then. The only difference was, Sammy'd come to terms with a lot of terrible stuff a long time ago, and that freed him up in some way. But Seth was caught right in the middle of it. He hadn't seen his way clear of anything yet, and it all hurt him a lot. Every day, it hurt him, and he was angry about it.

I guess I'd also have to say, lots of times he was angry with me too. I could never do things right for him—I was this snot-nosed kid Carlos had picked up somewhere, and everybody in The Company knew they were going to have to put up with me until Carlos came to his senses and dumped me. On good days, I think Seth thought about me about as much as he'd have thought about some lamppost Carlos had told him to train his camera on.

But then every once in a while this other thing happened between us. Some kind of tenderness, I guess is what it was—the kind only somebody who gets really angry can give you. The kind Carlos knew about too, in a different way. It never lasted very long, a few seconds or a minute, and after it happened I was never completely sure it'd happened—but it happened enough that, looking back on it now, I remember it, and I remember how it was important to me at the time.

The first real talk I ever had with Seth was one day in the collective. Carlos had gone out to do some errand, and the lady who was doing the movie about the deaf children singing wasn't there—she got depressed for weeks on end and couldn't work—so it was just the two of us. Seth was handling a strip of film, and he put it in the viewer.

"Here," he said. "Look at this."

I looked through the viewfinder and there I was, pretending I was dancing with this old floor lamp—I'd found it in a pile of junk somebody'd set out on the sidewalk, and I was just spoofing around. We were in between scenes. I never knew Seth had caught me with that. I'd been doing it just for myself.

"Recognize it?" he asked.

"I didn't know you were filming me. You sneak."

"What do you think of it?"

I shrugged. "Well, if you can't get a date," I said.

"Look at it again," he told me, so I played it back through.

"Well?" he asked.

"Well," I said.

"Don't you see, it's fabulous?"

"It is?"

He took the film out of the viewer and held it up. "It's terrific. And you know what? It's only you and me who's seen it. Carlos hasn't seen it. He'd give anything for a scene like this. It's exactly what he needs—and he has it and doesn't even know it yet."

There was white dandruff all down the front of the black turtleneck sweater he was wearing—if you ask me, I think he wore black as some kind of defiance.

"We could burn this," he said. "There's no record. Nobody'll ever know you made poetry by dancing with a floor lamp on Avenue C one winter morning in nineteen eighty. That could all just disappear. What do you say?"

"What're you getting at?" I didn't exactly follow Seth a lot of the time.

It was funny—I hadn't even remembered that little dance. If he hadn't got it on film, it would already be gone.

"Keep it," I said.

"Oh—definitely keep it," said Seth. "Definitely. And even you didn't know what you were doing, did you?"

"I never do," I told him.

"Let me tell you a secret," he said. "Nobody ever does. But the camera knows. That's the real secret—the camera always knows. That's why we invented the camera—so it would know exactly what we were up to, even if we didn't. Not just the main moments, the big picture—but the in-betweens. All that little stuff. Don't ever forget that, especially when you're around me."

It was one of those times when Seth would launch into something, and before I knew it he'd be sounding angry, and I didn't know why. I was just baffled.

I think Seth kept wanting to have completely dropped out of the world—he wanted not to care about anything except making movies, but the trouble was, he couldn't. He'd been through too many things, done too much stuff—civil rights stuff and antiwar stuff all through the sixties—and he kept getting angry about all those things. I think he smoked all his dope to keep things from making him angry but it didn't work. Before you knew it something else would come along and he'd start to care about that too—he'd get angry about all the ways it got fucked up. And I guess that caring somehow, now and then, included me. I think Seth made up his mind at some point—it was some way of staying alive with all his anger—that the one thing he had to do with his life was be Carlos's eyes. Why he ever decided that I don't know, but then why did any of us ever decide to do whatever it was we decided to do with Carlos? I don't have any answer. I've spent an awful lot of time thinking about it, and I just don't have any answer. I mean—why Seth or Sammy or Netta or Verbena didn't get the hell out any number of times before they actually did, I just don't know. I guess it's what made Carlos some kind of genius: keeping all those people together, and keeping them together through the kind of weird stuff they were doing, especially toward the end, when anybody else would've lost them in a week.

Part of the reason must've been that Carlos's brain was just always working. You couldn't tear yourself away from that. I remember lots of nights sitting around with him and Seth and Sammy and Verbena, where we'd spent all day working on a movie and everybody was exhausted. But Carlos wouldn't be content to relax; he'd be going on about all the other movies he wanted to make in the future, talking nonstop for hours with everybody else mostly wowed into just listening.

Lots of his movie ideas came from driving around the country in that van of his—which at a certain time in his life was one of his favorite things to do, though now he was too busy ever to leave New York with the one notable exception of that trip that took him through Owen, Kentucky—I always figured, no wonder he didn't travel much after that. Just too risky.

I always tried to imagine the Carlos back then, but I didn't meet with too much success. I only had the stories he told.

"There's this house in Nebraska," he told us, "near the Platte River—ordinary old farmhouse, but there's a secret. You go down into the cellar, only it's not a cellar, it's a cave—the house is built over a cave. You go down these steps that are carved into the side of the rock, maybe two hundred feet down you go, and then the steps disappear into water. Just at the water line, though, there's a cave room—they call it the blue room, because when you turn off the lantern or flashlight or whatever light you've taken down there with you, the room gives off this faint blue glow.

"The water level's always steady, though it must've been lower when the house was built, because if you look down in the water you can see the steps continuing down out of sight. And once, in the nineteen thirties, according to the old woman who lives in the house, the water started to rise. For no reason. It flooded the blue room and came all the way up the stairs—it just kept coming, rising about five feet a day, till they thought it was going to come right up to the cellar door. But it stopped just below it, and stayed there for a couple of days, and then receded again. No explanation.

"I want to make a movie about that old woman living alone in that house with that cellar that goes down who knows how deep.

"Then there's a man I met once, in Wyoming—it must've been nineteen sixty-seven. He claimed he had a petrified woman in his possession. I didn't believe it, but he took me there: I saw it, I touched it. It was a stone woman all right. He found it in the nineteen twenties up in the mountains. An Indian woman, hundreds of years old, calcified into solid stone. He wanted to sell it to me for five hundred dollars but who has five hundred dollars? I wonder—is he still alive? I can't even remember where he lives—it was this little tin shack up a steep dirt road. I remember, he had the petrified woman laid out on a long low table. There's a movie there—he's in love with the woman: living out there alone has put the zap on him. He tends to her, he starts to believe all sorts of crazy things."

I think he must've had a million movies all going at once inside him, and he was always incredibly frustrated because actually to make just a single one took so much time and energy that it meant a hundred other movies were never going to happen. So if you look at it one way, most of his best films never got made. They were all up there spinning around in his brain, and maybe he got to see them but the rest of us never did. We only heard him tell us what they looked like to him.

Actually shooting the movie was always the fastest part of the process for Carlos—he shot movies the way some hungry person'll gulp down a meal. It was getting the money together for the movie and then after it was shot editing it down that drove him crazy, because by the time he was editing he already had the whole thing in his head and so he was completely impatient to go on to the next movie. I guess if he could've had his way he'd've had the camera going twenty-four hours a day his whole life and somehow the money would be there and the editing would just happen and he could make movies as fast as he thought them up.

I N WARM WEATHER, CARLOS AND I'D CLIMB UP ONTO
the roof of our building. It was all tarry in most places, but there was
one place where somebody'd piled some tarps, so we'd sit up there and
drink cocktails and watch these sunsets that were like some movie in
technicolor—a really slow plot but one you could watch from beginning to end. Carlos said the color was because of pollution. "It's beautiful and it's killing us," he said. "What do you say to that?" Which I
guess is more or less what he thought about everything. He'd rigged up
a shower out on the fire escape in back, and we used to take showers out
there in full view of the other buildings. Since most of them were abandoned or burned out, it didn't matter. But it was great taking showers
outside, the water falling through the metal grate under your feet and
splashing down three stories to the ground. The only creepy thing was
that there were these two guys who used to sit out on their fire escape
about a hundred yards over from ours across this lot with broken bottles
and piles of bricks and these weedy trees growing up everywhere, and
they'd drink beer and watch us.

The first time Carlos kneeled down in front of me under the spray
from the shower head to blow me, I told him no way, those guys were
watching and you could tell they were all excited by what was going on.
But Carlos said they were too far away to see who we were, which was
true, and anyway they were enjoying it, and why shouldn't they? Which
was also true, I guess, and I have to admit I sort of got into it, letting
Carlos blow me while I was standing there with my hair hanging down
in my face and water running all over me and looking over at those
guys drinking beers and watching us. I thought, looking down at my

dick sliding in and out of Carlos's mouth, This is totally crazy, this is the craziest thing I've done yet. But then when I came, I remembered I was so into the feeling of it that I let out this Tarzan yell you could hear half a mile away. When those guys heard that, they started yelling, "Bravo," and applauding like we were some kind of show, which I guess we were, and yelling "Encore, encore." Then one of them yelled to Carlos, "Fuck him, fuck him!" and the other one did too, like a chant with their hands clapping, and before I knew it Carlos had me bent over and was fucking me like they told him to.

That was the summer of 1980, and though I didn't know it then, I guess it was a pretty wild summer for everybody; and nobody knew it at the time, but it was one of the last wild summers there was.

If you ask me, Did it bother me to get fucked with those two guys watching me and jerking off on that other fire escape? The answer's no. In fact, I could get pretty excited thinking about somebody wanting to jerk off while they were watching me. It made me feel like I did under those power lines that very first time, when I felt hooked into a million volts of power. And that was exactly what Carlos said when we finished and he was drying me off with a towel. "Powerful, powerful," he kept saying, like he'd felt the exact same thing.

I wondered why that could be—why fucking in full view of a couple of strangers, instead of making me feel clammy and squirmy, made me feel powerful instead.

I guess we must've had sex out there, with those two guys watching, about fifteen times that summer, and though they'd call out for us to come over to their apartment so we could all get stoned and get down, we never did.

In the afternoons, lots of times, we'd go up to Central Park and play soccer on this great big open meadow with these tall buildings rising up where Carlos said only people who were incredibly rich lived. I'd never been much on soccer or anything else really, but that summer I got to really like it. I got to really like running around and sweating and being out of breath. It didn't feel so great when you were doing it, but afterward you felt peaceful and sort of bright inside, and that was great. Carlos, it turned out, was really big on soccer—he played when he was a kid, and in fact all his life, and he was very good at it.

There was always this bunch of guys playing and you could just sort of join in with them—lots of Puerto Ricans especially. I'd never been with Puerto Ricans before. Carlos was friendly with them; it seemed like he knew a lot of them and they were always slapping him on the back or catching his arm to talk to him in between plays or while we were resting.

I used to imagine those rich people standing on their balconies and looking down at us playing soccer in that meadow in Central Park, and wishing they were down there with us instead of up there on their balconies, and I'd look up there and try to imagine how they were living their lives and stuff up there but I couldn't really. It was like they were living in some totally different city than we were. Which was fine—we probably both liked it better that way.

"So I didn't know you were such a soccer freak," I told Carlos one night after we'd been going up to the park for a few days. We were sitting up on the roof of the apartment watching the sunset.

He sort of laughed. "There's lots you don't know about me."

Which was definitely true—sometimes it made me dizzy to think about all the things I didn't know about him.

"So maybe it's time to change that," I said.

He just looked at me.

"It was a suggestion," I said.

"No, you're right," he told me. "I may be a criminal, but I got nothing to hide." Sometimes he went into this fake country drawl, which maybe was to imitate the way I talked or maybe not.

"Come on, you're not a criminal."

"You never know," he said.

"You wish," I told him.

"Yeah, I wish."

"So come on, give me the dope," I insisted.

"The dope?" He smiled, the way you smile when you think about things you haven't thought about in a long time. "Maybe I'm not so different from you," he said. "Did you ever think about that?"

I hadn't, because with a name like Carlos Reichart I figured there was no telling what his story was. I mean, where he came from and grew up and everything.

"Would you believe Ann Arbor, Michigan?" he said when I asked where.

I'd never heard of Ann Arbor, Michigan, but I told him, "I'll believe anything. You know that. Go ahead, make up something interesting. You know I'm just some teenage kid who gets bored."

"As far as I can tell," Carlos told me seriously, "you've got this very great capacity not to be bored."

It was one of those things he'd say every once in a while, like he wanted to throw me off-guard. And it always felt like that first swig of whisky, the way it lights you up from the inside out.

"But I really was born in Ann Arbor," he went on. "My father worked at the university. You could say he was a part-time janitor and a full-time alcoholic. It was terrible—back in the thirties he was a labor organizer, a real socialist with causes and ideals, but then after the war he just lost it. He got completely disillusioned with Russia and communism, and at the same time he was disgusted with things in this country, how everything seemed to be shutting down around him." We had this bottle of scotch we were drinking from, and I handed it to him to take a swig. I guess he was in some kind of mood that night, because after he took a swig he started to talk some more.

"My father drank himself to death," Carlos said. "I remember coming home from school in the afternoons and he'd be sitting on the front porch with a half-gallon bottle of the cheapest gin you could buy. He'd get up in the morning and drink till he passed out, which was usually around three in the afternoon. On really bad days he'd be sitting there with a shotgun across his lap and the bottle at his feet, because on those days he'd get up in the morning and announce very calmly to my mother and my brother and me at the breakfast table, I'm going to kill myself today. Then my brother, Adrian, and I'd go off to school, and we wouldn't know whether when we came home he'd have shot himself or our mother or both.

"So we were always worried, and I remember one day, I must've been in the fourth or fifth grade, there was this thunderstorm in the spring, tornado weather, and I suddenly got so nervous, because I had this incredibly vivid feeling my father was going to shoot my mother and then himself and we were going to come home after the storm and find them there. I couldn't keep still—I kept jumping up from my desk and pacing around the room. I'd walk over to the windows and watch the rain and how the wind was driving the rain down the street

in sheets, and the teacher kept telling me to sit down and I would, but only for a minute, then I'd get this uncontrollable anxiety and I'd jump up again.

"But he didn't shoot himself that day. In fact, he never ended up shooting anybody—he died of drink. He had what the doctors called a weeping liver, from all the gin. One day his whole system just collapsed.

"My mother found him dead in that chair on the front porch. It's odd—for some reason he didn't have his shotgun with him that day. I guess that morning he was feeling hopeful.

"It was very difficult for my mother, because she'd been afraid of him but she also loved him—though she'd spent ten years wishing he'd go on and die if that's what he wanted, because he made life so impossible for her. She cleaned houses to support us—the houses of her friends who felt sorry for her and gave her money. These were the friends she had back when she first got married and my father was sober and held a regular job and they were just like everybody else on the block.

"They broke my father," Carlos said. "They." He laughed. "Something broke him. The world we live in, I guess. What do the Irish say? The world'll break your heart. My mother was Irish. Is Irish, I should say. Hey, did I ever tell you how I got my name? Carlos."

"No, you never did," I said

Carlos was getting drunk. There was also this amazing sunset going on, though by now it was pretty much over—but earlier there were these big rays of sun shooting out from behind the clouds, only it wasn't so much rays of sun as these sort of blue-gray shadow rays, and if you were in the right mood that sunset was just plain scary it was so out of control.

"Not exactly what you'd expect some socialist Jew to name his kid, right? Carlos." He said it the way I guess the Spanish say it, rolling it around in his mouth and then spitting it out like he was gargling. "But it was the Spanish Civil War," he went on, "and my father was following it in the papers, magazines, any way he could—I think if he wasn't married he'd have been in the Abraham Lincoln Brigade in an instant. But he couldn't be, though he had some friends from Detroit and New York who were, and they all got killed."

He stopped and it seemed like he was thinking of something. About everybody getting killed, maybe.

"You were telling me who you got named for," I reminded him.

"Oh, right," he said. "Carlos Huesca was a communist organizer in Barcelona, my father had met him once when he was in America attending some international labor meeting, and when Franco's men killed him in '36, it made a great impression on my father. So when I came along a couple weeks later he named me Carlos. I'm proud of my name. All my movies are made for Carlos Huesca, if you want to know the truth. That's not completely true of course, but it's partly true. See, I'm carrying around certain obligations on this planet."

The sunset was pretty much completely gone now—it was in tatters like it ripped itself apart, it couldn't stand being so gorgeous. If we'd packed our scotch back downstairs and gone to bed right then, I'd have woken up next morning amazed at how much I'd gotten out of Carlos. But it turned out he wasn't through, he was only revving up. He chugged some scotch and wiped his mouth and sort of leaned back so his head was resting in my lap—I was sitting crosslegged on a beach towel we kept on the roof since it was tarry and sort of gross up there.

"I never told you about Adrian either, did I?" He had his eyes closed, and I looked down at his face, which from all the whisky looked peaceful.

"That was your brother," I said. I'd stopped drinking a while ago— a sip every now and then, but it was basically Carlos who was doing all the drinking.

"Did I tell you about Adrian?" He opened his eyes and looked at me.

"You mentioned he was your brother," I said. "That's all."

"When did I mention that?" He closed his eyes again, and I noticed how he had a sort of mole or freckle of some kind in the corner of his left eyelid I never noticed before, which you'd've thought I would've.

"Earlier," I told him.

"Mmm," he said, which I couldn't tell what that meant. He took a deep breath and said, "Adrian was two years older than me. When I was a kid I thought Adrian was the greatest."

"Where's he now?"

Carlos's eyes were still closed.

"He's dead," he said.

I didn't say anything because I didn't think there was anything to say. This was my favorite part of sunset, after it was gone and the breeze

from the river picked up a little and started to cool off the city. Carlos's brother was dead, but I was happy right there at that moment. Happy and content.

I guess Carlos didn't mind me not saying anything—he'd decided to talk about it whether I said anything or not. Sometimes in your life you feel completely close to somebody else, maybe three or four times in your life you really feel that way. It doesn't have to be when you're having sex with them. It's probably better when it's not, because then you know it's not the sex but something else that's a lot harder to put your finger on. But it was there right then, with Carlos's head in my lap and the sky going dark around us and lights coming on in all the buildings—this feeling of complete closeness, like whatever games we were usually playing with each other were just games—another kind of soccer you played with your life instead of a ball, but that's the only difference. And none of that mattered like this mattered. Which was just sitting there on that grungy roof together and talking in peaceful voices about whatever'd happened to us that we couldn't change even if we wanted to.

"He was the first person I ever had sex with," Carlos said. He opened his eyes and looked up at me, I guess to see what my reaction was.

"See?" he said. "I do have some surprises left."

I never doubted that for a minute. But still I didn't say anything. It didn't seem like I had to. I liked the way Carlos's head was resting there in my lap.

He sort of laughed. "I used to go crawl in bed with him," he said. "I guess it started when I was about eight or so, and our father took a real turn for the worse. About the time he started stationing himself on the front porch with the shotgun. And here's something interesting. Everybody knew about it, the local cop and the neighbors, but nobody did anything. It was out of some kind of respect for him, I think. Nobody blamed him for what happened to him."

"Talk about Adrian," I told him, because that was what I wanted to hear about.

"Well," Carlos said, "sometimes I'd wake up at night and hear my father walking around the house. He was so drunk he could hardly stand up, and so what you'd hear would be his shoulders rubbing against the wall when he walked down the hall, and then a thump when he'd lurch against the wall on the other side. He'd just walk around down-stairs like he was looking for something he couldn't find. He never came upstairs where we were, but I was always afraid he would."

Carlos drank some more whisky, though most if it dribbled down his chin and onto my pants, which were these thin billowy cotton things Carlos'd bought me a couple weeks before—he called them harem pants, and I wore them all the time around the apartment because they were cool. Carlos was so drunk he didn't know he was spilling whisky on my favorite pants, so I took the bottle from him and put it on the roof beside us.

I think what he really wanted to do was pass out—but I wanted to hear about him and his brother having sex.

"So how'd you have sex with your brother?" I asked, prodding him awake.

He looked groggy, like a little kid who's just waked up from a nap.

"Oh, sex," he said. "You know, Adrian was a very talented painter. When he was sixteen he started painting, and he went after it with a vengeance. Beautiful stuff, incomprehensible mystical stuff. I used to sit and watch him paint, and smell the turpentine, which was enough to give me a hard-on sometimes. He was the talented one. I'm just some tenth-rate jerk-off amateur who's trying to make up for him not being here anymore."

He reached for the scotch bottle but it was out of reach.

"I'm so fucking drunk," he said. "Are you fucking drunk?"

"Yeah," I said, even though I wasn't very drunk at all. I ran my fingers through his hair. I touched the tip of his nose with a fingertip.

"Did you ever have a brother?" he asked me. He was slurring his words a lot, but I thought his face was really great-looking in the dim light like that.

I told him about Ted.

"Ted," he said. "I'd like to meet him."

"I'll kill you if you touch my brother."

"I know where he lives," Carlos said. "I could go find him."

"I'll kill you," I teased, and bent down and kissed him—which is an odd angle to try to kiss somebody from, so after a minute I stopped and just put a couple of my fingers in his mouth. He sort of sucked on those a little, which was sexy, and I felt around his teeth and gums but after about a minute I realized he was totally passed out. He was even snoring.

To get on the roof you had to climb up this little ladder, which meant there was no way I was going to get him down tonight. So I got some blankets and stuff and we slept up there, which was cooler than the apartment anyway since it was the middle of August.

I never did find out any more about his brother, Adrian, how he died or whether they really had sex, or even if any of what he said was true in the first place. It'd be just like Carlos to make all that up, though for some reason I don't think he did. Whenever I'd mention it later he'd just say that whole evening never happened, it was all just a bad dream he barely recovered from—which if you'd seen the way he looked the next day, you'd agree.

He was so hung over he could hardly move, and I spent the whole day playing nurse, helping him find the black headband he put on when he had bad hangovers because he thought pressure on the brain would cure it, and when that didn't work getting him a cold washrag and laying it across his eyes the way my mom used to do when she was hung over, which didn't work either, and then going out to buy orange juice and soda and a bottle of aspirin he took about half of that afternoon. For some reason I was totally fine, like the way a tornado hits one house full on and the next one it skips right over for no reason you can figure out.

I 'VE BEEN WONDERING. IT'S ABOUT THREE WEEKS now since I started writing on all this: what's going to happen when I get through? The other day I thought, Tony, maybe this isn't what you should be doing. You let Earl put this thought in your head, but maybe it's not right. Because what I thought was—when I get through writing all this, I'm going to be used up. There's not going to be anything left of me.

Maybe I should leave things out. Then when I'm through, I'll still have some things left, parts of my life I never told about.

Like about the time I was married.

I've got my surprises too.

I'm very depressed tonight. Now that I've mentioned Monica, I guess I'm starting to use up even that part of my life. Maybe I want to use it all up. Have it all over and done with. Maybe that's why I'm writing everything down—so it really will be all used up.

That's what happens, isn't it? You start off full and then life just uses you up, it empties you out and there's nothing left. You've seen people like that—walking around, sitting on benches, sleeping on heating grates in the winter to try to keep warm through the night because they're all empty inside. I used to see them on the front porches back in Owen, or sitting in courthouse square on hot afternoons in summertime. It's what happens. It's like those wasps that came into my room here. Those leftover wasps from the summer, the way they swung around in here on those long lazy leftover flights of theirs. One morning they were all dead. Just like that. I must've picked about twelve of them up off the floor and flushed them down the toilet. I guess a cold snap or something hit the room in the middle of the night and that was that. Or maybe it was just their time. But I could tell from the first I saw them—they were leftovers, they were all used up.

There must be a way to keep from going empty like that. I'm sure that's what Carlos was looking for all the time—some way of filling himself back up. I know he woke up in the middle of the night sometimes to feel himself emptying out, one day at a time, and that's when the panic would set in—he'd have to find some kid somewhere to fuck who still had life in him, or he'd have to make a movie, or do anything to get it back, whatever it was that was emptying out of him. I didn't exactly know at that time—you could say it took me years to figure that out—but I know it now. And he infected me with it, I think. These days everybody talks about everybody infecting each other. But I think the real thing Carlos infected me with was that need to fill myself up again. To keep from going dry. When I think back about it now, in some way everything he did with me, and I don't just mean fucking me up the ass with that crazy scared energy of his, but everything, making those movies or even just knowing me, just sitting up on the roof watching the sunset or playing soccer in Central Park or even leaving me alone in that apartment with Sammy Finkelsztajn for weeks on end—all that was his way of using me up so he could try to get back something that was his. Somewhere in his past somebody must've done that same thing to him, which is how he got started on all this in the first place.

Like I say—maybe it's not that bad a thing if writing all this down uses me up for good. At least I'm not going to be out there doing it to other people. At least when I'm emptied out that'll just be it.

I remember something Sammy told me once about Carlos. Sammy was being very fatherly, which in his weird way I think he was always trying to be since he never had any children of his own, and with everything he'd seen he felt completely sorry for any children that ever got born into this world, including Carlos—but he used to say about Carlos, Carlos is burning his candle at three ends. Which I used to think about a lot—trying to picture it. And I finally figured it out. Those two flames burning at both ends and then the other one, the one that was Carlos's real life, that flame burning deep down inside the candle, eating it out from the heart and completely invisible to see.

FOR SOME REASON I'VE BEEN THINKING ABOUT various things, little odds and ends that don't fit in anywhere in particular—but I want to talk about them. It's my story, right? I can tell whatever I want to.

I've been thinking about the Paradise Grotto Lounge. It's something I haven't thought about in years, but back in Owen it was one of my favorite things. Though for some reason it always sort of spooked me just a little. I don't think I've talked much about Owen—the town itself—but it sat up on this little rise which kept it from flooding whenever the Pocohatchie River came out of its banks in the spring. Underneath this rise, like in most of Kentucky around there, were all these caves, most of them just small fingers you could go back about twenty-five feet in and then they closed off. But every once in a while, the cave would open up into something bigger.

The cave under Owen had an opening about the size of a door—in fact, there was a metal door somebody had fixed up so they could close the place off when they wanted. Once you went through that door you followed this corridor back about fifty feet—there were lights strung along the way to guide you—and then it opened up into this very large cavern that went maybe three hundred feet farther back, with a ceiling about twenty or twenty-five feet above your head. People said the cave went on back even after that, but nobody'd ever really explored it. Wallace used to love caves, and he kept trying to get me to explore some of the ones around Owen, but I was never that crazy about closed-up spaces.

I don't know who the first person was that found Paradise Grotto, which is what the cave was called, or when, but around the 1920s during Prohibition it used to be a speakeasy, and people would drive from about four counties around to drink there. That's when they put the metal door in, and the lights along the walls, and a long bar and tables and chairs. At the rear of the cavern, where the ground sloped down, there was a lake that some people said was bottomless, though I'm sure that's not true. Back in the twenties they had a platform built out on the water with a piano set up on it, and so when you went to the speakeasy there was this man sitting out in the middle of the water playing the piano for you. My mom told me about that. She used to go out there when she was a teenager in the fifties and they still had the piano on the raft then, though nobody played it. I don't know what happened to it—by the time I went there, there wasn't even any platform. But then by the time I went there, it was pretty rundown. You could tell it was once fixed up with colored tiles on the walls and stuff like that, but they'd let it go over the years. It wasn't a bar anymore, they only served soft drinks—but in the summer it was a great place to go and stay cool. There was always this breeze coming up from deep inside the ground, like water from a well. And this hollow wind sound.

Outside the cave, about fifty feet from the entrance, there was a concrete swimming pool where for a quarter you could go swimming. In the summers Ted and I were there practically all the time, from when it opened at ten in the morning till it closed at eight.

I remember this one thing we used to do—and I'd completely forgotten about it till just now. There were these openings along the side of the pool, right below the water level, where new water was always jetting into the pool to keep it full. I used to stand right up against one of those holes and pull my bathing trunks out so the water was jetting right down into my trunks. It was a weird squirmy feeling, and that was the first time in my life I ever came.

It was some kid my age who first showed me. He wasn't anybody I knew, I think he was visiting from somewhere and that's the only time I ever saw him. But I remember he swam up to me and just said right out, Want to see something fun? He nuzzled up to the concrete edge of the pool where the water was coming out and pulled his trunks down—that was the first time I ever saw anybody with a hard-on, except of course myself. I remember he and I spent all afternoon doing that, going from one spray nozzle to another, all the way around the pool, till my dick hurt with standing up so much. We didn't touch each other or anything, we just took turns at the nozzles and watched each other while we were doing it, and after that one day I never saw him again.

I showed Ted about it, but he was shy about me watching him. He'd always turn away so I couldn't see his hard-on—which I remember I was always really curious to see. Sometimes I'd catch him over at the far end of the pool up against the side, and I'd know what he was up to. I'd swim over hoping to catch a glimpse of his hard-on, though most of the time he'd see me coming and stuff himself back in. I always teased him when I caught him. I'd reach down and grope his hard little dick, which would get him all embarrassed and he'd swim away to another part of the pool. I'd chase him and we'd usually end up thrashing around in the deep end with me trying to grab him and him trying to twist away. We could spend hours doing that.

I hadn't thought of any of that for a long time, and now I wonder if other people saw us doing that with the water vents. Did they know what we were up to? I'd say probably yes, I know you're supposed to feel all shy about stuff like that, but I guess I've just never really cared if people saw me or not.

It's funny how Ted comes and goes in my head. There'll be times when I think back and I can't really remember anything about him at all, and then other times I'll remember something, like those swimming-pool games I'd completely forgotten about. It was like that the whole time I was in New York. I'd go for a while without thinking about him, but then I'd be walking down the street or taking a piss or anything—and suddenly I'd be thinking about him.

There was always this twinge I got when I thought about him, like I'd run out on him in some way I didn't feel good about. Like I just left him there. I never felt that way about my little sisters, but then they were too little to really be people yet. And I also never felt that way about my mom, because taking care of herself was the one thing she knew how to do really well. But Ted was different. When I thought about Ted I always got this empty feeling—the way when sometimes you look at the clear blue sky, and the light's just right, you get this feeling of emptiness but also something else, some feeling of being full up to overflowing with emptiness. If that makes any sense.

I thought about writing him a postcard or something, but then I never did—those first weeks and then months in the city just overwhelmed me, and even buying somebody a postcard and writing it and getting a stamp for it and then finding a mailbox to put it in—all those simple little things were way too much for me even to think about doing. It was all I could do to go out of the apartment to the little Cuban grocery store down the block and buy a six-pack.

But when *Next Year in Gomorrah* finally came out, I was feeling so great about being this big movie star and everything—I actually went out and bought a postcard of the Statue of Liberty, and I wrote on it that I was starring in this movie and I told Ted the title of it and he should watch for it. Which to look back on was a dumb thing to do, but how was I to know *Next Year in Gomorrah* wasn't exactly going to show up at the Arrowhead Drive-In on Route 24 any time soon?

I can't remember what else I said, but then how much can you say on a postcard anyway? I think I mentioned to him how I was sorry I just skipped out, and I hoped he didn't worry too much. I think I told him I was going to come visit him one day soon.

E VERY DEATH SERVES SOME PURPOSE," CARLOS ONCE
told me. It was another night when we were sitting on the roof of
the building. "There's no such thing," he said, "as a senseless death."
And he looked at me and grinned that tight grin of his, which the
instant he grinned it fell into something else that was sad.

I can't remember what we were talking about. I only remember that
one thing, because it made this tremendous impression on me.

T HE FIRST TIME I SAW *NEXT YEAR IN GOMORRAH* was in Montreal, Canada, in September 1980. Incredible to think that in just a year I went from being that kid on his bike who showed up on the last day of filming *Ur* to being the star of a movie. Though my name wasn't in the movie, nobody's name was in it because there weren't any credits—it just started up out of nowhere and ended that way too, like somebody'd found this piece of film and decided to show it to see what was on it.

It was a film festival where they were showing a bunch of movies. Carlos took me along to keep him company in the hotel and go to the receptions with him, and then to the screening of *Gomorrah*. Also to check out the other movies they were showing. If you thought Carlos's movies were strange, you should have seen some of the others, especially the one where they let a monkey operate the camera (at least that's what they said, and I'll have to admit that's what it looked like). Carlos's movie at least had a kind of story you could follow—even if nothing much happened, and you never exactly knew where it was coming from or where it was going, because it was like the beginning and the end got lost somehow. I personally probably wouldn't have paid money to see me and Sammy hang out on the alphabet avenues, but if other people wanted to that's fine with me.

There was this one movie that was really terrible, even worse—if you can believe it—than the one by the monkey. Carlos explained how they used the heel of a coke bottle instead of a camera lens to shoot it through, so it was all so blurry you couldn't tell anything about it—just these washed-out colors changing around like in a kaleidoscope and some woman talking nonsense. At the end of it Carlos turned to me and said in this really loud voice, so everybody could hear, "Remind me to wash the dildo when we get back to the hotel room." Which if you don't think that was the perfect thing to say, especially so loud that everybody could hear, then you probably wouldn't have liked Carlos all that much.

There in Montreal was the first time I saw the movie all the way through, though I'd seen bits and pieces here and there during the spring, and since like I said before we did the dialogue a couple of months after the camera stuff, it was hard to tell how it was all supposed to hang together until you saw the whole thing finished. Carlos was very proud of it, and he kept looking over at me in the movie theater to see if I was enjoying it. Which I was, even if I was sort of shocked when I saw how they'd done this treatment to make the film look really old and grainy, with scratches and blips and stuff in it. I didn't know he was going to do that. But it was fun to see how there was a kind of story hidden in there where I would've bet you money there wasn't, and how Carlos had picked that story out from all the other scenes Seth had shot that he decided not to use. Some of which were my personal favorites, like the one where we go down in the abandoned subway tunnel to visit a friend of Sammy's but can't find her, and instead we find this regular living room set up down in the tunnel, this old sofa and lamp and coffee table, and about a hundred rats swarming over it.

I don't remember much else about Montreal except watching the movie. I got really drunk on champagne at some reception where everybody was dressed in tuxedos except Carlos, who never wore anything in his life except jeans and a black T-shirt and black leather motorcycle jacket; and of course me, who's always been a bum. It was the first time I ever got drunk on champagne. The next day, I had the worst hangover of my life, so it was the last time I ever got drunk on champagne. In between getting drunk and getting hung over, though, I remember having some pretty wild sex with Carlos in the hotel swimming pool late at night when it was totally deserted.

I guess the movie was a pretty big hit with the people that go in for that sort of thing, because it got written up in a lot of papers, and then they showed it in New York at another festival that fall, and some magazine called *American Film* did a big fancy interview with Carlos.

It was this fall day when even in New York it was gorgeous and there were yellow leaves on the trees along the street—the interviewer came to the apartment, and since he said he'd buy lunch Carlos grabbed me and the three of us went to this little Polish restaurant. There were lots of restaurants like that in the neighborhood. I'd go by and see those old Polish men sitting in there, and always wonder what Sammy thought about them. He never had anything to do with any of them, even though he was Polish too. But I guess they weren't Jews like he was, and so he didn't trust them. There must've been too many things he remembered about living in Lodz for him ever to trust anything Polish anymore.

We ate this soup made out of beets, *borscht* they call it. I wasn't too thrilled with the idea of beet soup, but Carlos said it was the thing to have, and it was free, so I ate it and it wasn't bad.

The guy from *American Film* was this weasely, faggy-voiced guy with wire rims and curly black hair. He had a little tape recorder he set on the table, and a notepad with questions he'd written. He started right in, not giving Carlos a chance to eat or anything.

That was the first time I ever heard Carlos talk about his movies, and it was incredible. It was a Carlos I'd never seen before—the Carlos I knew would rather talk about dildoes than movies, and he never seemed to take anything all that seriously. I mean, this was somebody who thought being able to shoot a flame out of your rear end was just the greatest—and now here was this other Carlos talking very seriously about things I could hardly even understand. And the interviewer was loving it—he was rocking back and forth in his seat he was so excited, though partly I think that was this nervous tic of his. But it amazed me. When Carlos started talking, at first I thought he was pulling the guy's leg and what he was saying didn't make any sense. But then the interviewer started asking more questions, like he understood Carlos, and Carlos answered like he understood the question, and they went back and forth like that for about an hour. When it was over I was exhausted, and they seemed like they could go on and on—which is what the interviewer said, "I wish we could just go, on and on like this."

I started to understand why Carlos brought me along. He wanted me to hear him talk about the movie the way he did, because he wanted me to know those things but didn't think I'd listen if he just sat me down and tried to tell them to me directly.

I didn't say a thing through the whole lunch—I would've sounded too stupid. Plus, I figured the interviewer was so caught up in Carlos he didn't even know who I was. But then—this is funny. When the article came out a few months later, in the little introduction where he described the restaurant and what Carlos looked like and all, there I was big as life. Which I thought was a hoot, the way he described me.

I got Earl to find that interview for me in *American Film* magazine, and I want to put it in here so you can get an idea what it was like for this seventeen-year-old kid to sit there in that crowded little restaurant and listen to Carlos talk about this experience we'd all had, him and me and Sammy and all the others who were involved in it. The amazing thing was, what he'd experienced was totally different from what we experienced. Or at least what I did. If you'd asked me what that movie was about, I'd have said this old Jewish guy and this kid goofing in front of the camera. But sitting there listening to him talk, I suddenly started to see how, when Carlos looked at things, he saw them like everybody else, but at the same time he saw right through them too. I don't quite know how to put it. He saw what was on the other side of normal things.

That was scary. It made me think how much I was missing when I looked around at things, and how much Carlos was seeing. What it made me remember was one night when Carlos had come in, and I was reading some comic book. He took it right out of my hands where I was reading it, and stood there flipping through it. He looked sad; he shook his head. "You just don't know how many pictures there are they haven't put in that comic book of yours," he said. "Miles of pictures left out, for every one they show you."

He let it drop to the floor. At the time it didn't make too much sense, what he was saying—but in that little Polish restaurant that afternoon, it started to.

This is the way they printed it in *American Film,* the January 1981 issue.

Carlos Reichart had agreed to meet me at Veselka, a little Ukrainian restaurant on 2nd Avenue near his apartment. Veselka is bustling at midday, an amiable mix of old-timers and the trendy downtown crowd. Reichart entered the crowded room accompanied by Tony Blair, the sullenly attractive star of his latest film. There was an air of conspiracy about the two, a look of surprise as if they were thieves caught in the act. I half expected Reichart to challenge me, to glare at me defiantly, but he didn't. Instead he was charmingly cordial and guarded, at least initially—though as the interview progressed and things loosened up a bit I realized he was, in fact, glaring at me. This is a director whose intriguing quality is, for me, his concentration. When he first burst upon the scene with Burning City *in 1976, it seemed to many viewers as if he were intent on devouring film-making whole, transforming the entire genre with a single stroke. The intensity of his work is matched by the pace he sets for himself:* Burning City *(1976),* Season of Swine *(1977),* Mother Chicago *(1978),* Ur *(1979), and currently, at the New York Film Festival,* Next Year in Gomorrah.

AMERICAN FILM: *Some critics have complained that your films tend to proliferate images with an abandon that risks incoherence. That seems a criticism to which* Burning City *and* Ur *are particularly susceptible.*

CARLOS REICHART: *I seem to be an image-producing machine. You'll say this openness could also apply to someone who has nothing to say, but I hope that's not so in my case. The fact is that the series of films, beginning with* Burning City *through* Ur *and now this latest, has destroyed that need I had to identify myself sentimentally or ideologically with my subjects. I have to put my faith in a kindling of fantasy. Keeping my distance from my own mannerisms, my own stylistic quirks.*

AF: *Some have detected in that a decadent impulse.*

REICHART: *Oh I don't think so at all. I'd rather evoke the surrealist tradition of Cocteau or Buñuel, which seems to me particularly vitalist and, in Buñuel's case especially, fraught with overt political implications. The old surrealist tradition grafted onto the early American genius of a Keaton or Chaplin. But it's true what you say, to some extent, in that my primary, that is to say initial impulse was definitely toward the aesthetic, what I'd call the holiness of the image—but then we're talking the late fifties, early sixties. As you know I was a poet first. I had three books of poems out before I ever did any film work.*

AF: *And your first film work?*

REICHART: *Well, that's a complicated story, but basically it was these friends in New York I met through the antiwar movement and they knew Antonioni, who was going to be in the States shooting. There was this whole crew of people going over the script for that film, Sam Shepard was one of them, for example, and somehow they put me on the payroll for it and there I was, a script doctor when all I'd done before was write some poems and know some people.*

AF: *There was also the street theater work, which obviously prepared you in some way for that kind of work. How did that tie in?*

REICHART: *That was mostly improv with big doses of Brecht and good old-fashioned agitprop. I don't think we ever worked from a script, which perhaps prejudiced me against the rigidity of scripts because I still rely mostly on improv from my actors.*

AF: *But clearly it's improv that's carefully controlled, yes? One doesn't make film after film with the total "feel" of a Reichart film without being in some kind of control.*

REICHART: *You could say I believe in an ordered chaos. The strict rules of chance. The spontaneity of my actors is invariably well rehearsed, and as a result, I'm seldom surprised by the happy accidents as they occur along the way.*

AF: *Which is why you tend to work with the same people over and over.*

REICHART: *Well, that and the fact that these are the people I know—people I've been with since '68 or '69, Sammy Finkelstein and Netta Abramowitz and Verbena Gray, so they're all trained in improv, guerilla theater. It was the war that woke us all up. That made us start seeing the various structures—economic, cultural—that insinuate themselves within even casual you might almost say accidental images.*

AF: *Such as?*

REICHART: *Such as the structures of so-called normal life. The system of ideologies that buttresses that.*

AF: *Let's talk about Seth Rosenheim, who as cinematographer for all of your films has been widely praised.*

REICHART: *Oh, Seth's the absolute genius there. He's entirely responsible for the look of everything. I didn't even know about zooms when I started. I still don't, really (laughs). No, it's true. I think something up, I say to Seth can we do that? He either says we can do that or he says forget it.*

AF: *And in that case you forget it?*

REICHART: *(laughs) Absolutely.*

AF: *You must be the only director in America who dubs all his films. Why that curious practice?*

REICHART: *Well, I think dubbing enriches a character. It's part of my taste for pastiche—it raises a character out of the zone of naturalism. What I often* do is cross two nonprofessionals. I believe in polyvalence in a character. I like elaborating a character.

AF: Your latest film has been met with a certain amount of incomprehension but also a great deal of enthusiasm. Personally I find the film very mysterious, unsettling—like looking at an old photograph album and realizing everyone whose picture is in there is dead now.

REICHART: Next Year in Gomorrah is mysterious first and foremost because it's fragmentary. But its fragmentariness is in a sense symbolic—the general fragmentariness of our civilization as it will appear to some future civilization. This is the real mystery of the film and the world represented in it. Like an unknown landscape wrapped in a thick mist that clears here and there, but only for a short time.

AF: Hence the distressing of the actual film quality itself.

REICHART: Precisely. I wanted to suggest an ancient film, or fragment of film found, say, in a canister dug up from the ruins of one of our cities, pieced back together but heavily damaged, much of it beyond repair.

AF: One thinks of the Soviet reconstruction of Eisenstein's Beuzhin Meadow after the war.

REICHART: That hadn't occurred to me, but yes. An example closer to home would be the stills from von Stroheim's Greed that survive.

AF: Even though in certain ways Gomorrah is a comic film, it's also very sad.

REICHART: That's a personal impression. I agree it's not very funny, it makes you think more than laugh. But when it was put on in Montreal a month ago the audiences laughed a lot. I should say this too—Gomorrah is also about the end of a certain kind of film-making, I think. It's about the end of realism as a kind of limbo, and it evokes the ghost of realism, particularly in the beginning about two characters living life without thinking about it—humble humdrum and unaware. All the first part is an echo of realism, though naturally an idealized realism.

AF: Which brings in the whole question of Hollywood.

REICHART: I've never paid any attention to Hollywood, one way or the other. The main point is that in Gomorrah my love for reality is philosophical and reverent, but it is not necessarily naturalistic.

AF: How did you find Tony Blair?

REICHART: I met him by chance while doing Ur—he was there with some other boys watching us make the film and I noticed him at once. When I thought of doing Gomorrah I thought of him and Sammy Finkelstein without the slightest hesitation.

AF: *And you had worked with Finkelstein before?*

REICHART: *Again, he dates back to the street theater. We were in Washington Square, I think it was right after Cambodia, the incursions, and Sammy walked up to me at the end of a performance—I remember we were all dressed up in these extravagant costumes, we were supposed to be mythological birds or something, it was very magical—and he pointed right at me, poking me in the chest with his finger, and he said, "I'm with you." I took that to mean he was against the war too, but it didn't—it meant he was joining The Company whether we wanted him or not.*

AF: *That's a funny story. And that sort of feistiness comes across in his character in* Gomorrah.

REICHART: *Well, I hope. I took something of a chance, since there's always something iffy in asking someone who may be near death himself to act his own death.*

AF: *I remember the stories Satyajit Ray tells about the old village woman who played the grandmother in* Pather Panchali.

REICHART: *Well, especially in that culture. But in any culture—to face your own death is a serious thing. Not just the possibility of your own death but the thing itself. Which for me is montage. Death, I mean. Once life is finished it acquires a sense; up to that point its sense is suspended and therefore ambiguous. Though to be sincere I also have to say that for me death is important only if it's not justified and rationalized by reason.*

AF: *In an interview Barthes says that the cinema should not try to make sense but to suspend sense. Do you then agree with that, especially in connection with* Next Year in Gomorrah?

REICHART: *Yes, I'm always trying to suggest that. None of my films are supposed to have a finished sense. They always end with a question—I intend them to remain suspended.*

AF: *And the title? Clearly there's the implication of diaspora, the Holocaust...*

REICHART: *Oh, exactly, but here it's combined with a vision of Jerusalem that, even if you finally manage to achieve it, or rediscover it since it's really a kind of lost Eden, it's going to be ruined, it's going to disappear out from underneath you the instant you find it.*

AF: *So is New York* Gomorrah?

REICHART: *Is New York Gomorrah? I like that.*

"WHAT OTHER BOYS?" I REMEMBER ASKING HIM after that interview. We were walking down First Avenue and it was one of those great September days when you can just feel the sun in your bones.

"What other boys what?" Carlos asked. I thought the question was pretty clear.

"You said you met me with a bunch of other boys. Don't you even remember?"

"Well, I did meet you with a bunch of other boys, didn't I?"

"You met me in the laundromat. I was all by myself. You were doing your laundry and I was doing my laundry. You don't remember that?"

Carlos sort of frowned and then he laughed. "No, I don't remember," he said. "I have this very vivid image of you—you're on your bike with about three or four other kids. It's a very clear picture in my head. You were watching us do the shoot, and I asked you to hang around and you did."

It threw me, sort of—like another one of those things that when you think about them later, it seems like maybe you should've made something of it, but at the time you didn't think to. Still, it was something I went on about.

"You really don't remember." I was playing like I was hurt he didn't remember, and I guess I was hurt a little. All that stuff in the Nu-Way Laundromat was stuff I thought back to a lot, especially when I couldn't go to sleep and so I started to do those mind exercises Carlos had told me about that very first day, about thinking back to things and trying to be there all over again. It occurred to me—maybe every time I did that I was changing something about what really happened, and so if I thought back to it enough it'd be like rubbing your finger on something that's painted and wearing the paint away. It bothered me that Carlos was remembering something completely different, and I wondered if that was maybe because he didn't think back to it as much and so he hadn't rubbed as much away.

You probably know by now how I tend to get caught up thinking about one thing and I worry and worry it till it starts driving me crazy. I guess starting right that minute on the sidewalk, this one thing became the newest thing to drive me crazy. Trying to think—could I really not remember the way it was, in which case I was crazy, or was it Carlos who didn't remember, and then he was the crazy one? And how was I going to know one way or the other about it, since only the two of us were there and nobody else?

I was sure I was right. I had to be. That laundromat was something important for me to think back to a lot. It was the one instant where everything in my life changed, though I didn't know it at the time. I thought I was still living my same old life, but I wasn't. That life had stopped being there the instant Carlos walked in the door: I was already in some crazy new life without even knowing it.

It bothered me that Carlos could remember all that so completely differently. Unless he had some reason for not telling it the way it happened, in which case what was that reason? To keep it just between the two of us? Or because there were other things that got in the way of telling it straight that he knew about and I didn't? And so there I'd go off in another direction, worrying it out to the threadbare end and still not getting anywhere.

A few days after that interview, I happened to be alone with Seth. He was in the apartment going through some boxes of stuff Carlos stored for him there. I think he was kind of pissed off at not being able to find what he was looking for—which meant it probably wasn't exactly the best time in the world to try to have a conversation, but I went ahead and had one anyway.

"Seth," I said.

He didn't look around at me, he just kind of grunted and kept tossing stuff out of the box onto the floor.

"You remember that first time you met me, when I came to where you all were shooting, with Verbena and the pickup truck and everything?"

He emptied a box of tools out on the floor.

I told him how I remembered that day one way, with me being the only kid there, and Carlos remembered it completely different, and anyway that wasn't even the first time Carlos ever met me.

Seth must've found what he was looking for, because he stood up and turned around and looked at me. He was holding some camera-piece.

"Look, Tony," he said, and this is exactly what he said—"you are really pretty amazingly dumb."

It wasn't what I was expecting him to say. I just looked at him back.

"I don't understand," I said. And really, when I look back at it all, I guess he was right—I really was pretty amazingly dumb. But then, how was I supposed to know anything?

"You weren't exactly the first kid to come nosing around Carlos," Seth said like he was mad at me personally for that fact, "and you sure as hell aren't the last. So don't get any ideas."

All at once I completely knew what he was talking about. It came in a sort of rush right at me, and I'd never even thought about it before.

"Oh that," I said—like I knew what he meant all along.

Maybe Seth was pissed off at Carlos for some reason that day and that's why he told me, or maybe he would've told me the same thing anytime I'd asked him about it, but I hadn't ever asked before.

"See," he said, "I just think people have got a right to know certain things. So they can make their own decisions, if you know what I mean. But to do that they've got to know what's what."

"And you're going to tell me what's what," I said.

"Since no one else seems to want to? Yeah. Sure. Like I'm the one to do it. And like you didn't know Carlos has this sex thing for kids. I mean, you're not stupid."

"No, I'm not stupid," I said, though of course you might say I've always been stupid. This was a conversation we should've been having a long time ago.

"So—he gets them." Seth shrugged. "They just come around."

"What do you mean, they just come around?"

"Like you came around," he said. "That's Carlos. Whatever gets you through life, I say. Whatever takes you to hell and back again."

"So he was fucking around with some other kid besides me back in Owen?" It was like I was hearing myself do the talking but I wasn't really there.

"Who remembers Owen?" Seth waved his hand like Owen, Kentucky, bored him to death. It wouldn't exactly have been the first time in the world somebody had that reaction. "Owen was just some little town where we were making a movie."

"*I* was in Owen," I said.

Seth laughed. "Yeah," he said, "you were in Owen." He shook his head like he thought it was all too funny. "You wouldn't smoke my goddamned pot in Owen," he said. Like it was still some sore spot with him. "Sure there was some other kid in Owen. That's why we were in fucking Owen in the first place, some kid Carlos saw in the grocery store and he liked the looks of so that's where we were going to shoot the last part of the film. All so he can drive up and down the goddamned street looking for this kid, which I hate to say it, but it wasn't you."

"Who then?"

"How do I know who? I don't think Carlos ever found him. He wanted to write this script for him. He had it all worked out. This kid was going to be the star of his next movie. He always wanted to do a movie with a kid in it, and he never had."

It sort of made me light-headed, hearing all this for the first time. Like I probably should have sat down in a chair before he told it to me. "Look," Seth said, "I'm not saying you should do anything different, just because maybe now you know some things you didn't know before. But I'm betting you probably knew them. I'm right about that, aren't I? That you knew them."

It was odd—because suddenly it seemed like I *did* know them all along, I just never sat down and said them to myself.

"I guess I knew," I told him. "Yeah, I guess I guessed it."

He just nodded. He had these big eyes that made him look funny sometimes, and sometimes they made him look sad, and this time he looked sad. I thought how he wasn't a bad guy, Seth—just he had a terrible temper and was always at least a little bit stoned, so you never knew what he was going to do next.

"You've had some kind of time, haven't you?" he said, sort of out of the blue.

I knew he meant Sammy, and the way Carlos cooped me up with

him to see if we'd break—but we didn't, so Carlos went ahead and made the movie.

"Yeah," I said. "It's been some kind of time."

"But you're not sorry."

I shook my head. "Why should I be sorry? It's not over yet. Things are just starting up."

"You really think that?"

"I really do," I told him. I wasn't sure whether I did or not, but it seemed like the thing to say. Because the whole time we were talking my brain was racing ahead about five hundred miles an hour to all the things I never thought about till now. And now I had to say to myself Carlos was fucking around with other kids than me and what does that mean? And what my brain was saying was, Not much. Here I had the whisky and the sex and a bed to sleep in, and a movie I starred in and what more was I supposed to want than that? We had some kind of time together, me and Carlos—that was enough for me to say.

"So you'll be staying around?" Seth asked. He was using his gruff voice on me, which meant he was trying to be nice to me without being too nice. "No matter what?" he said—like he was anxious about it.

"Probably I will," I told him. "You can't get rid of me just like that." I smiled at him, the way I do when I'm being mean. "I'm going to be a star," I told him. "You just watch me."

"I'm watching you all the time," he said. "I'm the camera lens." We stood there looking at each other, me this kid who'd just turned eighteen about a week before and Seth, who must've been forty, with his big belly and his beard and him holding that stupid camera-piece that, now that he'd found it, he didn't exactly know what to do with anymore. Which I guess put the two of us in the exact same situation—not knowing what to do with what it was we'd just found.

It was some kind of understanding between us right then. I know he thought I was stupid and all, but I don't really care. Things wouldn't have worked out the way they did if it'd been any other way between us, and I think we both probably knew that, even at that instant we were standing there looking at each other. Because for a stupid kid I was always pretty smart, and Seth knew that.

"You can tell Carlos you told me," I said. "You can tell him I'm okay." I planned to figure out later, on my own, if that was true.

"You're sure you're okay?" Seth asked one last time while he was heading out the door. "You can stay at my place if you're not." Like he was afraid I was going to snuff myself or something all because Carlos was fucking some kid other than me.

"I'm fine," I told him. "You'll see how fine I am."

He sort of grumbled at that and then he was gone, and I was standing there in the middle of the apartment with the sun coming in through the windows and lighting up all the dust specks in the air so you couldn't believe you were always walking around breathing air that dirty, and the whole weight of it sort of hit me. I thought back to that night I tried to run away and then came back because I found out I couldn't run away, or I didn't want to—and I thought, I'd have gone completely insane if I found out about all this back then. But now it was just something that was happening and it wasn't going to be the end of the world. It was just part of me and Carlos, and I almost had to laugh, thinking about Carlos chasing that kid around Owen and coming up with me instead.

Still, I didn't feel too great, so I took a walk uptown— which you may be saying, Tony, that's what you always do when things don't go your way, and I guess that's true, but that's the way I am. It helps me to get out and look around and see what's what, to use Seth's phrase. So I went uptown to the library. I wanted to look at that picture I used to look at, the one of the guy my age feeding his little sister some soup in the ghetto. I hadn't gone back there since we'd made the movie, and it was really strange to see it again. It made me remember those times I spent in the winter talking with Sammy, which seemed like a dream now that the movie was made. Like making the movie emptied all that out of me the way you'd drain pus out of a sore. It made me sad to look at the picture and think that kid from Lodz was still dead whether I looked at his picture or we made that movie or not. He was still dead and I was still going on, and looking at him now was like looking at some old picture of me a long time after I'd stopped being that person anymore.

Though I guess you never completely lose it, that person you used to be, and so I hadn't lost him either. He was going to be with me a long time to come.

I put the book back on the shelf wondering if I'd ever come look at it again. Then I went on the few blocks to Central Park, where in the summer we played soccer but we didn't anymore because Carlos was always away during the day again and even though it was different now because I knew the city and got out and about a lot more, still it was sort of the same as it was back in the winter.

There were a few guys playing soccer, and even though they signaled me to join if I wanted, I didn't. With Carlos not there I didn't feel like I was part of it, even though it was great to watch those guys stampeding up and down and guiding the ball in between each other's legs, and the dust and sweat and you could hear their heavy breathing when they stopped for a time out. I sat down on this little hill where the grass was worn away and there were candy wrappers and I almost sat down on a used condom till I moved a ways away and sat down again—and I watched them play for maybe an hour, feeling sad and far away from everything, and just watching like it was a movie, and I remember thinking to myself how, number one, I wasn't angry with Carlos, and how, number two, I wasn't going to let him fuck with me anymore or fuck me either for that matter, and how, number three, if I was thinking that, then what Seth told me that afternoon must really hurt a lot inside and I thought I was taking it pretty well, but I guess I wasn't.

It's one more of those times when I should've just walked away from everything but I didn't. I was never very good at doing that, I guess— except maybe that time hearing Ted dry-humping his mattress put a move on me. Otherwise, with me it's sort of like those little animals that get hypnotized by looking into the eyes of bigger animals; they can't move, they just have to keep looking no matter what happens. I guess I was always one of the little animals. And Carlos—well, Carlos was Carlos.

By the time I got back to the apartment my throat was full up with looking at those soccer players. I was drunk with seeing them play the way they did, in and out of each other like they knew exactly what they were doing all the time—which they didn't: I'd played out there before so I knew. And I also remember this, vividly even though it's nearly ten years since then—by the time I got back to the apartment I was completely calm, and I knew what I was going to do.

When Carlos came in that night I was already in bed but I wasn't asleep, I was just lying there in the dark, peaceful, ready for what- ever was going to have to happen. Carlos didn't turn on the light—he undressed and slipped into the bed next to me. He didn't touch me or anything like he usually did. He just lay there next to me. We were both on our backs, looking up at the ceiling.

"So I hear you and Seth had a little dish-fest this afternoon," he said—like it was just a piece of gossip that didn't have anything in particular to do with him.

I felt strong. "Where'd you hear that?" I said.

Carlos reached over and turned on the light. At the same time, he said, "This pretty kid I was fucking up the ass told me."

It wasn't exactly what I expected him to say, and it made my heart go cold. He smiled that tight smile of his, and his Cherokee cheekbones rode up higher than ever, and it was like he was saying, Go on, fight me about it.

"Which one of them?" I said it as coolly as I could manage.

Carlos looked at me. I think I surprised him, matching him one for one like that.

Of course, I couldn't match him very long.

"Do you want to meet him?" he asked.

I felt the floor give way under me. I couldn't think of anything else but to risk it and say, "Sure, I'll meet him. Anytime you want me to."

Carlos grabbed me by the hair. "I knew I liked you," he said. "I knew there was something about you, and I wasn't wrong."

I started to get really mad.

"So all that stuff back in Owen, about the movie script and every-thing—you just made it up."

"I had to think fast," he said. "Otherwise I was going to lose you."

"Which maybe would've been better," I told him, "for the both of us."

"Definitely not," he said. "Absolutely definitely not."

"I can't believe it," I said. "You're fucking around with little kids."

I wanted it to sound like I was furious, though I knew I couldn't, exactly.

"You're not a very good actor sometimes," Carlos said.

Which made me sort of punch him in the shoulder, and he punched me back. It didn't go any further than that. We just lay there for another minute or so.

"But you're a very good person," he went on to say. "You're always a very good person, which means life is hard for you."

"And you're not a very good person?" I asked.

"Are you kidding? Anybody who thinks fucking is a way of life's not going to be a very good person."

I told him I thought fucking was a pretty good way of life. "It's sure gotten us some times, now hasn't it?"

"Oh, anything can get you by for a while," Carlos said.

He looked sadder than I'd ever seen him.

Sometimes it was pretty hard to talk to Carlos. You felt like he was lying on the bottom of some deep river and you were in a boat fishing for him with a long line and no bait. I told him, "If I learned anything from The Company, it is—you take things but you also have to give them back. Okay? Lots of people probably say they believe that, but I think I really do, Carlos. I think it was you and Sammy who taught me. that, even though at the time I didn't know that's what I was learning." Which was a kind of surprising thing for me to say—but as soon as I said it, I knew I meant it completely.

"I think I have faith in you," Carlos said. "I think that's the only way to put it."

"What do you mean, faith?" As usual, Carlos was about ten steps ahead of me. He was an incredibly reckless person in a lot of ways, but I think he also had this incredible sense of what he could do and what he couldn't do—and the whole time he was with somebody, he was letting the rope out, and tightening it up, and always playing right on the edge of things. When you think about it, it's amazing he didn't blow it more times than he did.

"I'm talking about having faith in how you see things. How things can be bigger than you or me, and how that doesn't seem to bother you the way it would bother most people. How I think maybe you know how to stand aside and watch yourself, and see what's what with yourself. Which is what makes you a such a terrific actor when you're not faking it."

Carlos must've been wondering if this time he'd let the rope out too far. I'm pretty sure he was scrambling for it, though that's looking back on it because he was always able to cover his tracks. But I wonder if he got scared at times like that, wondering what would happen—or whether if it all came apart he was just ready to shrug everything off. He was definitely some kind of survivor, but also I think sometimes he was sad about all the things he survived along the way. People he once knew but then made some kind of mistake with—Netta, for instance, and there were others I'd heard tell about, people who wouldn't have anything to do with Carlos anymore because one day Carlos took everything one step too far, and then that was it. I didn't know at the time what that step was, though eventually I found out too—but I knew, even then, that was what happened.

I think Carlos knew, deep down, that the way he lived his life meant the day would have to come when he'd go too far with everybody he ever liked. Knowing that made him sad, but he'd decided that was the way he had to be: he was going to try to hang on with people as long as he could, and then when it was time to pay the price, he'd pay the price.

But I don't think I knew that then, which is why I completely launched into him with both my fists. I took him by surprise—I think up to that point he thought he was winning and he was relieved, and then all of a sudden my punches knocked him completely off the bed onto the floor.

"Hey," he said, but before he could do anything I was on top of him, straddling him there on the floor next to the bed and slamming my fists into his face. It was a complete surprise to me too, since I'd never really beaten anybody up in my life before—but that's what you could say I was doing to Carlos right there, even though he was about fifty pounds heavier than me and worked out in a gym and if he wanted to, it would've been like that time back in the winter when he just grabbed my wrists together and there was nothing I could do. But he didn't do a single thing to fight back—he let me pummel him for a while, like he knew he deserved it and he was just going to lie there and take it. It made me even madder that he wasn't fighting back, because I think if I'm going to be honest I have to say—all I really wanted him to do was slam me once or twice and let that be that.

But he wouldn't do it, even though by now his nose was gushing blood and I had blood all over my fists and even on my chest. Under me I could feel his dick getting stiff, like he was loving all this. I hit him even harder, but that only made my dick start to get hard too, which was even worse because he could see it sticking up there in his face. It made him grin, and I was furious with my dick for getting hard, and even though I tried to make it go soft, I couldn't. The more I hit him, the harder I got—I was almost relieved when finally he must've decided enough was enough. He gathered me up in his arms and tossed me off him, and that was that. Which was fine with me because I was exhausted. I knew he wasn't going to hit me back or anything—whatever point we both needed to prove had just gotten proved and now there wasn't any need to prove anything more.

He got up off the floor and went into the kitchen, where I could hear him running the faucet. I sat on the floor for a while waiting, and then got back in bed like nothing happened. I was glad my hard-on was completely gone when he came back to the bed. I was relieved when I saw his was too.

"Nothing like a facial massage," he said when he lay down next to me.

"Did I hurt you?"

He laughed. Then he said, "Ouch."

"You deserved it," I told him. I wasn't mad at him anymore. I guess I got that out of my system.

"Go to sleep," he said. "First thing tomorrow we're going to Brooklyn."

That was news to me. "Why're we going to Brooklyn?" I asked.

"We've got things to do," he said in this completely matter-of-fact voice, like nothing had happened between us. "You and me. I've got some things to show you. I need your help."

"You need my help?" I couldn't really imagine what kind of help Carlos would be needing from me, especially right now.

"I'm making a new movie," he said, just like that. "I need your help."

So there it was. I guess maybe I should've known, at least been able to guess—but I didn't. I would've thought he would've told me.

"You're making a movie," I said. "You're making a movie and you didn't tell me."

"I was waiting for the time to be right," he said, and he even sounded like he believed it, though I wasn't sure I did.

I had to laugh. "You're crazy," I told him, leaning on my elbow to look at him where he was lying there with his face starting to puff up where I hit him. "You're totally crazy."

"It's been said. Look, do you want to be in this movie? I really need you to be in this movie."

"What's it about?" Like that was the question to ask about Carlos's movies.

"It's different," he said. "You'll see tomorrow."

"And this kid you're fucking up the ass?" I said. "Is he in the movie too?"

"It's got a cast of thousands," Carlos said. "It's biblical, it's an epic."

"Are you kidding with me or what?"

"No," he said. "I'm not. Just wait and see."

So we lay there for a while, him not making any move to touch me like he usually did, and me not making any move either. We didn't know each other anymore—that's what it felt like, this horrible cold clammy feeling starting somewhere around my heart and spreading out into my arms and my legs. Even the night which used to be summer, or the end of summer, didn't seem that warm anymore.

I had one more question. I waited a little while before I asked it, maybe because I was hoping he'd go to sleep and then I wouldn't have to ask it. But finally I did have to ask it anyway.

"Carlos," I said, "you're not going to fuck me anymore, are you?" It made my throat really dry to say that, but I had to.

He didn't say anything for a minute, like he was thinking—then he said, "No, I'm not."

"That's amazing," I said. "That's just amazing."

"That's what they say," Carlos said. "That's what they say about life. It wouldn't be a good idea, would it?"

Of course he was completely right, even if it was what I thought before when I was walking in the park.

"It wouldn't be a good idea," I said. "No."

I hadn't thought I was going to say that when the time came. I was used to deciding things and then having to undecide them as soon as I was around Carlos, but this time was different. Something had changed. I couldn't put my finger on it but there it was. I remember once I was walking down Main Street in Owen and suddenly the temperature got ten degrees colder. Some kind of front moving through, I guess, but it was spooky—one minute it was seventy and the next instant it was sixty and if you took a step backward to step back into the seventy-degree air you couldn't do it, you couldn't find where that old weather went to. And that's what it was like—some sudden dip in the temperature between us that happened just like that. Or we both suddenly grew up in some way, and things couldn't be the same as they used to be anymore. I felt a lot older lying there next to Carlos, not touching him—sad about what was all of a sudden put behind us, but also I was feeling this kind of respect. Respect for both of us in some strange way.

I guess all of it was just one more thing he set me up for. But if you spend your life going around looking for traps, you're going to miss everything else.

I 'VE GONE DOWN INTO SOME KIND OF UNDERGROUND cavern. In the dream it's a carnival ride where you get in this little roller coaster car, and you go by all these scenes of people doing things. It's supposed to be a horror ride, only the scenes are ordinary scenes from a factory—assembly lines and machines and people working the machines, and the whole place is humming with this quiet powerful hum behind everything, which is the power source for the factory. Then while we're gliding by these scenes in the little car, I somehow know it's not a carnival ride, it's only supposed to look like one. Because actually it's an underground factory where aliens from outer space are making human beings, and the only reason I'm there is because they don't think anybody who goes on this ride is going to guess that's what's going on down here, so the aliens think they can be safe and get away with what they're doing right under everybody's noses.

Then I remember thinking, if the aliens are making all these human beings in this underground factory, then how can you know if the people around you are real, or if they're just made by the outer space aliens in this factory too? What if everybody around you's been made by the aliens, and there's only you left?

And then I'm thinking, what if you can't tell whether you were made in the factory or not? What if I'm not real either? Then how am I going to know? What if all the human beings in the world are made by aliens in an underground factory and we just think we're human beings but we're really not? But also we really are, because then that's all a human being is—something made by aliens in their underground factory. The instant I think that, I know I'll never be able to know even when I wake up. Because if I was actually down in that underground factory, the aliens did something to my memory to make me think it was only a dream. That's their way of protecting themselves. I'll remember it and then I'll remember it was just a dream I had, so it can't be real and not to worry. So even if I catch on, like I'm catching on now, still I'll never know for sure and that's when I wake up.

I bolted up in bed completely covered in sweat, with this prickling all up and down my arms and legs. They know I know. That's what I immediately thought. They know I've figured it out and they're out to find me, they're going to take me down into the factory and re-make me so I won't remember them.

I lay there completely still for a while. All there was was the hum you hear all the time here at night, I guess it's the Eddy's heating system— this humming sound that's almost regular but not quite. If you listen to it like I do at night, you notice it keeps going in and out of phase with itself. After a while the dream started to fade, so I wasn't scared anymore—and now today it's just another dream. But I want to hold onto it. I have this feeling I figured out something in that dream— I stumbled across something nobody else had caught onto. Not about the underground factory exactly, but something else—the way you aren't in control, but just act like it because you see everybody else is doing the same only they don't know it.

NEXT MORNING WE TOOK THE TRAIN OUT TO Brooklyn, some neighborhood down by the water, which, if I thought the alphabets looked bad, I hadn't even started to see bad yet. There was this totally rundown-looking warehouse, but when Carlos let us into it, I was just astounded. It was like opening a door to what you think is just some regular room in a house, and suddenly you're on another planet. Carlos and The Company had gone and turned the whole inside of that warehouse into this crazy, beautiful city in the desert.

From where I stood at the door of the warehouse, it was all sand stretching back in these low dunes with some palm trees here and there and at the far end of the warehouse—which was huge, the size of a football field—there was this city rising up on a hill, all spires and walls and turrets like in a fairy tale. And behind that a light blue sky.

Still holding a hammer in her hand and nails in her mouth, Verbena came walking over to us. "Oh hello, children," she said, like she wasn't expecting us. "Welcome to Sodom." She was wearing this enormous hot pink running suit she just barely fit into.

"You're looking at a masterpiece," Carlos told me. I wasn't sure whether he meant her running suit or the stage set. Which either way you had to give it to her, they were both pretty fantastic. And I told her so.

"Honey," she said, "there's a very beautiful soul trapped inside this body."

"I like your body just fine," I told her. And I meant it. I was always glad to see Verbena, even if she didn't always remember my name.

"Stroll on around," she told me, "hang out in the cafés, visit the whorehouses. For angels, no visas required."

What was amazing were the shapes of those buildings, all piled up topsy-turvy on top of each other, and the colors, these chalky reds and greens, like once they were bright but from lots of hands touching them they wore down to the dull color they were now. You'll say it was just a stage set made out of cardboard and plaster of paris, and you'll be right— but if you haven't seen it you won't know how there was something about it that put its spell on you and made you feel empty and sad and faraway.

"Amazing," I told Carlos while he was walking me through the set that first time—we were climbing the scaffolding up to the platform at the top. "I never knew anything like this was going on."

"Ever read the Bible?" he asked. Which I never did.

"The story of Sodom and Gomorrah," he said.

"Like in the last movie," I mentioned.

"Except all different." We'd made it to the top of the town, which was all built on stilts so if you looked at it from the desert down below, it looked like it was on a steep hillside, but now from the top looking down you could see it wasn't a town at all, it was just lumber and heavy cardboard latched together and all painted up. Down below I could see Verbena talking with Sammy. She was doing the talking. I couldn't hear what she was telling him, but I could see he was busy banging the palm of his hand against his forehead in some kind of response.

"Not much of a view," I joked.

"God wanted to send his angels to Sodom to see if there was a single just man living there. But the angels fell into the trap of the Sodomites—the trap of sexual knowledge, sex as knowledge, since in the Bible 'to know' means both—and so out of jealousy God rained fire on the Cities of the Plain."

"You're not planning on burning all this down?"

"Not exactly, no. I'm not following the Bible all that carefully. You might say I'm doing some long overdue revising on that old book. The angels'll probably take one look around and just settle down, live happily ever after inside those human bodies of theirs. If that's what angels do. I haven't worked everything out yet."

"Let me guess," I said. I'd seen it coming a mile away. "I'm supposed to play one of the angels." But Carlos didn't answer me—instead he said, "Remember back last summer, how we hooked the shower up on the fire escape?"

Carlos never reminisced about the things we did together.

"Yeah," I said. I was touched he wanted to remember that.

"That was pretty fun."

He put his hand on my shoulder, and one more time I remembered, We're never going to have sex again—which all morning had been a bell chiming inside me, every fifteen minutes or so, that thought—it's over, it's finished, whatever this is, it's something else now.

"You know," he said, almost like he was reading my mind, "fucking's just something that happens. It's like everything else."

I didn't exactly see what that had to do with the fire escape. Or with the angels.

"Fucking's just a motion, an activity, see? It's a set of physical principles."

"What are you talking about?" I asked him.

He turned and looked at me, holding both my shoulders with his hands and looking into my eyes.

"This is really, really important," he said. "I really need you. I really need you to do this for me."

"Do what?"

"You remember how we'd get going out there sometimes, out under the water with it pouring down all over us and before we knew it we'd be fucking? And there were those guys who used to watch, and it didn't really matter whether they were watching or not, it didn't have anything to do with what we were doing, so they could see us doing anything they wanted to and it didn't affect what we were doing one bit. And you even sort of liked it that they were watching, I remember you got into it because it gave them some kind of pleasure without taking anything away from your pleasure, in fact it even increased your pleasure because you knew how it was pleasuring them too without you doing anything different to your own pleasure than you'd normally do."

Carlos said all that really fast—it came pouring out of him like it'd been dammed up and now he was relieved to let it go.

I realized exactly what he wanted me to do. "So you're making some porn movie," I said. "I told you I wasn't going to be in any porn movie, no way."

"I know you said that. But think about it—you were a very different person back then, Tony. There was lots you didn't know. I think you know more about yourself now," Carlos went on. "And about making movies. You're an actor, Tony. A very good actor. You understand about acting. Anyway, *porn* is hardly the word for it. Did you ever see a porn movie with a set like this? You don't exactly go building a city right out of Piero della Francesca just to shoot a porn movie there."

It was odd being way up there near the roof and looking down on all that scaffolding and stuff, and knowing if you were down below and looking up it'd seem like we were two people standing on the very top ramparts of this fantastically strange and beautiful-looking city.

"So what is it if it's not a porn movie?" I asked Carlos. "You want me to take my clothes off, right? You want me to have sex where the camera can film it, right, and Seth can see everything I'm doing with my dick hard, and everybody else can too, and besides, who'm I supposed to be having sex with since you said last night we weren't ever going to do it anymore?"

"And we aren't," Carlos said. "We can't. You understand why we can't."

I did, unfortunately—which didn't mean I didn't still feel like I'd gotten totally dumped for some new kid he had the hots for.

"We have to put everything else behind us," he went on. "We have to make the best movie we can."

I remembered the way Verbena shot flame from her butt. And Sammy shivering his way through all those February days because he thought Carlos's movie should get made. So who was I to say no, just because I wasn't crazy about waving my dick around in front of Seth's camera?

"I'm not pressuring you," Carlos said. "I want you to think about it. I want us to make the most amazing movie we can make. It's not porn—you'll see that. It's going to be something terrific and beautiful and when it's over, years from now, when you're lying on your deathbed, you'll be glad you had something to do with it."

As I'm sure you know by now, I can be talked into anything, especially if it was Carlos doing the talking; so though I said, "I'm not going to let you pressure me," I think Carlos knew as well as I did there was no way I was going to say no. Because I really had meant it when I told Seth the day before that things weren't over, they were just starting out—and if Carlos wanted me to make a porn film with him, if that was where we were going to go, well than that's where we were going.

So we came back down from the top of the city, scaling our way down those little streets that weren't really streets, and looking back every once in a while to see the city start to look more and more like a real city the more we came down out of it.

In front of the city—the part of the warehouse that was done up to look like a desert—a kid about my own age was sitting. So this was the famous kid Carlos was fucking up the ass these days. He was sitting on a fake rock underneath a fake palm tree. I'll always remember that first glimpse I had of him: smoking a cigarette, looking completely out of place there but at the same time relaxed, like he didn't care where he was. Like he was this person who carried around whatever he needed right there with him, and so it didn't matter.

So much for first impressions.

"Scott," Carlos called to him, and Scott got up and came over to where we were. You have to imagine the two of us there, Scott in the prep school outfit he was still wearing since he'd hopped the train in from Connecticut that morning, spiffy and rich to the core with this sullen spoiled look on his face and a haircut he must've paid twenty-five dollars for—and then scruffy me with my hair pretty long and nothing but jeans and a T-shirt and these gorgeous snakeskin cowboy boots Carlos had gotten for me back in the spring, which I wore all the time.

Scott smiled and ran his hand through his blond hair and let it fall back in place, which I guess you can do if you have a fancy haircut. And I have to admit, he had this really great smile. He wasn't very big—he looked only fifteen or so, but I found out later he was seventeen. This wiry little body and thin clear face with one single bright red pimple on his cheekbone. In the meantime he was checking me out too—looking me up and down, I guess to see what he was getting into. And I could tell he was nodding to himself and saying, Yeah, I can do this, no problem—even before we'd said a single word.

"So I guess we're making this big movie together," he said.

He stood around with his hands on his hips, completely relaxed like we'd known each other forever. I still didn't know what to do; part of me wanted to bolt from all this, while the other part was holding steady, thinking, Okay, let's see what happens. Let's see exactly what Carlos has come up with this time. Because I never doubted he really had come up with something. Even though I was furious with him and also it was a little painful to be standing here with this kid he'd just dumped me for, at the same time I knew there was a movie here, and Carlos wouldn't be putting us through all this if there wasn't.

I remember suddenly thinking, I don't care whether Carlos wants me to fuck this kid or not—I'm going to fuck him. It came like a bolt of lightning and I was completely sure of it and completely sure I could do it. I'd never fucked anybody in my life before—and now I was urgent at the thought of fucking this kid, sinking my dick into him till I had him sobbing and moaning. I felt in control for once. I was somebody who could take some kind of revenge.

That sounds like bragging, and I admit it. But I could also see Scott was the kind of person anybody could do anything with and he wouldn't care. Even before I knew anything about him, I could see it written all over him.

"Can we get to work now?" Carlos said abruptly. It was like him not to even ask me how I was feeling about all this—just to plow on ahead like everything had to be fine. He did this sad smile that tried to be funny but wasn't. Then the three of us sat down in the sand. Verbena had brought dump trucks of real sand and dumped them on the floor to make the desert, and while Carlos talked I kept running my hands through that sand which was once just sand on a beach somewhere. Looking up at that city on the hill which wasn't a city but just lumber and plaster and paper, I kept thinking how nobody driving by the warehouse on the outside could ever in a million years guess what was going on inside.

"This is a perfect moment," Carlos said to both of us. "It's holy." He reached out and took my hand and Scott's hand and held them together, covering them with both his hands and holding tight. "This is the movie we're going to make, and it's going to take all our self-control and self-lessness and our love to do it. We're going to have to give up everything, and only if we really do manage to give up everything is the audience going to know that. You probably want to hear what it's about, why the city on the hill, why the silly costumes you haven't even seen yet, but don't worry, those'll come later. Right now you don't know any of that. Think of it like a dream you're just starting to have; you're starting to find your way around inside it, and you start to think this dream is your own body you're moving around inside of, this is what the dream is, it's your own body, what your own body can do. It's a way of thinking about that body, it's a vision of that body—you could call it a porno-theology, the holy life locked inside muscles and skin—and then all that turned inside out, like a glove, and spilled out into the iconography of the Bible, the Renaissance, all our ways of thinking up to now, the present. Can you see that? What can you do with it?"

It was like Carlos was trying to hypnotize us, which I think was more or less working on Scott, who just sat there nodding. Whatever Carlos said was fine with him, he could listen all day to it. As for me, well, I could tell from the word go Carlos didn't have any idea what he was saying. But that was okay: I knew he was trying to talk his way into something that maybe one day would make sense, but he wasn't there yet. It was something I totally recognized from making *Gomorrah* with him. There weren't any exact words yet for what he wanted to say. There wouldn't be any till he made the movie, and then the movie would be exactly his way of saying it.

In eight months, I told myself, he'll be telling some interviewer all this stuff he's telling us now, and that interviewer'll be eating it up. It'll mean something then.

It's what I always respected about Carlos—the way he was always looking for some way into places nobody'd gone before. Right then I knew I had to be in this movie. I had to help him get wherever it was he was going.

Scott on the other hand was willing to try anything just for the kicks of it.

"I love this instant right now," Carlos said. "The way you're sitting here, you don't know a thing about each other. There's only one moment like this between two people who are just meeting, and this is it, this is that one perfect moment where everything goes from here. Can we start filming? Can we take it from here?"

He motioned with his hand and Seth was there with the camera, the guys who were working on the city cleared out of the way and the klieg lights were on and there we were, we were making Carlos's movie.

I wished I had a long, long swig of whisky somewhere to slug—because my heart was thumping away in my chest like no tomorrow. Scott was smiling his pretty smile at the camera like he had no idea what was going on, and I think he probably didn't. Carlos stood up and moved away behind Seth, who was zeroing in on us. I think I told you before how Carlos was scared to death of being caught on camera even for a few frames that could get cut out anyway. It was this thing he had—like some primitive tribes, Seth always said, who're afraid for their souls.

"Just remember," Carlos was saying to me and Scott sitting there on camera in the sand in front of this fake city in a warehouse in Brooklyn, "it's reality, whatever happens, reality definitely is the sum total of all this."

Scott looked at me and smiled. "So, it's nice to meet you," he said. I had to laugh. I was scared to death, because I knew it was all up to me. That was why Carlos needed me—nothing was going to happen unless I made it happen. And if something did happen, and it was interesting, then that was the only thing that counted.

Well—then let's make things interesting, I remember thinking. I reached out and touched Scott's cheek with the tips of my fingers, barely grazing the skin. Scott seemed completely indifferent to that, it didn't even register on him. I put my other hand up and touched his other cheek, stroking both his cheeks, which were completely smooth—he didn't even have the slightest trace of a beard yet.

I'd never untied somebody's tie before, and it's not as easy as you might think—but finally I managed to get it loose. He kept looking right into my eyes, and I kept looking into his—the way Carlos always did to me. Was that where Scott learned it too? I had to wonder. I unbuttoned the top button of his shirt; suddenly he turned his head to the side and looked up at the ceiling. Then he did this peculiar, sweet thing. He started singing. I don't know what it was—he was singing very quietly and it faded in and out so you could only hear parts of it, and I don't know who he was singing to, but it was like some little child singing. It scared me half to death.

Carlos was going wild. I could see him out of the corner of my eye, behind Seth and the camera. He'd taken a handkerchief out of his pocket, and he was gnawing on it, he was so excited at what was going on. It made me excited too—I concentrated on unbuttoning Scott's shirt, one button at a time, and sliding my hand in between the cloth and his skin. He wasn't wearing any T-shirt, and his skin was ice cold. I found one of his nipples, and rubbed it till its little nub got completely hard and I felt the gooseflesh around it. Scott was still singing—he'd forget a little of his song, and then remember and pick up wherever he could. I thought he could be some kind of mechanical doll, especially with his skin so cold and hard; and I could feel his ribs, the way his skin stretched tight between them.

I wondered if this was giving Scott any kind of hard-on—I was completely stiff in my jeans and it was even a little painful, the way my dick didn't have the room it wanted—but looking down at the front of his pants I couldn't tell. I remember it seemed important to me to know, and I half wanted to grope him down there. But I remembered what Carlos said about all this—how everything was happening here between us for the first time, and after that there wasn't another first time. I had to make it last as long as I could, I had to use that self-control Carlos was talking about. Which was definitely some kind of exciting thing to do.

Scott wriggled his shoulders to help me slide his jacket off him. Then both my hands were inside his shirt and I felt up under his arms to pinch his little tufts of hair. His ice-cold body was sweating something furious. I rubbed my hands down his sides, his hip bones just under the waist of his khakis. He was still singing, but then every once in a while he'd catch his breath, especially when my fingers would slide under his waistband to graze his bush of hair down there. He's got to have a hard-on, I thought—I was fixated on that hard-on, and whether he had one or not.

But I shied away from his dick. I was trying to go really slow and stretch things out like maybe time itself was slow motion in here and if we could stretch it out thinner and thinner we'd fall right through. I liked that idea a lot, which sounds like I was drunk or something—but I wasn't. I was the most stone-sober I ever felt in my whole life. I wanted to cry I felt so sober.

I unbuttoned Scott's shirt cuffs, then I pushed his shirt back on his shoulders and peeled it off. I touched his arms at the bend of the elbow. It made him stop singing. "No," he mumbled in this groggy way, the way somebody would if you bothered them in their deep sleep.

That did it. All this time we'd been sitting facing each other in the sand. Now, grabbing Scott by his belt loops, I yanked us both up so we were standing face to face. It wasn't the smoothest thing in the world—

we both sort of stumbled our way up—but I didn't want us sitting in the sand anymore. I wanted us standing with that city in the background so Seth could get a shot of us there.

I was facing the camera and I could see Carlos off to the side watching. I looked over to him—and then I kissed Scott. I thought it was probably what Carlos wanted—but it was also exactly what I wanted. I wanted to get back at him for everything there was to get back for.

I pushed with my tongue and it went right into Scott's mouth. He tasted like metal, this flat hard taste, but when I put my arms around him he went liquid—his little ice-cold body went flowing in against me in some kind of motion the whole time, his crotch rubbing up against mine, grinding away at me in fact.

He definitely had a hard-on—I could feel it jutting up hard inside his pants. I broke away to catch my breath from that amazing kiss. Scott was breathing pretty hard, and I was too—my head rushing and my dick aching down in my jeans. He pulled back and looked at me with these solemn kid's eyes. It was a kind of breather in this little war we were fighting with each other. His lips looked all swollen up from our kissing, and when he licked them I couldn't stand it any longer. I moved right in against him and undid his pants and slipped both my hands down in there where it was warm, the only part of his whole body that was warm.

And there it was—I had both my hands around this slim little hard dick. "Oh," he said, and he leaned over and bit me on the side of the neck, just a light bite. Then he was sucking on my skin while my hands felt on down in his pants to his balls that were tight and little and all clenched up under his dick. I went ahead and shoved his pants and underwear down—he was wearing these skimpy sky blue things, which I guess is what prep school kids wear. He did a step or two, and then he was out of them, we were both stepping all over them in the sand. He was going crazy on my neck and both my hands were crazy on his dick, moving up and down on it in these big slow pulls.

We broke apart and stood there looking at each other, Scott without a stitch and me still all buttoned up. There was something great about that. I wanted to throw him down in the sand and step all over him, I wanted to show him exactly who was in control here. But before I could do anything, his dick started to completely go soft. I remember—I was really distressed. It was some kind of insult to me, that he'd go limp just like that. But before I could think what to do, Scott had already gone and made the next move.

He turned around, grabbed his ankles, and bent over. I'd never seen anybody's asshole before, and it took me off-guard. I could hear Carlos saying, "That's it, that's it. Now zoom," while I just stood there and gaped. I'd tried to touch Carlos's asshole once or twice because I was curious, but I think I mentioned how that was always off-limits. Now here was this asshole, all pink and puckery and staring right up at me. For a minute I was stunned—like a bird when a cat gets it. My dick completely wilted down to the size of my finger, and I remember thinking, some porn movie this is going to turn out to be where nobody can get it up. I could see Carlos motioning me to turn us so the camera could still get the city in the background. I grabbed Scott's hips and scooted him around a little; then I took my finger and ran it along the crack of his ass where the camera could see. Very slowly, barely touching it—it was something I'd wanted to do to somebody for a long time. When I got to his hole my finger sank right in. I hadn't expected that, but before I knew it my finger was all the way in.

I pulled out, then I stuck two fingers in. Scott groaned and lurched forward a little, but I still had my other hand on his hip so I caught him. I twisted those fingers around. It was amazing how slick it was when you got up in there—like animal innards, which I guess is exactly what it was. He was making noises like I was hurting him some, and that made me go at it even more. I got another finger up in there, then four fingers. I rammed my hand in all the way up to my thumb, and he made this low sound like some animal that's caught in a trap. Like some wolf chewing its leg off, I remembering thinking.

This was making my dick get hard again—especially since I kept shoving those fingers up his ass, paying him back for I wasn't even sure what. But that groan I was wrenching out of him was sweet.

When my fingers came out of Scott's butt for about the twentieth time, I noticed something that sort of made me stop. They had this gook on them, shit mixed with some blood is what it was. It made me go soft all over again and sick to my stomach—which he must've known somehow, because he twisted away from me and threw himself on the sand on his back. It was like he'd washed up on some shore.

There'd been a shipwreck; he'd almost got drowned.

I don't know exactly why I did what I did next. I pulled out my dick and pissed all over him. I pissed on his face and on his chest and in his hair and on his dick, I pissed like I was never going to stop pissing and if you ask me why I did it, I can't tell you. I just did it and it happened and then it was over, Scott was lying there covered in my piss and the sand around him turning dark with it, little grains of sand stuck to his sides where it splattered and my fingers still gooey with his shit and blood. Then Carlos was beside me, touching me on the shoulder and laughing, saying, "Beautiful, beautiful, beautiful—you break my heart." Which I thought might be a joke till I looked at his face and saw he really was crying, these big round tears rolling down his cheeks—and he was laughing and howling like a maniac and wiping at his eyes with the flat of his hand.

I MENTIONED THOSE SNAKESKIN BOOTS CARLOS GOT for me, and that I wore all the time. I remember, after I left The Company and was living in Tennessee, I used to keep those boots on a shelf in the closet. I never wore them, because they looked too good. What I mean is, they were great cowboy boots for New York City, but anybody who wore anything like that in Memphis would've been spotted for a fag in about two seconds.

I can remember exactly when Carlos got them for me. There'd been this nighttime spring thunderstorm over the city, and the air was cool, and when Carlos came back to the apartment—it was late—he was totally drenched from having been caught out in the rain, and he had these boots wrapped up in newspaper. He dumped them on the bed where I was lying, not asleep at all because of the thunderstorm and enjoying the way the cool fresh air was coming in through the windows.

"Where'd you find these?"

"Real snakeskin. For you."

"You're kidding." I could tell right away they were fantastic boots. "You steal them, or what?"

"Would I do a thing like that?" Carlos sat down on the edge of the bed and picked up one of the boots to look at it. It was all sleek and shiny with little scales, like snakeskin's supposed to be. "I just happened to see them, I thought they were completely you."

It was great to hear Carlos say that. I always had the feeling he hardly even thought about me and now here he was calling something "completely me." I think now he probably stole them, or took them off somebody who owed him money as a way of putting them in their place.

But who knows? Maybe he really did walk into some store somewhere and buy them for me because he thought I might like to have them. It's something I'll never know—at the time I was way too happy with those boots to ask any more questions about them. I remember I hopped right out of bed and tried them on—walking around the apartment in them, loving the feel and the look. I must've been a hilarious sight, stalking around with no clothes on, just those boots. But Carlos didn't laugh. I think he was as impressed with how great they looked as I was.

They're the only things Carlos ever gave me. I mean, he gave me lots, but not stuff I could hold in my hands. Carlos never cared about possessions like that. He was a person who was totally content to live in this rundown loft with basically just a mattress to sleep on and a couple pairs of jeans and some T-shirts. He was trying to travel as light as he could, and I think he felt sorry for all those people whose lives got so tangled up in the things they owned that they weren't ever able to do anything else except spend all their time keeping their possessions together. I think in some way that's what all his movies were about— how even one pair of snakeskin boots can ruin your life if you're not careful.

I guess by the time he gave me those, he thought he could trust me to be careful. I remember I wore them all the time—even in the hot summers—and some years later, when I was living in Tennessee, I used to take them out of the closet every once in a while just to look at them. They were all silvery-gray colored, and each one of the little scales caught the light a different way. You could study that snakeskin for hours and never get tired of looking at it. The other thing I liked was how tough they were, even though I know from when I was a kid and used to tromp around in the woods how a snakeskin after it's been shed is the most delicate thing in the world.

But after I left New York I never put them on again, even on those nights when I'd find myself wondering where Carlos was that moment, what he was doing, and I'd wish I was there with him whatever he was doing. I didn't care, I just wanted to be with him. Those were the nights I'd stop at the liquor store on the way home from work and buy a pint of Canadian Club for old times. I'd park my truck on the river bluff—this little park called Tom Lee Park—and watch the Mississippi flow past, and Arkansas in the distance on the other side. In the middle of the park, I remember, there was this monument to Tom Lee—a piece of rock that said on it, A WORTHY NEGRO. Tom Lee was this slave who swam out in the Mississippi when some riverboat caught on fire and saved a bunch of white people from drowning. And he got drowned himself.

I felt completely lonely, like I'd made some wrong turn and gotten very lost. Even though now my life was what you'd call normal and not crazy like it used to be with Carlos, still I felt like there was this wrong turn I'd made. I had a job and a house to go home to and Monica waiting for me and everything. Still, I'd watch the river go past with pieces of lumber and garbage floating in the current, and I'd think about Carlos and it all seemed so far away, like it was a dream that had happened to me but that was all. Those were the nights I might've gone home and dragged those boots out of the closet and put them on, but I never did. It would've been too depressing, and no telling what I might've done once I had them on.

After I left Carlos, there was only one time I ever put those boots back on—but that'll have to be for later.

S O FAR AS I KNOW, CARLOS NEVER TRIED TO RELEASE
The Gospel According to Sodom, which is what he called the movie
we made in the warehouse. He edited it down and everything like he
was going to release it, but then he never did. He kept it to himself,
like some secret diary where he'd put down all his dreams, or maybe I
should say nightmares, about me and Scott.

Probably he'd have gotten into some kind of legal trouble if he
released it—but that can't be the reason why he held onto it.

I know it was an important movie for him to make. Looking back
on everything, I guess you could say everything really started there. I
mean, everything that went on building up till the end, when it finally
came down. Or if it didn't start with *The Gospel,* then at least that's
where it came up to the surface. It was in all the other movies too, but
Carlos never gave it free reign till he locked us in that warehouse for
those three days to see what he could make happen. And even though in
the next couple of movies he made after *The Gospel* he pulled back a lot
from what he'd learned, still there it was inside him, and just knowing
that freed him up.

I also have to say this—I don't think Carlos could've learned the
things he did without me and Scott, and so in some sense I'm partly
to blame for things that happened later. I'm not walking away from
it—I'm taking the blame. Plus, I want to say for the record that I think
Carlos did exactly what he had to do, all the way up through that last
movie, *Boys of Life.* Considering everything that happened, you might
not expect me to say that. But I do say it. And I also say—I did exactly
what I had to do, too.

Which is jumping way ahead to the end—and I'll get there soon enough anyway.

About *The Gospel:* I know there've always been lots of rumors about that movie, mostly from people who weren't there when we made it, and so couldn't have known anything. But there was something about this being Carlos's secret movie that set everybody whispering about the way it was made, the kinds of things Carlos made us do. Making things sound worse than they really were. First off, he didn't make us do anything. Everything we did, we made up on the spot. You could say, we wanted to do it. The shit scene, for example. It's true Scott squatted down over me and dropped this turd right on my chest, and it's true he dabbled around in it a little and even tasted it. But Carlos never made us eat each other's shit. I know some people testified that at my trial, and I know they did it because they thought they were helping me out by saying things like that about Carlos—but they're wrong, and they know it. Just like those same people who later said Carlos hypnotized us before we did scenes like that, so we'd do whatever he wanted us to without being able to resist. But that's also not true. I'll say here for the record that it's not true, and if Scott decided to eat his shit off my chest then that was something he decided to do, and there might've been a lot of reasons for it or maybe there wasn't any reason at all, it was just something he did—but still he was the one who decided to do it.

I think some people who knew Carlos just a little, who talked to him only once or twice, probably figured that here was this guy who, if he wanted to hypnotize somebody, probably could. But finally that's wishful thinking, and Carlos never did any of that—no matter what some of my so-called friends from The Company say.

You didn't find Seth saying things like that on any witness stand. And if anybody was the one to know, it was Seth. How're you going to trust what a few sound men and stagehands have to say over Seth and his camera?

It is true about the fisting scene—I ended up doing that to Scott, but it was something he wanted. Talk about somebody totally into their ass. It's the only time in my life I ever fisted somebody: I could feel his warm slick insides throbbing around me, and I remember I had this feeling I could just keep going, there wasn't anything to stop me from turning him inside out if I wanted to.

The movie wasn't all like that. There was some very funny stuff in it too—like Sammy's part. He was supposed to be king of that painted city, and he got carried around through the whole movie on this throne by these four black men. He'd sit there dressed up in this gold lamé bathrobe, with an onion-dome crown perched on his head. "I'm touring the properties," he'd say, making these blessing motions with his hands like the Pope. "My dominions," he'd say. "Onions for the minions of my dominions."

Also there were the angel wings Verbena strapped on our shoulders, these big gaudy peacock-feather things which were the only clothes Scott and I had on for those three whole days. We had a lot of fun with stuff like that—the huge chandelier throne that lowered down from the ceiling so Scott and I could sail away to heaven, and all the dildoes Sammy kept pulling out of the pockets of his robe to offer us whenever we tried to have a serious conversation with him. "Accept the bounty of my kingdom, fair strangers," he'd say, and bow to us.

There was also the stuff with the pistol.

I know the pistol story's part of the Carlos legend everybody likes to talk about, but everybody gets it totally wrong. And besides, it happened to me, not them.

It was the end of the second day, and everything would've been going fine, I guess, if I hadn't seen this one thing that really upset me. Scott and I'd done some pretty heavy stuff with each other by then, including this one scene with one of the dildoes Sammy'd presented us with, this monster thing Scott went and worked up into me. None too gently, I have to say—like he was paying me back.

Afterward, I was walking around letting my guts calm down a little, feeling both incredibly lifted up and also totally emptied out. I'd wandered over to the corner of the warehouse where we'd tossed our clothes that first day, and then I saw Scott. He was sitting on this pile of tarpaulins, with nothing on except his peacock-feather angel wings. At first I thought he was jerking off—which would've been a little strange, considering. I took about three more steps toward him and then I stopped. He had a belt wrapped around his arm, and he was making a fist, flexing it. He drew a little blood from his arm up into the syringe and held it there, then eased it back into his arm, and when he did that he kind of shivered.

It's something I'll remember till I die, that shiver. I didn't move. I couldn't. I could hear Verbena or somebody hammering something somewhere up in the rafters, but the sound was so hollow it didn't fill the space of that warehouse at all. After what seemed like forever but was probably about fifteen seconds, Scott pulled the syringe out of his arm and laid it in a little case that was open on his lap. Then he undid the belt and wound it into loops, and laid it on his folded-up trousers.

He didn't see me, and I backed away without making a sound. But I went straight to Carlos and told him I was getting out, I couldn't stand this anymore.

He was sitting down, writing some stuff in a little notebook. He didn't even look up.

"You can't get out," he said. He was completely calm about it. "It's too late," he said.

"Of course I can," I told him. "This is a free country. I can walk out any time I want to."

"Try it," he said.

That's when he pulled out the pistol.

My heart stopped. "I don't believe it," I told him. "You're crazy." I was yelling at him. "Can't you understand about people's lives? People's lives aren't movies."

"I'm not making movies," Carlos said. He was still sitting, and still completely calm. And still pointing the pistol right at me.

I'm sure I was a sight. Standing there in front of him completely naked except for those stupid peacock-feather angel wings.

"Then what do you think you're making?" I said.

"I'm making reality," Carlos said. "I'm trying to make a little bit of reality."

"You *are* crazy," I told him. It was the first time I ever stood up to him like that. "You don't know what's what anymore."

"Or maybe you're afraid I actually do," Carlos said. "And that scares you to death, doesn't it? That I took some dumb little fucked-up country kid and showed him some ways of looking at things he never even thought about, and now he doesn't know what to do with all that. He doesn't know how to use it, and so he's afraid of what he sees. He closes his eyes, because he's afraid what he sees all around him might really be reality. And so he wants to run away."

"There's not anything real in your movies, Carlos, there's not anything there," I told him, sick in the pit of my stomach to know all of a sudden that he was right and I was wrong, that it really was reality, me and Sammy wandering the alphabets, me and Scott fucking in some warehouse in Brooklyn—all that was just as much reality as anything else, and what's worse, it was my life. I'd lived through all those things and they were just as real as anything that ever happened to me. And if all those things could happen and be my life then anything else could too.

Carlos was also right that I was scared to death. Plus he had that pistol.

"All right, all right," I told him. "I'll stay."

"I knew you would." He grinned that tight grin of his, then he put the pistol away. He'd never even stood up in the whole argument. But I could see he was embarrassed, like the instant he pulled that pistol was the one single time in his life he hadn't trusted me, and he was ashamed of that.

I was fine for the moment. I told everybody within earshot I was fine, not to worry. But as soon as I got away from Carlos and found a place to sit down and put myself back together, I started trembling all over just thinking about what had happened. He must've known I was going to be upset, because I hadn't been sitting there three minutes before he came over. He sat down beside me and put his arm around me, which with those angel wings was clumsy to do.

"I guess angels don't hug much," he said.

"Angels don't do a lot of things. They don't even exist."

"Look," he told me. "I'm sorry. I'm really sorry. I don't know what happened."

"You have a gun," I told him. I still couldn't believe he was carrying a gun.

He took it out. "Go ahead," he said, "it's all yours. Shoot me—I deserve it."

"I don't want to shoot you, are you crazy?"

He forced me to take the gun in my hand anyway.

"Put it to my head," he said. "Pull the trigger."

He took my hand where I was holding the gun and dragged it over to his temple. "There," he said. "Go on, pull the trigger."

I threw the gun down on the floor—it made a clattery noise on the concrete.

"So we're even," he said.

I looked at him. "We're not ever going to be even," I had to tell him. And I guess he knew that. He stood up and put his hands in his pockets like he didn't know what to do next.

"I know it's hard," he said. "It's impossible. We have to keep on going in spite of all that. There was this newspaper, a revolutionary newspaper back a hundred years ago, and its motto was this—its motto said *Pessimism of the mind, optimism of the will.* Do you understand what that means?"

I did understand, sort of.

"We have to keep living that way," Carlos said. "Every single one of us. You and me and Scott and all of us. Until we drop down dead." He picked up the gun and put it back in his pocket.

And that was that. Maybe I should've pulled the trigger—when I look back on it, I think that maybe he really did want me to shoot him right then and there. But I wasn't about to do that. It wouldn't have made any sense to do it.

When I thought about it, it made complete sense that Scott was shooting junk—I should've guessed it from the start, the way he couldn't keep his dick hard for more than half a minute at any one time. It was frustrating—I used to nibble at it like it was some little fish I was trying to slurp down, but nothing would happen. After a while it'd usually start to crank up, and I'd think, Oh good. It'd get about halfway there and then die down again. The whole three days I kept trying to work him back into a hard-on like he'd had for a couple of minutes that first time when I was undressing him, but I never did.

One last thing I should mention about that movie—how the last scene we did for it was in a way just the reverse of the first scene we shot. We unstrapped those dumb angel wings we'd been wearing for the last three days. I pulled on my jeans and T-shirt, Scott got back in his prep school outfit. I remember watching him disappear inside his clothes, till he turned back into this prep school kid anybody could see walking down the street and never know about. But underneath all those clothes was still his dick I'd sucked on and his balls I'd licked, and under the balls that smooth hard cord of muscle running back to his asshole I'd been inside of, and past that—all his insides I'd felt my way up into.

"See you around," he said, like we'd just met and nothing else ever happened, it was just some fever he'd had.

"Yeah, see you around," I told him. He didn't hug me or shake my hand or anything—though he did hug Carlos. Carlos held him like that, facing me and looking over Scott's shoulder right into my eyes for the longest time—this look I can still remember but have no idea what it meant, only that I think I knew it from seeing it in some of those pictures in the library book Sammy took me to see that time.

E ARL WAS IN HERE AGAIN TODAY, BRINGING ME A
couple of articles I'd asked him for. He took the opportunity to
get out those pictures of his kids one more time. Does he really not
remember he's showed them to me?

Today he said, "I love my boys. I don't ever want anything to
happen to them. But they're growing up, Tony. I can't stop that. I came
home yesterday and my wife, Doreen, was crazy—out of her head
crazy. You see, the boys went out on their bikes—they ride around the
block, but we don't let them go farther than that. So they went out on
their bikes, but they didn't come back. It was seven o'clock, pitch dark,
and they still weren't back. 'Boys'll be boys,' I told her. But Tony, I had
this fright. Sure, they got back okay—turned out they'd been at some
friend's house. He'd got this electric train set for his birthday, and they
went and forgot all about the time. You know: boys'll be boys.

"But Doreen was furious. She went out in the backyard and cut a
switch, and she switched them right there in the kitchen. Made them
take their pants down and everything. And you know what one of them
said? He turned to his mother and said, 'Now what do you think this
is gonna prove?'

"I guess I understand why Doreen was so furious. She loves those
boys as much as I do. But I got this awful feeling, Tony—like I was
looking into the future. You know how you can't hold onto anything?
That's what I was looking at."

Looking at Earl's face while he told me all that, I realized something.
I'd seen that look before: this woman on the jury, who kept looking at
me the same way. For three weeks, no matter who was on the witness

stand or what was getting said, she just kept looking at me—this black woman, I guess about sixty, sixty-five. One thing about her—she wore a turquoise-blue dress one day, and a green dress the next, and then back to the turquoise and then the day after that it'd be the green one again. All through that trial, only two dresses. And the same pillbox hat: rainbow-colored, made out of feathers. You could tell life hadn't been too great to her. But there she was, doing her jury duty. And looking at me the whole time like I had some kind of answer to all the stuff that was getting said. Like everything that got said was some kind of question to her, and she was desperate to know the answer.

I've got lots of reasons for writing all this, but that old black woman's one of them. Earl too. I don't imagine I can clear anything up for either of them, but I can at least try to tell my side of things the way they really happened—even if it does make me look bad sometimes. Because I feel sick to my stomach when I think about what went on at that trial. It was my trial, right? I should at least've called a few of the shots. But I didn't. I let my lawyer do everything the way he wanted. I let him stand up there and call Carlos a "totally unnecessary human being." I let him say that. I let him tell the jury, with his voice all emotional like a preacher's when he gets to the part of the sermon where he asks for money, how Carlos went and took this young kid, practically stole him out of his mother's house. How he destroyed my life, and then wasn't content to just throw me away when he was finished with me, but had to go on hounding me even when I tried to find some normal life for myself.

I let my lawyer say that, I guess because I was scared and anything he could say to convince those people sitting there on the jury that what I did was what I had to do, then I was going to let him say it. I didn't know any better. I was too scared of dying.

For the record, I'm taking back everything my lawyer said. This time around, I'm trying to get it right.

DURING THOSE THREE YEARS BETWEEN THE TIME we finished making *The Gospel* and when I met Monica, we made what lots of people think are some of Carlos's best movies: *The Only Bitterness of Anna,* which was Verbena's big acting role and I had only this tiny part in; *Creeping Bent,* starring me and Sammy, which we filmed on that old estate up the Hudson River; and *Cloud Pavane,* that documentary he did about people living down in the subway tunnels. They were tamer than *The Gospel,* which is why they got released and shown around. But like I said earlier, without making *The Gospel* and then stashing it away like it was some kind of wound he didn't want anybody else to know about, he couldn't have made any of the others.

During all that time Carlos and I never had sex again after that night when he said we shouldn't. That changed lots of things between us. It was pretty hard for me for a while, just to have it end like that. Making *The Gospel,* though, put some kind of barrier between the way we used to be, and the way we were now, and it didn't really seem like either of us could go back. Once I'd fucked Scott, that was sort of it between us—for us to have sex anymore might've been fun, but it also would've been pointless. Even I could understand that.

It freed me up, in sort of the same way that going with Sammy to the public library that first time had freed me up. It wasn't long after we made *The Gospel* before I was going out on my own and getting dates. That was Carlos's word for it—he treated my dates the way he'd treated my running all over the city that first winter: like some great adventure that I'd learn tons from. And he was right.

He'd always say, "So, do you have a date?" Which meant, Was I planning to go out to Uncle Charlie's or the St. Mark's Baths and pick somebody up and fuck them? And lots of nights—or afternoons, or even mornings—the answer was yes. I guess I just sort of said, Fuck it, and once I said that I wasn't scared anymore. I didn't mind going out all hours of the night all over the city, just looking around to see what was what. And once you start looking, at least in New York, it's all there— the bars, the clubs, the baths. If I couldn't have Carlos, then I was going to have everything else.

I had bike messengers and telephone repairmen, and a cop, and a businessman from Uganda in the Plaza Hotel, who paid me six hundred dollars. I had models who were doing shoots for GQ, and a ballet dancer and about twenty different waiters. I had two French sailors from the SS Joan of Arc, and a graduate student from NYU who was writing his dissertation on the early films of Carlos Reichart and of course had no idea who I was. I had a fifteen-year-old Puerto Rican drag queen who said his name was Ramonda Ramrod with the biggest dick I ever saw, and a Pakistani cab driver who took me to Queens and we did it in the back of his cab parked on the shoulder of the BQE in broad daylight.

I never stopped wanting Carlos to fuck me again, but he never did. He'd gone on to other things, and I had to respect that. I had to respect him for knowing where things stopped. It didn't change anything else between us. In fact, you could say the instant he stopped fucking me, Carlos started treating me like one of the important people in The Company, somebody he depended on, like Sammy or Verbena or Seth. I started to understand how that was Carlos's pattern with people—he set his mark on them, and then when he knew he had them, he went on to collect somebody else. I don't resent that—I think I did for a while, but I don't anymore.

I think I even remember the exact instant I stopped resenting it. I'd been at this bar and got picked up by some guy I didn't find all that great-looking, but that didn't matter. During the big sleep—which is what I call those years—I was interested in just seeing whatever would happen and I didn't really care with who. So we were walking down the Bowery toward this guy's apartment—it was late at night, probably four o'clock—and somebody was coming toward us along the sidewalk, hands in his pockets, and I thought to myself how that person looked completely lonely and sad.

Then I saw it was Carlos. I don't know where he was coming from—
he might have been up all night editing and just taken the train in from
Brooklyn. Maybe he'd been trailing some boy around town but he'd
finally lost the scent. Who knows? We didn't say anything—but we
looked at each other and just nodded as we passed. It was like we were
saying to each other, Well, what do you know? Like we knew everything we had to say, so there wasn't any reason to stop and talk.

The guy I was with—I've completely forgotten everything about
him—didn't know a thing about what was happening, and that was
the way it should be. It was still me and Carlos, however things looked,
and we both knew that. I remember thinking, almost saying it out loud
while we walked on down the street, You've got me in your hands,
Carlos, you know you've got me in your hands.

One other big thing happened to me in all that time: I stopped
drinking. I mean, I didn't stop drinking totally, but I changed
a lot from that kid I used to be, who couldn't get through the day
without taking a couple of shots of Canadian Club every hour to
keep me steady. Now, a couple of beers and I was content. No more
Canadian Club. It's funny, but part of what stopped me from drinking
was hanging out in bars trying to pick up guys I thought were sexy.
The last thing I wanted was to be sloshed in Uncle Charlie's—there
was too much to pay attention to.

It's hard to put my finger on why I stopped being the drunkard kid
I was and started being some kind of adult, but I think it started in that
warehouse in Brooklyn. I don't know whether Carlos knew it at the
time, but those three days he locked me up in that warehouse were the
longest time in five years I'd gone without a drink, and it was pretty
severe. To be honest—the main reason I wanted to leave there, that time
Carlos pulled the pistol on me, wasn't because I'd seen Scott shooting
up. That was just an excuse. The real reason was, I needed a drink, and
I was embarrassed to tell Carlos I was dying for a drink, I was out of
control for a drink. So when I saw Scott with his needle, that did it.

Actually, Carlos must've known what was going on with me. That
must've been one of the reasons he locked me up there in the first place.
I'll never know for sure, but what happened was, when I came out of that
warehouse after those three days, my first thought was that I had to get
to the nearest bar and slug something into my system to keep it going.

I remember standing there on the street outside that warehouse, with everybody packing the van to go back to Manhattan, and wondering how soon I was going to be able to snatch a drink somewhere. Wondering whether there might be some bar around the corner where I could just disappear.

I set out to see. At the end of the street, under these concrete piers that held up an elevated expressway, there was this stripped-down car. I wandered over to it—everything you could take out of it had gotten taken away, there was nothing left. And it'd been burned too— it was this rusty-black color. So while Carlos and Seth and Verbena were loading the camera equipment, I climbed inside that car skeleton. I don't know why I did—it was odd sitting in there, not going anywhere. There were a bunch of needle works lying around on the floorboard, and a couple of condoms—which made me remember this story I'd heard, I can't remember where, of somebody who went around picking up used condoms off the ground and sucking the come out of them. I just sat there and looked at those condoms and thought about that. It didn't make me sad or gross me out or anything—it was just something to think about while I could hear Carlos's voice talking in the distance, and then Verbena, and the sounds of them loading the van. I thought about all the things that must've happened in that burned-out car, and how nobody would ever know.

I picked up one of those condoms from off the floor and held it between my fingers. It'd been there for a while, whatever come was in its tip dried up a long time ago. But I remembered something from way back—what Carlos had once said to me the first time he ever gave me a blow job, when he said how your come holds all the information there is about you, and I thought about the dried-up come in that condom and how that was true here too, only here it was just thrown away, all that information.

When it was time to leave Carlos came over to me—I guess he'd seen me sitting there in that car, but he hadn't wanted to bother me. He probably figured I'd earned a few minutes to myself.

"Tony, you okay?" he asked me, leaning in at the window.

"Dad," I told him, "you never gave me a car for my birthday."

It just came into my head to say that.

"Your old dad's not a rich man," Carlos said, playing along with it. I don't know whether he thought it was odd or not. "Your old dad gives you what he can."

"I know," I told him.

And I think I did know. I felt fine. I felt quiet. When we got back to Manhattan I didn't go to a bar like I'd planned. I went home and fell asleep for a long time, and when I woke up I wasn't an alcoholic anymore, which was the first time in probably six years.

Of course I've never stopped drinking completely. But even though there were always nights where I'd drift back to the Canadian Club, it was only once every three months or so and then I was back on the wagon again. It's some old self I have to get out of my system, and when I drain it dry, then that's it.

One other thing I should say here too, which somehow in my mind's all connected up with me not drinking anymore. About a month or so after we finished making *The Gospel,* Carlos dumped Scott Farris just like he dumped me. It was all for still some other kid who I don't think I ever met—there were a bunch of them in those years, though they never lasted very long. And for Scott, some pretty bad things happened one after the other. He got into big trouble back at his prep school for dealing, and there was some trial where he fingered somebody completely other than Carlos—which I'm sure is some twisted-up story if only I knew it—and then he ended up in a detox program.

Seth was the one who told me all that—Carlos never said a word about it, even during the trial when he must've been pretty nervous that anything could happen. But Carlos and I never talked about Scott after *The Gospel*—it was like he never existed. When I say Carlos dumped Scott the way he dumped me, *dump*'s not the right word, even though I probably would've felt like it was exactly the right word at the time. You could say he eased us back down—that's more what it was than dumping, because I have to say about Carlos that you never for an instant got the sense he stopped loving you just because he moved on to somebody else. In fact, I think I only started to understand that he loved me after he did dump me.

I think now that in some way he had to move through that stage of completely desperate fucking with somebody before he learned how to love them. Maybe I'm trying to make myself feel better—I don't see any reason why I should at this point, but maybe I still am. But I really think whatever relation we had with each other grew up the instant he moved on to Scott. I think in a way what it told me was—all right, from now on you're going to have help, you know where help is, but the only person who's going to save you is you. Because, like I said, I basically stopped drinking, and for a while I even got this on-again off-again job working in a paint supply store on Second Avenue—which Carlos didn't ask me to do, I just did it because I thought I needed to. I started to go around thinking about myself as this regular person who's got his head down against the wind but he's determined to make it. And I think the same thing went for Scott too, what with the detox program and everything. I think if you asked him he'd give Carlos some kind of credit too.

Every once in a while over the next few years I'd run into Scott. Whenever that happened, we were always friendly—I don't think he blamed me for the movie at all, I think in fact he felt like we'd been through this certain thing together, and that was some bond we had.

I think it was some kind of politeness on both our parts that we never talked about Carlos, even though something would come up now and then and we'd both just look at each other and know.

I remember the one time we ever did talk about Carlos. It was in the winter, late at night, and I'd wandered into this bar off Christopher Street. I wasn't drinking, I was just checking out various places to see if there was anybody I wanted to go home with. Or not even go home with—just guys to meet and talk to. And there was Scott sitting at the bar drinking some tropical-looking fag drink. Once the prep school kid, always the prep school kid. He had on this black leather jacket that looked great.

I edged in beside him at the bar.

"So, Tony Blair," he said.

I was always surprised when he remembered my name. In lots of ways it was like we didn't know anything about each other—though it was also strange to look at him and think, I've pissed on this guy's face. I've had my fist inside him.

Scott had had a few drinks already. I was standing with my foot on the lower rung of his bar stool, and he took my knee and pulled it in so it rested against his crotch. I was a little surprised by that, but I kept my knee there.

It's odd how one thing'll trigger something else. What I remembered the instant he did that was something I always told myself I meant to ask Scott if I ever saw him again, but then whenever I did see him, I'd forget. But this night I remembered it.

"That junk you used to be on," I asked him. "Who got that stuff for you?"

He just looked at me like he didn't know what I was talking about.

"Carlos got it for you, didn't he? You can tell me. I never see Carlos these days."

Scott smiled that smile of his that was going to get him through life. I put some pressure on his crotch with my knee, which I guess he liked. He ordered himself another drink.

"Don't you want anything?" he asked me. "I'll buy."

"I want to know if Carlos was giving dope to little kids. That's what I want."

"You mean me in particular?"

"Yeah. For starters."

He swirled his new drink with the little umbrella that was stuck in it. I'd have been embarrassed to drink something like that, but he was smiling at it like it was some friend of his.

"If it wasn't for Carlos," he told me, "I wouldn't have gone into detox like I did. How's that for an answer?"

I didn't know how that was for an answer.

"You're saying he's the one who got you off drugs? But he was selling drugs, wasn't he? That's how he came up with the money for his movies. He sold drugs to little kids. Tell me I've figured it out."

It was something that just hit me one day after we'd finished making *The Gospel,* and though I thought about it a lot, I knew I couldn't ask anybody in The Company. It'd get back to Carlos, and if it was something Carlos didn't want me to know about, then maybe it was because he was protecting me, and I had to respect that.

"Beats me." Scott shrugged. "I don't know anything about making movies. All I know is, they're expensive. But everything's expensive. And you know why? It's the Japanese. Where I work, this sushi restaurant, I take a look around me, and all my bosses—you know, the guys with the money—they're all Japanese. All I hear is Japanese, and I think—so this is just what it would be like if the Japs won the war."

There was a rip in my jeans about halfway up my thigh, and while we talked he slid his finger in that hole and sort of rubbed my skin. It felt nice, though his finger was still as ice cold as it used to be. He looked up at me and kind of laughed.

"So how about it?" he said.

I hadn't seen Scott in about a year—I'd run into him a total of maybe five times since we finished the movie back in 1980 and this was, I think, the winter of '82. He looked a lot older. He wasn't nearly as cute as he used to be.

We went back to his apartment—this tiny little room with nothing in it but a mattress and a lot of fancy stereo equipment—and I fucked him, and then because by that time he was off the junk that'd kept him from being able to keep a hard-on the whole time we were doing the movie, he fucked me too.

That was the last time I saw him, because not too long after that I left the city for good.

CREEPING BENT IS THE NAME OF SOME KIND OF plant, but that didn't have anything to do with the movie *Creeping Bent*. Carlos just liked the name. He thought it sounded spooky, so he took it and made it into The Company's biggest production ever—bigger even than the city Verbena built in the warehouse.

This old lady named Mrs. Jarique owned a huge mansion about seventy-five miles up the Hudson River from New York—somehow Carlos had talked her into letting us use the place. I mean, move up there for the months of August and September and live with her, and film a whole movie there. Some people say she was just some crazy old lady Carlos took advantage of—and maybe she *was* crazy. Anybody who'd let The Company live in their house for two months has got to be crazy, right?

Friulia, the place was called—the biggest house I ever saw in my life, three stories that rambled along the top of a hill overlooking the river. There were towers and turrets, and balconies jutting out all over. Even though it was down on its luck, still you could tell it'd once been something. There was fancy carved wood everywhere, and marble, and Persian carpets that Sammy, who knew about carpets, got all excited over and told us to be careful not to ruin. The only time I ever saw him yell at Carlos was when Carlos started to track mud across one of those carpets one day—not paying attention, because Carlos never paid much mind to things like that. And it was interesting how Sammy could turn Carlos into a little kid with just a couple of words. Carlos went slinking off with this look on his face I'd never seen before, like Sammy'd caught him at something. Caught him in the act of being Carlos, maybe. But after that day, the carpets started to figure in Seth's camera work—all those tight little curls of design, where anything could be hidden in them and you wouldn't know it. In fact, the movie starts and ends with a carpet—all those vines and flower shapes shown close-up, so they fill up the screen, and then gradually pulling back to show how the design's all locked in together.

Mrs. Jarique was so old she couldn't walk—there was this very nice black man named Maurice who wheeled her around. Not that she ever wanted to go anywhere much—but sometimes, when it was nice out, she loved to sit on the terrace and look at the river. It's something I've spent a lot of time doing—not looking at that river, but at the Mississippi—and I know how nothing can make you think like looking at the way a river goes by. How it just keeps on going and nothing can stop it. There's worse to do than looking at a river.

I think she liked me, Mrs. Jarique, though she couldn't ever remember my name—she called me Tommy or Tim or sometimes names that weren't even close to Tony. Phillip was one of her favorites. And she called me Matthew sometimes. I never knew whether those were people she knew once upon a time, and she was so old now that everything blurred together, or whether she just plain couldn't remember my name.

She was always startling me with the things she said. I'd be walking by her wheelchair and she'd sing out, "Have you ever been in Guatemala? I went dancing in Guatemala once. My father's ship anchored off the coast for a month, and we went dancing every night."

I think probably most of what she said was true—who'd make up a story about dancing in Guatemala? She was so rich—at least she had been at some time in her life—that she'd probably been everywhere she said she had.

We moved right in on her. After all those years cooped up in that dingy apartment on Avenue C, it was terrific to be out in the country, and have all this space around you, and green trees and a huge empty lawn with nothing cluttering it up. There were about twelve, maybe fifteen of us in all who went up there for the movie, and we each had our own separate bedroom. That was how huge Friulia was.

Some of those rooms hadn't been used in ages. In mine, there was this bouquet of flowers that must've been there twenty years. All I had to do was breathe on it and those flowers fell apart. The outside wall had leaked water over the years, and the wallpaper— this red velvet stuff, all fuzzy to the touch—had ugly splotches on it.

I remember the first day we where there, we were comparing our rooms. Sammy was saying how his room had a whole suit of armor in it, and he saw a mouse too, which ran under the bed. Verbena's room had a balcony off it, and a set of secret stairs that went up to a locked door.

"Well," I told them, "I got fungus from outer space living all over the wall in my room."

Carlos wasn't paying too much attention to us—he was writing things down in his little spiral notebook. But when I said that, he perked up. "Let's see," he said. "Let's see, let's see, I knew this would happen"— and we all went traipsing up to my room, which was on the third floor. When he saw that wallpaper, and the big water stains that'd turned the red velvet black and green, he went wild. "It's perfect," he said. "The fungus from outer space. Of course, of course," he kept saying, and dancing around the room in the way he'd sometimes do when he saw something happening on camera that he hadn't expected, but that once it happened he loved to see.

None of us knew at the time what the movie was going to be about— Carlos never told us anything till he started shooting. His movies always made themselves up as they went along. I don't have to tell you how the fungus from outer space ended up playing a major part. In some way, I guess you could say it turned into the creeping bent the movie's name was about.

In the movie, the house is some kind of way station for these creatures from other planets, or another dimension, or maybe they're just dreams—like in all Carlos's movies, you're never sure. It's done with puppets—great big puppets Verbena designed. I helped her sew them down in New York, sitting in her kitchen listening to salsa music come through the wall from next door.

The aliens—if that's what they are—have been passing through the house for years. It's something Sammy and I, who live there, have gotten totally used to. They're real to us—we have conversations with them, though they don't exactly talk back to us. But now something's happened, something's gone wrong, and they're trapped here on their way through to other places. Stranded.

And the house keeps getting bigger. Outside, it stays the same—but inside, there start to be all these rooms Sammy and I never knew were there. Somehow, by trying to get out, the aliens keep adding new rooms on the house. Every morning, Sammy and I find new rooms, or a new staircase where there wasn't one the night before—it leads to a floor of the house that's impossible to be there, but it's there anyway. The house isn't a hundred times, it's a million times bigger than we thought.

We go in one room and it's the inside of an opera house—we went down to the Bardavon in Poughkeepsie to shoot that scene. Another time we find a room that, when we go inside it, is like being outdoors in a field—only it's still just another room in the house, and at the other end of the outdoors there's another door that leads you back into another room. And the puppets are everywhere—they're part of the furniture, the walls, they're in the air. When I open up a jar of mustard, the aliens—or whoever they are—come spilling out, inflating up to full size right before my eyes.

It's Carlos's most gorgeous movie, because of the house, which Carlos somehow makes seem to have more rooms than it does, and also because of Verbena's puppets. I wish I could paste some pictures in here of those puppets, because if you've never seen them then you can't know how bizarre and pretty they were. Sort of like huge jellyfish, only decorated all over with seashells and half-moons and old lace. Like somebody's gone and dipped a jellyfish in a vat of trinkets from a junk store.

Mrs. Jarique loved the puppets. She'd sit there and applaud when we did scenes with them, and she'd shout things at them. "The Great Wall of China," she'd shout. "Madame Li, 1923. And the spoiled gown. Egg stains. The Great Wall."

Carlos didn't mind, since we never did sync sound anyway. She could yell her head off at those puppets for all he cared. And I think he kind of liked it that she yelled like that—it got us all in some kind of mood.

While we were filming up there, a hurricane came through. What it started out as was this tropical depression in the Atlantic Ocean that Verbena somehow took notice of. She was always skittish about the weather: she'd lived through a tornado when she was a little girl, and the man who lived next door got killed when the wind picked him up and slammed him into a tree. Verbena saw it, or that's what she always said. For some reason, she got fixated on this one particular tropical depression: she said she had a feeling about it, right from the start. None of us paid it any mind till it got upgraded into a tropical storm and started heading north. When Verbena heard that, she made us keep the radio on the whole day, tracking it while it turned from a storm into a hurricane out over the water somewhere and still kept moving toward New York.

"Just you wait," Verbena said. "We're sitting in a natural hurricane funnel here. The Hudson Valley. You look at any map and you'll see. Storm'll come gusting up that river," she predicted.

What especially worried her were the suspension bridges we saw out the train window on the way up. Every one of those bridges was going to buck and sway and finally break loose in the storm. Barges were going to get tossed around like toys in a bathtub.

For two whole days, while the hurricane moved closer, she kept us going.

Even Mrs. Jarique got into the act. "Tierra del Fuego," she told us. "Land of fire. We were sick for days. Seasick. Ask him."

Sometimes she thought Sammy was the captain of the ship we were all sailing on.

"It's true," he told everybody. "We were all seasick, every one of us. But we made it, didn't we?"

"Naked Indians," Mrs. Jarique said. "Go ahead, tell them."

"Naked Indians," said Sammy, like he believed every word of it.

As the storm got closer, the radio talked about it more and more.

"If it's going to be so bad up here, what about New York?" I asked the rest of the group.

We all tried to imagine the streets underwater, like Verbena said they'd be.

"Phone booths'll be floating down the streets," Seth said.

"Beds with people in them," said Sammy.

"Thousands'll drown in the subway," Verbena told us. We were all a little giddy with being out of the city after living cooped up there so long. The open space got to us, and we were doing what I'd never have thought: we were missing New York.

It was a way to let off energy from the movie. We knew that. Every movie we made, there was always something we came up with to keep the craziness down in between scenes, whether it was that endless mission we were always on during *Gomorrah* to find Sammy a coffee-shop, or the time we spent with a Ouija board when we were making *The Only Bitterness of Anna,* trying to get in touch with spirits.

When the hurricane finally came, it was nothing—a rainstorm that went on all night, and some trees that got knocked down. We woke up the next morning and the sun was shining, and it was cool.

V ERBENA WAS THE PERSON I HUNG OUT WITH MOST
during those years from 1980 to 1983. I went over to her place
in Brooklyn a lot. Not the place with the pigeons on the roof. That
building got torn down, and T.J and his pigeons moved to the Bronx,
where his cousin lived in a high-rise that had a perfect roof for pigeons.

Verbena's new apartment was on the same block as the old one, but it
was totally different. Nothing from the old place was there anymore—
the pot plants had died, and she'd given everything else away. It was
something she did every couple of years—to "keep from getting stale,"
she said. In the new place, there were books everywhere—I wouldn't've
said Verbena was much of a reader, but it turned out she was always
reading books on magic and astrology, and she knew all about casting
spells and reading palms and doing people's birth charts. On the walls
she had posters showing the planets and the various stars that influence
you, and also the body and all the systems inside the body.

There was a card table by the front windows that was completely
covered in plants—leggy things with big strange blossoms that smelled
up the whole apartment. There was always some kind of incense burning
too, and underneath the smell of the flowers and the incense there was
this other smell that I have to call the Verbena smell, this moist sweet
sweaty smell that was the smell of her big body. It was a smell I kind of
liked—though probably most people wouldn't. But it made me feel at
home, if that makes any sense—a homey smell.

There was this window in her kitchen that looked out across the
empty lot full of bricks and broken bottles where her old building had
been. By day it was pretty ugly, but come late afternoon it was an open

space that let the light in. I'd sit there, and she'd cook rice and black beans, which I loved, and slice some raw onions to go on top. It was very peaceful, just the two of us and the little TV set that was always running but with the sound off—"my fireplace," Verbena used to say. We'd talk a lot, and she'd smoke jimson, this stuff country people used to smoke back in Kentucky when they had colds. Verbena said it was better than pot, once you got used to how strong it was—plus it was completely legal, not that that made any difference to her. She had some cousin of hers send packets up from Alabama, and she kept it in a mason jar on the kitchen table.

Every time I'd go over there she'd roll some and offer it to me, but I never joined in—I'm one of those people who's never been able to get high. Not that I didn't try over the years. I used to completely disgust Seth when we'd sit up half the night smoking—he'd be so stoned he couldn't even talk, and nothing happening to me except a headache. The couple of times I tried jimson, it was the same. Verbena always teased me, though: "Shy girl," she'd say, "you're getting high just like everybody else. Your brain's just not fine-tuned enough to know that's what happening to it."

"I've always been a clod," I admitted.

"Some clod," she said. "This clod is definitely high heels all the way."

It didn't matter to me that I couldn't get high, though it might've been fun to get buzzed with Verbena once in a while. But by the time I was hanging out with her, I was pretty much straight all the time. It was like I'd had this other life we could both sit and look back on.

She told me one evening, "You know how we was all of us pulling for you."

She was sitting in this bright blue robe she used to wear, and her hair was pulled back from her head in this tight bun. The jimson smoke made the kitchen smell like some field had just been mowed.

"Pulling for me how?" I asked her.

"I mean, to see you make it through," she said. I knew she must be talking about Carlos.

"Through to the other side," she said. She sort of cocked an eyebrow while she looked at me.

I understood how it meant "through to the other side of Carlos."

Because there were people who didn't make it through, and they fell away, they got lost. But if you made it through to the other side, like Netta and Sammy and Seth and Verbena had done, then you were there for good.

"Sometimes I want it to be like it used to be. Before I made it through."

"You miss him," she said.

"I miss getting fucked, if you want to know the truth." I'd always been able to be completely open with Verbena. Part of it was just who she was—the most generous person in the world. And part of it was remembering her shooting fire out of her butt, because if you can't talk to somebody like that about getting fucked, then who can you?

Most of the time we didn't talk about Carlos—but it was like she was sitting up with me till missing him wore off. It was like some assignment he gave her to do. In the meantime, she kept me entertained telling me all about herself—which could be pretty wild, at least when I was in the mood to believe what she was saying.

"I was raised up on conjure," she told me one night. "My daddy was Doctor Jim Jordan. Don't pretend you never heard about him—he was the most famous root doctor in the whole South. Even in Kentucky they heard about him. And he was growing me to follow in his footsteps."

"So can you really do spells?" I asked her. I thought there might be some use for a spell or two to throw on Carlos.

"Anybody can do spells," she told me. "Making them work— that's where the living's at."

"So could you make them work?"

"I used to help," she said. "I used to stand around with the slop bucket when people came to be cured of lizards and such like that would get in their stomachs."

"People would really have lizards in their stomachs?"

"That's what they thought they had. So who's to say they don't, if getting rid of that lizard's going to make them feel better. My daddy'd conjure that lizard out, and usually what'd happen was, they'd commence to vomiting. I was there with my slop bucket to catch it. Then I'd be out the door fast so I could throw that nasty stuff away."

"Was there ever a lizard in it?" I could never tell how much Verbena was playing with me.

"Sometimes when I was already out the door, my daddy called me back. He'd say come on back here and let's see that lizard that came on out of there."

"And would there be one?"

"Sometimes there was a lizard in there," Verbena said. "Sure there was a lizard sometimes. I remember it." She smiled her smile that had three or four teeth in it—she always looked sly even when she was telling some kind of truth. She lifted her jimson cigarette to her lips and took a drag. She had these big costume jewelry rings on every one of her fingers.

"Daddy was fighting off dirty work all the time," she reminisced. "We had each one of the rooms in that house all papered with newspaper to keep busy the witches that were coming there."

"What're you talking about, newspaper?" I asked. It was something I always thought black people did because they couldn't afford regular wallpaper.

"How'd you live so long?" Verbena asked me. "Anybody knowing the first thing about conjure can tell you—you put newspapers up on the walls, witches have to count every single letter up there before they can start their work. And if you can keep those witches counting till dawn, well then that's all she wrote. Ain't no more dirty work there. Same reason to wear a checkered shirt. My daddy was never without his checkered shirt, summer or winter—to keep them witches counting."

"Did you know any witches?"

She laughed this big deep man's laugh.

"I knew some home girls who came pretty close, the way they kept crossing me."

It never made any sense to me how Verbena got from there to here, even when she told me.

"It was around the year 1962," she said. "I remember I was seventeen years old—I was sitting on the steps of Rasco Thomas's store drinking this nice cold grape Nehi through a straw—I remember it exactly, how I was there with two other of my girlfriends, and there was Carlos, this thin white boy who'd come down from up North with a bunch of other college kids, all fired up about things. And they were trying to organize. Nobody I knew wanted to get organized, especially not by no fool white boy from up North. Here he was wearing this black shirt buttoned right up to the collar, and the sleeves rolled down even though it was the middle of the summer. He said he was looking for volunteers—he was asking us what we could do to help out with the cause, and I was being very haughty so I said, I can conjure the lizard right out of an ailing person's belly. I remember he looked right at me and you know what he said? I just had to laugh. He was so *serious*. He said to me—Well, there's a lizard stuck in the belly of this country of ours, and if you can conjure it out then why don't you get down here and help me do it?"

Verbena hooted, she still thought it was so funny. I felt sorry for Carlos there in his silly black shirt with the collar all buttoned up. "My girlfriends just laughed and laughed," Verbena went on. "He was a talker, see, and he just won. He put me right down. You should've seen him—he was only maybe a year older than me, all goofy and dead serious, and wanting to stay up all night and talk about anything instead of going to sleep. He was afraid to go to sleep, he was afraid he was going to miss out on something.

"And *believe* in stuff! I never saw anybody believe so much stuff as him. If he thought it was going to help to go conjuring some lizard out of America, then he was going to believe we could do it. He'd make me stay up all night with him trying to figure out how to do it."

"1962," I said. "I was probably just being born right then. Probably that exact same night. It's been a long time since then."

"It's been a long hard time," Verbena agreed. "Lots of things went wrong—got all twisted up." She shook her head. "Sometimes it kills me," she said, "just to think about."

"Do you think he's..." I trailed off because I didn't know exactly what it was I wanted to ask her. Still doing whatever he was doing, I guess is what I wanted to say. It was so strange to think of Carlos coming all that way to here from where he used to be—that goofy kid out of college.

"Oh, he's still conjuring," she said. It wasn't what I expected her to say. "He's got his back right up against that wall, and he's losing but he's still fighting. He knows he's losing but as long as he doesn't stop fighting they can't tear him apart."

I remember it scared me. I remember thinking about all those movies he'd made, like they were newspaper sheets pasted up on the wall.

THERE'S SOMETHING I HAVEN'T BEEN TELLING about. Not that I'm superstitious, but every time I go to talk about this dream, something stops me. Ever since I started writing all this, it's been shadowing me—or maybe I should say, it's something I've brought out of the shadows by writing all this stuff. Some nights it's the only dream I have; other nights I dream other dreams that happen around it but when I wake up I can only remember little pieces of those dreams, while this one's so vivid it's like something I've actually seen, and not a dream I had.

It's the woods behind the trailer, back in Owen where all my dreams are. Night, and I'm alone in the trailer, I'm washing dishes and I look out the window: down where the woods start, about fifty feet from the back of the trailer, there's this man. He's just standing there, leaning against a tree. He's waiting.

When I look closer, I realize it's a man's body but not a man's head. He's wearing some kind of mask that makes his head twice as big as normal, like those mud masks you see in *National Geographic* that some tribe in Africa wears to scare away strangers—this big mud mask with huge eyes and a sad hole for a mouth. The color of the mask is chalky white and you somehow know if you touched that mask with your hand you'd leave fingerprints. The chalky white would rub off on your fingers.

Only it's not a mask. It's his real head.

Most of the time he's wearing this rumpled brown suit. His hands are in his pockets. Sometimes he's wearing a yellow shirt, and sometimes he's bare-chested. There're these white marks on his chest, like somebody drew lines where his ribs are.

He doesn't come any closer to the house than where he is, he just stands there. But he's watching me.

Sometimes I remember that crazy old man with the golf club, from back in New York. But it isn't him. I don't know who it is, and I don't know what he wants—though in the dream I know I have something that's his, it's in the trailer somewhere and he wants it back. It's something I found out in the woods and took home with me, but it was a long time ago and now I've forgotten what it was. I'd give it to him if I knew, but I don't. So he just stands there.

It's some terrible disease that's done this to his face, made it all white and bloated up and puffy. He's come to show me what it's done to him—somehow it's because of that thing of his I have, that I don't know what it is. And I'm afraid to look at myself in the mirror, because when I look at my hands they're all chalky like his face is, and what if my face looks like his, a mask but it's really my face?

It's so vivid, sometimes I wake up and I think there must be a window to my cell where in the middle of the night I've actually gotten up to look out, and I've seen him waiting out there.

I don't know why I've been afraid to tell that dream. It's just a dream, one more bad dream for somebody who's always had bad dreams. They're just part of the night for me. But I've never had a dream that kept leaving its mark on me, the way when you get chalk on your hand, everywhere you touch you leave fingerprints. Maybe I'm afraid that's what I've been doing for the last ten years, leaving marks everywhere I touched, and now it's coming back to haunt me.

I MET MONICA IN THIS BAR EVERYBODY CALLED THE V Bar—it had some long Polish name nobody knew how to say, but it started with a V so that's what everybody called it. Carlos and The Company never went there. Not for any reason, they just never did, which is probably why I was always there in those days—to get away from them for a while, to get some free space.

It was one of those incredibly hot July days in the city when everything turns into an oven and you spend all your time trying to think how to get maybe one degree cooler than you are. Not that one degree cooler makes any difference when it's ninety-seven degrees plus no breeze and the humidity's wringing you out like a sweatrag. I grew up in Owen, Kentucky—I should know about hot summers. But there's nothing like a hot summer in New York.

I'd taken to dipping around midafternoon into the V Bar, where it was cool and dark, and I'd hang out way into the night playing the pinball machine and sort of keeping to myself. I liked it that nobody in that bar knew who I was or anything about me, and I didn't tell anybody anything either. Not that I was going to walk up to some stranger and say, Do you know what I do? Do you know any strung-out kids I can take to see Carlos, so maybe he'll put them in some movie of his and give them dope in exchange? I guess I preferred to keep my fun and business separate from each other. I guess by that point I wanted to have my own life in addition to The Company.

Carlos was doing this series of shorts at the time, which he later put together into a longer movie called *Atomic Pictographs*. Basically it was a bunch of jerk-off footage of runaway kids, only Carlos as usual managed

to take something dumb like that and turn it into something unforget-
table by this process of tinting the film, which was complicated and you
had to do it by hand—but it meant that not every detail in the movie
was in black-and-white. Some things had this pale watercolor look to
them—maybe a ray of sun or the tiles on the floor or a flower. And it
kept changing, so you were sure that flower had been yellow a minute
ago but now it was red, and then a minute later it'd be black-and-white.
So you kept thinking you were going crazy imagining colors where
really there hadn't been anything there all along except black and white.
Plus it was always little details you wouldn't otherwise notice—and that
was the real action of the movie, not the jerking off, which became just
another part of the scenery.

Carlos had found this abandoned Catholic church out in the South
Bronx—one of those neighborhoods even the priests and nuns had to
call it quits on. It was this great building, dark and cool inside, with
pigeons in the rafters and big pools of water on the floor, and off the
sides of the aisle there were these little chapels. Of course they didn't
have altars in them anymore—anything that could've been taken out
of that church had been carried off a long time ago. But Verbena, with
her totally amazing eye for that sort of thing, went and outfitted those
chapels with flowers and candles and masks, so they looked like a cross
between some voodoo shrine and a window at Macy's. Carlos filmed
boys jerking off like they were statues of saints—or maybe just department store mannequins—that'd come to life.

I wasn't in on any of that, really. My job was to hang around Port
Authority and nab runaway kids right when they got off the bus
from New Jersey or wherever, and before they knew what hit them
I'd have them over in the South Bronx. Most of the time they went
along with it—they were too dazed to do anything else. Though
every once in a while I'd get some kid who'd totally freak when we
got out there and he saw what was up. Whenever that happened it
was my job to take him out of the neighborhood and drop him somewhere. Anywhere.

If you want me to say I feel bad about all that—I don't. It didn't do
any harm, they were back in Manhattan in four hours with some cash
in their pocket. Plus, all they did was jerk off—they weren't going to
get AIDS from jerking off in front of a camera. If most of them were

going to get AIDS, it was probably from shooting up somewhere and not jerking off in some deserted Catholic church.

But I was trying to tell you about Monica. It's perfect, the way talking about her leads right back to Carlos and his movies—even though Carlos and Monica never once even laid eyes on each other, and in fact she'd never even heard of Carlos Reichart before she read about things in the newspaper. And he never in his life heard about her.

I was playing pinball the way I always did, with a nice cold Rolling Rock set down there beside me to swig every once in a while—and suddenly there was this girl leaning over my shoulder to watch. I remember it completely: even though it was a hundred degrees outside, she was wearing a blue flannel shirt and tight jeans and cowboy boots. She had these high hard cheekbones, almost like there was Indian blood in her somewhere, though I don't actually think there was, and she had this long very limp blonde hair that came down past her shoulders. You could say she was kind of tough-looking, more like a boy than a girl— but from the first instant I saw her, I liked that. There was something sassy about this girl who—except for her long white-blonde hair, and maybe even that too—looked like she could be a boy.

She asked me, Was I was planning ever to get off the machine or did I usually play all day on a quarter? I don't want to brag, because I know being good at pinball doesn't mean a thing, but I have to say, I was a great pinball player. Always had been, from back in Owen when Wallace and I'd play the machines in that hole-in-the-wall arcade on Main Street. Wallace taught me all his tricks, and then I went and improved on them till I could play for hours on a single ball. Something in me'd go on automatic pilot when I got in front of a machine—my brain would completely turn off, and that automatic thing in me would just keep reacting like lightning to the little silver ball. Over the course of the spring and summer 1983 I must've upped the top score of that machine in the V Bar by about six million points.

"You want to play?" I asked her, flipping the ball into one more tour of duty. "I'm done. I can get off anytime." It really didn't matter to me—I played all the time. So if somebody else wanted to use the machine, which in the V Bar wasn't all that frequent, I never had any problem with that.

"No, I don't want to play," she told me. It wasn't unfriendly or anything. It was a statement of fact. "I've just been watching you to see how long you could keep going."

"A pretty long time," I admitted.

"You spend a lot of time at that machine?"

"A pretty lot of time, yeah."

I wasn't used to talking to somebody while I was playing, so I was getting a little annoyed. There'd been a couple of close calls since she came over, but I'd managed to save them. Not that I could go on doing that forever.

"Well, I was watching you for a pretty long time," she said. "My name's Monica, by the way."

"Tony, and I got my hands full in case you hadn't noticed." The instant I said that, the ball that'd been going wild in the outfield suddenly shot right down the gulch and was gone.

"Shit," I said. Monica laughed. "So what's funny?"

"Nothing," she said. "I had a bet that if I talked to you I could get you to lose."

"Yeah? For how much?"

"Twenty-five bucks." She looked around. It was her turn to say, "Shit."

"Now what?" I asked.

"They ran out on me. I can't believe it—they just left."

"Who?"

"The guy who was going to pay me twenty-five dollars."

"Do you know who he was?"

"I just met him. We were just talking, and he pointed you out."

"So we both lose," I told her. "That'll teach you." Though I wondered who the guy could've been—if he knew me.

"Nothing teaches me anything," she said. She sort of gave her head this proud shake. "That's why I'm still me. Hey, you want another beer? I'll buy you another one. Sorry for wrecking your game."

"It's not like it was my last chance or anything."

We sat in a booth and drank Rolling Rocks.

"Where're you from?" I asked her.

"Guess," she said.

"I can't guess. I'm no good at guessing anything."

"Well, then—Tennessee. And I think you are too."

It sort of took me by surprise that she said that.

"Kentucky," I told her.

"Same thing. It's nice to hear—you sound like home."

It was probably four years since I'd talked to somebody from Kentucky, or even Tennessee for that matter. It hadn't ever occurred to me to miss the way people talked there, but now that she said it, she did sound familiar. She sort of brought things back.

"So what're you doing up here?" I asked her. I'd gotten it into my head that, except for people like me and Verbena, nobody got out of the South, especially not to end up in the alphabets.

"I could ask you the same thing," she said. "And I probably will. But if you want to know—I came here to be a singer."

"I thought people went to Nashville to do that."

"I can't stand country music," she told me. "All that whining and garbage. I want to be a rock star."

It made me laugh. She didn't look much like a rock star.

"So what's funny? I'm down on my luck. It happens to everybody—it takes time, and then you get a break and after that you're on your way."

"I don't think it happens that way."

"I don't either much anymore," she admitted. "Now my ambition is—be a waitress the rest of my life. That's my new career goal." I liked the way she didn't take herself all that seriously. It made me feel comfortable with her.

"So how's the new career going?" I asked.

"I got fired last week. But I'm starting this new job on Monday, a place called Veselka."

"I know Veselka," I said. It was where Carlos and I went when he did that interview for *American Film*.

"How do you know Veselka?" she asked me. Like it mattered any.

Suddenly I didn't know what to say. Not for any reason I can think of even now, I couldn't bring myself to mention Carlos's name. I just couldn't do it. And when that happened, a whole area of my life suddenly closed off and Monica was never going to know about it. At least for a long time.

All I said was, "Oh, I just know Veselka because it's in the neighborhood."

"Well, that's where I work now," Monica said, "so any time you want to find me, I'll be there. Until I get fired from there too."

"Who'd fire you from a place like that?" I asked. Veselka was nothing but a cabbage restaurant.

"You'd be surprised. All these places, sooner or later they want you to do things. They've all got some scam going in the background somewhere. Like this Moroccan guy I was working for—before I knew it, he had me running heroin for him. I said, forget it, and walked out of there. If you don't watch out for yourself, Tony, you're in over your head in a minute. As for me, there're just lots of things I don't do. I don't run drugs, for one thing. I got to keep up my self-respect. It's all I got." She smiled. "But it's mine."

"I know how that is," I told her. I sort of liked her, even if I could tell right off we were totally different from each other.

"Yeah," she said, "around here, you probably know how it is as much as I do. It's sickening. Somebody's got to do something."

Suddenly I saw how maybe she was right. What I said earlier about it not bothering me, what I was doing with those kids at Port Authority—I guess that's not completely true. It did bother me. It bothered me how Carlos was using those kids and then unloading them, and even though I bought it when he said how it wasn't hurting them any, still it was a lousy thing to be doing. How was I going to tell somebody like Monica I was into stuff like that? That I was part of the problem? When what I wanted, right now, was to be on the other side of it, where she was.

I liked sitting there talking to somebody my own age for a change. Somebody normal, who wasn't into kids jerking off or conjuring or the Lodz ghetto or anything like that. I didn't want to ruin it by telling her I was a movie pimp.

We'd finished our Rolling Rocks, and Monica ordered us another round. "Sometimes," she said, "I wonder why I ever left." While she talked, she tore the label off the bottle in little shreds. I saw how she'd bitten her fingernails down to nothing. I liked that about her. "I mean home," she said. "Why I left home. See, I really love my mom and dad." It could've been the bottle she was talking to, but I knew it wasn't. It was just her way of talking to me. "I just ran out on them," she said. "They needed me and I just ran out. I couldn't deal. I couldn't deal with what they were going through."

"I'm not totally following you," I told her. All the while I was thinking, it figures—sit down with some stranger in New York and before you know it you've got an earful of trouble. I thought maybe I should've gone on playing pinball without saying a word. Not let any of it touch you—that'd been my motto for a while.

"I had this brother, Gary," she said, "and then he died."

She didn't say anything more. She just kept peeling little strips of paper off the Rolling Rock label.

Everybody I knew seemed to have a dead brother. Carlos had one, if you could believe what he said, and Sammy'd lost both his brothers in the ghetto, and now here was Monica.

"I'm sorry," she said. "I get all upset about this. I don't talk to people about it. I came away to New York so I could be with people who didn't know anything about it, and now here I am telling you all about it first thing."

"Tell me about it," I said. "You can talk to me about it."

I didn't totally mean it, but I never know what to say to things like that.

"He was the greatest brother," she said. "He was so much fun. I always wanted to be his brother instead of his sister. Does that sound weird? But then we could pal around together. Everywhere. He was a year older. I wanted to travel all over the country with him—that's what we were planning to do. He'd even bought a motorcycle. We were going to go to New York. Or he was—I never told him how I was planning to come along. I never got a chance to."

There was this long pause. Somebody was going to town on my pinball machine, and it was making a racket in the background.

"What happened?" I asked her. I didn't know if that's what I was supposed to ask or not. For some reason all this was making me shake, like I'd got a chill from it.

She kept tearing at that label with her bitten-down nails. "It was starting to rain," she said. "He went around a curve too fast, I guess, and he spilled. It tore him all up—they wouldn't even let us see him, he was so torn up."

Nothing terrible like that had ever happened in my life. I didn't have anything to say. I always felt a little in awe of people like that— it's what I felt whenever I talked to Sammy, or even that night Carlos told me about his brother, Adrian. I always thought—those people are different from me. They're better, because terrible things've happened to them. I don't know why I thought that, but I did.

I looked at Monica. She was studying the little pile the torn-up label had made. She didn't know I was watching her, or maybe she did know—but the look on her face was terrible. I thought—this is what Carlos is always looking for in his movies, one single instant like this, the look on Monica's face. And now here it's happening in some dark little bar on Seventh Street where Carlos'll never go. It's happening, and there's no Seth, there's no camera—there's only me. I'm the only person here to see it. To make it somehow count.

It made me dizzy to think that.

"I'm sorry about your brother," I said. I reached out and patted the top of her hand; I let my hand lie on top of hers for a minute.

"I didn't mean to bring all that up," she said. She looked at me, and she was smiling. "You must think I'm a total mope to go talking like that."

"I'm glad you thought you could say it to me," I said. And I was glad. I'd seen deep down inside her, the way Carlos saw things. I'd never done that with somebody before.

M ONICA'D MENTIONED HOW HER BAND WAS
playing later in the week, and would I like to go? "I'll put you
on the list," she told me. "They'll let you in without a cover." Which
was how I ended up as one of about fifteen people in the audience to
hear the band Valve Lash at CBGB's on a rainy Thursday night.

It was always something to me, how many different scenes there
were in New York. I got around; there was the Adonis, where I'd go
with Carlos to see a porn flick or maybe catch some kid's strip show;
there were the West Village bars, where I cruised, and the baths, and
the V Bar for pinball. I would've said I knew the city pretty well. But I
didn't know the half of it—maybe nobody ever does. I'd never been in
a music club in the city before.

I got to CBGB's late—I kept waiting for the rain to end, because
there wasn't any umbrella in the apartment, and I didn't want to show
up drenched. But it never did stop, so finally I gave up and walked
over to the Bowery in the downpour. Valve Lash was already on stage
and revved up when I came in, Monica standing out there in front
and these four guys on guitars and drums backing her up. They were
all in jeans and white T-shirts—except for Monica, who was wearing
this bright blue cowgirl outfit with fringe, and a white cowboy hat.
With her long white-blonde hair it looked pretty dopey. All four of the
guys were wearing sunglasses—it was some statement they'd decided
to make about something. I could tell they were a little rattled by
not having any audience. In between songs they kept lifting up their
sunglasses so they could see, and looking out at the empty room. But
nobody else came in after me, I guess because of the rain. Or maybe

people had heard them before and that's why they stayed away.

Valve Lash was this thing to do with car engines, Monica'd told me earlier, but since I didn't know anything about car engines it didn't mean much to me. The lead guitarist, Matt, was the one who thought the name up. But it was Monica who did everything else; she wrote all the words and all the music, which sounded just like country music to me, even though she'd told me she hated country music and wanted to be a rock star. I've never paid that much attention to music, I can take it or leave it, so I never could tell whether Valve Lash was as terrible as it sounded, or whether it was supposed to be good. Not that I'd have said that to Monica in a million years, even if she asked me to be honest—which, fortunately or not, she never one single time asked me to be.

There was something that got to me, though, seeing her up there singing her heart out with nobody listening. She was putting everything she had into it. She'd hold the microphone in both hands and sort of croon into it, country-style—it sent chills up your spine, not that that was what she wanted, but that was what happened and it was very effective. You felt, here was this person who was hurting from loneliness and calling out and there was nobody there for her. I could identify with that. I felt that way most of the time—giving everything I had, whether it was Carlos in a movie or somebody I'd just picked up for the night in some bar, and then feeling like nothing ever came back home to me.

Maybe I was just pissed off at the way the guys in the band were wearing sunglasses. They didn't care if nothing came back to them. Monica deserved better than that.

She was really happy to see me—it made me glad I'd gotten completely drenched. She wanted to hug me.

"Don't," I said. "I smell like some dog."

"I like dogs," she said, and threw her arms around me. I could feel her breasts against my chest.

She introduced me to Matt, who offered me some coke if I wanted any—but I didn't. "Hey, pretty good, what?" he said, putting his arm around Monica and kissing her hair. I sort of nodded in agreement, since I wasn't completely sure. I'd applauded as loud as I could, and so had the other fifteen or so people in the room, but we got a little swallowed up in all that empty space. "In this city, nineteen hundred and eighty-three," Matt told me, "you gotta have some hot chick like this up there. Otherwise you get a bunch of fags. It's a crying shame. Who wants a bunch of fags?"

Monica swatted at him playfully.

"Fags," I remember saying. "Who needs them?" It was my idea of a joke, sort of. I didn't like Matt, but for some reason I wanted him to like me. I wanted them all to like me.

After we'd helped Matt load the equipment in the van, Monica and I went to her apartment. It had stopped raining—it was one of those wonderful nights with slick streets reflecting all the lights, and the air cool. She was starved, she said, singing always made her grow together—which was what she always said when she meant she was hungry.

"You're going to think I'm plain crazy," she said, "but there's this thing, I do it after every gig. I don't know why—luck, I guess. See that Chinese restaurant there on the corner?" There was this hole in the wall, WING FAT CHOW said the yellow sign over the door. "I go in here after every gig and get take-out moo shoo pork." She laughed. "It's not even very good. In fact, it's really salty and greasy and you get an MSG high from it. But I guess I always think if I don't go through this little ritual, then it'll be the last gig I ever get."

"You're funny," I told her. "Anyway, that's fine. I'm growing together too. And I like salt and grease. It's what I'm made out of." She was walking along swinging her arms in these big motions, like she was some little girl. I could tell she was really relieved to be through singing for the night, though I could also tell she was pretty disappointed in the audience. But she was being brave, and I liked that.

"I never told anybody except you. So now you're part of my good luck."

"First time that ever happened," I told her.

"Stick with me and it won't be the last. Anyway, when we get back to the apartment, I have this little present to give you."

"But we only just met," I said.

"Well, that's okay. I can still give you a present, can't I?"

For a minute I was nervous. Suddenly there was this little whine of sex between us. You could barely hear it, but it was there, and I didn't quite know what to do about it. It'd been years since I used to follow women around. Whatever it was I'd been looking for in those days faded away from me, and I never thought about women any more.

Verbena was the only woman I had anything to do with, and I didn't exactly think of her as a woman. Women just didn't seem necessary—at least not to fuck.

But fucking wasn't what Monica had in mind. She let us into her apartment—there were about ten locks she had to undo to get in, and once we were in, it wasn't clear to me what she was afraid was going to get stolen. The place was tiny—a mattress and a chair and a beat-up dresser took up most of the room. The window faced right onto a brick wall.

"Let's light candles," she said. "I love candlelight." I noticed there were candles all over the room—stuck in beer bottles, or big fat ones the size of tin cans. I sat on the bed while she got them lit. Then she started pulling a guitar case out from under the dresser.

"What're you gonna do?" I asked her. I figured there'd been enough singing tonight.

She strummed a few chords, and cleared her throat. "This is for you," she said. "This is what I saw when I saw you playing pinball in the V Bar." And she started to play.

It was this mournful song, like all the middle-of-the-night truckers' songs I used to hear on the radio in Owen. This is for me, I thought—not sure what to make of that, not sure at all.

"You wrote it?" I said. "The music and the words and everything?" I have to admit, I was impressed. And also a little alarmed.

"'Lone Steel Ball on a Roll,'" she said. "Think it'll be a hit?"

"Catchy title," I said. "I can't believe you wrote me a song."

"I was thinking about you," she said. "It just sort of came to me."

I told her it sounded like country music to me, and I thought she hated country music.

She sort of pursed her lips. "It's not country music," she said. "It has this special edge to it. That's why I could never get a break in a place like Nashville. They don't understand my kind of thing there."

It sort of broke my heart, the way she said that, because I could see right then and there how she was telling herself these stories so she could keep on going, and deep down she knew she wasn't ever going to go anywhere with those songs. I've never been very good at figuring out what exactly it is I like about people. Most people probably would've found Monica pretty plain to look at, and totally out of place in New York, and fairly good at pretending to herself things weren't really the way she knew they were—but something happened to me, I saw some poor kind of spark that was about to go out in her, and I thought if I could breathe on it, then maybe it'd stay lit a little while longer.

Or maybe I'm the one who's fairly good at pretending about the reasons for the things I do.

In any case, over the next few weeks she wrote me a lot of songs. "You're my muse," she told me. "Tony my music muse." I didn't really know what to do—I kept wishing they'd stop coming to her, but I knew it made her happy for them to be coming, and to tell the truth, I liked somebody to be crooning these sad sappy songs to me. It was always a big deal when she'd finished a new one—she'd invite me over and light the candles and open a bottle of wine. We'd sit cross-legged on her bed, facing each other, both barefoot. She'd cradle her guitar that had a horse and a rose stenciled on it. I'd feel shy and watch her toes, how she'd painted them red, maybe to make up for her fingernails that she bit down to nothing. I always noticed that her second toe was longer than her big toe, and even though I know a lot of people are like that, still I felt weird noticing it, like it was something a little freakish.

"You're not going to like this one," she'd always say, hefting her guitar and picking at some moody chord.

"Try me," I'd tell her. She'd clear her throat, and hum a note, and then she'd close her eyes and start in. Only then would I look at her face—that thin high-cheeked boy's face that could've been Cherokee if it wasn't for the white-blonde hair falling down around it.

Her songs all sounded pretty much the same to me—country and sad.

I guess it's a good thing I have this terrible memory for music. If I didn't, I'd probably be hearing those songs in my head right now, and then I'd feel even more terrible than I already do. Though there's this one song I keep hearing here in the Eddy. I'm never sure where it's coming from, maybe from Earl's radio down the corridor; I keep meaning to ask him but then I never do. It's a country music station, and usually I can't hear it, it's just this hum in the background—but some-days it's like a door's been left open somewhere, and I can hear it really clearly. A mixed blessing, I guess you'd call it. It makes me homesick, a little—but homesick for where, I can't exactly say. Homesick for somewhere I think I should've been, but never was.

The worst is how I keep imagining it's a song Monica wrote, how she's gone and recorded a hit and now it's playing on all the radios in America. It's not impossible, is it? Some record producer reads a mention in the newspapers about Tony Blair's wife writing songs, and thinks, Hey, this'll sell. And I wouldn't've heard about it—they'd have kept it from me—only I recognize something about that song that says Monica loud and clear.

I keep imagining what would've happened if she'd gone on writing songs.

It's this sad melody, the kind of sappy thing that'll drive you crazy if you listen to it enough—but I have to say, when I listen to it I remember Monica singing those sweet dumb songs to me in her dingy little apartment with the candles burning and boxes of take-out Chinese food, and I remember sitting there listening to them and thinking how this was somebody who was falling in love with me and what could I do?

In a way, that's how I think of my whole time with Monica—what could I do? Everything fell into some kind of place between us, one step at a time, and I kept knowing in some part of me how it was all completely wrong and I should get out. But I kept saying at every step, what can I do? I was tired of Carlos and his movies. I was exhausted by the bars. I kept hearing these scary things about some new disease that was starting to infect New York, and people like me—this is what they were saying—were its prime target. I didn't know whether I believed all that stuff or not, but still it was worrying. It made me think about whether this might not be a pretty good time to jump ship. Nobody'd said it had to last forever, what I was doing. Maybe this was the time to make some kind of change.

I guess I'd finally gotten to the point where I wanted somebody to be singing songs to me. I could hear Carlos saying, "Nowhere's safe, Tony, there's nothing safe," but what I wanted, after all those years, was to try and be safe just for a little while.

I MENTIONED THE ADONIS THEATER, WHERE CARLOS used to take me for his idea of a night on the town. I never thought about it at the time, but the only movies I ever saw Carlos watch were porn movies. I think that's the only kind he really enjoyed, at least after a certain point. All the others just seemed like fancy wastes of time. I remember hearing him tell Seth, when Seth was going on about some new German movie he'd seen at a film festival: "Oh, I remember when I used to be interested in movies. Now it's just life I'm interested in." Which at the time struck me as sort of strange for a movie director to go around saying, but now I think I understand. All of it was life for Carlos. Everything that happened.

W E'D KNOWN EACH OTHER ABOUT A MONTH before anything actually happened in the sex department. I remember we'd been out one night, first at the V Bar, then this place next door called The Blue and Gold, and then another bar called Radio Bar. Even though I wasn't drinking much in those days, mostly only beer, we'd had a fair amount, and at the Radio Bar we even did these shots of bourbon with our beer. Bourbon's something I'd always hated—but Monica, being from Tennessee and all, just loved it.

I don't know when it started, but I got to noticing how she kept touching me, and I kept touching her too. Brushing up against each other, holding onto each other's arms when we were talking to each other. She was telling me some crazy story about shooting water moccasins at this lake in Mississippi where she went with her dad and brother fishing sometimes. Her dad got the idea they should clean the lake up, so they took a shotgun out in the boat and went along the bank where the water moccasins liked to hide in among the tangled-up tree roots.

"So Gary spotted this cottonmouth gliding along toward the boat," Monica said, "and he grabbed the gun and aimed right at it and pulled the trigger. And you know what happened?" Thinking about it made her laugh. She leaned her head against my shoulder.

The way she'd been telling it, the story seemed incredibly funny— or maybe I was just drunk.

"So what happened?" I asked her. She was trying to catch her breath, gasping from laughing so hard.

"He pulled the trigger," she said, "and the recoil knocked the whole boat over. Flipped all three of us right out into the water."

"Great," I said. "Right in the middle of the moccasins."

"Right smack in the middle," she said. "All three of us were yelling our heads off, we were each of us so convinced a cottonmouth was heading right toward us."

"But you survived?"

"We survived," she said. "But we gave up that notion about cleaning up the lake."

"And now you're here," I told her.

"Now I'm here," she said.

"So it had a happy ending, you could say," I told her.

"You could say," she said. She looked at me—this look that made me remember that her brother had died.

"Let's go," I told her. "Let's go back to your place for a nightcap."

I was drunker than I'd been in months. It was fun to be drinking again, it brought back old times.

"I don't have any beer back at my place," Monica said.

"Is that a problem?"

"No problem," she said and ordered two beers from the bar. "Here," she told me. "Hide it under your shirt." The bottle was ice-cold against my belly, but it was a good feeling. I remember concentrating on that feeling even after we were outside the bar and had pulled our beers out into the open. I could feel that patch of cold fading on my skin the whole time we were walking east along Seventh Street, taking swigs of Rolling Rock, and suddenly she put her arm through mine—just slid it through and all at once I knew definitely that we were going to have sex when we got back to her apartment. It was this cool wave passing through me even though it was early September and sticky hot even in the middle of the night. I remember saying to myself, "I'm finally going to get laid by a girl." It was odd, after all this time and everything that'd happened—it made me think back to Owen, to Wallace and those girls we used to go out with. I thought—if I hadn't met Carlos, maybe this is how my life would've gone. The only thing that's happened, I'd tell myself, is that now at the ripe age of twenty-one I'm finally back on track.

I remember being really impatient at the door to Monica's apartment while she fiddled with all the locks. I wanted to be inside that apartment and know what was going to happen next—so I leaned over and kissed the back of her neck, through her hair.

"Hey," she said, and put her hand to the back of her neck, and I kissed her fingers. That made her sort of giggle, and I knew everything was going to be okay, that we really were on the same wavelength with each other and so I could relax while she undid the rest of the locks.

Once we got inside we didn't say a word—we went right to her bed and undressed, and since it was so hot we just lay down on top of the sheets. Only then did we both start touching each other and kissing all over, like it was something we'd wanted to do for weeks but we weren't sure the other person wanted it. I touched her breasts, which brought back Cindy and the back seat of Wallace's car in Owen, and how I used to get so excited when I'd manage to slip a hand up her blouse—it was great to be squeezing a girl's breasts again, it was great to feel how they just filled up your palm when you cupped your hand around them. I remember thinking, Why doesn't everybody have these, they're so much fun?

Otherwise it was pretty much like touching anybody's body that didn't have much hair on it—till I made what I guess was the big mistake of running my hand down her stomach and between her legs. Suddenly it was the most depressing thing. There wasn't any dick down there, and I thought with this kind of panic, What'm I supposed to do? There's nothing to do anything *with*. I felt so empty—I should've known right then how we were never going to be meeting each other on equal terms. I should've gotten out of it right then and there before the damage was done. But you never know these things till later. I kept feeling around down there trying to find something to do something with. Finally she grabbed my dick and said, "Go ahead, go ahead and put your johnson up me."

She always had these other words for things.

"My what?" I said.

"This thing." And she helped me stuff my dick up inside her.

Since that first time with Scott three years before, I'd gotten pretty used to putting my dick up lots of assholes—but I'd never been inside a cunt before. And it wasn't exactly what I'd expected it to be. She was so loose I felt totally lost up there, I felt like it was going to slip right out. Plus I kept getting limp inside her because there wasn't anything to hold me to being hard. When that happened, my dick did go on and slip out of her. But she just took it in her hand, which made it get hard again, and then she slipped it back into her.

The whole time we kept kissing and breathing right into each other's faces, which was kind of great.

"Yeah," she said when I finally got it in and managed to keep hard for a while. I was moving around inside her but I couldn't feel a thing, just at the base of my dick where the muscles at the opening to her cunt were clamped around it. For the rest, I might as well have been floating in space.

But she seemed to be enjoying it. She kept tossing her head back and forth and moaning, and then I started to go soft again. I pulled out and turned her over so I could put it up her asshole, where I was used to and knew it'd keep me hard.

"Hey," she said, "pervert." And she sort of slapped me away.

So we lay there a while panting, and kissing now and then, and I thought, well, so that's that. It wasn't going to do any good trying to put it back in her cunt—I was totally limp.

I wanted to cry, I felt so alone right then. But she did the sweetest thing—she took my soft dick and went down on it with her mouth, and in about a minute and a half she had me coming in this way that felt really good.

I slept there in her apartment that night—if you can call it sleep, since the guy who lived above her practiced his saxophone the whole night long. He'd been playing when we came in, this loud raucous stuff that was all honks and squeaks—but of course I was too excited by other things to pay much attention. But once we'd settled down to go to sleep—I guess in all sex took about ten minutes between us, though by then we were both completely drenched in sweat—you could hear his sax coming loud and clear down through the ceiling.

Monica was sound asleep almost immediately, but all I could do was lie there and try to follow the ups and downs of that sax, try to figure out where the melody was in there with all those other notes. It wasn't so different, I guess, from watching one of Carlos's movies, though that only occurs to me now. At the time I wasn't thinking of Carlos one bit.

Next morning, when morning finally came, I asked Monica how she could stand it.

"Stand what?" I guess I'd drifted off to sleep sometime, because she was already up and standing in the shower. Only a little trickle of water was coming down—it hardly seemed worth it.

"The *noise!*" I yelled.

"Oh, Dominic. Yeah, well, you forget about it. He's really famous, you know. He's a smack addict, he washes dishes at this restaurant, and then he plays all night."

"So what's famous about that?" I asked.

"Just listen to me," Monica told me. She was in a bad mood, the way I guess you're always in a bad mood after you have sex with somebody you're already known before, and you're trying to figure out how things are going to be different from now on with them. "He gives this one single concert every year," she said. "People come from all over to hear him."

I could tell she felt that having that guy practicing upstairs was part of her apartment, like furniture.

While she was finishing her shower, I found a couple of bagels in the refrigerator, and since she didn't have a toaster I fried them in some margarine. She must've thought that was fine. We drank coffee and ate those bagels, and stuff was okay between us—the sex hadn't upset anything between us at all.

M ONICA WAS ALWAYS GETTING SCHEMES IN HER head. She'd decide there was some band in Hoboken we had to catch, and so off we'd go. Or some deli in Brooklyn somebody told her about. It was her way of organizing her life. I was always happy to go along—it reminded me of my early days in the city when I used to go everywhere. There was something okay about showing up with Monica in these different parts of the city I hadn't been in for years—places I couldn't have found again for the life of me, but when I got there I recognized I'd been there before.

I was still doing work for The Company, but I was showing up less and less. Since Carlos was right in the middle of editing *Atomic Pictographs,* that was fine: from here on out, the movie was up to him and Seth alone. So I don't think he even missed me in those months. And he was used to me not sleeping over in the apartment; it'd been years since I stayed there regularly. These days I slept at Verbena's more than I slept at Carlos's.

Verbena was the one person in The Company I didn't have any problem introducing Monica to. "The only thing is," I told her before I brought Monica by the first time, "Monica's not Company material, if you know what I mean."

Verbena looked at me—this quick look that showed me she knew what I was talking about.

"There isn't any Company," I told Verbena. "You're an old drug connection, from before I went straight. Got that?"

"I always get the glamor parts," she said. But she went along. I think it probably wasn't the first time she'd gone along with something like that. And she and Monica got along great. I was a little worried at first, that my only friend in the whole city was this huge black woman, but Monica took Verbena totally in stride. "She reminds me of this maid, Louise, we used to have when I was little," she told me. "Louise used to steal spare change from the dresser, so we had to let her go."

One day Monica heard about a car lot in Jersey City from some friend of hers who had a friend who bought a car there cheap. She decided that what we should do with our Saturday was grab Verbena and go car shopping in New Jersey.

She'd gotten these complicated directions to the lot: once we got off the PATH train we had to take a bus, and then in the middle of nowhere change from that bus to another bus. It took us an hour and a half at least just to get there.

The whole time I kept thinking back to when my mom used to take us to the shopping center in Paducah on Saturday afternoons, just for something to do, and Ted and me'd spend a couple hours wandering around the Woolworth's trying to see who could pocket the most candy.

Car Country, the place in Jersey City was called. It was one of about ten used-car lots on this one street, all looking more or less the same, with an American flag flying over each one, only Car Country had the biggest flag. About the size of a football field.

It was incredibly windy that day. The flags were all snapping on their flagpoles like no tomorrow.

Our salesman was this guy with this name that sounded like Esta-chio—I never did hear it right. He was one of those people who I think actually likes being a used-car salesman. He'd sold to so many people who didn't have enough money to buy a real car that he didn't think the cars he was selling were junk. In fact, it seemed like the junkier they were, the more he liked them.

He was totally bald, but he had this huge mustache that looked like somebody'd gone and glued a hairbrush to his face.

The first car he showed us he said was his definite favorite—this shiny black Edsel he just got last week from some old man in Paramus who kept this car parked in his garage for twenty-five years. We could check the odometer, he said—less than ten thousand miles.

"They can turn those things back," Monica said.

"Not on your life," Estachio said. "Ten thousand miles—guaranteed."

Monica walked around the car, looking it up and down. "An Edsel," she said. "What do you know?" She ran her hand along the hood. "So how much're you asking?" I thought it was pretty hilarious; Monica acting like she knew what she was talking about. But then it occurred to me—maybe she really does know about cars. I think I liked it that just about everything I thought about her at first turned out to be wrong in one way or another later on. Usually in little ways, but just enough to keep me guessing.

The salesman thought about it. "Six hundred bucks," he said. "Prime condition. And after all, it's an Edsel. What more can you want?"

I didn't get what all the fuss was about—it just looked like a boxy old car to me. But Monica knew all about it.

"That's just great," she said. "An Edsel. You know," she told me and Verbena, "they named it for Henry Ford's son, and it was supposed to be the car of the future. They designed everything special, just for it. But then nobody bought it, it was too far ahead of its time, so they stopped making it after only a year. But now they wish they'd kept on making them."

Verbena said she thought it was the perfect car for us. "The car of the future," she said.

I wasn't so sure. I kicked the front tire.

"Why're you doing that?" Monica asked me.

I shrugged. I thought it was what you were supposed to do.

"They only do that in the movies," Monica told me.

"That's where he learned it," Verbena said, "was in the movies."

I looked at her—this quick look. But it was a look I didn't even need to give her. As soon as she said what she said, she realized it was thin ice. What I liked about Verbena was, you could depend on her not to make mistakes, which was why I trusted her to hang around with.

Monica of course didn't notice a thing. She was busy climbing into the car to sit behind the steering wheel. Estachio leaned in on top of her, pointing to the odometer he was so proud about.

"It's a really ugly car," I told Verbena.

"Honey, it's historic," she said. "Like me. You can put up with a little ugliness for the sake of the historical."

"I think you're this piece of beautiful history," I told Verbena, and she swatted at me. It wasn't something she ever did when Monica was watching, I noticed.

"This Edsel's not the cheapest thing in the world," Estachio was telling Monica. "You want cheap, I can show you cheap. But not every car's an Edsel. All those dreams that went into it."

It was funny—I could tell he really wanted to be talking to me instead of her, but she was the one who seemed to know something about cars. I think he was confused. He kept looking at me like he wanted me to be in this conversation too.

I asked him if there was anything cheaper than six hundred.

He looked disappointed. I guess everybody always asked him that.

He put his hands in his pockets. The wind was blowing all of us around like crazy. Verbena was hanging onto her hat with one hand and her skirt with the other—still, it seemed like acres of maroon skirt were billowing out like a sail.

"Woo," she said every time another gust of wind would lift up first her hat and then her skirt. She was flapping in the wind like some flag.

Monica didn't really notice the wind. That always impressed me about her—when she started concentrating on something, she totally concentrated on it. This afternoon she was concentrating on cars.

"We want an automatic," she said. "It doesn't have to have an air conditioner, but it has to have a radio. And four doors. And American-made."

"Where'd you learn so much about cars?" I asked her.

"I keep my ears open," she said. "How come you don't know anything about them?"

"I live in New York," I told her.

"You didn't grow up in New York. You're a Southerner like me. We got cars in our blood."

I remembered how much I used to like Wallace's pickup when I was a kid. It made me think maybe Monica was right—if I'd never left Kentucky, I'd probably be crazy about cars. There were a lot of things that would've been different if I'd never left Kentucky. I had to start wondering, right there in that used-car lot in Jersey City, about all the things that would've been different. I'd probably be settled down and married if I'd kept on living in Kentucky. I'd have kids. I'd be working as a penitentiary guard.

Verbena'd found this lime green Cadillac parked over in the corner of the lot. "Check this girl out," she called to me, stroking one of the fins with her hand. "Picture taking this shark down the highway."

"You should buy a car too," I told her. "We could drag race."

"Drag my butt," she said. "What're you thinking about getting a car for anyway? Don't tell me you're going to up and leave us now?"

"Leave?" I said. "Where's there to go?"

With Monica talking to Estachio, Verbena and I could say whatever we wanted. The wind would blow all our words away anyway.

"So what's up with you and this Monica girl?" she said.

I'd been wondering when she was going to ask me.

"Does it bother you?" I asked. I'd never brought any of the guys I was seeing around, probably because usually I never saw them for more than a night or two and so we didn't have to think of other things to do with our time than have sex.

"It's not like somebody blowing cigar smoke in my face," Verbena said. "Anyway, I'm not your momma, thank the lord. But surprised—yes. I'm a little surprised."

"Maybe I'm a little surprised too," I admitted. "But it's nice to be surprised, right?"

"It's nice to be surprised," she said. "Some of us done went and built our whole careers around it. And I'm happy for you. You've done your work here. You don't want to stick around forever. You got your own life to live now."

"I haven't said anything to Carlos," I told her. Not that he'd have minded—I would've been the one who minded, not him.

"You're still stuck on that man, aren't you?" Verbena asked me. A gust of wind rocked us. Dust and newspapers were swirling around in an empty part of the lot.

"I'll always be stuck on him," I had to say. "He's still got me."

The wind was carrying those newspapers higher and higher, like birds, like T.J.'s pigeons.

Verbena looked sad. Where she was standing she couldn't see that little cyclone of wind. I could tell she didn't want to hear what I just told her.

"I tell you what," she said. "This is your old Verbena talking, but you can trust me, right? What I say is, buy the cheapest car you can find here today, and take that nice girl Monica and head for as far away from here as you can get. Keep driving till you think Carlos'll never find you, and then drive some more after that. It's what you got to do."

"He found me in Owen, Kentucky," I said. "Remember that? If he could find me in Owen, he'll find me anywhere."

"The man casts a mean shadow," she admitted. "He's a total eclipse you're never going to get out from under. But you need to get to where you can at least see it. See around it. And shy girl, you can't do that here. You ain't ever going to be able to."

"Hey," Monica was calling to us. "Hey, come here."

She was standing by the ugliest car in the world.

"Two hundred dollars," she said. "1976 Buick Century. King of the highway. Built to last."

"It's half rusted through," I told her.

"Half rusted through," she said, "it's still solider than any other car you'll find." Estachio was nodding—he was very enthusiastic, even though he looked kind of disturbed that Monica instead of him was the one making me a sales pitch.

"I would describe the color," Verbena said, "as shit brown. If I was asked to do so."

"Nobody's asking," Monica said. "What about it, Tony? Do we got the two hundred? Can we do it?"

It looked like the kind of car people back in Owen drove. I'd never seen an uglier car.

"A mean shadow," was all Verbena said.

Monica looked at me. "A little joke," I told her. "It's nothing." I felt sick in my stomach. I reached in my pocket and pulled out my cash. "Look," I said, "I got twenty dollars. That's everything. What've you got on you?"

"A hundred," she said. "How about selling it to us for a hundred twenty?" she asked Estachio.

"A hundred seventy-five," he said.

"We only have a hundred twenty." She took my twenty and put it with her money and waved it in Estachio's face. He looked away, across the street at another car lot. He tapped on his cheek with his finger.

"A hundred fifty," he said.

"Listen to what I'm saying," Monica told him. She kept waving her wad of cash in his face. "A hundred twenty dollars. Count it."

"A hundred fifty," he said.

"This is making me weary," said Verbena. A flip of wind took her dress clean over her head. But she didn't even pay attention. She rummaged around in her pocketbook. "Why do I have a jar of pimentos in here?" she asked us all, holding it up. Then she dropped it back in her pocketbook and pulled out some dollar bills. "Ten, twenty, thirty," she said, counting them out to Monica.

"Verbena," I said. "What're you doing?"

She snapped her pocketbook shut, and reached up behind her with one hand and pulled her dress down. "There used to be this thing," she said, "called the Underground Railroad. You ever heard of that? The Underground Railroad?"

None of us ever had.

"Well, it don't matter," she said. "This here's been a whistle stop on the Underground Railroad. If you ever want to know."

"Verbena," I said, "I don't know what you're talking about, but thank you for the money. I'll pay you back."

"You'll get that car on the highway," she said. "If you want to pay me back, you'll drive like a demon till you hit the Mason-Dixon line, and then you'll just keep on going."

I GUESS IT SAYS SOMETHING ABOUT ME HOW I'VE never left anywhere normally—I've always just slipped off, so when you turn around I'm gone. Maybe it's the best way, though I'll never know since I never tried anything different. Anyway, that's the way I left New York—I just slipped off. I told Monica I'd meet her at six in the morning at her place. That whole night, I couldn't sleep. I lay in bed even more excited than if this was some new movie I was about to start. When five o'clock dragged around, I slipped into my jeans and T-shirt, and the snakeskin boots I've told you about already—that was all I took with me.

Carlos was sound asleep in the so-called back room, the one Sammy and Netta used to share. There was somebody with him in there, probably some kid—I didn't look in to find out. Our schedules were so totally different these days, we didn't see each other that much. I didn't really even know what he was up to half the time anymore.

I'd have thought I might've taken one last look around the place I'd called home for the last four years, but I didn't. I guess I sort of nodded my respect to Carlos asleep in the other room, and I remember thinking that I hoped whoever he was with had made him happy last night, and also thinking how the poor kid probably hadn't, because who could? But I wasn't feeling sentimental—I was just out of there, out on the street at dawn—just about the only time I ever saw dawn on Avenue C from the sleep side of it. There was a streetsweeper truck moving along with its brushes whirring. Streetsweepers never came in that neighborhood—it must've been lost, or maybe the driver was in the neighborhood to buy drugs. Probably from Rafe or Nicky or somebody like that—money that'd end up going for another of Carlos's movies.

Monica'd overslept, which was a little disappointing. I waited around her apartment while she took a shower. She'd packed everything she wanted to take in four big duffel bags, plus her guitar.

"So where's your stuff?" she asked me. She was letting me dry her hair with a towel—something I always liked to do.

"I'm not taking any."

"What d'you mean, you're not taking any?"

"Like I said—I got all I need." I spread my arms out wide to show her, but she wasn't too impressed. I think for the first time since she met me, she thought I was maybe a little too weird. I think she was wondering whether she should have second thoughts, even though it was sort of her idea in the first place and I was just going along with it because what else could you do?

"You're sure?" she said. "We can stop off and pick stuff up."

"Completely sure," I told her. "I'm free as a bird."

"You're crazy as a loon," she told me. "I love you. You're completely insane."

And we were off. It was so long since I'd driven I could hardly remember how, but it was early, and we were going against the rush-hour traffic pouring in from New Jersey.

"Bye bye, suckers," Monica called out the open window as we dived into the Lincoln Tunnel. In four years I hadn't been out of the city except twice, that time we went to Montreal for the film festival, and when we were shooting *Creeping Bent* on that estate up the Hudson—and both those times I was with Carlos, so in a way they didn't count. Carlos somehow managed to carry the city with him wherever he went. No matter where you were, if you were with him then in some way you weren't out of the city. Even I suppose if you were in Owen, Kentucky. He'd lived in the city there so long something had rubbed off—some kind of hectic nervous energy, this power line talking craziness that'll always be different from country craziness, which is slow and deep and hardly ever says a thing.

We drove down through New Jersey, cut across Pennsylvania and West Virginia—WILD, WONDERFUL WEST VIRGINIA said the sign at the border—and by night we were in eastern Kentucky. We stopped at some little motel in the middle of nowhere. I think the fat old country woman behind the counter thought we'd just gotten married or some-thing, the way she was all friendly to us—and we might as well have, the way we went at each other that night. It was the best sex I ever had with Monica—I guess because we both wanted so bad for it to work out. I know I was really trying hard, and I think it did work out, I think it was probably just great.

But then after she'd dropped off to sleep it sort of hit me what it was I was doing. I wasn't freaked out, exactly—but I do remember saying to myself, Tony, you've just made a pretty big move. I think sitting there next to her in bed with the light on—she was completely conked out, but then she'd been the one to do most of the driving that day—I wasn't sure this was what I wanted to be doing. But I knew I was already into it. This was a girl I really liked a lot, she was nice to me and she made me feel like she needed me. Still—I remember doing this crazy thing. I picked up the phone book that was on the nightstand next to the bed, and I stayed up for hours reading that book, all night in fact—all those names of people I didn't know, all those little eastern Kentucky towns I didn't even know where they were. Looking, I guess, for somebody, anybody, I could call.

The next day, around the middle of the afternoon, we got to Owen. We'd planned it that way—to stop through there on the way to Memphis. I don't know what I thought I was going to find—I hadn't heard from anybody in Owen, not my mom or Ted or anybody, in the nearly five years since I'd been away. To tell the truth, part of me dreaded going back—I felt guilty about all those people I just walked out on. Part of me was still seeing it as a completely selfish thing to've done. But I was also nervous—to see Ted again, to see him after five years. It was hard to think of him as being any more than fourteen like he was when I left, and now he'd be nineteen. I had this terrible fear I might see him walking down the street and not even recognize him, he'd look so different.

I don't think I'd have gone back if it hadn't been that Monica wanted us to. She was always trying to get me to talk about it, which I never wanted to do. From the very first time we met, she had this big thing about us both being from the South—like it was fate we were meant to be together.

Not much had changed in Owen. There was the brick school, and the playground; and the lumberyard where Wallace and I worked loading pallets; and the Nu-Way Laundromat, which looked even seedier than when I used to go there. The only thing that was different was the one thing I'd known was going to be different, the one thing that had to be. My mom wasn't living in Owen anymore. Nobody knew where she went. The house trailer was still there—but new people were living in it, this black family that'd gone and turned the front yard into a trash heap with all these bright plastic toys and hubcaps and just plain junk they'd let pile up. The woman who came to the door of the trailer was even fatter than Verbena, if that's possible. She just barely fit in the door, and not at all into these purple sweatpants she was trying to wear. But she turned out to be nice. She told me she didn't know my mom, that she'd gotten the trailer from some cousin of hers who'd lived in it for about a year, but then he moved away to Louisville and so she moved in.

She was impressed when we told her we'd driven down from New York. "I'd just love to go to New York City," she told us. "Broadway, Harlem, the Statue of Liberty. But I'll never get to go. I'll be stuck here till the day I die." She looked like she was about thirty.

"You never know," Monica told her. "You could always just hop a bus. That's what I did."

"I got these four kids," the woman said. "I got responsibilities. My traveling days are over and I never even traveled. But ya'll come inside, have a cup of coffee. I never met anybody from New York except my cousin Billy, and he's a fool."

I couldn't stand the thought of going in that trailer. "We've got to be pushing on," I explained. Though Monica went inside—she had to use the bathroom.

"Disgusting," she reported when we were back in the car. "Worse than a Texaco station."

I told her I didn't want to hear about it.

"Well, at least I got to see where you grew up," she said. "I never believed it when you said you lived in a house trailer. Are you upset your mom wasn't there?"

I didn't tell her I was relieved.

I N LAST NIGHT'S DREAM—AND I DON'T WANT TO write this down, but I guess I have to, because I promised myself to write everything down—I'm lying on a mattress on the floor with Ted. I think it's somewhere in New York, it's vaguely familiar but I can't place it. I'm not just lying with Ted, we're fucking—or rather I'm fucking him, this long slow-motion fuck that feels really good and completely realistic, the way dreams can sometimes feel. Then I get up from the mattress and walk over to this little washbasin that's in the same room, and I start washing my dick off with warm water.

When I turn around, there's Ted lying on the mattress where I left him—only it's like he's been burned, his skin is all charred black, and where it's not black it's bright pink. It's like the skin on some swollen-up overcooked hot dog. He's holding himself by his arms, sort of rocking back and forth and looking at me with these big pleading eyes. I know I have to get him to a hospital right away because something terrible's wrong with him, but in the dream I also know the hospital's not going to do any good, and Ted knows it too. This terrible sickness he has is beyond any hospital's helping it.

I can't tell you how horrible it looks, his skin all black and blistered up like it's going to pop open.

The other thing we both know in the dream is—I'm somehow the cause of what's happened to him.

M ONICA'S DAD RAN THIS ADVERTISING AGENCY that'd made lots of money putting these great ugly billboards up all over the city. He was always getting petitions from people who thought that they were eyesores and that he was ruining the city.

That's what we talked about the first time I met them: billboards. We sat in the living room of their big fancy new house. The part of the city where they lived was called Germantown.

"It's the only part of Memphis the blacks haven't gone and ruined," Monica's mother told me. That was about her only contribution to the conversation that first time, and even though I never got to know her all that well—I never felt very comfortable around Monica's parents—what she said that first time always stuck with me. I always thought about her living room, which was done up completely in white—white sofa, white armchairs, white carpet, white curtains. I thought about how the blacks certainly hadn't managed to ruin that living room yet. I tried to imagine Verbana sitting on one of those sofas, I tried to imagine her rearing back and letting loose with one of her stories about conjure. Or farting some flame out of her butt to catch those curtains on fire.

Mr. Nolan was this pudgy man, completely bald. Monica'd got her looks from her mom, who was thin and had those same high Indian cheekbones I liked in Monica so much. Only her mom wore these prissy-looking glasses that completely ruined her looks—at least I thought so, and I always got the feeling Monica's dad thought so too.

"Donald Nolan," he introduced himself that first time. He shook my hand. "You can call me Don," he said.

I wanted to say, "Well you can call me Tony," but I didn't.

"Billboards," he told me when we'd settled into those big white armchairs and Monica's mom had served both of us mugs of beer on a tray. Don was in the middle of this big fight—in fact, the whole five years I knew him he was in the middle of this fight to keep his billboards.

"They don't know it, but we're doing this city a service," he explained to me. I was trying hard to be polite, but I also kept yawning away in spite of myself. I'm sure he noticed, but I think he was used to people yawning when he talked to them. "We're getting products out there so people can see them. That's what you've got to do. People don't know about it, it don't sell. It's simple as that. You got to tell 'em about it if you're gonna distribute the merchandise."

For an instant I thought about what Carlos would've said if he'd been sitting there in that white living room. But it'd only have been something rude. He'd have started talking about dildoes or race riots or something. I put Carlos out of my head. Anyway, he'd arranged his whole life so he'd never have to sit in a white living room and talk to somebody's parents.

Then I thought—that's where he's wrong, that's where he's missing out. Sometimes Carlos seemed like the most depressingly selfish person in the world, not to be able to sit in a living room and listen to somebody's parents talk about whatever they wanted to talk about.

I could do a pretty good job of pushing him out of my head in those days—it was a skill I'd developed.

"Now Memphis," Mr. Nolan told me, "Memphis is the distribution capital of America. Lots of products go through here on their way to somewhere else. Did you know that?"

I didn't know anything.

"And so it goes hand in hand, see? Distribution, advertising. You can't tell me a few signs are going to ruin this city. This is America, this is free enterprise."

It was true when you drove down the interstate you could hardly see anything for all the billboards.

"Anyway," he said, "I'm not just out for profit. You can make those signs speak to the community. This last Christmas, for example, I put up four billboards at my own cost to remind people of the holidays. Put people in the holiday mood while they're going out shopping.

"Bring back memories of old-time Christmases. Now who's going to complain about that? And for Fourth of July I put up this beautiful sign with a flag, to make people proud about being Americans. I'd say you've got to be pretty much of a spoilsport not to like a billboard with a flag."

There was a picture of Monica's brother, Gary, on the little table next to my armchair. He had those same high cheekbones like Monica, but his hair was darker and his lips fuller—they were almost pouty they were so full. He was sort of a great-looking kid, in his way, and now he was dead. I tried to fathom all that, while Monica's dad talked on about billboards, but I couldn't.

I could hear Monica and her mother talking away in the kitchen, and I wondered what they were talking about. I had this fantasy Monica was asking her mother about sex, whether there was more to it than what she and I managed to do. I had this fantasy her mother was telling her to get me to put it up her butt sometime for a change.

"There's lots of future to this business," Don was saying. "We could get you in at the bottom. Work yourself up."

"I appreciate that," I told him. "I'll think about it. Let me take some time to think."

I knew immediately there was no way I was going to work for Monica's dad.

"Well," Don said when Monica and her mother had finished their little talk in the kitchen. I think he was pretty relieved for our conversation to be over. They never liked me all that much, Monica's parents. They were just glad to have their little girl back in Memphis, and if I was what it took to get her back there, then they were going to be grateful to me.

"You think about it," Don told me. "Son, it was awfully nice to meet you." He shook my hand like I'd passed some kind of test.

"Nice to meet you too, Don," I told him. I guess I emphasized the "Don" a little more than I should have, because Monica gave me this little warning glance. Even though she wasn't crazy about her parents, she always thought I was making fun of her if I made fun of them, so I pretty much had to toe the line. I dearly wanted to have called him "Mr. Nolan" just to see what kind of distance that would've put between us. But Monica had said if they liked me, they'd probably help us out. I guess I've always wanted people to like me, which is probably my downfall.

Actually, I have to say this about Monica. Even though she didn't think she liked her parents very much, really she liked them a lot. She spent all her time trying to make them happy, which I guess is a good thing to do if you don't have anything else. They'd had a hard time of it. Monica told me her dad was never the same since Gary died. He got the skitters, was what she said—meaning everything had been going along just fine, and then his life had hit this patch of ice and went into a tailspin. He'd never gotten over that. He kept waiting for another patch, and no matter how long he went without hitting another, or how many billboards he put up, you could see he wasn't ever going to get his confidence back.

Monica's mom had her problems too. She was one of those teeto-talers who'd have been a better person if she drank, but she wouldn't because she was terrified of becoming an alcoholic. She was forever telling Monica how, if you were a latent alcoholic, even one sip of liquor would have you hooked, so you'd better not risk it. Beer she thought was okay—she didn't drink it herself, but Don did, and she'd serve it to him without making a fuss. Anything stronger, though, she completely disapproved of. Which I always thought was something of a hoot, since Monica once told me her mom couldn't sleep at night without her dose of this stuff called NyQuil. I don't know whether you know about NyQuil—it was something I was acquainted with in Owen, when I'd buy it at the drugstore if I couldn't get anything else to drink. If you look at the label, you'll see it's basically straight alcohol with a little cough medicine mixed in. I can tell you, it's pretty potent stuff—it even comes with this plastic top that's like a shotglass, which I guess shows somebody somewhere has a sense of humor.

Maybe I should've gotten a job in billboards and been some sort of second son to that family, but I didn't. Instead I got this job working at a lumber company called Mad Joe's. You might've thought its name meant to say Joe was crazy, but it just meant he was mad as in angry—not angry the deep way Seth was angry, just bad mood angry. But that was okay, I could live around Mad Joe's being mad. I've always been able to sort of go to sleep on my feet, automatic pilot—and anyway, there's not much to selling wood. It's not like hustling kids at Port Authority.

It was amazing how quickly I put that whole Port Authority thing behind me. My whole life's been walking in and out of different situations like that—and then once they're over, I've always just put them behind me. It's my great talent. Though every once in a while some kid would come into the store in these dirty jeans and work shirt, a baseball cap cocked back on his head, and I'd catch myself sizing him up, thinking how Carlos would really go for that one. But I felt ashamed when I did that. I told myself, you've put all that behind you now. You've closed that door.

Monica always called sex "the wild thing," and I think for her it really was the wild thing. That depressed me. If only she knew about the really wild things. But I never told her about any of the wild things I'd done. Maybe I hinted I'd had to do a little hustling when I first got to the city, but she wasn't too shocked by that. She knew how guys could get taken advantage of—it was one of the things she had against New York, all those queers out hustling kids who didn't know any better. She had her own set of standards, and I'm positive she never got involved in any stuff like that. She told me Matt from Valve Lash was the only guy she was involved with in New York, and all they did was fool around. Whatever that means. I think whatever I might've told her about myself—it was way back when we were first getting to know each other—she just totally put out of her head and forgot. Which was something she was always good at, especially when it didn't fit into her story of things.

I don't think we were ever very good at the wild thing together— I'd feel sorry for anybody who thought we were. Though Monica never seemed to notice how bad it was; or if she did, she never let on. "You're a great driver," she used to say to me all the time, which I always thought was meant to be some kind of compliment.

The only nights it was ever any good between us was when I'd take a bottle out to Tom Lee Park after work, and sit on the bluffs and think about stuff. I mentioned this earlier. I never wanted to be with anybody when I drank, I just wanted to be alone to practice that old exercise Carlos told me about the very first day we ever met: "Try to think back farther and farther and see if you can follow one single thought all the way back to its beginning." He was right, too—I could learn all sorts of things just by doing that one thing. I'd stay out there a long time, sometimes till two or three in the morning.

I was always honest with Monica and told her about the river bluff—that I went out there to think—but I don't think she ever quite believed me. I think part of her would've almost preferred me to be cheating on her with some other woman—at least that'd be something she could understand. But sitting with a bottle of whisky and just thinking about things was frightening to her. She just didn't know where that sort of thing might end up taking me. I think somewhere deep down she knew that even though to everybody else it looked like she had me, she really didn't have me at all. She could never put her finger on what it was—and I never gave her any clues, because whether she had me or not didn't really seem to me to make much difference, since I was there with her anyway.

Gradually we fell into this joke about an imaginary woman I was having this affair with. It was less scary than thinking about the river bluff—maybe for both of us. My woman was a waitress at a barbeque joint, she was forty-five years old and chain-smoked—Monica claimed she could smell it on me when I came in. She had three children, and a husband who was a truck driver, and we'd check into the Alamo Plaza motel to do our version of the wild thing. When I think about it, the whole thing was a little weird. We'd go on and on about this woman—Monica had decided her name was Velma, and I think in some way we both knew exactly what we were doing, and how we could get in some kind of high spirits making things up about her but underneath all that there was something else, some kind of fright.

Monica didn't play her guitar much anymore—only when she was waiting up for me. That night at CBGB's was the high point of her music career, and once we were back in Memphis she gave up on her ambitions—I guess those songs she wrote me back in New York did her in, and once the music was used up inside her, that was it. It wasn't something we ever talked about. When I think about it now, I realize we never talked about much of anything. We just kept falling into one pattern after another, sort of like the way we fell in with each other from the start. She'd spend Thursday evenings and all day Sundays at her parents' house, or she'd go out to the malls with this mousey high school friend of hers, Lisa, who I couldn't stand to be around. I'd get home from work and, especially if Lisa was there, which she was a lot,

I'd go out to the shed to try my hand at a little carpentry, or if I was really depressed I'd sit on my workbench and jerk off and watch how my come spattered the sawdust on the floor. And then there were the days I'd detour by a liquor store and find myself in Tom Lee Park watching the river roll by.

Usually Monica had fallen asleep on the floor, propped up against the seat of the sofa. Her guitar would be in her lap, and four or five beer cans beside her. My shutting the door would wake her. She could come awake instantly—not like most people, who have to swim a ways up from sleep before they surface. She'd smile and say in this bright voice, "So, you were out with your girl again."

"Yeah," I'd play along. "Velma was pretty hot tonight. There was no resisting her. We broke one of the motel beds and had to pick ourselves up and move over to the other one."

She'd shake her head. "Men," she'd say.

"Women," I'd tell her.

I guess it was some way of reminding ourselves of something. She'd grab my leg and wrestle me down to the floor, which I always kind of liked—I'd let myself go down without much of a fight, and we'd tussle there on the rug in front of the sofa, giggling like little kids because we were both drunk—we'd both gotten drunk in our own separate ways so this sort of thing could have a chance to happen, and she knew that as much as I did. We'd wrestle each other out of our clothes, and by that time I'd have a walloping hard-on—which was something I had a little trouble some of the time finding my way to with Monica. Those were about the only nights the wild thing got halfway wild, and I guess for Monica it was often enough to keep her going.

I have to admit I used to feel this tremendous relief when I got back home those nights, like there was something I'd just barely escaped. I'd cling to Monica for dear life, this totally crazy fear that I was being swept down the Mississippi River and hanging on tight to one of those tree trunks I'd sometimes see slamming along out in the current, their roots looking like they'd been torn right up from the ground in some terrible flood somewhere.

OUR WEDDING TOOK PLACE IN THE SPRING OF 1985, this cool gray May afternoon, the kind that always made me remember when I was a kid. I used to love those days—everything looking shaggy with new leaves, and you knew it was going to rain later in the afternoon. The whole day was just waiting for it to happen. I used to get drunk on afternoons like that, and then fall asleep on the sofa and when I'd wake up it'd be raining outside the windows, this gentle rain falling down. That was a great way to wake up. An hour later I'd usually have a headache—but right when I woke up, it was great.

I guess I got talked into it, or I should say I let myself get talked into it. Getting married, I mean—though I could mean most of the things I've ever done in my life, and definitely everything I did with Monica. Everybody's got some special talent, I guess, and Monica's was talking me into things. I don't think she even knew she was doing it—it was just the way she was. And it wasn't a bad thing, really. In fact, I've always liked being talked into things, it always made me feel like I was worth something to somebody.

We'd rented this little apartment in midtown for cheap, I guess because there were some welfare apartments across the street and nobody wanted to live near those. It was an okay place—we didn't have much furniture, which didn't bother me because I'd been living in a place without much furniture for years, but it made Monica nervous. "I want to feel like somebody lives here," she said. So we spent Saturdays going to yard sales. Personally, I can't think of anything more depressing—I hated seeing all some family's junk piled up for sale in their front yard. If you don't want it, just throw it away, I always thought. There was something indecent about going and selling it.

Maybe that sounds strange for somebody like me to say, but it's what I always felt. I'd take one look at those old books and records, and clothes, and toys, and a lamp or a bookcase—and I'd feel like I knew way too much about the people who owned them. I didn't like knowing so much about total strangers. And I didn't like bringing their lives into our apartment, which is what I felt like was happening every time we bought another coffee table off of somebody's front lawn.

I remembered Carlos's apartment, that tent bedroom we had there—how with just a mattress and some good fucking we managed to fill the place up with ourselves, and that was enough. Sometimes I'd hear Carlos saying one single word to me: *baggage*. And I knew what he meant.

I said something like that to Monica once—not about Carlos, because she never heard that name pass my lips, but about the furniture. "I sort of liked it better empty," I think is what I said. We'd spent two hours lugging this ugly green second-hand sofa up two flights of stairs. Monica looked at me and said, "Sometimes you're just weird, Tony. Do you know that?" It was her theory that New York was what had made me weird, but now that we were back home, as she called it, things were going to get better.

The one thing I was excited to get was a big color TV. I think I told you how, the whole time I was growing up, we didn't have a TV. And Carlos never did either, for different reasons. So when we got a TV I thought, This is it. I've arrived. I'd spent my whole life thinking about how ordinary people came home from work at night and watched TV, about all the great shows they could watch, all the channels there were to choose from.

It was the way everybody else could live except me, up till the day I bought that Zenith.

I have to say this—TV's the most disappointing thing that ever happened to me. Maybe when I was younger it would've been perfect, but by the time I was twenty-three and got my first TV I was no good for it anymore. The waiting for it had worn it out.

I guess if I'd never met Carlos, I'd probably've been duped like everybody else. Monica could sit for hours and watch anything—it was one of those things that made me realize she'd never be able to understand anything about me, really, if she was somebody who could sit and watch TV like that. It was her upbringing, I guess. Her parents liked nothing more than for the two of us to come over for an evening of TV watching—Thursday night was the best night for that, they claimed. All the good shows were on then. I'd take one look at what was on, and go in some other room like it was something I was allergic to. I'd work on fixing the leaky faucets around the house, or wiring a new telephone jack—any kind of tinkering to keep my hands busy and my brain out of the reach of the TV set. One look and I could tell the big secret: TV was just another kind of drinking, and there're lots worse kinds of drinking than booze.

During a commercial one Saturday night, Monica turned to me and said, "I think you and me should take the old plunger." I've told you how Monica had her own words for things.

"What's the old plunger?" I asked her. I thought maybe she was referring to some clogged drain I hadn't gotten around to yet.

She looked at me with this sort of smirk. "Get married, stupid." She was sipping beer through a straw—which always drove me crazy to see, but she liked to do that sometimes.

I was a little surprised. "Oh," I said. "Says who?"

She shrugged like it'd been my idea instead of hers. "We're not getting any younger," she said. She was three years older than me.

"What's that got to do with it?" I asked.

"Well, it's true. It's a fact of life."

"Yeah? So? Are you trying to drive me crazy?"

She flicked her straw at me. "What's wrong with us getting married? It wouldn't change anything."

"If it's not broke, don't fix it," I said.

"That's as dumb as me saying 'We're not getting any younger,'" she pointed out.

Which was true. I liked it when she wouldn't let me get away with things.

"It wouldn't have to be for a while," she said. "We could think about it."

"Like how long a while?" We'd been living in Memphis about two years by then.

"Like May a while," she said. "It'd be fun. The parents want to pay for everything—they like you a lot, they say we deserve some big splash we'll never forget. We'll have a great honeymoon. Think about it. We could go to Mexico. Acapulco."

"I don't want to go to Mexico," I told her. "What's in Mexico except a bunch of desert?"

"We can go anywhere," she said. "It doesn't have to be Mexico. Plus," she added, like it was some afterthought, "they'll give us some money to buy a house."

"They really said that?" I couldn't believe they'd do something like that.

She only nodded. She was playing with that straw in her beer bottle.

"You mean, a house to own?" I could still hear Carlos's voice saying, "baggage." At the same time, it was like some door opening up, a door I'd always thought would be shut. I'd never in my life lived in a regular house, except that thing that leaked before we got the house trailer in Owen. The idea of a house—lots of rooms, a yard to mow, maybe space in a garage where I could build things in my spare time. Some woods in back where I could go be alone and think.

"No kids," I told her. I'd seen too much happen to want kids.

"That's not something we have to talk about right now," she said. I remember she put her hand on my knee. "So what do you say?"

I still wonder whether she knew that a house was the one button she could punch with me. Probably she did—Monica's always been smart that way.

I remember I was a little pissed she'd been talking to her parents about it, and they had everything planned out, but the idea of a house totally did me in.

I took a deep breath. "Okay," I said. "We'll do it."

"So do you love me?" she asked. In general, she wasn't too pushy on things like that. What she didn't know, I think she always figured, wouldn't hurt her.

I took the straw out of her beer bottle and flicked it at her. She jumped when the little drop of beer spattered on her face.

I knew even when I said it that I didn't really mean it. If I'd thought I did, that would be one thing. But I didn't think it for one instant, even at the time. "I love you," I said.

I'd never said anything like that to Carlos. I never said it to anybody in my life, and I'm sorry I said it to Monica. Monica, I'm sorry. There're lots of things I'm sorry about, but I'm sorriest about that, Monica. You won't believe me when I say that—and I wouldn't either if I was you—

but I really am sorry. It's the most despicable thing I ever did.

Looking back on everything, I'm a little surprised her parents were so set on her marrying me—they must've seen what a scruffy, sullen sort of guy I was. But then who knows what they were thinking? Monica always told me her mother thought I was charming—which is a hoot if there ever was one. At least I managed to get through the wedding without upsetting anybody too much, except myself. All I kept thinking was—the last time I was in a church, it was in the South Bronx, and it wasn't exactly a wedding. I kept thinking about the cool damp smell in that church, and the pools of rainwater where the floor had sunk and the pigeons flapping in the rafters.

At the little reception at the Nolans' house, I didn't even get drunk. In fact, I didn't have a single drink. They were serving champagne, and I guess it was some kind of luck that the only time I ever drank champagne before, I got the worst hangover of my life, so this time I wasn't even tempted. Plus I must've known if I had anything to drink, I'd probably have kept on drinking till who knows what I might've done?

I smiled and shook a lot of hands of Monica's relatives. You could divide them into the ones with high cheekbones like Monica and her mother, and the round-faced ones like Don. Everybody in America does this, I told myself. At some time in their life, everybody has to do this.

The only time I nearly lost it was driving away from the reception toward the airport: our honeymoon turned out to be a week at Disney World, which was okay with me—definitely better than Mexico. Along both sides of the highway, Don's company had put up these huge billboards. I was looking at those signs, thinking how ugly they were—but also how it was the money from them that was paying for my new house and everything—when the next one I saw said, in big script letters, BEST WISHES TO MONICA AND TONY! In the background there was this pastel picture of wedding bells and a church steeple. I nearly had a heart attack. At the same time Monica was saying, "Dad's totally crazy. He's got to be totally crazy. Is that not the sweetest thing?" And I guess maybe it was—but I've never been a sweet person in my life, so I'll never understand those things.

"Be sure and mention it to him when we get back," she was telling me. "He'll love it that we saw it."

I remember thinking, Yeah, he'll have it papered over in an hour with some other ad he can make money off of.

All I can say is—I was wrong. We flew back from Disney World a week later and that stupid sign was still up, and it stayed up for the next six months. I'd see it whenever I drove by there to deliver stuff down to South Memphis for the lumberyard. Don was always trying to figure out ways to tell Monica he loved her—which I guess is all anybody can ever do, even if it's billboards.

I GUESS YOU COULD SAY WE HAD A PRETTY GOOD marriage. Once she'd gotten everything official, I think Monica had what she wanted, and so she was willing not to badger me for anything more and risk spoiling everything. It's hard to describe, but she sort of became a different person after the wedding. She backed off from things a little. She settled in.

She liked to cook—which is something I never cared about, but I pretended this sudden interest. She bought cookbooks—French, Italian, Californian. Even Indian, though I had to be honest and mention how everything she cooked out of that one gave me the runs. But as for the rest, she was pretty good at gourmet food. It was something she and Lisa gabbed about all the time—cooking shows on TV, and recipes, and where to buy what weird vegetables you never heard of before. I was a little sorry the days of shoplifting cans of Spam and packages of Oreos were over—though it's also true you could get pretty tired of eating those kinds of things all the time.

What was fun about being married to Monica was the ways I could make her happy. I mean, happy the way ordinary people are happy. With Carlos there was never anything like that I could do, unless it was crazy stuff in front of Seth's camera like fist-fucking a kid I'd never met before inside some run-down warehouse. With Monica, I could do it just by coming home with a bouquet of flowers—which may sound dumb, but after a while in your life it's a relief to know that something simple like buying flowers is going to solve some things for you. She wouldn't ever have bought flowers just for herself, but it made her so happy that there was somebody out there to buy them for her. Plus I always thought flowers made the house look nice. I'd go in a florist's and wish I could buy a pickup truckload of flowers to put everywhere through the house so you wouldn't even be able to tell it was a house anymore—you'd think it was the outdoors, only it'd still be indoors.

Which is something Verbena might've done for a movie set. I have to admit that every once in a while I'd think back to those movies we made, and I'd just have to shake my head. I wondered what had ever happened to them—if Verbena was still designing sets, and Seth still poking around with his movie camera, and if Carlos was out there somewhere making it all up for them as he went along.

Whenever I'd get to thinking about that kind of stuff, I'd go out to my workshop in back. Working at Mad Joe's, I could pick up tools for a discount, so I had a bunch. Plus scrap-ends of lumber that otherwise were just going to get tossed out. Only trouble was, I never knew what to build. I'd start things—a coffee table, a cabinet for the kitchen, even a canoe—but then I'd lose interest. Most nights I'd find myself sitting out there with my pocketknife and some stick of wood, whittling away at it, not sure what it was I was making. Sometimes what I ended up with looked like a little stick figure of a person, or a face, but most times it was just curves and corners and things that'd keep changing their shape the more I'd whittle them down. Because I never knew where to stop. I'd just keep seeing how the wood kept changing under my knife blade, and before I knew it, I'd whittle the stick down to nothing.

I think I mentioned that I used to jerk off out there a lot, too.

Monica would joke with Lisa about how I spent all my time in that workshop but I never seemed to get anything done.

"I'm a slow worker," I told her. But I think she somehow must've understood something, because even though she wanted that coffee table and that kitchen cabinet, she never got on my case about them, and, for the record, I give her credit for that. I wasn't the easiest person to live with. I never hit it off with her parents, or her friends like Lisa, and I never had any friends of my own. I wasn't there for her the way a regular husband is supposed to be. You could say I didn't care enough about our marriage, but that's not true. Monica saved me from something, or at least she almost did, and I never stopped being grateful to her. We never talked about things like that. It wasn't the way we were with each other, not even in the beginning, and the longer time passed, the less we were like that. But I think she guessed more than she ever said, and so we didn't need to talk.

Since I've been at the Eddy, I've gotten one letter from her—which, to tell the truth, is more than I expected and more than I deserve. I sort of wish I still had that letter, but I don't. When I got it, I let it lie around about a week at least before I finally worked myself up to open it. And then I read it really quickly, just skimming down the pages, afraid to look at it too carefully. It made me think about when I was little and the few times I ever went to see a movie; if it was a horror flick, in the scary parts I'd sort of squint my eyes so I could just barely see what was going on, and if something happened that I didn't want to see—like somebody opening a closet door and there was the zombie—I could shut my eyes in no time. That's the way it was with Monica's letter. I read it in kind of a squint, so I could hurry and pass over the parts I didn't want to see.

I have to say she let me off easy. She told me she supported me totally, and I had all her prayers. She told me she thought she knew me, but now she knew she never did, and that hurt her a lot, but she guessed I had my reasons and finally they probably hurt me more than they hurt her. She said she thought I'd understand if she told me she had to pick up the pieces and get on with her life. The counselor she'd been going to had given her this book about the seven stages of grief, and it was doing her good to read it.

I understood all that. I remember I tore the letter up into these little squares—not emotional or anything, just feeling like it was what I had to do. Then I flushed it down the toilet.

Actually, I think I was afraid if I left that letter lying around I'd wake up in the middle of the night to find it glowing with some blue light, or the pages rustling around the room like a whirlwind had taken them up. You know the kind of dreams I have—I wasn't about to keep that letter in there with me. Besides, even though I'd squinted, I knew everything it said. I didn't have to ever read that letter ever again.

But that's all in the future. During the three years we were married, we had an ordinary kind of life. She'd taken to calling me Tone after we got married. It sort of drove me crazy, especially when I'd hear her talking to Lisa about Tone this and Tone that. But what could I do? That's my wife talking about me, I used to say to myself, and it sounded so strange that I had to stop saying it or it'd pitch me into a mood I couldn't get out of for days. My wife. Monica's husband, Tony. Tone. I never thought about the way I used to live—all those guys I was out on the streets every night looking for like my life depended on it. It was like all that never existed.

Except for this one time. There was a Halloween party we went to at Lisa's house. I hadn't wanted to go, but Monica pointed out how we never went much of anywhere, so I said okay. It was another way of buying her flowers. I wasn't too keen on getting dressed up. From making all those movies with Carlos, I'd ended up in enough different costumes to last me my whole life. But Monica really got into it. We went around to the Salvation Army, where she found herself this fur coat some moths had had a field day with and a pillbox hat with peacock feathers on it. "I wouldn't even think about putting those things on my body," I told her. "You'll get worms or something." But she was slipping into that coat like no tomorrow.

"They dry clean them, silly," she said. "Before they hang them on the rack."

"I'm not getting into any of this stuff," I told her, and I folded my arms to show her I was firm about it. Which of course never worked for a second with Monica. She grabbed me by the elbow and took me over to the men's rack where all these suits were hanging. Hideous stuff— one of those suits was made out of this bright green cloth that was shiny like some insect wing. A bunch of them were sky blue or lemon yellow. There was one the color of mustard that's been in the refrigerator too long, and that was the one Monica took a liking to. "Yecch," I told her. There was a jacket, and pants, and a vest, all the same mustard color.

"Yes," she said.

"No," I told her flat out. "Do you want me to go around looking like some Chelsea Avenue pimp or what?"

"It's dress-up. Nobody's supposed to know who you are."

I didn't like it, but the whole suit only cost eight dollars, and Monica'd made her mind up. "And a hat," she said, taking one off the shelf and squeezing it down on my head. She looked at it, and sort of squinted, and screwed up her nose. "Nope," she said, lifting it off by the brim and sticking another one on there, and then another, till finally she found the one she liked.

"You look so cute in hats, Tone. You should wear them all the time."

"Very funny," I said.

We looked like two total tramps in all that get-up. "I just hope we don't get picked up by the cops," I told her when we were driving over to Lisa's. "It'll be the slammer for sure."

"It's Halloween," she said. "Everybody's wearing a costume tonight. Just look at the drivers of all the other cars."

I did, but so far as I could see, they all looked completely normal. But I didn't say that to Monica.

At the party, some people were in costume, but lots weren't. It sort of annoyed me that I'd had to come in one when other people weren't going to. Lisa was dolled up to look like a whore, though when I mentioned that to Monica she told me, no, Lisa was supposed to be Sleeping Beauty. I wanted to say I'd seen a lot of drag queens do a better Sleeping Beauty, and with no sleep either. But I didn't.

There were a couple of witches in the room, and somebody with a sheet over his head was trying to be a ghost. One guy had a Lone Ranger costume on, complete with two six-shooters. Somebody else was decked out in a tabby-cat mask with big whiskers and a silver spandex body suit that fit him like a glove. His body had great definition—you had to give him that. He definitely worked out in a gym somewhere.

The doorbell rang, and some jerk outfitted to look like a computer walked in. He'd fixed a cardboard box around his waist to look like a disk drive, and another one over his head, which was supposed to be the screen, and he was holding a keyboard in one hand. Everybody seemed to think it was the greatest costume they'd ever seen.

"Tony and me, we're Bohemians," Monica was explaining to a bunch of people. "Bohos is what they call them in New York. That's where Tony and I met. New York City, and I can tell you there were Bohos everywhere you turned."

I could tell she was impressing everybody with her talk. It sort of depressed me, though, so I went outside on the deck where the night air was cool. There's something I always like about fall, the leaves turning and coming down. I couldn't see them because it was night, but I could hear the dry sound they made when they fell. From inside Lisa's house I could hear music on the stereo, and people talking, but out there on the deck it was the leaves falling I could hear louder than anything—leaves falling in the dark where nobody could see them.

"So—it's a Boho," I heard this voice say behind me. I turned around and probably didn't look too thrilled.

"Just kidding." It was the man with the cat mask.

I shrugged. I wasn't all that interested in talking to a guy wearing a cat mask, even if he did have a great body under his silver spandex.

"You know," he said, "I think we know one another."

I looked at the cat mask.

"I'm pretty sure I'd remember," I said.

He pushed the mask up over the top of his head and grinned at me.

I did know him. I didn't know his name, but I knew he owned some outfit that built fences around swimming pools. He was in Mad Joe's a fair amount to buy stuff. I guess I'd always sort of noticed him—he was about forty, this wiry frame and gray hair cut real short. He didn't remind me of Carlos—nobody I ever met ever reminded me of Carlos. But I have to say, whenever he came into Mad Joe's, I got this whiff of something, some itch of electric current I used to know back when I was living the life I lived in New York. The Boho life, Monica was probably calling it inside at that very instant.

I guess that's why I'd look at him the way I did whenever he was in the store. And he must've noticed it. I didn't think I was being too obvious about it, but I guess I was—because before I knew what was happening he was touching me. It was this brazen thing—he just reached out and grabbed my crotch. It took me totally off-guard. I backed up against the deck railing.

"Whoa there," I told him. "You're pretty off-limits."

He didn't take his hand off me. He just looked at me.

I guess I should've thrown a punch at him just then, or something like that—but I didn't. I've always respected people who knew exactly what they wanted.

"I could just tell about you," he said.

"There's not anything to tell," I told him.

He'd moved in against me and put his arms around my waist. It was all sort of sudden, and before I knew it he was pressing his crotch up against mine. He was getting a hard-on, and I guess I was too.

"You've got me all wrong," I said. "You're barking up the wrong tree."

"I'm a cat," he said. "I don't bark. You know you want it, don't you?"

"No, I don't know that," I told him.

He'd worked his hand down the back of my pants, and his finger was creeping up on my asshole.

"I really don't want this," I said.

"I've always thought cocks speak louder than words," he told me, pressing himself against me so I knew he could feel my hard-on there.

His middle finger had wormed its way up my asshole, and now he started sliding it in and out of me, like he was fucking me. I think I leaned my head against his shoulder and just let him go on with it. I couldn't do anything else. I didn't want to. It brought back too many memories, and I knew what I'd always know—how my body didn't really belong to me sometimes, it was just something I was inside of. Meanwhile the cat man was humping himself against me, and I was humping back. He put his tongue inside my ear and that did it—I went crazy shooting off inside my mustard-colored Boho trousers. I bit his shoulder to keep from crying out, and he bit my ear. I don't know whether he came too or not, because at that instant Mr. Computer came out the back door with a beer in one hand and that stupid keyboard in the other. The cat man and I broke apart like nothing had happened, and I'm sure Mr. Computer didn't notice a thing.

"Aren't you guys chilly?" he asked. "Anyway, you're wasting your time out here. All the hot chicks are indoors."

"We'll be in in a sec," the cat man said. "We're out here looking for shooting stars. And I think maybe we found one."

When Mr. Computer had squeezed his way back indoors, the cat man said in this totally normal voice, like we were talking swimming pool fences, "You should stop by my place sometime. We could have something pretty hot going on."

I shook my head. "I don't think so." I was still tingling where his finger'd been up my asshole. To tell the truth, I wanted to bend over right there and get fucked like I hadn't gotten fucked in two years—but I also felt suddenly empty and terrible inside. "I'm a married man," I told him. "I've got these responsibilities."

He shrugged. "I'm married too. Everybody has to live their own life."

And that was true. We walked back into the party and headed for different corners of the room and stayed like that the rest of the night.

And even though he came into Mad Joe's about every other week like nothing ever happened, I made sure not to look his way. I guess he got the message—or maybe he was content with that little bit of trick or treat he got from me at Lisa's party, and decided just to settle for that.

THERE WAS THIS ONE PARTICULAR STREET IN Memphis I used to drive down every day on my way to work. I didn't have to drive down it—in fact, it was a couple blocks out of my way—but on the corner was this movie theater, one of those big old-fashioned kinds you don't see anymore. It was all closed up when I first got to town, but then somebody bought it and opened it up to show foreign movies. There was a big marquee out front, and every three or four days they'd be showing a different movie.

Every time I drove by there and saw some new movie playing, I'd feel like this fugitive who's gotten himself a new identity and is hiding out—but he knows sooner or later he's going to walk out his front door and there'll be some car he doesn't recognize parked across the street, and then he'll know they've tracked him down. A year went by, three years—but some day, I knew, one of Carlos's movies was going to show up on that marquee.

M ONICA'S DAD LOVED TO GO FISHING. THERE WAS this lake down in Mississippi, about twenty miles south of Memphis, where he'd been going since he was a boy. It was the lake where Monica's brother, Gary, tried to roust out the water moccasins with the shotgun.

"Fishing?" I said when Monica told me her dad wanted us to go out with him sometime. "It's the middle of winter."

"Winter's the best time," Monica said. "When it's cold and early in the morning—that's when the fish're biting."

"My idea of fun," I said. "When it's cold and early in the morning."

"Dawn," she said. "I told him we'd go next Saturday."

I always tried to be a good husband. Monica dragged me out of bed while it was still pitch dark, and we sat in the kitchen drinking coffee waiting for her dad to come by and pick us up.

"What're you doing?" she asked me.

I was eating coffee beans. "If I'm gonna make it," I said, "I better be all charged up. There better be some light socket out there to plug me in to."

"Fishing's relaxing," she told me. "You'll scare the fish away if you get nervous."

"I'm always nervous," I said. "I'll be especially nervous in a boat in the middle of a lake full of water moccasins."

"Don't be stupid," she told me. "Snakes sleep in the wintertime."

On our way out of Memphis we drove past Graceland. I'd never been by there before—I didn't even know it was there. Don couldn't believe it. "They've got billboards from here to the North Carolina border advertising Graceland," he said. "First thing you see when you come into the state's a billboard in the shape of a pink Cadillac. COME HOME TO GRACELAND, it says."

"I never noticed them," I had to tell him.

Along Elvis Presley Boulevard, there were billboards everywhere—cars, liquor, plane flights to Mexico. They were selling everything. At five o'clock on a Saturday morning, the street was totally deserted except for those big lit-up signs. There was this huge cut-out of Elvis playing the guitar, about fifty feet tall. It was probably the only billboard in town Don hadn't put up, and he was jealous. "Does that make some kind of statement or what?" he said. He craned his head around to keep his eye on that sign as long as he could while we drove past. He didn't want to let it go. I turned around too—but from behind, it wasn't Elvis anymore. It was just some scaffolding and you couldn't tell what it was supposed to be.

Once we crossed over into Mississippi, Memphis sort of trailed off, like it lost interest in being a city anymore. We went driving through this country of sharecropper shacks half-falling down, and tacky little country stores with rusty gas pumps in front—but mostly just cotton fields as far as you could see. It was about dawn when we turned down a dirt road that headed back into some woods, and after a while we came to the lake. There was a tarpapered cabin there, up on stilts—a ladder led up to the door, and a sign that was tacked there said SHANGRI-LA. Signs were posted up everywhere, pieces of plywood with big lettering, like somebody'd gone hog-wild with a paintbrush one afternoon. NO TRESPASSING BY ORDER OF THE ROYAL TISHOMINGO HUNTING & FISHING CLUB, said one sign. Another said, KEEP ON DUMPING TRASH HERE & THERE WON'T BE NO MORE FISHING.

There was trash all around the cabin—tin cans, newspapers, tires. It was a pretty unappealing place. Cypress trees were growing out in the lake; their knobby brown knees stuck up out of the water the way the stubs of all those old piers do along the Hudson River in New York.

Inside the cabin a big Confederate flag with burn holes in it draped along one wall. Two men were sitting at a table drinking. When we came in, they jumped up and slapped Don on the back and hugged him with these great bearhugs. "How's it going, buddy?" they said—not talking but shouting, whooping it up. They must've been drinking a while—coffee mugs full of whisky. Their faces were all red, and they moved around the cabin in these big sloppy motions, pulling out a couple of folding chairs for us from under a pile of tarps, getting out some more coffee mugs from a cabinet that hung on the wall.

"This is my girl, Monica," Don told them. One of the men pulled out a bottle and splashed a little whisky in each of the mugs.

"You was wee-high last time I saw you," the man said. He patted her on the head. "You remember me?"

"Sure I remember you," Monica told him. She picked up her coffee mug and swirled the whisky around in it. Then she gulped it right down. What I always loved about Monica was, nothing ever fazed her. She just entered right into things. "You're Sonny," she told the man. "You have that soybean farm. And you're Ross, right? You were the restaurant man. You ran for the senate that time. You're famous."

"Used to be," Ross said, "used to be. Not famous anymore."

I could tell she impressed him, though. "Your girl's got her head screwed on," Ross told Don.

"Like her old man," Don said. "And this here's my girl's husband, Tony." He grabbed me by the arm like I was some trophy he was showing off. Which I guess I was.

Ross and Sonny both looked me up and down, but they didn't say anything.

"Been out yet?" Don asked them.

"Too fucking cold," said Ross. "If you'll pardon my French."

"You got a fine accent there," Don said. He held out his mug for more. I'd never seen him drink whisky, only beer. It flushed his face right up. "I'd take you for a native with an accent like that," he told Ross.

"I'm not a fishing man," Ross said. "I'm a hunting man."

"Don't believe a word," Sonny said. "He just came down here to get drunk. Get away from the wife and kids."

"A man's gotta do what a man's gotta do," said Ross. He was a big shaggy man, and I tried to imagine him running for the senate—making speeches, kissing babies, shaking people's hands. Both those guys made me nervous. The way they looked me over, I got this feeling they could see right through me to something they didn't like. But they were too polite to say it. I'd got out of the habit of people looking through me—in New York it always happened, but usually in Memphis I fit in fine, like I'd always been here. Sometimes I even felt like Monica'd been this net the South threw up to pull me back where I belonged.

Sonny and Ross were keeping up this loud back-and-forth with Monica and Don. It was like I wasn't there with them, which was fine. I walked around the cabin looking at stuff. There were a couple of bags of groceries—breakfast makings—sitting on the table, and a little camp stove. On one of the walls somebody'd taken an old signboard that used to have an Indian's head painted on it, some hook-nosed chief in his war bonnet, and they painted over that with white paint; then they painted the rules of the Royal Tishomingo Hunting & Fishing Club in red paint—but the white was so thin you could still see the old Indian peering through. The rules said:

1. *No Ladies*
2. *No Niggers*
3. *A good time will be had by all*
4. *No shooting of firearms in the cabin*
5. *Please do not gut fish inside the cabin*
6. *No spitting or pissing indoors*
7. *Shut out the lights when you leave*
8. *What lights?*

"Here Tony, my man"—Sonny was nudging me with the whisky bottle—"it's gonna freeze your ass out on the water."

"Tony's tough," Don said. "He lived up in New York City."

"New York, New York," sang Ross. I guess he thought he was Frank Sinatra. "City of queers and niggers," he sang in this gravelly voice.

"My own damn daughter went to live in New York for a while," Don told Ross.

"That's how I met Tony," Monica said.

"City of queers and niggers and kikes," Ross sang. Then he said, "The Trilateral Commission runs that fucking city. Did you know that? They elect the mayor and the city council. There hasn't been a free election up there in years. It's all faked. Tony, you ever come across the Trilateral Commission up there?"

"I never heard of it," I told him.

"They keep a low profile," he said. "They're very smart. They know what they're doing."

"Who's they?" I asked.

"Jewish banking establishment. Communist Party. It goes back to the 1940s. Franklin Roosevelt. Their front's the Rockefeller Foundation, but really they're everywhere. Infiltration. Basically it's your large Jewish population up there."

"It's true," Monica said, "half the people you meet up there turn out to be Jewish when you get to know them."

"And the other half," I added, "are a bunch of queers." I didn't mean to say that—it just seemed like the right thing. The way Monica said what she'd said—to fit in.

"See what I mean?" Ross told her. "You were lucky to meet a normal white man like Tony up there."

She smiled—her best smile, her Cherokee-Indian-cheekbone smile—and what I thought just then was: It's not New York anymore. I'm not a fag. I'm just Tony Blair, that's all I am. And suddenly I was remembering something Carlos told me once, a long time ago, after I first got to New York, how when they started putting people in the camps, like they did to the Jews back in Sammy's hometown, I wasn't going to have to worry. I'd just disappear back to Kentucky and everything would be fine. Suddenly I remembered him saying that so vividly.

I have to admit I liked the feel of whisky in my stomach at seven o'clock in the morning. I hadn't gotten drunk in the morning in years, and it felt great to have it go to my head like that.

"You sure you're not going out?" Don was saying. "There's a lake of fine fish out there just waiting to be breakfast."

"Too damn cold," Ross said again. He held up his mug. "I got my own warm fireside here. I'd be some kind of fool to go leaving it."

"Well, that kind of puts the fishing up to us," Don told him.

"Somebody's gotta do it," Sonny told us.

I got the feeling they could talk with each other like that all day, without saying a thing. They could live their whole lives that way.

"Ya'll hurry back," Ross yelled to us as we went down to the water and the motorboat that was moored on a little falling-down pier. "I'll scramble you up a little breakfast."

It took us forever to get the motor on the motorboat started. I say us—it was Monica who finally figured out what the problem was. I spent the whole time looking around at how the lake had washed out the tree roots along the bank. It was one of those times when it comes over you—you think it's just odd you're here. That's all—it's just odd to be here at this exact moment.

Trouble was, all of a sudden I desperately wanted to get drunk.

Not with Ross or Sonny; not with Monica and her dad either. Just curled up drunk away by myself somewhere.

When I breathed out I could see my silvery breath. Now that it was light, you could see it was cloudy—it looked like snow or probably cold rain. Everything was silver-gray—my breath, and the lake and the sky and the tree trunks by the edge of the water. The boat. Only Monica in her red jacket wasn't gray. That spot of bright red in the middle of all that gray was the most depressing thing of all.

"How was that for blotto?" Monica said once we were out on the lake. She liked to drink now and then, but she hated drunks. It was something I guess she got from her mom. "Stinko heaven back there," she said. "What is it? Seven o'clock in the morning?"

"Good solid fellows," Don told her. "Backbone people."

"I think that Ross guy is crazy," I said. I never said anything like that around Don—it just didn't seem worth disagreeing with him about things. I guess that's the worst thing you can say about somebody, that you just don't have the energy to want to bother with them. It's why Don always thought I was sort of feeble. He was used to having friendly arguments with people, the kind where you agree not to disagree too much. It was the way he got on with his friends.

"Everybody's crazy," Don said. "What you got to do is look at what made them crazy."

"Yeah," I said. "I have this feeling Ross was crazy when he was born."

"There you got it totally wrong, Tony. Ross is a deep-down good person who got derailed for doing something that wasn't his fault."

I'd never seen Don spark like that, like I'd gone and said something that offended him. But I wasn't letting go—I guess I was pissed at being dragged out here to go fishing in the middle of the winter. I guess I was hating all of this stuff.

"What do you mean, derailed?" I said.

Don looked down in the bottom of the boat, where there was water. We'd bailed some before coming out—but not completely.

"I mean thrown off track," he said. "I mean, like somebody came round and lifted him up and tossed him in a ditch."

"Oh," I said. I kept tugging on my line, not that there was any point to it, but it was something to do. The water was this oily gray color.

"Ever hear of The Delta Hut?" Don asked me. He was sitting in the middle of the boat, fooling with the bait. "Nah," he said, "you wouldn't have."

I hadn't, either.

"Well, it was some fine restaurant," he said. "Ross is one fine cook. All sorts of your famous people ate there—movie stars, politicians. There was this register in front where you could sign, and you wouldn't believe some of the names that were in that book. Frank Sinatra, Danny Kaye. Dale Evans."

I waited for him to go on, but he just sat there threading the bait on his hook like it was some kind of sewing job. Monica wasn't paying us any attention—she was concentrating on her line that fed out into the water. I don't think she wanted to listen to all this.

"So this restaurant," I said.

"Well," Don said, "he was set up. Bunch of college kids from New York City, do-gooders—came down on a bus. Got all hepped up about things. Help the Negroes, that sort of stuff. Lord knows how they found The Delta Hut, but they did. Decided to walk all over Ross in the name of so-called civil rights."

Monica wasn't looking at her dad, but she wasn't looking at me either. I'd really wandered into it this time.

"Tell me what happened," I said. I remembered Verbena's stories about Carlos in Alabama, how he thought he could make everything better. I remembered those water moccasins Monica's brother tried to shoot with a shotgun in this very lake. I don't know why I remembered those two things together like that, but I did.

"Well," Don said. "What do you expect? There was this ugly scene. Everybody knows it was ugly—Ross knows it was ugly, he'll be the first person to tell you. But he was set up for it. Now you tell me—what was a man like him supposed to do, a couple of colored boys from up North trying to bust their way into his place to get dinner? See—The Delta

Hut wasn't exactly on Main Street. It was this place for people who knew about it, not for everybody. It wasn't advertising itself, it wasn't throwing itself in the face of the Negroes."

Don was really going at his bait, threading it on that hook. There wasn't too much left of it. "I'm not prejudiced," he said. "You know me, so you know I'm not prejudiced. I'm just telling you this so you can see Ross's point of view. Everybody always hears the Negroes' point of view, and I'll be the first to admit they have a right to their own point of view, but nobody ever hears Ross's point of view. His point of view just got censored out of all the books, no different than what they do in Communist countries."

"I don't understand," I said. "What did they do?" It was starting to drizzle, the way a cloudy day can shade into this fine rain without your hardly noticing it. And in fact Monica and Don didn't seem to be noticing it. But I could tell we were going to have full-fledged rain out there.

"Those fellows," Don said, "went in there looking to get beat up. That's my opinion. I wasn't there. I don't know what happened for sure, and there're fifty different stories, depending. But if you ask me what's my opinion, that's it."

"You're telling me he went and beat up some black guys who wanted to eat at his restaurant?" I said.

The cold was making us all look pretty miserable out on that water. Don especially looked pretty miserable. He gave up trying to get that bait on the hook. He threw it down on the floor of the boat and just sat there. We all could tell now how it was starting to rain.

"You have to understand," he told me. "This was 1964. You weren't even born in 1964."

"Well," I said, "just barely."

"Look," Don said, "what I'm saying is, here's this man minding his own business. He's not hurting anybody. And then they make a big case out of it—this bunch of Jews from New York. Lawyers volunteering their time to help the blacks. They go and back him into a corner so he looks like some kind of monster and..."

"I think," Monica said, "I've got a fish."

Don looked over the side of the boat at where she was tugging her line. The rain was stinging into the water. "You got a fish all right," Don said. "You got a big one."

I don't know why I'm telling all this. I don't know why we were even talking about it out there. It's got nothing to do with fishing. It's got nothing to do with sitting around out there in the freezing cold and rain, waiting for something to happen and then nothing—except, somebody, maybe it was Ross, started shooting off a gun in the distance. Drunk and shooting at tin cans, I guess. We were out there maybe two hours and caught two little fish whose names I forget, and which we threw back in, and Monica's catfish, which we kept, this big ugly flat thing with whiskers and a dull shine to its body.

When we got back, Ross had made good on his promise. That shack was all steamy with him cooking on a greasy black griddle. Sonny was passed out on a cot with an army blanket pulled over him. Ross had opened another bottle of whisky. This one was Canadian Club.

Good old Canadian Club, I thought. We used to be acquainted. We used to be good friends. I poured myself some in a coffee cup. The wind and the wet had gone and chilled me right through. I remember thinking about a lot of things—Sammy eating those tomatoes of his with some kind of delicious old man's greed, Verbena and her jimson weed, her conjure stories, and T.J., the way his birds shot off the roof to then come funneling back down like water in a spout. I remember thinking about Carlos sending me out to scout those runaway kids at Port Authority to bring them back to the South Bronx, to that empty abandoned old church we were using for his movie.

It was a great breakfast Ross cooked there for us, one of the best I ever ate—scrambled eggs with hot sauce, and sausage, and salty ham and redeye gravy and cheese grits and cornbread, and of course that catfish from the lake that Monica gutted right there into a slop bucket.

It all made me want to throw up.

S O EARL'S FINALLY GONE AND PLAYED HIS HAND—
which I knew would have to happen sooner or later but it's always
a surprise when it does. This whole time, he's been moving in on me—
he's probably a pretty good hunter out there in the woods with his rifle.
Patient. But then when he gets a chance, he bags his game with a clean
shot. I guess that's how they told him to go after me—bag him with a
clean shot.

He showed up yesterday with his Bible, and my heart sank. You
think you've got a mystery on your hands, and it turns out to be just
another person out to save your soul.

"Tony," he asked me, "do you know the story of Cain and Abel?"
He hefted his Bible, I guess to show me it was inside there somewhere.

"I know lots of stories," I told him. "Some better than others."

"This is one of the famous ones," he said. "It's about these two
brothers. One's a farmer and the other one raises sheep and goats. So
they each have a different sacrifice to give up to God. Abel gives goats,
and Cain gives grain from the field. God likes the goat sacrifice better,
because meat's better than vegetables. It's more serious. Which makes
Cain jealous, because it's not his fault all he had was grain to give. But
God's not listening. He wants meat. So Cain kills his brother, Abel. And
God punishes Cain. You're never going to have a home anymore, he
tells him. No matter where you go, you're not going to have a home."

"I've heard that story," I told Earl. "It's a stupid story. It's got nothing
to do with me."

He looked disappointed, like he was sure I'd understand. "I want to
save your soul," he said. It was the same thing I used to hear years ago

in the bars in New York—only then it was "I want to fuck you." I've always liked people who are direct.

"You've got one, you know," he went on. "Your soul's beautiful. I can see it inside you, Tony. I can see it in your life. You see, there's no reason why you have to be going through all this. All you have to do is to ask God, and he'll set you free."

I could tell he really believed what he was telling me—the same way all those guys used to believe it when they said I was good-looking.

What could I do? "I hate to tell you this, Earl," I had to say, "because you're a nice guy, you've been pretty decent to me and everything, and I like you. But you got to understand one thing. This soul of mine— forget it, okay? Maybe it looks to you like it's there, but it's not. Maybe in some people, and that's their business. But not me, Earl. Not me. And you know what? I don't miss it. It's like somebody missing having a long furry tail that they never had in the first place. That's the amount I miss it."

I could tell Earl wasn't believing me. He thought all this was something sin was making me say.

"Aren't you sorry for anything?" he asked. He was holding that Bible of his like it was some kind of weapon, which I guess in some way it was.

"Sure," I told him. "I'm sorry about a lot of things. I'd be crazy if I wasn't. And I'm not crazy. So yeah. I'm sorry about all of it. But you know what? At the same time I'm not. I'm not sorry about any of it. It's what happened, because something had to happen, and so why not that? At least we were alive. That's what counts, isn't it? To be alive?"

We'd never talked like this, and I could tell Earl wasn't understanding a thing I was saying to him. That's one thing you can always count on Earl for. Still, I hoped it'd upset him a little.

"I just want to read you something out of here," he told me. He flipped through his Bible to where I could see he'd marked sentences with a yellow highlighter. It made me feel sorry for him: how he was trying to muddle his way through all this stuff he didn't understand.

"Then there were brought unto him little children," Earl read to me, *"that he should put his hands on them, and pray."* I'd never heard Earl read from a book before, and he kept stumbling over the words—but then, the Bible's not written in regular English anyway. While he read, he

followed the words along with his finger. *"And the disciples rebuked them,"* he read me. *"But Jesus said, Suffer little children and forbid them not, to come unto me; for of such is the kingdom of heaven."*

"That's just a lot of words," I said. "Come on and tell me what you're really trying to get at."

Earl closed his Bible and looked at me. He has these big sad eyes and bags under them like he doesn't get much sleep at night. He sat down on my bunk, which he'd never done before. I was sitting on the little stool at the foot of the bed, and it sort of surprised me when he sat down.

"My wife took my kids from me," he said. "She just took them away from me."

It wasn't what I'd guessed he was going to say next.

"I didn't know," I told him. "I'm really sorry about that." Which I meant.

Sometimes when you downshift on a car, you feel like you're inside this river that's widening out—that's what it was like. Downshifting.

"She said I wasn't fit, Tony. You've been around. Do you think I'm fit?"

"Sure I think you're fit," I told him.

"They're in Ohio now," he said. "Last time I saw my kids was Christmastime. She accused me of brainwashing them."

"Brainwashing?" I said. I could tell how all this was eating at him. For some reason, people've always wanted to sit me down and tell me their stories.

"You remind me of my boys," he said.

"No," I told him. I was shaking my head. "I'm sure I don't. You've got nice kids."

But he was off on his own track, and he was going to follow it through.

"Sometimes," he went on, "when I lie down at night, I find myself having these thoughts, Tony. Like a dream, but it's not a dream—my eyes are wide open and I'm still awake. But I see it so clear. There I am with my rifle, and I'm hunting. It's the rifle I had when I was a kid, I haven't shot that thing in fifteen years. But now I'm hunting, like I used to do, only it's not deer or nothing. I'm hunting my wife and my kids. And when I find them I'm gonna shoot them. I'm gonna watch them go down—not a sound, they just sink down to their knees and go pitching forward. I go over to where they are: turn them over, lay them out, side by side facing up. And their eyes are open—that's something I notice, how they're staring up at me with these totally black eyes like deer eyes."

I thought it was all pretty scary—stuff I didn't want to know. I wanted to ask him, did he ever jerk off, thinking about things like that? But I didn't ask. I told him, "Everybody has bad dreams. You should see some of my dreams."

At least I could give him the comfort of my perspective.

"See," Earl reminded me, "this isn't a dream. I told you, my eyes are open. I stand there looking down at them; then I take out my knife and slit open their bellies, like you'd gut a deer. But you know what? It's not blood and guts inside—it's money. It's dollar bills, and then I remember how I stored that money there, inside my kids, instead of putting it in the bank. I'd gone and forgot that."

He started laughing—this out-of-control laugh, which I knew meant he didn't find any of it very funny. And I had to laugh too—not a laugh like Earl's, but just laughing along with him as far as I could go, and then him laughing his way along to whatever craziness it was taking him to. But all of a sudden Earl wasn't laughing. He was looking at me with this pleading look, like in the next instant I was going to blow him away, and here he was begging some kind of mercy.

His Bible was one of those floppy soft-covered kinds, and he was rolling it up between his hands like he was about to swat something with it.

"Someday I'm going to wake up and think I was just dreaming again, and then I'm going to turn on the TV and find out I really went and did something. What makes me think things like that, Tony? Like sometimes I'm going crazy. It scares me to death."

He was looking at me like I was really somebody who could tell him about that.

"It's probably really hard," I told him, "not seeing your kids and everything." I didn't know what on earth to say. "You probably feel really rotten about your wife taking them off like that. I never knew about that."

"I go and read in my Bible," Earl said, "how the sins of the fathers get visited on the sons, even down through three generations—and I wonder, why does that have to be like that? What does all that mean?"

I really had to laugh that time. "You're asking totally the wrong person, Earl," I told him. "I don't know anything. If I knew anything, I wouldn't be here."

That didn't put him off any.

"Look, Tony," he told me. "Could we pray? Would you pray with me?"

"No way," I said. What I thought was—even though you've got this belly on you like no tomorrow and your dick's too scary to think about, I'd still probably rather go down on you than go praying with you. I'd gotten through this much of life without praying, and I wasn't about to start yet.

"If we just believe in the Lord, Tony, in Jesus Christ, and we pray, then there'll be a way to get through all this. You and me both, Tony. We need each other. You got to admit that. We need each other to pray together. To pray for each other together."

So this was where being a penitentiary guard got you. Asking to pray with prisoners.

I had this sudden picture: it was the last time in my life I ever prayed. Not that it was much of a prayer—just the last time I remember closing my eyes and saying the words, because I was still too young to really know any better, even though all the time I knew better. I must've been about eight and we were visiting my mom's mother across the border in Tennessee. We'd go down there on a Saturday night, stay over for Sunday School the next morning, then drive back after Sunday dinner. My mom was never a church person—as you can probably tell—but her mom was, though that didn't stop that old lady from being a pretty mean bitch most of the time. She used to shoot at stray cats when they came in her yard, and she fixed razor blades on the stems of her shrubs because one Halloween night somebody pulled up something she'd just planted, and if they ever did that again they were going to get what was coming to them. But she was a firm believer in church, which probably goes hand in hand with shooting stray cats, and so whenever we visited her, we'd do the right thing. Church, that is. I hated it. This creepy old man named Mr. Polk taught the Sunday School class, which they held in this Quonset hut that was an annex to the regular building. He always used to come into the Sunday School room with this wet spot on his trousers where he'd peed before class and didn't shake himself dry. He'd stand in front of this easel and draw us pictures with colored chalk while he talked: Bible scenes, I guess to keep us entertained. His favorite was Jonah and the whale. He'd draw this man you could see crouched down inside the whale's belly, like he was sleeping there. It always made me think of stomach cancer—I don't know why. Everybody thought Mr. Polk was the greatest because he drew those pictures and then colored them in, and the person who answered the most Bible questions right got to keep the picture of the day. I never paid much attention. I used to watch that wet spot on Mr. Polk's trousers, and I always knew Sunday School was almost over when that spot'd had time to completely dry up.

He always made us close our eyes and say the same prayer—though I've gone and totally forgotten what the words were.

But that was my experience praying, so I was pretty surprised when Earl was down on his knees before I knew it. "Hey," I said, "don't do that."

"I want to pray for you," he said. He was so insistent.

"It's not going to do any good," I told him. "Not for me or for you either."

I'd stood up, I guess in surprise at seeing him go down like that. I stood there looking down at him—it'd make a pretty odd sight, the two of us, if somebody came along right then. "Dear Jesus," he was saying, with his eyes shut tight and this look on his face like some-body was hurting him—that look Carlos used to like in porn magazines when some young guy's getting it from behind. Only this was Earl, and he was praying. "Save this young man," he said. "Let your might and forgiveness, oh Lord, release him from this hell of bondage."

"Oh please," I wanted to tell him. "If you really want to go releasing me, hand over the keys." Not that I was particularly itching to escape from a place I pretty much thought I deserved to be in.

So I didn't say anything, though I did have to wonder where he'd learned to pray like that. It didn't sound anything like the Earl I knew. I guess I've tried to respect other people's needs, whether it's butt-fucking or praying, and I could see this was something Earl needed to do. And to do in front of me. Probably he'd been looking for somebody like me for a long time, ever since he started thinking those thoughts of his and getting turned on by them. I sort of admired him that he'd finally got up the nerve to try and save me—provided that's really what he thought he was doing.

I wasn't about to go along with it, though. From start to finish, the whole scene was more about him than it was about me anyway. Plus—it was a little embarrassing. For some reason what I kept thinking about through the whole thing was this restaurant we used to go to after church with my mom's mom—I guess that makes her my grandmother, but I never thought about her that way. It had this huge catfish on the roof to advertise it, a really ugly thing with this pink underbelly and spots all over it like huge freckles, and that big gaping mouth and whiskers the size of straightened-out clothes hangers. It had this hungry look that could make you never want to eat again.

I'd think about Jonah, but what I thought it looked like now was Earl, and the hungry way those prayers were coming out of his mouth. How he was gasping to breathe out of his element.

"I'm not going to pray with you," I told him. "I've got more respect for what I did than that."

Earl was starting to realize this wasn't going to work so well with me. He opened his eyes that'd been shut tight, and that gasping look went off his face.

Suddenly he seemed really hurt, like he'd tried to pick me up and I'd snubbed him. I knew that look from the bars. It all comes down to the same thing, I remember thinking—the same thing dressed up in a million different disguises.

Earl picked himself off the floor. His face was all red, and he was panting a little. I was sorry for him that this whole thing had backfired like it did.

"Don't go worrying about me," I told him. "I'll be okay. Your kids'll be okay. Nothing's going to happen to them. You're not going to do anything to them."

He just stood and looked at me for a minute—in that instant I thought I could tell he hated me.

"Suit yourself," he said.

"I've always tried to suit myself," I told him. "It's the only thing I ever had going for me."

It must've broken whatever special thing Earl thought there was between us. He's been by a couple of times since that day, and he's not exactly unfriendly—but there's this distance. Like he's embarrassed at what happened. Or maybe it's that he's pissed he tried something and it didn't work out.

Sometimes I have to wonder what Earl's going to think when he reads all this stuff I've written down in here. Because, like it or not, he was the one who first put me up to it. He never asks me about it, but he knows these pages are piling up, and he must be curious to find out what they say.

I wonder, Was he really trying to save my soul like he said he was? Did he really think that was what he was doing?

I WISH I COULD SAY I'D FELT SOME TWINGE THE morning of that particular day, but I didn't. I'd gotten so I didn't even notice what was on the marquee of that movie theater I drove past all the time. I know some part of me always looked up there just to make sure, but I couldn't actually have told you the names of any of the movies. It was just this force of habit.

My first thought was, There must be some kind of fire. Starting about a block from the theater, the sidewalk was suddenly full of people milling about, and there were blue police barricades set up to keep them from spilling into the street even though a fair number were in the street already. About ten police cars had pulled up with their lights flashing, and I was looking for smoke to be billowing from the building. Instead, what I saw was the marquee, and this thrill of sheer fright plunged right down to the bottom of my stomach. There it was—not even Carlos's name but just the name of the movie, *Boys of Life,* which I knew at once had to be Carlos's movie because that was a name he'd thought about calling *The Gospel According to Sodom* but then didn't.

I was trying to take in about ten different things all at once. It wasn't any fire that crowd of people was in the street because of—if there was any fire, it was the movie that was the fire. That's why they were all there. I had this crazy thought—Carlos is here, he's making some kind of big entrance, though I knew Carlos wasn't the kind of person to make a big entrance anywhere. Then I thought—he finally went and released *The Gospel* starring me and Scott Farris, and everybody in Memphis knows it's me and I'm dead.

But that passed in a flash, because I was starting to register all the signs people were carrying, these big handpainted signs almost the size of small billboards that it took five or six people to hoist aloft. WANTED FOR MURDER AND TORTURE OF CHILDREN read this one sign. MEMPHIANS FOR MORALITY said another, and another said ART IS NOT A LICENSE TO KILL.

There was every kind of person out there in that crowd—blacks and whites, fat women in pants suits, serious-looking men in business suits, a couple of winos who were along for the ride. There was even a bunch of children wearing cardboard haloes and linked together with this paper chain, and adults stood over them with a banner that read, CHILD ABUSE IS SOUL MURDER.

Carlos had made a lot of movies, and I figured he'd kept on making them after I left—but they never, at least during the time I was with him, raised this kind of stir. It was something he'd love, I thought, and I loved it too—all those moral Memphians taking to the streets. I felt proud of Carlos, whatever it was he'd gone and done to shake people up like that. Whatever balance it was he'd finally found some way to tip.

I parked the pickup in an empty parking lot across the street where a building really had burned a few weeks before, RE-OPENING SOON: WE'RE GETTING OFF OUR ASHES said a sign, which seemed a little optimistic since the building was nothing but a burned-out shell these days.

Some of the people had started holding hands and singing "Onward, Christian Soldiers." They were swaying back and forth in a kind of chain that started to stretch across the street, until some policemen stepped in to force them back up onto the sidewalk. This fat woman with a big wooden cross tied by a leather thong around her neck kept calling out, with her hands cupped around her mouth, "Carlos Reichart, you repent! Carlos Reichart, you repent!" Like he could hear her or something.

It felt totally strange to hear Carlos's name come out of that lady's mouth. It was like something that might happen in the worst dream you could ever imagine having. Or maybe in one of Carlos's movies.

"Carlos," I said aloud in this normal tone of voice. I hadn't said that name in years, and I kind of liked saying it aloud like that on a sidewalk in midtown Memphis. So I kept on. I wandered around in the crowd a little, just saying "Carlos, Carlos, Carlos," like I was some little kid who was lost and looking for him.

"Who's Carlos Reichart?" I asked this black man in a three-piece suit. He had this huge gold watch chain hanging across his belly. I think maybe he was a preacher of some kind.

"Don't you read the newspapers? Don't you watch TV?" he asked.

Neither of those were things I ever did.

The blue police barricades were a funnel leading to the open front door of the theater, and people lined them on both sides. A few folks were going into the theater, and whenever they did, they hurried in with a police escort while people in the crowd yelled "Shame!" at them. One little man in a bow tie kept trying to give away Bibles to the people going in, and even though the police kept leading him away by the arm, in a minute he was right back where he had been and trying to hand them out like his life depended on it.

None of the people hurrying into the place took the Bibles, or even dared to look at the crowd that was shouting at them.

I had to see that movie. I knew that. It was because I was still crazy about Carlos and I thought about him all the time even though I was always telling myself I never thought about him and that was all in the past. It was like I'd drawn a tarpaulin over that heap of stuff that was my whole life back then, and I thought I'd made it go away—but if I lifted up even a little corner of that tarp, there it all still was, bright and crazy and alive as ever. I'm crazy about Carlos, I thought. I'm still crazy about him. Like it was some great discovery I'd just made when really I knew it all along and it was what had been killing me for years.

"Carlos," I said one last time, and then I ran down that gauntlet of shouting people past the little man with the Bibles and the police barricades, right toward the theater entrance.

"Whoa," this cop said in a really loud voice. He grabbed me by my T-shirt and held me there. "Where you think you're going?" he asked me.

"The movie," I told him. *"Boys of Life.* A Carlos Reichart movie." It felt good to say that.

He just held me there. I could see the pores on his nose, how there were blackheads there he should pop.

"You sure?" His eyes were glaring at me.

"I'm sure," I told him.

He held me a second more, and then he winked at me. It took me totally by surprise. "Good," he said in this voice meant just for me to hear, and he sort of shoved me along toward the ticket booth.

Inside, the theater was about half full. Everybody there seemed really nervous—no wonder, considering what they'd gone through to get inside, and they were probably all trying to figure how they were going to get out now that they were in.

I was thrilled and scared and totally singing inside, my heart was beating like no tomorrow, and under my arms cold sweat kept dripping down. Where I was sitting, there weren't any people around me, and even though I was dying to hear what they knew about all this, I couldn't. All I could hear was this one pretentious man telling the woman next to him, about five different times, not to worry, it was all staged, he was sure of that. At first I thought he was talking about the crowd, but then I realized it was the movie he was talking about.

You idiot, I remember thinking to myself, there's no such thing as staging in Carlos's movies. What happens there, one way or another, it's all definitely reality.

I also remember, as the lights went down, linking the fingers of my hands together, and unlinking them, and linking them again. Then the theater was totally dark and the movie started.

I felt like I was waiting to meet Carlos in person, even though I knew I wouldn't even glimpse him. He'd never be in his own movie—the whole time I was with him, he never let anybody take a picture of him if he could help it.

At first you couldn't tell what you were seeing—it was this close up that was so close up it wasn't anything anymore. Then the camera pulled back a little and you saw it was somebody's arm, and a knife, and the knife blade was moving along the arm so this seam of blood just opened up. It was like somebody peeling back a pair of lips, and out came this red blood which you knew was real. There wasn't any way to fake it. It really was somebody slicing his arm open with a knife. The camera pulled back even more and you could see that person sitting on a rock in the middle of the desert.

Then I saw it was Carlos.

The camera circled around him very slowly, all the way around him. He was totally alone on that rock in the desert, barefoot, without a shirt, wearing just this beat-up pair of jeans. And that black headband he used to wear sometimes—to put pressure, he always said, on his brain. He was fixing a tourniquet, holding one end of the cloth in his teeth and pulling it tight, I guess so he could control the flow of blood from his arm. In front of him was a low table—sort of an easel—and the camera focused in on that. Carlos took a little paintbrush, the kind you use to paint model airplanes, and dipped it into the blood that was welling up along his arm. Then he started to write with the paintbrush on a big piece of paper that was spread out on the easel.

I watched him write out the whole thing in his own blood on that big sheet of paper there in front of him. The whole time he was still bleeding, probably getting faint. It was a race against time to see if he could finish writing that thing down before he passed out, and in fact the last part of the writing was very shaky and then he did pass out. He slumped down onto the easel, and the blood from his arm smeared across the paper, and then the easel fell over because of his weight on it and he crumpled to the ground.

The camera didn't really seem to care about all this. It moved in and studied Carlos's face for a while. His eyes were shut and his mouth hung open and a fly was crawling on his lower lip. It was like that camera wondered in this cool detached way who this man was, but it didn't really care all that much whether he was alive anymore, or dead.

Then the picture faded to black and the rest of the movie started.

All of which was just agony to watch—it must've taken Carlos fifteen minutes to write what he wrote in his blood, very slowly, very carefully. Plus what he was writing was so horrible that you didn't know whether or not to believe it, and at the same time you knew it must be true, because why would somebody write something like that in his own blood if it wasn't true? But then when the rest of the movie started, there wasn't time to think about that anymore. You just had to put it on hold to deal with later.

You see shots of the desert, sleepy little Mexican villages. It's all peaceful-feeling. A tree, a donkey standing under it. This bright blue lizard sunning itself on a rock. It goes on and on. An old woman walking along bent over under a huge sack of something on her back. Some vultures are making lazy circles in the sky over something out there that must be dead or dying. I remember all these things completely vividly.

The regional governor—or maybe he's some drug lord, or a Nazi war criminal who's in hiding, or even a rabbi gone beserk—whoever he is, he's collecting the most beautiful boys to take into his hacienda. He's convinced the world's coming to an end, but his hacienda's going to be saved. An angel's come to tell him this. They walk in the garden in a rainstorm, and they talk. These bells in the distance are ringing—all the bells in the village, plus goat bells and cow bells and the wind chimes that are hanging from the arches of the hacienda—so you can barely hear what the governor and the angel say to each other. Their voices come and go over the bells. The angel's barefoot, dressed all in white and wearing a floppy straw hat like you'd think some young Mexican farmer would wear. He promises to help the governor, but he says God's going to want some of the boys for his own. "You never know who God's going to want," he says. "That's why the bells ring. God gets greedy whenever it rains on the earth."

The governor is played by Carlos. It's not Carlos's voice—he dubbed it like he dubbed all his voices. But it's Carlos's body. I used to know that body better even than my own. I guess, after that first scene, I got over the shock of seeing him act in his own movie—not to say I wasn't shocked from beginning to end by what I saw. But I accepted it. I told myself if he was finally in one of his own movies, then he was probably doing what he needed to do and he didn't have any choice.

When the rainstorm's over but the bells are still ringing, Carlos takes the angel by the hand and they make love in this beautiful bedroom in a big canopy bed with flowers and hundreds of candles burning and plaster statues that start bleeding for no reason—you just notice there's blood running down a face or a hand where you're sure there wasn't any before.

It made me queasy to see Carlos and the angel undress each other like they did—these long quiet motions and the bells still ringing. I remember thinking what a great body that angel had, all smooth and hard like I liked bodies and the candles coloring his skin honey-colored. And it was nice, I also remember thinking, to see Verbena was still on board after all those years. At least I thought that bedroom was probably her doing.

I have to say—I was so nervous through all this, if somebody'd coughed or touched me on the shoulder in that theater I'd have died of a heart attack. Which might've been the best thing. It made me miserable to see all this, though I was getting a hard-on in spite of myself. Carlos looked older, his bald spot was bigger, and he had this flower tattoo around one of his nipples. It set him apart in some way from the Carlos I used to know, and I wondered if Rafe had anything to do with him getting that tattoo. Then there was his dick, sliding in and out of the angel's butt—I squirmed to remember what it felt like having Carlos's dick rooting around inside me like that, all the things it made me feel. But I couldn't remember—I'd had too many dicks inside me since then, and then none for three years now, and all I was seeing on the movie screen in front of me was just a picture—it wasn't real like that dick that had sent me places I'd never known you could go out there under the power lines that first time years ago when I was just the crazy needy kid I used to be.

I can't say when it first started to happen—I was just starting to calm down a little and get used to the things I was seeing up there. The candle light was wavery and dim, and mostly it was just arms and legs and backs and a dick that could've been anybody's dick sliding in and out of what could've been anybody's asshole. Anyway, I've never been all that good with faces in the first place—I've always said, if I see somebody I know from one city walking down the street in some other city, I wouldn't even recognize them. Not even my own brother.

It'd been eight years since I saw Ted. He was only fourteen when I left Owen, and lots of things can happen in eight years. I knew it was impossible, even when it suddenly clicked. It had to be impossible. I kept looking and looking at that angel, and most of the time he looked like some complete stranger I'd never seen before in my life, but other times—the way he smiled like the camera was always catching him off-guard—there was this terrible feeling I got.

This all makes me really uncomfortable to talk about. What I have to say is, by the time Carlos and the angel finished making love in that room with all the candles and bleeding statues, I knew it was Ted, even though I still couldn't see how it could possibly be Ted. There were even long stretches through the rest of the movie when I was able to convince myself I had it all wrong, and it was the pressure of watching Carlos in a movie that was making me see things. It just seemed impossible even somebody like Carlos could've come up with Ted, especially when he'd never even met him. And I also couldn't imagine Ted ever being in any movie like *Boys of Life*. But then I remembered the sorts of things Carlos had been able to talk me into, and I'd start feeling cold all over again. Carlos would still be Carlos, I knew, even after all these years. If he wanted you to do something in one of his movies, he'd find a way of getting you to do it. He'd even make you think it was what you'd been wanting to do all along.

I've done some pretty wild things in my time, which you already know about, but nothing I ever did got me ready to see the kinds of things I saw in that next hour and a half, once Carlos and Ted got those boys rounded up and started in on them. I remember being aware other people were getting up and leaving the theater, so that when the lights finally went up I was about the only one still in there.

I'd been thinking I couldn't stand this, I couldn't stand to see another kid get fucked and then his tongue cut out or his dick lopped off, or shit on or hanged. I didn't care whether all this was about how consumer society does to our minds what the Nazis did to people's bodies, or any of the other stuff the movie kept saying it was about in these voiceovers that came and went during the torture scenes. I didn't care whether the torture scenes were staged or real or what. And just when I couldn't stand it anymore, that was the end. We were back outside the hacienda, everything looked so peaceful you'd never in a million years guess the kind of stuff that was going on behind those white plaster walls. Under this desert-looking tree these two little girls were playing a flute and a violin, the way little kids play who just barely know how, and these two little boys are dancing with each other, like they're this old-fashioned couple dancing some waltz.

"What're you doing tomorrow?" the girl who's playing the violin asks one of the little boys.

He starts to answer her, but then the screen goes black and it just says in white letters against the black, IN MEMORIAM TED BLAIR 1966-1986.

"No!" I remember yelling at that screen, this deep yell that started way down inside me and just went and went till there was no yell left. And before I knew it the words were off the screen, like maybe they'd never been there in the first place. I'd only imagined them—and that was the end.

In one of the rows behind me, this woman was crying. The man she was with, the man with the pretentious voice, kept hugging her and saying, "It's only a movie. It's not real, it's only a movie."

One of the ushers peeked in the door—I guess he heard my yell.

"Everything okay in here?" he asked me. He was wearing this stupid uniform—blue pants, red jacket—and carrying a flashlight.

"What did that say on the screen?" I asked him.

"What did what say?"

"There at the end," I told him.

But he just shrugged. He hadn't seen it. "Personally," he said, "I don't think people have any business watching stuff like that, is what I think."

"Well fuck you," I told him. It was some last bit of loyalty to Carlos.

"You can't talk like that in here," he warned me.

Out in the lobby, a few brave people had made it in for the next show. I could hear the crowd outside shouting "Shame! Shame!" but it was dark by now, so I couldn't see them. It felt like there were thousands of them, though.

I didn't know what to do. I could see the usher keeping his eye on me. For a minute I thought, Maybe this is what having a heart attack feels like—I was all out of breath, my chest was throbbing like somebody was sitting on it. I climbed the stairs up to the projection booth.

A girl who looked like a college student was in there. She was rewinding the movie.

I think I startled her—the way I tore into the booth without knocking or anything.

"This is private up here," she said. "Employees only."

"Look," I told her, "Can you play back just the last minute of that movie? Just the very end. It's very very important to me."

Even though they had the air conditioning on full blast in that theater, I was sweating like crazy—which in fact is what she probably thought I was.

"It's already rewinding," she said. She was very edgy with me, I think she was trying to figure out how to make a dash for it if I tried anything. "Nothing I can do," she told me. "You can stay and watch it again. You don't have to buy a new ticket."

I could hear the usher coming up the stairs behind me. "Okay," I told her. "Sorry to bother you."

The usher gave me this hard look. He was holding his flashlight like a club. I think I was making everybody extremely nervous—which I didn't want to do, they were already nervous enough with that crowd outside. It was just that I was out of my head there for a few minutes.

"I'll watch the movie again," I told the usher. "She just told me I could." He looked at me as I passed by him and hefted his flashlight like it was going to keep me in line.

The second time, it was worse. Everything started to come together, the ending with the beginning and all the things I'd figured out in between. I was crying through most of it, which I guess was a good thing, because the more I cried the calmer I got. I knew what the worst was going to be—there couldn't be any surprises this time around. It was like I was already starting to grieve.

Ted, I was crying, Ted, Ted. Because there was my brother, there he was, and he was dead.

I should put in here, for the record, what Carlos wrote at the beginning, that poem he made out of his own blood and then passed out from.

> *Maybe it was silly how I hugged that tree*
> *the winter I drove out of Hermillosa*
> *so drunk I could barely see*
> *& laughed where I nailed him down*
> *nailed his dick down because they called*
> *yesterday from the hospital where he died*
> *a week after I nailed him & I hugged that tree*
> *& cried I held on tight to my boy*
> *wanted to make him live wanted to love him again*
> *see his face like all God's face light up*
> *Drunk crying 50 years old I went down in the dirt*
> *where his blood spilled I got the dirt in my eyes*
> *in my nose my mouth into cockhole*
> *& asshole I burrowed into my boy's blood crying*
> *where I nailed his dick to a tree.*

I think I mentioned somewhere earlier how Carlos wrote three books of poems before he ever made his first movie, and nobody ever paid any attention to those poems. I guess you could say it took Ted Blair to finally make Carlos into a poet anybody'd ever heard of.

ANYBODY WHO SAW ME COME REELING OUT OF that theater probably thought I was completely drunk. And I was, in a way. I managed to climb into my truck—but then I just sat there for the longest time. I couldn't start the engine, and even if I had I wouldn't've known where to go or what to do. I kept thinking, This is it, this is it. But I didn't know what It was. I only knew something had happened that finished everything else. Everything that'd started a long time ago and been working itself out till now.

The crowd outside had all disappeared by then—I guess they figured there's only so much you can do, and anyway most of them had to go to work the next day. Pretty soon even the people who'd been in the theater had driven away too, and I was alone there in the parking lot. I don't know how long I'd been sitting there before a police car pulled up next to me and stopped. I guess they were patrolling pretty thoroughly that night. Probably he thought I had a can of gasoline and was going to torch the place, but that was the furthest thing from my mind. Still, I had the strangest feeling—like finally, after all these years, I'd been caught. And I wasn't going to put up a fight—I just sat there like some fugitive who's been run to ground.

The policeman looked a little jumpy, but he rested his elbows on the window of my truck to try and hide it. He was smiling this goofy smile, like it embarrassed him to be doing this. "Anything wrong?" he asked.

Like I could tell him what was wrong.

"I'm fine," I told him.

"That's good," said the policeman. He still seemed embarrassed. "This lot is, uh, closed right now. We had a little ruckus here this afternoon, so if you wouldn't mind parking somewhere else that'd be just fine."

"I know," I told him. "I was just going."

He sort of nodded, like he didn't really believe me and was wondering what he was supposed to do next. Off in the distance there was a siren, but we both realized after a second that it didn't have anything to do with us. I started the truck's engine up. He nodded again, and I eased the truck away from him. It must've been midnight. The streets were empty, and I felt like I was about to explode.

I kept trying to remember Ted, but I couldn't. Ted the way he'd been when he was my brother. But all I could see was that movie, and who he was in that movie—the bad angel dressed all in white who tortures and kills pretty-looking Mexican boys. No Ted I could recognize, but it was Ted, it was Ted playing his part in the movie, it was Ted who was somehow dead now, I didn't know how. It was the Ted I'd recognized even before the movie came to an end. I tried to think about things we did together when we were kids, and what he looked like then—but everything was a blank. That movie took it right away from me.

The only thing I knew was, when I was a kid and Ted was a kid I was crazy about him. I was in love with him. I never knew it, but I was in love with him and of course you can't be in love with your brother, not the way I was in love with him when we used to swim around together in the pool outside the Paradise Grotto.

Everything else, Carlos and New York and the bars and Monica—it all just followed from me loving Ted when we were kids. That started it, because if I hadn't loved Ted I wouldn't've felt so shut out and sad hearing him dry-humping the mattress all alone in that trailer of ours, and with Carlos I wasn't alone that way. It was the natural thing for me to take off with Carlos the way I did and be in his movies or any of the other scenes he ever sprung on me down through all those years, and however Carlos came to find Ted wouldn't've happened if I hadn't known Carlos in the first place, and Ted wouldn't be dead now.

I didn't have any idea where I was driving—I was just driving around aimlessly, though where I ended up was at Tom Lee Park on the river bluff.

It was after midnight, and nobody was around except this one car with its lights off—and you could tell by the way it was rocking what was going on in there. In front of me I could see the monument to Tom Lee: A WORTHY NEGRO. I don't know why I did what I did next, but suddenly I was out of the truck and scrambling down the steep bank to the river. Before I knew it I was in the water, up to my knees, to my waist—and then the river current took hold of me like a fist taking me up. It knocked me under and when I came bobbing up I could see the lights in the skyscrapers up on the bluff, and I knew the river was shooting me downstream.

I hadn't swum in years. I guess maybe I was hoping if I drowned then that would solve everything and I wouldn't have to do anything. Actually, I don't think I was thinking much of anything. I was just doing something because I didn't have any idea what else to do.

I kept managing to come up for air, though I kept getting these mouthfuls of ugly-tasting water too—and I tried to swim toward shore. But the river kept pushing me on—I could see the bank sliding past, incredibly fast—and the river went on tugging me out into the current no matter how hard I kept trying to swim against it. I thought about just letting go and having it carry me. I used to watch all that river running past and think how it went to New Orleans and then out into the ocean, and it used to comfort me somehow to think that—but I never thought I'd be in the middle of it.

I guess I wanted something I thought the river was going to give me, but then when it didn't I started fighting it. I must've gotten carried about a mile downstream, because I remember going past the piers of the Interstate 55 bridge, and when the current pressed around those piers it let me get some momentum and I drove on in toward shore.

I was trembling all over, coughing up big spews of muddy water, and my wallet was gone. But I'd been down in the river and come back again. I was laughing too, I think—and maybe crying some. And just gasping and gasping at all those lungs full of night air. I lay on my back there on the muddy sand. It was a hazy night, and the sky was all orange with the glow of the city. I felt like if I was supposed to've died right then, I would have. But I wasn't supposed to, and so I was still alive. Ted was dead, but here I was still alive.

And somewhere Carlos was alive too.

I knew I had to find him. Whether he knew it or not, he wanted me to find him—and I was going to do it.

I guess I felt all sorts of things, but mostly just amazed, if that makes any sense. Amazed by everything. Stunned by it, the way you might be stunned to look up at some night sky way out in the country and see all those clear stars pressing down on you, and their light that's coming from so far away that some of those stars are completely burned out before their light ever gets to you. Which is all something I know because Carlos once told it to me, I think on the roof of that apartment in New York—how the stars are like ghosts, and people can be the same way, their light can come to you from a long way off and reach you only after they've already gone and burned themselves out completely.

I had this terrific headache, and a long scratch down my left arm that was bleeding. I took off my T-shirt and tried to wrap it into some kind of tourniquet—but the cloth was so wet it didn't really work, so I decided it wasn't bleeding that bad and I'd let it alone. I guess making that tourniquet was just something to do while my head finished clearing up.

I didn't quite know where I was—south of the bridge, but that was all I was sure about. I picked myself up and the first thing I saw in the dark in front of me was some woods, and when I walked toward them I saw that in the middle of trees was this boat, an old steamboat. It didn't make any sense. The boards had all split apart, trees were growing up through it and it was covered in vines. For a minute it seemed completely impossible. I thought maybe I really was dead after all, with dead being just some place where nothing made sense, where there were boats sitting high and dry in the woods with trees growing up through their hulls.

But I wasn't dead. I went on past that boat which turned out to be real—at least I think it was real. Somebody should maybe go below the bluffs south of the Interstate 55 bridge in Memphis and see if there really is an old steamboat in the woods. The bluff turned out not to be as steep as I thought, and I was able to scramble on up to the top. Then the river was down below me again—this dark flat plain I couldn't believe I'd almost lost my life in just a few minutes ago.

It took me about an hour to walk back to where the truck was. I didn't pass a soul—there was that eerie late-at-night feeling when you think it's completely possible everybody else has died, and you're the only one left. The only sign of life was that car in the parking lot of Tom Lee Park, just where it was when I left and still rocking back and forth on its springs. I wondered if the whole time I was drowning those two people had kept on fucking, not knowing for an instant anything else was happening in the world. I liked those two in that car—I didn't know anything about them, I never would, but somehow I thought maybe it was their living it up like they did that'd saved me in the river, and they'd never know it.

I was pretty much dried off, though there was this film of mud on me, and when I ran my hand through my hair it was all stiff and tangled. When I got in the truck and looked in the mirror, I was shocked—it was still me, still my face—but it also didn't have a thing to do with me. I don't know whether being in the river added something, or took something away, but I think I'd have to say that ever since that moment there's been something different about me that's never quite gotten back straight.

Which if you think I'm trying to get out of something here, I'm not.

What happened next was, I passed out. Maybe it was the shock of everything finally settling in, or maybe just sheer exhaustion from my fight with the river—but the next thing I knew, it was dawn and I was slumped over the steering wheel like some dead man. For a minute, in that hazy gray light, I was disoriented—but then something in me snapped to. I hooked into this pure sharp electricity that everybody must have stored away somewhere deep in them, but they never stumble on it.

What it did most of all was focus. I know some people will say, Tony, everything's a muddle from here on out—but I didn't feel that way, and I still don't. For me it was like looking through the sharpest lens there is.

The first thing I had to do, before anything else, was find a library. That's what I mean by focus: the night before, I'd just been reeling, but now it was completely clear to me that I had to find out exactly what happened to Ted, and some newspaper somewhere was going to be able to tell me.

I'll spare you the details—only to say that it was the first time I'd been in a library since the one in New York where I used to study those pictures from the ghetto, so I didn't have any idea how to go about finding what I wanted. But I ended up getting all the help I needed from this nice lady named Miss Kieling who had a big birthmark that covered half of one side of her face, which I guess is maybe why she became a librarian.

She must've figured I was some homeless lunatic from the streets, considering the state of my clothes and mud in my hair and all, but it didn't seem to faze her any. She'd heard about *Boys of Life;* she said there'd been a lot in the papers about it a few months back. Once she'd set me up in front of the microfilm machine, with the *New York Times* for the year 1987, it wasn't all that hard to find what I needed. I scrolled down through those pages like they were some kind of time-lapse movie about the days passing and passing, and then before I knew it I'd stumbled on the first of a whole series of articles, starting at the beginning of April 1987 and going to the end of May, about Carlos's trial, which was taking place in Hermillosa, Mexico.

Here, for the record, is one of those articles—thanks again to Earl, who found it in the microfilm section in some library in Albany, and who, I keep telling him, should get some job as a detective. But he won't do it—he likes being a prison guard too much. I guess he likes being around people like me.

BIZARRE CASE IN MEXICO

HERMILLOSA, Mexico, May 18—A Mexican court today acquitted the American film director Carlos Reichart of charges of kidnapping, assault and reckless endangerment in the 1986 death of Theodore Blair, a 23-year-old actor who had worked with Reichart on several films.

The trial attracted considerable attention both in Mexico and in the United States, due in part to the lingering mystery surrounding the actual events of Blair's death.

Blair was admitted to the Hospital Santa Maria de Los Angeles on July 1, suffering from numerous lacerations and contusions which appeared, according to doctors, to have stemmed from some type of ritual mutilation. Also present were massive internal injuries.

Contradictions

After Blair's death, Reichart surrendered himself to Sonoran authorities, claiming that he had held Blair captive for a week in which he repeatedly sodomized and tortured Blair. According to Reichart, Blair managed to escape his captivity when a door was left unlocked.

Complicating the case, however, was a signed statement by Blair, deposited with Dr. Hermann Perez of the Hospital Santa Maria de Los Angeles shortly before Blair's death, to the effect that Carlos Reichart was in no way responsible for the events which led to Blair's death.

Further confusing the

situation is the fact that sources at Santa Maria de Los Angeles indicate Reichart accompanied Blair to the hospital on July I, and was with him frequently during the next several days. Blair died on July 9.

At first reluctant to pursue the case, Mexican authorities reportedly decided to prosecute when Mr. Reichart's past became more fully known to them. In I984 Reichart was charged by the state of New York with soliciting minors for the purposes of filming obscene acts. The charges were later dropped. In 1985 allegations surfaced that in 1980 Reichart had held two boys virtual prisoner for several days, and had forced them at gunpoint to perform sexual acts. These acts were allegedly filmed, though a search of Reichart's Manhattan apartment failed to uncover any evidence of this. No charges were ever filed in connection with the allegations.

Death by Method Acting?

Reichart's insistence on his own guilt was contradicted by testimony from various of his associates, several of whom remarked on Mr. Blair's self-destructive propensities.

The Mexican court ruled today that the evidence in Mr. Blair's case indicated death by misadventure rather than any demonstrable criminal misconduct on Reichart's part. The judge admonished Reichart, however, that "grave misjudgments of conduct" had been made by Reichart and his associates, and that many of his actions, while not necessarily illegal per se, nonetheless carry with them "a volatile moral taint that provokes disgust and outrage."

At 23, Theodore Blair had attracted considerable critical attention in three films by Carlos Reichart, *Zouf!*, *An American Purgative*, and *Theo-Porn-Kolossal*. His striking physical beauty combined with an air of romantic dissolution was compared to such figures as Nijinski, Sal Mineo and Antonin Artaud. Some critics considered him the most brilliant member of The Company, that extraordinary ensemble of actors Reichart assembled beginning in the late 1960s, which provided him with a seemingly endless pool of talent. The Company also included in its ranks such celebrated performers as Netta Abramowitz, the transvestite Verbena Gray, and the late Samuel Finckelsztajn.

Extreme physical hardships, orchestrated mental duress and other techniques imposed on his actors served to create what Reichart called "a theater of reality"— a heightened method of improvisational acting.

Controversial Career

Reichart, 49, self-proclaimed "anarchist, theologian and pornographer," is the director of a number of critically acclaimed films including *Mother Chicago*, *Ur*, *The Only Bitterness of Anna*, and *Creeping Bent*. These lively, hallucinatory films have often shocked even sophisticated audiences, especially Reichart's more recent work. His 1987 film, *Theo-Porn-Kolossal*, was named by the New York Film Critics Circle as "perhaps the most important independent film of the last decade." The film's explicit homoerotic and sadomasochistic content, however, caused protest at screenings in several American cities.

In 1984 Reichart was awarded a special medal for lifetime achievement at the Barcelona Film Festival in Spain.

It's funny how you can get used to something. Maybe it was because I was still totally exhausted and in some kind of shock from the night before, but reading those articles I felt calm, like I was reading something that took place a long time ago. You probably want me to say I was howling—but I wasn't. I guess somewhere in the night this door just shut on Ted, and I knew he was gone. I wasn't any more upset about him being dead than I'd be about Abraham Lincoln, or Tom Lee for that matter—anybody who'd been dead a hundred or a thousand years. It was just this fact, like a river's a fact, or a mountain.

When I got back to the house, it was about noon. Monica's car wasn't there—and it was only then, not seeing her car in the driveway where I expected it to be, that I realized I hadn't thought of her once since everything started to come down. On the kitchen table there was this note saying she was at her parents, please call. It said she was worried sick.

I know I should've called—because as it turns out, in the year since then I've only talked with her through her lawyer, and I understand why she feels that way. But that morning—what was I going to say? That the Tony she thought she knew was just this thing pasted over some other Tony, and now it's come unglued? That this other Tony had things he needed to do that didn't have anything to do with anything she could know about? Nothing I could say to her would even begin to make any sense.

So instead I took this long hot shower. It felt really good, and I just stood there in that water luxuriating for a while, getting the soreness out of my body from the night before. That same electric focus still had me in its grip. I put on some clean jeans, and a black T-shirt, and I reached way back in the back of the closet and pulled out those snakeskin boots Carlos got for me once, back in some other life.

ONE THING I KEPT THINKING ABOUT, ALL THE WAY to New York: one little detail that was in that newspaper article I read, the part where it talked about the famous members of The Company over the years, and the words "the transvestite Verbena Gray" lost in there amidst everything else.

You know how you focus on one single thing to keep from thinking about everything else? I kept turning that one thing over and over in my head, saying to myself, How could I not have known that? After all those years, all those afternoons I spent hanging out with her in her apartment, and eating her black bean soup and listening to her talk about conjure and star charts—how could I not have known? And if I missed something so obvious as that, then what else had I gone and missed along the way?

Maybe it wasn't true, what the article said. And if that wasn't true, then the rest of what it said about other things wasn't true either—but I knew that wasn't the case, and that all of it must be true. And I knew that there must've been lots that went on right under my nose, all along, and I never knew about it. Most of the things I thought I'd known about those people, I probably was wrong about in one way or another. I should just tell you that, for the record.

THE NEIGHBORHOOD WAS CHANGED. FIVE YEARS had passed since I was in the alphabets last, and it wasn't so rundown anymore. There were these fancy-looking restaurants stuck in between the slums, and lots of the people walking on the streets were the kinds of people who, you can just tell by looking, know they're hot stuff. The kinds of people I always hated about New York.

It was sad to see, especially because being away so long I could look at those people and see what they couldn't—that they were all going around putting on an attitude because they were scared to death of AIDS, and some of them even had it in their bodies though they didn't know that yet. But they were carrying it around, it was eating away at them and all the time these big posters on the walls of buildings telling them SILENCE = DEATH, and they couldn't hear it. I knew Carlos must've gone wild when he first saw those posters, since that was his whole life, SILENCE = DEATH.

Carlos's building was about the only one on his whole block that looked exactly the same—like everything that'd happened had happened around it but couldn't touch that building. The instant I caught sight of it I knew Carlos had to still be living there. It was like some force of his personality was protecting that building from change. I wondered if he was still showering out on the fire escape in the summers—only now it was probably in full view of the people eating at some new restaurant garden. But he still wouldn't care. I had this sudden picture in my head of Carlos standing on the roof of the building pissing down on them while they ate their fancy meals and yelling, "Eat the rich!"

When I got to the top of the stairs—still piss-smelling after all these years—I waited there at the door, which, if Carlos was still living there, I knew would be unlocked. There'd never been any doorhandle on it, and still wasn't. When I'd caught my breath, I just pushed and the door swung open like it always used to.

Carlos was standing at the front windows with his back to me.

"It's funny," he said, almost like he was talking to himself. He didn't turn around, but I knew he was talking to me. "I saw you coming. I saw you walking up the street. I don't know why I walked to the window just then, but I did. And I saw you coming."

He turned around.

"So how're you doing, Tony?"

It took me totally off-guard, his saying that. Maybe he did see me, and maybe he didn't. With Carlos you just never knew. But already, like always, he had all the advantage.

I noticed somebody'd taken the plastic down off those windows, and it was true—you could see out them like you never could all the time I lived there. They were open wide and a breeze was coming through.

I didn't say anything—I just stood there looking at him, which must've made him nervous. He grinned that grin of his that flashed and then went sad, and held his hands out, palms up—like he was showing me he didn't have anything to offer.

"I had to come," I finally said.

"I knew you would," he told me, "sooner or later. I'm glad you did."

What came next just burst out of him. "Tony, Tony, Tony," he said. "Oh, it's good to see you." I think it was the most sincere I ever heard Carlos in all my years. And I completely believed him—not that it was going to make any difference. But I still believe he was happier to see me right then than he'd ever been to see anybody in his whole life.

And I was happy to see him too. I had this insane idea that now that I was with him again, everything was going to be okay—somehow Ted would have to be still safe and alive and living back in Owen, Kentucky, where nobody had ever heard of Carlos Reichart. And as for me, Carlos and I were going to pick up right where we left off years ago like nothing had ever happened to make things go wrong.

"Can't we get out of this apartment?" he asked, like it was suddenly this idea he had. "The heat's killing me."

"Okay," I told him. "We should walk." I'd always hated that

apartment, and to be there again brought back all those winter days I used to sit there feeling trapped—by the city outside the windows, and by Sammy, and all that whisky I used to drink every day. The streets were where I'd always escaped to. Out there, I felt in some kind of control again—and I think Carlos knew that.

You know how murderers claim they don't remember anything? Well, I remember everything. I remember every word we said that night, the whole time we were walking up Broadway toward Central Park, and then when we were in the park, and everything else. You might expect me to say I wish I didn't remember it—but I don't say that. It's important to me to be able to remember it. Not because it makes me feel any better, or any worse either, but just because I think you have to look at life whatever it looks like, and you can't ever look away from it because when you start to do that, you start to die. Carlos knew that— it was the one terrible lesson he taught—and I learned it from him. Whatever you might think about that, it's something nobody that ever learned it can go and unlearn. And so I remember everything.

Neither of us even knew where to start. I'd rehearsed all this in my head about a thousand times on the drive up from Tennessee, but of course all that just disappeared once I was back in Carlos's presence. He was older, I could tell—he'd always seemed younger than somebody in his forties, more like somebody who was thirty, but now that he was fifty his age had sort of caught up with him all at once. Plus he'd lost weight, not that he ever had that much extra to lose. But it made his face look older.

It took a while for us to figure out what to say. He was the one that finally got it started, of course.

"Sammy passed away from us," he said. It was as good a starting place as any.

"I know," I said. "But tell me about it anyway."

"Well, it was a couple of years ago. He and Seth went up to Pough-keepsie to visit this friend. They took the train, and when they got to the station in Poughkeepsie Sammy said he was very tired and could he sit down and rest? So he sat down on a bench in the waiting room, and Seth went out to get a taxicab, and when he came back Sammy was lying down on the bench. Seth tried to wake him up but he couldn't."

I knew that train station—I'd been in and out of it a lot when we were filming *Creeping Bent* up on the Hudson, back in the fall of 1982. I could see the benches where Sammy would've laid down, and the high ceiling and grimy red brick—it was this big empty depressing room. So that was the last thing he saw, after everything else he'd seen in his life. I felt sorry for Sammy, but I also felt—I don't know why—glad for him that he was finally gone off this planet. Even though he loved being alive, I think he was probably glad too—not to have to go through being alive anymore.

We'd turned onto Broadway and were walking uptown. It was a warm night, lots of people were out, and it was great to be back in the city after all those years.

"He said he wrote you," Carlos said. At first I thought he was still talking about Sammy.

"After he got your card he wrote you a letter." Neither of us broke our stride even for an instant. We just kept on walking up Broadway. "But you never answered back," Carlos said.

"I never got any letters," I told him. I remembered how I waited for Ted to write me back after I sent him that postcard all those years ago, but he never did, and I finally gave up waiting and decided the card never got to him. I also remembered how happy I'd been to write Ted and tell him I was in this movie, and how I was going to be famous. I remember actually believing that—that I was going to be famous because I'd been in that movie.

Carlos shrugged. "Nobody ever delivers any mail to that apartment," he said. "It's why the rent's so cheap. Even the postman's on drugs. He probably threw those letters in the trash can. But it's better now. You noticed, didn't you—how it's all better now? Gentrified. I could make a fortune going co-op on that dump." He grinned his Carlos grin, and neither of us knew it but that was the last time he'd ever grin like that.

"I'd like to think I've been truthful," he said abruptly.

"You were always truthful with me," I told him, and I meant it.

"Even when I was being a monster," he said, "I was a truthful monster."

"Maybe," I told him. I thought about it. "Definitely," I had to say. "Even when you were being a monster—which a lot of the time you were. But you know that."

Three fire trucks went by us, one after the other, and then an ambulance. Somewhere people were burning up but here we were walking up Broadway toward Central Park and the night was muggy even though it was the end of September, tail-end of the hottest summer in years.

"Of course I know it," Carlos said. "I've always known it. Anybody who tries to be truthful in this country gets turned into some kind of monster. That's why I let you go. I didn't want to just shoo you away, because then you'd come back. I wanted you to go for good, which meant I wanted you to learn that you wanted to go away. Which I think you did learn, because you went."

"You're right," I said. "I fucking went and got the hell out. I got married, Carlos. I moved to Memphis and I work in a lumberyard and I love my wife."

"And look what happened," Carlos said in this quiet voice. We both sort of stopped there on the street and I just looked at him. We'd reached that point we both knew we had to reach.

I took this breath, and felt all queasy inside. "How did it happen?" I asked him.

"You've got a right to know," he told me. We were walking again— it was just this brief pause where we couldn't move.

"I have to know," I told him, "one way or another."

"It happened," he said, "like some bad movie. It happened like a story out of the Bible. There was a knock on the door—literally. One day there was a knock on the door and I opened it and there you were, only it wasn't you, it was Ted. He'd come looking for you. Or I should say, he'd come to New York and he had a postcard he said you'd sent him once, with the address of the apartment on it, and so he thought he should come look for you. And you have to admit, he came to the right place.

"He was a little down on his luck, you might say. I don't think Owen, Kentucky, quite prepared either of the Blair brothers for New York. He had that same dazed look you did when you first came here."

That dazed look was news to me.

"You have to understand, Tony—I was good." He said it almost like a cry. "I sent you away, I let you grow up. I did that, and it was hard, but we both got through it, we were both fine. And then you just left me. One day you just weren't there anymore."

I didn't remind him how he was the one who dumped me. He seemed to have forgotten all that.

"And then there's this knock on the door," he went on, "and here you are all over again. Standing there looking like an angel, and I thought, My God, if this is a test I'm lost. I can't do it. I fail."

"So let me guess," I accused him. "You offered to let him crash at your place for a while. Till he got on his feet. Then you put the moves on him, didn't you? You put the same moves on him you put on me."

"It takes two to fuck, Tony. Even you know that." It was a tone I remembered him taking with me now and again—sounding like he was disappointed in me for not figuring something out that was obvious to everybody else. I wasn't letting him get away with it this time.

"It takes two people for a rape too," I said. "Or a murder. You had all the cards. Ted was just a kid."

"He was nearly twenty years old when he came to New York, Tony. You forget, in this country, you reach the magic age of eighteen and suddenly you're an adult. Just one day, even one minute past the age of eighteen and you're not a child anymore. And if you want to talk cards—we've all got cards, Tony. We've got different cards, and we put our different cards on the table. Haven't you learned that yet? We put our different cards on the table and whatever comes up comes up."

"I'm not going to believe that," I told him. We were both raising our voices. It was the kind of conversation you walk past in New York and wonder what's going on. "I'm just not going to believe somebody like you who's smart and famous and fifty years old and some kid who— maybe he's twenty but he's still a kid—doesn't know anything about anything are going to have equal cards. You can try to get out of it all you want, but I'm not going to believe that one."

Carlos was raising his voice too. "You want to know who held all the cards?" he shouted at me. "The one thing you're scared to death to know? You did, that's who. Ted did. I never had anything. To be eighteen or sixteen or whatever, to be young and pretty and have a dick that works—in this country, that's to have everything. Faggot, breeder, I don't care what you are. That's the way the whole thing's set up, baby. It brings everything else to its knees."

I shook my head.

"You're still crazy," I said. "You're a crazy fucking lunatic, and you killed my brother."

The instant I said that, Carlos shoved me against the wall of the building we were walking past. He was wiry and strong, like he'd always been. "First of all," he told me, talking right into my face, almost hissing, "nobody killed your brother. There's nobody to blame it on. Get that through your head or you're not going to understand anything. It was just something that happened, and he knew it could happen but that didn't stop him from doing it. Your brother was a wise kid, Tony— he was the wisest, bravest person I ever knew. He took after you that way. He had this fantastic courage to live inside his body, and that's what he did, right to the very end. I spent my whole life looking, but I never met anybody who let himself go so far with everything. He was a genius, Tony."

All this talk sounded totally crazy to me. It sounded like Carlos talking about Carlos and not about Ted. I couldn't recognize my little brother in any of the stuff Carlos was saying.

He went on, though.

"You know what all my work was about—you were part of it, you even started to show me the way. But Ted—Ted just knew it from the inside out."

I had this sick feeling all at once—I remembered me and Scott in that warehouse in Brooklyn, and those kids in the abandoned church in the Bronx, and suddenly I thought I knew what Carlos was talking about. Carlos wouldn't have known Ted without me. He wouldn't've known what to do with him.

"Are you trying to say I'm the one who killed him?" It was something I had to say, it was where everything was leading.

Carlos went limp—he let go of me where he'd grabbed the neck of my T-shirt with both hands.

"I'm sorry about Ted," he said in this exhausted voice. "What happened to Ted was a terrible thing."

"What did happen, out there in the desert?"

We were walking again—I guess because there wasn't any use in just standing there, and Carlos seemed to have some deep energy that night that was moving him on, not letting him stop to reconsider. In Times Square some of the movies and plays were letting out. Milling all around us were tourists, Japanese businessmen, and the hustlers and prostitutes hanging out in doorways. XXX ALL MALE BURLESQUE said the marquees on the movie theaters we'd go to whenever we went on what Carlos used to joke were our dates.

"Tell me where you saw *Boys of Life*. Where'd it finally track you down?"

I had this insight. "You wanted it to track me down, didn't you?"

"That was the only reason," Carlos said. "Otherwise I would've burned it."

A pretty kid in bright red sweatpants and a black T-shirt was leaning against a mailbox, saying in this quiet voice to everybody who was walking by, "Hundred bucks for the night, hundred bucks for the night." He said it to us as we walked by, and I saw Carlos look him over out of the corner of his eye.

"Memphis," I said. "It tracked me down all the way to this little movie house in Memphis. And I had no idea—I just got to the end and everything blew up in my face."

"I'm sorry," Carlos touched my arm. "I had to let you know, whatever the price was."

I didn't tell him about the river. I didn't think that was something he needed to know.

"Everything I've ever done," he went on, "it's been for love. You understand that, don't you? Wanting, having, giving up—it's all been love."

"Don't get off the point. Talk about Ted," I commanded him.

But all he said was, "Remember when you fist-fucked Scott Farris? Do you remember that?"

I think I said earlier how Carlos never mentioned Scott after we finished that movie, like it was something we were both ashamed of.

"I remember it," I had to tell him.

"Then tell me I'm not making this up. Tell me there wasn't this instant when you had your fist up inside him and suddenly you realized there was nothing to stop you from going all the way on up, there was nothing to stop you from touching his heart, and pushing yourself all the way up inside him till you disappeared into him, and then you'd *be* him, his skin would be your skin and his insides would be your insides and you'd be looking out at the world through the eyes in his skull."

It touched some kind of memory in me that made me nervous.

"Carlos," I told him, "you're insane. That's just insane talk."

"Think about it, Tony. Think how far you could really go with that if you dared. No more fear, no more shame, no more being alone. None of that mattering anymore. Think about finding somebody who was willing to go all the way with that."

"You're talking about Ted," I said.

"I'm talking about Ted. I'm talking about being out in that desert with a group of people completely dedicated to the idea that they could push themselves beyond their physical and mental limitations. I'm talking about things we did in that desert nobody's even imagined being able to do. A kind of trust, Tony, that's like a white light.

"Imagine this." His voice was quivering, he was so caught up in what he was saying. "Imagine being buried alive. Building a coffin out of wood—you cut the trees down, you saw the boards, you nail the thing together. Then you take your shovel, and you dig a hole. Just for yourself. When you've got your hole dug, you gather your friends and you have a big feast. You eat all your favorite foods. You drink some wine. Then you lie down inside that coffin you made for yourself, and your friends nail the lid shut, and they lower you down into that hole and shovel dirt in on top of you. And you trust them to dig you back up in time. That kind of trust is absolute discipline. With that kind of trust, if you focused it enough, if you practiced—you could do anything. You could fly."

He looked at me with this look that killed me, this look of complete happiness. He said, "And we did, Tony. We flew. Out there in the desert, at night—we actually flew through the air."

I thought about what Verbena had said once about Carlos—so much belief, she'd said—and it was true. He could believe anything, almost enough to make those things he believed come true. It was frightening, it was wonderful—it was what completely took me about him the first time I met him, and I have to admit it almost took me now. I remembered that first day in the laundromat—how he stared at me, like he knew if he wanted me bad enough, and just focused on that want, then he'd get me. And he did. And that was the way he'd been living his life ever since.

"That's not the Ted who was my little brother," I told Carlos flat out.

Carlos sounded tired. "I knew Ted a lot better than you ever did," he told me. "Maybe that hurts, but it's true."

And it did hurt—because I knew when he said it how it was completely true. He'd taken Ted away from me. I'd shown him how he could do that, and he went and he did it.

"We went and we went," Carlos was saying. "Every day it was a little farther. I would've stopped—but Ted wanted to keep going. He had what you could call this cosmic sense of adventure. And so we just went. I guess we went so far we couldn't find our way back. He wanted to die, Tony. He was ready to find out what it was like. But he was happy— your brother was very happy. There was this special light in him that went on shining to the very end, even there in that little hospital."

We'd reached the edge of Central Park. We plunged on ahead, and suddenly, that wonderful thing about Central Park—all the city just fell away. We were wandering in these big dark woods in the middle of the city, but the city was miles from us, another planet. Around us, in the bushes, I knew men were cruising for each other, hungry for something even AIDS wasn't scaring them away from.

A lot of things still didn't make sense.

"But why did you tell them you killed him down in Mexico, if now you're saying you didn't do it?"

It wasn't that I thought he was lying to me—I just plain didn't understand.

"I can't help you," he told me. "Some things you can't explain. It was just what I had to do," he said. "I lost somebody I loved a lot."

We'd come to this open space, and now I knew exactly where we were. Carlos loved to come here—it was where we used to play soccer.

"Tony, Tony," he said. He stopped walking and looked at me. "I lost you," he said. "You were the one I lost."

Suddenly he was holding me—this bearhug so tight I was frightened. But it felt great for him to smother me like that. We just stood there, sort of rocking back and forth and holding onto each other in the dark. His hands were moving up and down my back, my butt, and I was pressing up against him like I used to do. If we could just hug each other hard enough, we could squeeze out everything that was between us there. There'd be nothing left except just us.

I was getting a hard-on. I didn't want it to happen—or I guess I *did* want it to happen, because there it was. And Carlos knew it too. He was always expert with his hands, leading me exactly where he wanted me to go, no matter where that was—and that was exactly what he was doing. He kissed the side of my face, and then his tongue was in my ear, and I just lost it—all this pent-up stuff inside me letting go. I arched my hips up against his, so he could feel me there, and then he was on his knees in front of me—he was unzipping my pants.

I'd dreamed about this and jerked off about it so many times—it was the one thing I could always think of that would make me come whenever I'd jerk off. It was Carlos, who'd always had me exactly where he wanted. And I wanted to be exactly there.

Then I remembered Ted, and it was this black door crashing closed on top of everything. "No," I remember saying, and I took Carlos's head in both my hands and tried to push him away. But it didn't work. He'd managed to pull my dick out of my pants, and just when he touched his tongue to it I reeled back like some electric shock.

I hated this man. I hated how he stepped into my life and ruined everything he touched and then just walked out without ever looking back. I hated every single thing that'd happened to me in my life since I met Carlos in the Nu-Way Laundromat.

Carlos was still on his knees, crawling toward me even while I was stepping back from him. It was ridiculous. Behind us there was this fence—one of those snaking things, pickets wired together, that they unroll across the lawns in Central Park, I guess for some kind of crowd control. Anyway, I didn't see it in the dark—I sort of stepped back on it. One of the pickets snapped under my foot, and then I went crashing down backward on top of it.

Which hurt a lot, and suddenly that made me completely furious. "Fuck! Goddamn it!" I yelled out. Carlos on his knees there was laughing. Maybe he knew how pathetic all this was, or maybe he knew exactly what was going to happen next and he was laughing because he was so relieved, he was laughing because he was happy. He was walking right toward the bullets and he wasn't afraid anymore. He was singing.

I remember I pulled myself up to my feet just as he reached me and wrapped his arms around my calves. Then I guess I must've reached down and grabbed the fence picket where I'd broken it, and just wrenched the whole thing right out of the wire that attached it to the rest of the fence. I don't really remember any of that, and I don't see how I could've had the strength to pull that picket off the wire—but I guess I did, because there it was in my hand. Before I knew anything else I was slamming it into the side of Carlos's head—holding it like a bat, and swinging, and the whole time he kept clinging to my legs like some nightmare that wouldn't go away. I hit him probably ten times in the side of the head, each time connecting with this loud *thwack!*—and he'd groan, the way you groan when somebody pushes their dick in you and it both hurts and feels fantastic. Like death, some people would say.

Then the picket splintered in two.

Carlos seemed stunned. He wasn't bleeding, as far as I could tell. He wasn't doing anything—just holding onto my legs, and sort of swaying back and forth like he needed me to hold him up. I remember what I felt was this insane annoyance, like all I wanted was for this just to go away from me. I pushed at Carlos, but he wouldn't budge, and I couldn't untangle myself from him. The more I tried, the more furious I got—not with Carlos, but just the whole situation. I took the half of the splintered picket I was still holding and I poked at him with it. I guess I poked him pretty hard, because the sharp splintered-off end of it slid right into the side of his neck. I was horrified, and suddenly there was blood everywhere. Plus he started making this gurgling sound, and when I tried to pull the picket out, it was stuck. I kept feeling like this bleeding was something Carlos kept doing to annoy me, and it made me angrier and angrier. I gave the picket a tug, and this time it came out— and because he still wouldn't let go of me I poked him again and again, as hard as I could, and I could feel it going into him each time I poked him. He'd let go of me by this point, and was in this weird position on his knees with his back bent way back, so his whole chest was exposed to me, and I guess what happened was, I hit his heart. Suddenly there was this explosion of blood all over both of us: Carlos gave this groan from deep in his throat and blood was spurting out his mouth, and that groan went deeper and deeper in his throat till it trailed away. After that he didn't move anymore.

Where he'd tried to blow me, my dick was still sticking out of my pants, and though I don't remember this, and I wish more than anything in the world it wasn't true, I must've come about the time I stabbed Carlos in the heart. Because the police investigator found my semen mixed in with the blood all over Carlos's hair and his face.

ONE OF MY FIRST MEMORIES—MAYBE THE VERY first—is this winter night when my dad woke me up and said to come outside. I must've been only two or three years old, because I remember my dad lifting me up out of bed in his arms, and carrying me out into the front yard. Me on one arm, and Ted, who was just a baby, on the other. We stood out there in the cold, on the patchy grass in front of the trailer, and my dad said, "Look up there, you'll never see anything like this again."

I looked, and up there in the night these big sheets of color were folding down across the sky, red and green and blue, like wispy curtains some wind was blowing. And no sound—just these long snaky gauzes of color and the cold air, and I was shivering not because I was freezing, which I was, but because I was scared. I didn't want to take my eyes off that sky. But I had to—I remember craning my head around to look at the woods, and then back at the sky, and then the woods again. Because I thought something was in the woods, watching us, ready to come out at us, and those lights in the sky had something to do with whatever was in the woods. If I didn't keep watching for it, if I got too caught up in watching the lights, then it was going to get us.

It's one of the few times I remember being with my dad. I think I used to remember a lot more, but now for some reason I've forgotten it all. I can't remember a thing about him except that night, and the Red River Valley song he used to sing, and then the way, which was years later, he used to tug Ted out from under the bed whenever he'd come home angry at our mom.

I've never been sure whether any of that with the night and the sky really happened, or whether it was just something I dreamed, maybe my first dream ever. My mom wasn't out there on the lawn with us—at least I don't remember her. It was just the three of us. Whenever I'd ask her about it, years later after my dad left us, she'd tell me nothing like that ever happened—I must've dreamed it. But I sometimes think maybe when we were little she used to go away and leave us with our dad, and then who knows what happened with just him and us? Ted of course was too young to remember anything, and anyway it was something I never asked him.

Carlos was the one who finally told me about the aurora borealis—how winds from outer space are pouring over the world all the time, how they scatter down these weird lights that sometimes on winter nights shower from the North Pole even as far south as Kentucky, maybe once every twenty years. How I was lucky to have seen that; most people go through their lives and they never see anything like that. He told me about the Eskimos, too, who live in the far north—how they believe those lights come from some other world, where the spirits of the dead go on living. How those lights can come snaking down to the ground and carry you away if you get caught out in them. Those ghost lights that can dazzle you and you'll never come back.

T HERE'S NOT A WHOLE LOT MORE TO TELL.
I was stunned, I was out of breath, my dick was aching, and my whole front was covered in Carlos's blood. One thing you never realize till you're covered with somebody's blood is how fast it dries. It starts to cake up on your skin in no time—something I guess only murderers and a few other people would know.

The first thing I did was find a policeman. I knew exactly what I'd done, I knew Carlos was dead, so I wasn't about to go pretending it didn't happen. I probably could have. I probably could've walked out of there and disappeared and nobody would've known. Maybe I was taking my cue from Carlos one last time, but this was some blame I wasn't going to shirk. At least one thing I think you can say about me is, I've always taken some kind of responsibility for whatever I did. I've always tried to live with the things I decided, whether it was my brain deciding them or my body. Still, it was me, and I lived with it and never regretted any of it.

The policeman I found was this black man with one of those pot bellies every policeman you see's got—I guess from swaggering around all day.

"I killed somebody back in the park," I said. "You'll want to get an ambulance up here, but it's not going to do any good."

He just looked at me, like I was trying to put something over on him. I guess it was then that he saw, even in the dark, how I was covered in blood.

He stepped back a couple of steps and said, "Oh my God." Then he pulled his pistol out of his holster and pointed it at me, which I guess is what they teach you to do. But then I guess he felt a little silly since I wasn't doing anything. I was just standing there with blood all over me, and he'd probably seen worse. So he just held the pistol without pointing it at me.

"I don't believe this," he said.

"It's for real," I told him. "It's definitely reality."

We walked over to his car, and he radioed for some other officers, and then we waited by the car till they got there. He offered me a cigarette, but I don't smoke. I guess what I felt mainly was just relief—I hadn't known what was going to happen, and now I did. Carlos wasn't going to touch me anymore.

It's been a year since all that. The trial was a foregone conclusion, though I understand there were people out there—Earl's definitely one of them—who thought I should've gotten off on the grounds Carlos Reichart was the sort that needed killing. I don't happen to think they're right, but that's not here nor there. What is here is all the thinking I've been able to do, and what I want to say may sound strange for somebody's murderer to say, but I know now that I did to Carlos exactly what he wanted me to. I may have thought it was what I wanted to do, and maybe it was—but it was definitely what he wanted.

I don't know why he decided it was time, or why he wanted to go out the way he did. I don't know whether it was because of all the stuff with Ted, or whether Ted was just part of it too, part of his way of going out. But I'm positive that some day came when he made this decision, and once he decided that, he looked around for the most loyal person he could think of to help him.

Or maybe he only recognized it was already decided the minute he faced it happening in me—the way he knew Seth would always manage to get it on film when something real was going on, and I was just being his decision for him.

But there I was. Here I still am. He's got me in his hands—from the very first instant in the Nu-Way Laundromat that day ten years ago in the rain, he's still got me. To the very end.

You've probably noticed how I have this habit of not saying goodbye—just out the door at some crack of dawn. What I'm remembering right now is the very end of *Next Year in Gomorrah*, my favorite movie of Carlos's—maybe because it was the first one I ever made with him, and everything seemed clear and okay back then. The ocean, waves, and a little boat out on the waves. Some seagulls flying in this gray morning light. Then you hear the character played by me—it's not my voice, of course, it's somebody else's voice dubbed—saying, "I decided to go with them, a ship running guns or contraband. I never knew exactly what. But I heard for the first time the names of Silifke... Mersin...On the docks at Antakya a young Jew introduced himself and told me that in the year..."

Then in the middle of the sentence that voice just stops talking, there's no more ocean, no more boat or flying seagulls—the screen's just blank.

It's the way I've always left.

ABOUT THE AUTHOR

Paul Elliott Russell is the author of seven novels.

He grew up in Memphis, Tennessee, in a neighborhood called Scenic Hills. After graduating from Raleigh-Egypt High School in 1974, he attended Oberlin College in Ohio, and also spent time in Germany and London. He then went on to study at Cornell University, earning an MFA in Creative Writing in 1982 and a PhD in English in 1983. He has taught at Vassar College, The College of William & Mary, and the University of Exeter.

The Unreal Life of Sergey Nabokov, published by Cleis Press, won the 2012 Ferro-Grumley Award for Fiction. The same title received a Silver Medal for the Independent Publisher Book Award in the Literary Fiction category, and was a Finalist for the Lambda Literary Award. Russell also received the Ferro-Grumley Award for Fiction in 2000 for *The Coming Storm*. His 1994 novel *Sea of Tranquillity* was chosen as one of the 100 Best Gay and Lesbian Novels of All Time by the Triangle Publishing Group. Other Russell novels include *The Salt Point* (1991*)*, *War Against the Animals* (2003) and *Immaculate Blue* (2015).

His nonfiction book, *The Gay 100: A Ranking of the Most Influential Gay Men and Lesbians, Past and Present* (1995), has been translated into ten languages. He's published poetry, essays and short fiction, and *edited Best Gay Erotica 2013.*

Russell received a National Endowment for the Arts Creative Writers Fellowship in 1993.

Read more about him at paulrussellwriter.com.

"Picaresque and symbolic, raffish yet lyrical, told in one of the most compelling and authentic vernacular voices in American literature— Tony Blair is the peer of Huck Finn and Holden Caulfield...an awesome achievement."

—*Booklist*

"A vivid and often compelling work. Many of its scenes are startling in their beauty and haunting in their horror."

—Harlan Greene, author of
What the Dead Remember and *Why We Never Danced the Charleston*

"A powerful coming-of-age story, a tragedy about an emotionally battered gay youth with appeal that easily extends beyond a gay readership.... Russell has crafted a timely, involving tale that explores the outer limits of gay sexuality and the point at which art or artiness slides into exploitation."

—*Publishers Weekly*

"Paul Russell's stunning achievement...irresistibly we are led into the dark, beautiful, disturbing world of filmmaker Carlos Reichart and are asked to watch in what becomes a terrifying and thrilling complicity."

—Carole Maso, author of *The Art Lover*

"This is no treacly account of boyish victims and demonic older men, but a forthright vision of love's darkest possibilities."

—Dorothy Allison, author of *Trash* and *Bastard Out of Carolina*

"Chilling...contains powerful scenes that display Russell's talent."

—*Los Angeles Book Review*

"A deeply disturbing novel, full of scenes that leave you queasy and uncertain whether you should keep reading. But you do.... Russell is an artist."

—*The Lexington Herald-Leader*

"A provocative but balanced study of the artist as pioneer in the far reaches of human experience."

—*San Francisco Chronicle*

"A kind of long *examen de conscience* that is both personal and historical... Russell has a keen sense of moral and psychological nuance, and all his characters are presented as richly complex beings."

—George Stambolian, editor of the *Men on Men* anthologies

"The hero of Paul Russell's new novel says he can be 'talked into anything.' He can also talk *about* it all, in a tone that has an eerily consistent believability. The book is a tremendous feat."

—Thomas Mallon, author of *Aurora 7* and *Arts and Sciences*

"Paul Russell strikes again! Readers who enjoyed *The Salt Point* will find even deeper pleasure in *Boys of Life*. Frankly explicit, funny and sweet and tragic by turns, it is a rich and compelling adventure."

—Dan McCall, author of *Jack the Bear*